CAPTIVE AND CAPTOR

The big man stood in the creek, washing the paint from his face and body. Cherish had never seen a naked man before. Muscles rippled as he scrubbed himself, the dawn light glistening on the droplets running down his brown skin.

Something on the creek bank caught her eye. A pistol in a holster near a pile of clothes. If she could get her hands on that, she could hold him at gunpoint. She slipped around, grabbed the pistol out of its holster.

At the sound, he whirled around, cursing.

"Now we see who is the captive." She held the gun with both hands, trying not to look at the virile body as she reached for a towel, tossed it at him. "Get out and get your clothes on."

"Or you'll do what?" His tone was arrogant. He tossed the towel to one side, started toward her naked.

"Stop or I'll shoot you!" She tried to concentrate on his face, too aware of his nakedness as he strode toward her.

His hand reached out quick as a rattler's strike, jerked the gun from her hands.

She turned to run, but he grabbed her and they struggled on the slippery bank. She lost her footing and they both fell.

"You sneaking savage!" She bit and scratched and fought him, very aware of his hot, wet skin touching hers. He easily ended up on top, pinning her hands above her head.

Before she realized his intent, he bent his head and kissed her. . . .

DISCOVER DEANA JAMES!

GEORGINA GENTRY

NEVADA DAWN

ZEBRA BOOKS
KENSINGTON PUBLISHING CORP.

ZEBRA BOOKS are published by

Kensington Publishing Corp.
475 Park Avenue South
New York, NY 10016

First Printing: December, 1993

Printed in the United States of America

How sharper than a serpent's tooth. . . . How many parents have lain awake nights feeling guilty and wondering; what did I do wrong? What could I have done differently? If you have ever agonized over a child gone wrong or maybe you were that rebellious child, dear reader, I wrote this story just for you. . . .

One

One May night, 1887

If he couldn't have the rich white man's daughter, once again he'd steal his gold.

On a rise overlooking the railroad tracks in the lonely Nevada night, he sat his pinto stallion surrounded by his war party.

The moonlight shone on his lithe, half-naked frame, the war paint on his massive bare chest and handsome face. From his Paiute chief father, he had inherited his size and strength, but it was his beautiful Cheyenne-Spanish mother who had given him his fiery, passionate nature.

His Medicine Hat stallion snorted and stamped its hooves, moving under him, impatient to run with the night wind. Its natural coloring, with spots on its head and chest thought magic by many tribes, was painted as garishly as its rider, with red handprints and other coup marks. The brave patted the stallion's neck and watched the far horizon. He took a deep breath of the scent of cactus and sagebrush,

7

listened to the sounds borne on the wind. To the east, he heard the echo of the coming train, its whistle lonely as a coyote singing. "It comes now," he grunted in a mixture of Paiute and border Spanish to his men. They nodded, confident in his leadership.

The moonlight reflected off the mountains in the distance, the metal tracks gleaming below them like two silver ribbons. White men and a Mexican rode with him also. To the old *gringo,* he said in English, "Ben, is the track blocked, the wood ready?"

The old Southerner took out his harmonica, played an off-key tune as he nodded. "Charlie'll set the blaze when he sees the signal. That Trans-Western will have plenty of time to stop when it comes 'round the bend."

"It is good." He intended to steal the train's gold, but he didn't want to hurt the innocent. "It is the fifth month, it means luck."

To the Paiute, five was a magic number. Perhaps this raid would be special. In the distance, the sound of the laboring engine drifted faintly to where they waited on the rise overlooking the track. The Nevada night brought the scent of smoke from the iron horse to mingle with the slight fragrance of desert flowers.

A cloud drifted across the moon. He looked up at the wispy, almost scarlet shadow. Blood on the moon foretells bad luck, he thought with a shiver, and almost crossed himself. Old habits died hard. Once he had lived as a white man, but that had been years ago, before . . .

He could not think about her now; he would enjoy his revenge, think of the gold and how it would feed the desperate braves who rode with him. Even though they feared robbing the Iron Horse would bring them bad medicine, greedy government policies and corrupt Indian agents had brought desperation to these remnants of his father's people. Over the rise to the east, the train chugged like a long black snake. Its headlight gleamed through the darkness like one yellow eye as it crawled across the desolate stretch.

"Now?" Mex asked in Spanish.

The big warrior nodded, reached for an arrow, and said a silent little prayer. Whether he prayed to the white man's God or the primitive gods of his father's people, he couldn't be sure. He hoped luck rode with them tonight.

The Mexican outlaw struck a match even as the warrior put the arrow to his bow. For just a moment his rippling muscles tensed as he pulled the string taut and thought how much better he was with a pearl-handled forty-five. Still, the wood felt natural to his big hands. Mex lit the cloth-wrapped arrowhead and the warrior pulled and let go, sending the flaming beacon in a powerful arc across the desert sky to alert Charlie Whitley waiting in the brush on the other side of the tracks. Even as the train rounded the bend in the distance, the tinder-dry wood piled on the tracks roared into flame.

Between his powerful thighs, the leader felt the mustang stallion snort and stamp its hooves. "Easy, Sky Climber," he said, patting the spotted neck.

Sired by the greatest wild mustang stud of the Sierra Nevada mountains, the beautiful horse was always eager and impatient to run.

He felt his own heart beat faster as he shifted his tall frame, feeling the cool desert wind like a kiss on his almost naked body. The moonlight reflected off the ring on his hand. A white man's ring. The memories came flooding back and they hurt even now, after all these years. He pushed the troubling thoughts away and concentrated on the train moving along the gleaming rails. The engineer had not yet seen the burning barricade, but when he topped the next rise, he would have to throw on his brakes.

Jack Whitley cursed, the sweat gleaming on his white face. "I hope they got an express car full of gold so we can make one last haul and quit!"

The warrior didn't answer as he watched the train. He expected to be killed eventually and he accepted it; wasn't even sure he cared anymore. He didn't rob Trans-Western Railroad for the money; his needs were simple. Yet he got some satisfaction in knowing the starving Paiutes who followed him could use the salt, flour, and warm blankets the gold could buy.

His heart beating faster at the coming danger, he signaled his men. With the braves yelping their war chants, the little band galloped down off the rise toward the train so they could be there when it reached the flaming barricade and screeched to a stop.

* * *

Inside the Blassingames' ornate private railroad car, Cherish stood modeling the lavish white wedding gown for half a dozen awestruck friends. "Well, what do you think? Will Pierce like it?"

The elegant young ladies paused in their ohhs and aahs. "Like it?" Hetty gushed. "Why, Cherish Blassingame, it is absolutely the most beautiful dress anyone ever had. I'll bet Frances Cleveland didn't have such a lovely dress!"

"She didn't," Cherish said. "Don't you remember Daddy and I were invited to the reception last year when the President married his ward?"

"Oh, you get invited to things we only dream of," Agnes said. The other girls nodded and giggled in agreement.

"Well, maybe a back East shopping trip for my trousseau wasn't such a bad idea after all." She surveyed herself critically in the mirror at the end of the swaying car and readjusted the imported lace veil on her blond curls. She felt almost guilty that she didn't look forward to this wedding with as much excitement as her friends. "Are all of you happy with your bridesmaid's dresses?"

"Oh, yes!" the pretty, well-bred ladies chimed in. "Taking a shopping trip in your father's private car was a lot more fun than just staying in California and having seamstresses make our gowns."

Cherish shrugged and stared at her reflection critically. "After all, Daddy does own the railroad, and it was his suggestion that I bring you along."

The railcar swayed lightly and the whistle blew. Only a few more hours, she thought, and the train will be arriving in Sacramento. Daddy and Pierce would be at the station to meet them early in the morning. This would certainly be the biggest wedding California ever saw, but then the public would expect the president of Trans-Western Railroad to host a lavish celebration when his only child married.

Hetty wrinkled her freckled nose and sighed. "Is it true you'll be going to England on your honeymoon?"

"Of course." Cherish studied the satin bodice in the mirror. "It's Victoria's Golden Jubilee and Daddy has promised to present us to the queen."

She didn't want to take Daddy along on her honeymoon, but Pierce didn't seem to mind. And after all, she thought guiltily, her birth had cost Amos Blassingame his beautiful young wife. He often reminded Cherish of that.

Plump Gladys reached for a bonbon. "So are you and your handsome groom going to live on his family's ranch?"

She would like that, but Pierce Randolph was ambitious and Daddy had promised to put his power and influence behind him. "Daddy's asked us to live with him, and after all, the house is so big and empty." As she began unbuttoning the tiny buttons at her throat she wondered if Pierce's rogue brother would show up for the wedding. No one really knew where he was. "You know there's some talk of Pierce running for office."

"As well as he's doing in business, he's probably looking for new worlds to conquer," Hetty said with a trace of envy and plopped down in a chair. "He's such a catch, Cherish!"

She continued to undo the tiny buttons, not answering, but no one seemed to notice. They were giggling and chattering among themselves. What more could a bride want? Nothing, she supposed; certainly any of her friends, as rich and privileged as they all were, would be delighted to change places with her as she walked down that aisle less than a month from now.

Her musings were interrupted by the long shriek of the whistle as if the engineer were attempting to scare a cow off the tracks. "What on earth—?"

She never finished. The brakes screamed as the whistle blasted a warning. The swaying train hurtled forward even though she felt the engineer applying the brakes. The girls around her shrieked and fell as they scurried in confusion.

Cherish grabbed for the back of a plush scarlet chair, but it didn't halt her tumble. For a long moment, everyone clung to whatever they could grab while the brakes protested, furniture overturned and glass crashed to the floor. Cherish could only imagine the sparks flying in the darkness as the engineer put steel against steel, fighting to stop the train.

Daddy would certainly fire an engineer over this, Cherish thought, sprawled on the floor in her wedding dress, her veil slightly askew. No doubt the man had been drinking or had fallen asleep.

Even as the train slid to a halt and protesting steel was abruptly silenced and replaced with the hiss of blowing steam, Cherish heard a faint sound, almost like thunder. "Is anyone hurt?" She stumbled to her feet, surveyed her dress that was by now falling off her bare shoulders.

"Oh, Cherish," Hetty gasped, staring at the dress, "there's a smudge on the skirt and I think a tiny tear in the lace. Some employee's head will roll over this! Your father will be so mad—"

"Hush!" Cherish held up her hand for silence. "Do you hear anything?"

"Sounds like pounding drums," Gladys answered.

Cherish paused, stared out at the cool, clear night. They were in an isolated stretch of the hostile terrain, probably not much help around if hitting a buffalo or a wild mustang had caused the engine to derail. "Alma," she gestured to her plump black maid, "go find the conductor and see what the problem is, how long we'll be here."

"Yes'um. Is you hurt, Miss Cherish?"

Cherish shook her head, waved her away. "Fiddlesticks, no. The dress may have a few smudges, that's all."

"That's an expensive dress, Miss Cherish. You papa gonna be powerful upset."

But not with me, Cherish thought, he was only upset with those who didn't do exactly as he wanted. She had learned that long ago. "Go see how long we're going to be stuck here and if we can get help."

The maid disappeared into the next car even as a slow thunder built outside.

Agnes put her round face against the window. "Oh, there's help coming already. I see horses and riders."

14

"The cavalry!" Her friends cried and crowded to the windows, "Oh, what an adventure we'll have to tell when we get home."

"Cavalry?" Cherish asked with puzzlement, "why would there be cavalry—?"

"Well, riders, anyway," Agnes pouted as if her word was being questioned, "they're just as plain as day riding toward us."

Cherish lifted her full skirts and ran to the window, ignoring the dress now falling off her shoulders. How like Daddy to send the army to escort them the last few miles. It was the sort of grand gesture he would make. They didn't really need an escort, this route hadn't been plagued by bandits like some other routes had. She peered out at the riders reining up around the stalled train. The moon lit the scene clearly now. A strangely marked pinto stallion gleamed in the light as it galloped up to the coach. It was ridden by a big, half-naked man, his dark features smeared with scarlet paint.

She blinked. No, her eyes must be playing tricks. She looked again, backed away from the window, hand to her mouth. "Indians! Our train's been waylaid by Indians!"

Immediately the little group of privileged ladies set up a hysterical shriek.

"Hush now!" Cherish commanded. "We'll all hide and they'll never know we're here. They're probably after the gold shipment or weapons; things like that, and—"

The door was kicked open even as her friends scattered, squealing in terror. Cherish stood frozen, clutching her dress to her bosom as the big savage and his war party strode into the car, gaping in surprise at what they'd found.

She was going to be raped in her snowy white wedding gown, Cherish thought with dismay. Maybe she'd be lucky if he only raped her; he and his savages might kill and scalp them all! The silly girls screamed, but the leader only looked around as if disappointed to find the private car full of swooning ladies. Just who had he expected to find in the railroad president's private car?

One of the men moved toward the girls as if to grab them, but the tall warrior snapped an order in a language she didn't understand and he retreated, looking angry.

Abruptly, his dark gaze swept over Cherish. His eyes widened for a long moment as if he could not quite believe what he saw; a white girl in an elegant wedding dress cowering before him. Cherish glared back at him with more spirit than she felt. He hesitated a split second, then strode toward her.

"Don't touch me!" She retreated against the wall, feeling foolish and terrified. Of course she couldn't expect him to understand, but her defiant tone seemed to make him hesitate. For only a moment, he stood looking down at her, his face a grim frown, his features disguised by the scarlet and ocher paint.

"Please . . ." She felt almost faint with terror. "Please, let us go. I'm on my way home to be married. Soldiers will come after you if you hurt us!"

He hesitated, almost smiled; or was it only a grimace?

Maybe he spoke some English. She drew herself up to her full height, although she was petite. "My daddy is a heap big chief. Leave now while you can!"

He muttered something, it might have been a curse, before he reached out, jerked the veil from her blond hair, threw it to one side.

He was going to rape her here before everyone, Cherish thought in a frightened daze, grabbing for her dress as the white satin slid off her bare shoulders. She glared back at him. Before she realized what he intended, he grasped her naked shoulders, looking down into her brown eyes.

She felt anger, outrage and panic at the heat of his hands on her skin. Even Pierce had never touched her so intimately.

Tearing a ribbon from her dress, the brave twisted her hands behind her back and tied them. Now she stood helplessly looking up at him, the wedding dress sliding down her arms, revealing the swell of her bosom under her lace chemise. "What—what are you going to do?"

He didn't answer. Instead, he picked her up, light as a plaything, held her in his arms a long moment. Bare pale flesh touched dark skin. "Stop! You can't do this! Do you know who I am? Let me go or you'll regret it when my father calls Wells Fargo, the whole War Department, and the governor!"

The brave ignored her mixed threats and pleas, held her even tighter. She could feel his heart beating against her naked breast.

"How dare you?" she fumed, now too angry at

17

the damage to her dress to be fearful and cautious. "This is a Worth original, do you hear? It cost a fortune!"

He didn't answer and she was certain he didn't understand a word she said. A slight smile crossed his lean face as he swung her up and threw her across his shoulder like a sack of grain. She felt the hot power of his muscular shoulder beneath her soft, half-naked form.

Oh, the indignity of it all! Her long hair hung in a tangle and with her hands tied behind her back, her full breasts were in danger of falling completely out of the torn satin dress that dragged the floor. He wheeled and started out of the railcar. She craned her neck to look back in horror at her cowering, silent friends. Even her maid stared in open-mouthed disbelief that anyone would have the effrontery to touch the only child of one of the richest, most powerful men on the West Coast.

He was abducting her! For a moment, Cherish couldn't believe that fact, and then the cool night air touched her as he went to the open door, paused. Now fear and fury overcame her. "How dare you! Put me down, put me down this instant! You can't do this; do you know who my daddy is?"

However, her captor paid her protests not the slightest heed as he carried her from the train slung across his shoulder. She looked back in desperate appeal to her friends and train crew. "Help me! Someone do something!"

They were all helpless, she realized. The few guards had been disarmed and stood with their hands high. As her captor carried her out into the night, she saw the wide-eyed conductor's shock, the faces of her friends pressed against the window staring out. Cherish had never felt such terror and such fury. How dare they come into her private car without being invited? How dare this savage put his hands on her so familiarly? She felt the heat of his broad back through the thin white satin covering her breasts and the power of his arm across her legs.

The long train of her snowy wedding dress trailed in the dust as he strode toward his horse. Daddy would see him hang for this! He'd have the army combing the countryside. She twisted her head, saw men coming with the express box. Why, they were robbing Daddy's train like common outlaws. She'd never thought about Indians robbing a train before. Matter of fact, in her sheltered young life, she'd hardly thought about Indians at all.

If only she could make them understand how influential and important Daddy was, what the dire consequences would be, they might reconsider and let her go. "Put me down! Put me down, do you hear me? My daddy is president of this railroad and I'm about to be married! You'll be hunted down like dogs if you dare touch me!"

The leader didn't indicate that he heard her. Perhaps he doesn't speak any English, she thought. Maybe if she screamed loud enough, there might be some soldiers in the area who would hear her. At least it was worth a try; all the Indians could do was kill her and it looked as if she was headed for a fate worse than death anyway. Cherish shuddered as he walked toward his horse. She didn't even want to think about it. She began to scream.

He promptly tore off a bit of the hem of her dress. "My dress!" Now she really was upset.

Was that just the slightest hint of a smile on his lips? She got out one more scream and with the next, he stuffed the torn bit of white satin in her mouth. She was terrified, she was angry, she was stifled.

Cherish struggled to pull her hands free, but only succeeded in causing her unbuttoned dress to slide further down her bare shoulders. How ironic, to be raped and murdered in the symbol of her innocence when Pierce had waited all these years to take her virginity. For just a moment as she looked up at the savage, their gazes locked, and there was something about him . . . no, of course not. Perhaps he looked somewhat like one of Daddy's Mexican stable boys. Yes, that had to be it.

Maybe the soldiers would come riding after them if there were any in the area and she'd be rescued. Wouldn't it be a grand adventure to recount to her bored rich friends? Cherish tried to concentrate on that thought to keep from giving way to hysteria as the big brave lifted her to his saddle, climbed up behind her. What a beautiful, strangely marked horse, she thought in a daze. No doubt besides being a robber, he was also a horse thief.

Now the leader signaled his men and they rode out, scattering like dry leaves in all directions. Cherish twisted her head to look back over her shoulder at the train. Against the lighted windows of her elegant car, Hetty pressed her freckled nose and Agnes's round, plump face stared out at her.

This couldn't be happening; no one would dare abduct the daughter of the president of Trans-Western Railroad, they'd all be afraid of her father's money and power. This simple savage probably had never even heard of Amos Blassingame. Had he merely lusted after her? She had seen the intense look of his dark eyes when he stared into hers. Or had he understood enough English to realize from her shrieks that he had inadvertently captured a rich prize worth more than the strongbox in the express car? Maybe they intended to hold her for ransom. In that case, at least they wouldn't kill her. As for the other thing . . . Cherish shuddered. She wouldn't think about that just now.

The fiery stallion surged beneath her as it ran. Its master held the reins in one hand and clasped Cherish with the other. The gold ring on his hand gleamed in the moonlight. What white man had he scalped and murdered to get that?

His strength pulled her against his bare chest and his hand felt warm on her waist up under her breast. When he leaned forward, she felt his breath warm on her naked shoulder. She had a sudden vision of herself staked out in the torn remnants of her wedding gown while this war party took turns raping her. Daddy and Pierce always protected her from every inconvenience, every discomfort, but now she might be in a spot where money and power weren't going to do her any good.

Perhaps she could bargain with the savage leader.

21

How much were her life and her virginity worth in gold? If she got raped but escaped with her life, would it change Pierce Randolph's feelings about her? Of course not! Pierce loved her. Wouldn't his first thought be to get his beloved returned safely without caring whether some savage chieftain had lain with his bride?

They galloped through the night. Could this be real? Any minute now, she would wake up back in her own bed in her own railcar, surrounded by servants, or maybe in Daddy's Sacramento mansion, safe, sound, rich and protected. Somehow, she knew that wasn't going to happen. Maybe this kidnapping was her fault. If she'd kept her mouth shut, maybe the savages would have stolen a few things from the train and ridden away. She abruptly felt guilty. Daddy often made her feel that way when she didn't do exactly as she was told. Yes, maybe it was her own fault the Indians had singled her out to kidnap.

The leader cradled her close against his muscular, almost naked body as they rode. The big hands seemed to burn into her waist and when she moved, her breast brushed against his knuckles. Maybe he wasn't aware of it. Then she felt the outline of his prominent maleness through the skimpy loincloth he wore. Her face burned as she realized he was as keenly aware of her body as she was of his.

She'd see the arrogant savage hanged for this. No man had ever dared be so familiar, not even Pierce. In fact, she'd only been kissed twice, the second time a prim kiss by her fiancé, after she had finally been worn down by both Daddy and Pierce into accepting his proposal.

The horses' hooves seemed to drum like thunder as they galloped away into the desolate hills. Come morning, the governor would have a thousand soldiers, Wells Fargo, and lawmen searching for her. By then, it might be too late. Cherish shuddered at the thought. He won't dare harm me, she reminded herself, because of who she was. The Randolphs were rich and important, too, and Pierce would leave no stone unturned to bring this savage to justice.

She tried to concentrate on her indignation to control her fear. Her mouth tasted so dry from the gag, she was choking. She would concentrate on her anger, not her fear. She'd probably have a difficult time getting a new original Worth gown in time for her wedding. If she could get this scrap of cloth out of her mouth, she'd give him a piece of her mind for shredding the imported satin.

Cherish felt the heat of his hand holding her tightly against his swollen manhood. Think of something else; anything except that it felt like a big, iron bar against her body. There was nothing she could do but let him cradle her face against his bare chest. He smelled of horses, smoke, and sun. It wasn't unpleasant, but it certainly was different from the fine cologne Pierce wore.

She was cold in the night air, and try as she might, she couldn't stop herself from trembling. Immediately, he pulled her even closer against his big, warm body. At least maybe he didn't intend to share her with the others. Would it be any better to only be raped by one warrior? Then she remembered the way he had glared at her as if he hated her and she knew better than to expect mercy.

How far had they come? There was no way to tell and she didn't know the country anyway. It might take hours before the crew could clear the tracks or send someone down the line where they might find a telegraph. Her heart sank as she realized these savages might have cut the telegraph wires and damaged the track to delay pursuit for hours. By then, the war party would be swallowed up by this fierce, wild country. Cherish could disappear without a trace, never to be seen again. The wind picked up and she realized that it was blowing their tracks behind them, losing them in the shifting sands.

Besides, the way the Indians had scattered in different directions, the posse could go off in a dozen diverse ways and maybe never track them up into the hills where they were heading. She thought of being out here at this man's mercy for countless years if the ransom didn't come. Would he use her as a slave of his passion? She was only vaguely aware of what it was that men and women did in bed together. The girls at Miss Priddy's Female Academy in Boston sometimes giggled about it, but having been raised by dour servants, Cherish was quite innocent.

She was so very, very tired and there was nothing she could do but let him mold her small frame against his big one as they rode. With her hands tied behind her and the dress half off, when he held her against his naked chest, she felt her bare breast touch his rippling dark skin. It seemed to burn like fire against her nipple and there was nothing she could do about it. Trussed and mute, if he wanted to put his hands all over her, fondle her breasts, touch her in the most intimate manner, she'd be helpless to stop him.

Now, however, he seemed to be concentrating on his riding. As weary and as frightened as she was, Cherish found herself dozing off as they galloped through the night. Periodically, she would come awake with a start to find herself cradled against that wide, muscular chest. She must stay awake, she reminded herself, try to remember some landmarks. Maybe she could escape when no one was looking. Then all she would have to do was find the posse that would be combing the whole state of Nevada looking for her. It gave her hope and she concentrated on it, even though she saw nothing but a blur of starlit sky and dim mountains.

After what must have been hours, they rode up a narrow trail near a river, through a rocky pass and into a valley. By now she was only vaguely aware of landmarks. She knew there were Indian lodges, camp fires, dogs barking, shadowy people and horses neighing. He reined in.

The leader gave orders in a language she didn't understand. A woman called out to him in Spanish, laughing and teasing, but a bit angry. At least there were other women here. Could she expect help from them? Maybe if she offered a bribe. . . .

The warrior slid from his big stallion, reached up

25

to grab her. His hands almost encircled her waist; she felt the heat of them through the bedraggled wedding dress as he lifted her to the ground. When she looked up at him, he was looking at her breasts, almost bare now. With her hands tied behind her, Cherish was helpless to do anything to protect her modesty.

A handsome older warrior with gray streaks in his hair took the horse, led it away. Her captor lifted her with no more thought than if he'd been handling a bundle of old clothes, threw her across his broad shoulder again. She felt her long hair trailing almost to the ground and the white satin dragged in the dirt as he walked.

Oh, fiddlesticks! Where was he taking her? She couldn't see anything but felt his hard muscles ripple against her face. One of his arms held her legs and the other went up to clasp her hips. How dare he put his hand there? Then she realized her naked breast was against his bare back, her nipple rubbing his brown skin as he strode across the ground. Was he taking her now to share her with his warriors? Cherish had a sudden vision of her self staked out helpless, spread-eagled by a fire. Never in her whole sheltered life had she been at any man's mercy.

Instead of throwing her down by a camp fire, the brave stooped to clear the door as he carried her into a lodge. He slid her from his shoulder, lay her down on a blanket by the fire, stood looking down at her without a word. He didn't need to say anything. The heat in his dark eyes, the prominence of his manhood under the skimpy loincloth, let her

26

know exactly what he was thinking. With her hands tied behind her and the gag in place, she couldn't even beg for mercy or threaten him with her father. She begged him with her eyes, but the way he glared down at her let her know that she could expect no mercy; no mercy at all!

Two

Cherish looked up at the savage, wondering how much English he spoke. He took the gag from her mouth.

"Please," she implored, "oh, please. . . ."

"So you know the word?" He did not smile and his tone was arrogant. Somehow, there was almost something familiar about his voice.

Please. Admittedly, it was not a word she used often. When as a child, she had tried to be friendly to the servants' children, Amos Blassingame had made it clear she was not to mingle or be democratic to those beneath her. He hadn't struggled to reach success so that his only child could befriend ragamuffins.

If at least this savage spoke a little English, she might reason with him; no, bribe him. The Trans-Western fortune might save her chastity yet. "I—I want to go home," she implored. "My father is rich; he'll pay you well."

In the firelight, the half-shadowed face was grotesque with scarlet and ocher paint. "Money; don't need. Steal plenty from train."

"What—what can I offer to go free?" she asked, heart beating hard in fear.

His smoldering look swept over her in a manner that almost seemed to reach out and touch her naked skin with its intensity. "What I want, I think maybe you not want to give."

"You don't mean—?" Cherish cowered back against the side of the lodge. With her hands tied behind her with a ribbon from her own dress, he could do anything he wanted, including. . . . If she hadn't been so terrified, the idea would have been laughable; elegant Cherish Blassingame, distantly related to dukes and earls, having her body bartered for her freedom. "That's—that's absurd!"

"Is it?" His tone told her he was enjoying her discomfort. His gaze swept over her torn and soiled dress.

That reminded her all over again that the original she wore had been damaged beyond repair, and after she'd gone all the way back East for it. The thought almost made her anger overwhelm her fear. "My daddy will give you many blankets and supplies for my safe return. Otherwise, he and the man I am to marry will hunt you down and kill you like a coyote!"

"Must find me first." He almost smiled. "White girl, too proud. I like you better when you beg."

"You don't know who I am! If you don't return me unharmed, Daddy will have soldiers, many soldiers looking for me. They won't stop till they find me!"

He shook his head, the slightest smile crossing his hard mouth. "Not find. Secret valley. Look forever; never find."

Was that possible? Cherish wondered with a sinking heart as she looked up at him. He seemed pretty sure of it. "What do you want of me?"

"You know, I think." He reached out and touched her face. Cherish shrank back as far as she could against the lodge wall but still his big hand stroked her cheek.

She closed her eyes, afraid of the way his dark eyes burned into hers. His fingers stroked her cheek almost as if he were stroking a little pet dog. "Please let me go," she whispered. "I can't stay; I'm to be married."

"Fancy dress ruined; forget marriage." He almost seemed to be pleased with himself.

The arrogant savage! She gritted her teeth, imagining the army rescuing her, capturing him. She wanted him flogged. Cherish closed her eyes and imagined him tied to a post. The captain would hand her the whip. "Here, Miss Cherish, for ruining a fine Worth wedding gown and inconveniencing a lady, that should be about fifty lashes."

In her mind, she held the whip and surveyed his naked back. Even his back looked arrogant. No man, not even a savage, had ever treated her with such effrontery. She would concentrate on the punishment he would get for daring to kidnap her, that would keep her mind off the feel of his warm hand stroking her cheek. She imagined bringing the whip back, bringing it down as hard as she could on those rippling brown muscles.

"What white girl thinking?"

His words brought her out of her vision of cutting his back to ribbons, wrapping that lash around his lean, naked hips while he fought his restraints and begged for mercy. She opened her eyes wide, looked up at him, so very close to her face. No, this man wouldn't beg if he were beaten to death. She hated him worse for that than she did for tearing her dress, kidnapping her. It was not proper for a simple savage to have more pride than the rich gentry of California.

"I must go back, be married," she tried to reason with him. "My Daddy will give you much money and many presents." Now he had her talking like he did.

"Always 'Daddy.' What about future husband? What he give?"

"Nothing, unless I am returned unharmed." She couldn't bring herself to say "not raped." Cherish struggled to keep her voice calm as his hand continued to stroke her face. "He, too, is from a rich and powerful family."

The Indian smiled ever so slightly. "Rich, but maybe not powerful. I got his woman in my lodge. In my power."

Oh, my God. What could she do now? His logic was unmistakably correct and he wasn't at all impressed by talk of money or power. Her mouth tasted so dry, she thought she might choke. His hand

31

cupped her chin, forced her to look up at him, although she tried to look away. Maybe she would be lucky to just get out of this alive—if she got out of this alive. If gold meant nothing to him and he wasn't afraid the army might track him down and hang him, he could amuse himself with her body at his leisure.

If Cherish hadn't been so angry and terrified, she would have laughed at the irony. Half the eligible young gentry of the West had begged and pleaded for her hand in marriage, each hoping to be the one. Amos Blassingame had looked over each contender with a critical eye before urging her to select Pierce Randolph. Now that which Pierce hungered for was about to be taken unceremoniously on a blanket in a crude Indian lodge out in the savage wilderness. "What—what is it you expect from me?"

"Besides learning to say 'please'?" He smiled again, displaying even white teeth in the shadows. "Let me think on it." He stared at the dress. "Who is the man?"

She looked up at him, confused, exhausted, and uncertain what he was asking. "Oh, you mean the man I'm to marry? Why, a very rich and important white man; Pierce Randolph."

Something in his face changed abruptly. For a split second, she thought he would strike her. Without warning, he reached out, caught the front of the exquisite white satin, tore it away with a loud rip.

Now she was really terrified. Cherish cowered, naked to the waist. With her hands tied behind her, she couldn't even cover her breasts from his bold stare. She might as well be a slave on an auction block. What had caused his fury? She had no idea, she could only huddle with her blond hair half hiding her full, naked breasts while his gaze swept over her as if she were a whore to be bartered for his pleasure. He reached out and tangled his dark hand in her light hair, twisted her face up so that her fearful gaze looked into his smoldering one.

For a long, heart-stopping moment, they looked into each other's eyes and again she had that slight sense of familiarity, yet there was no way she could have met this war-painted brave in her safe, protected world. He would rape her now, she thought, and wondered if he could hear her heart pounding, see it beating beneath her bare breast. Instead, after a long moment, he let go of her, turned without a word and strode from the lodge.

Cherish took a deep, shuddering breath and willed herself not to cry. What was it she had said? Why had he seemed familiar? Her mind went back over all the servants and employees the Blassingames and Trans-Western had employed over the years. No, she didn't think he had ever worked for Daddy, but maybe there had been a Mexican stable boy or two who might resemble him; yes, that had to be it. At least she was safe for the moment.

She looked down at her shredded dress and got angry all over again. Fiddlesticks. If she did survive this, there wouldn't be time to order another original, she'd probably have to make do with a wedding gown by a local seamstress. At least it would delay the nuptials. It occurred to her as she struggled to peek through the doorway that she had small misgivings she hadn't even been willing to admit to herself. Daddy was so enthused about his future son-in-law that she would have felt guilty even voicing her doubts.

Cherish peered out the lodge door and watched the big savage stride to a camp fire and sit down. It didn't seem to be as large a camp as she had first thought. Was there any possibility of escape? The idea was too daring. To keep from giving way to terror and despair, she would plan appropriate ways to punish this Indian who had dared put his hands on her, stared with obvious lust at her breasts. Surely a giant rescue mission would soon be underway.

What to do now? There was nothing she could do but wait and hope the war party had left a trail the posse could follow. With a sinking heart, Cherish remembered the way the wind had blown along their trail, blotting out the tracks. Money would buy anything—including people, Daddy always said so. While her abductor said he had no interest in gold, she didn't believe him. Surely he had kidnapped her in hopes of a big ransom. She must continue to impress upon him, if she could, that the ransom might not be paid if she were harmed in any way.

She was so very tired and it still seemed to be a long time until dawn. Peering out the entrance, she saw that the camp appeared to be asleep and the big savage sat before the fire as if he did not intend to move for a long time. She must conserve her strength for tomorrow and whatever that might bring. Cherish lay down on the blanket as best she could, close to the small, crackling fire. Exhaustion was fast surpassing her fear. She would close her eyes for just a moment and think about happier times she had known.

Happier times. She sighed as she realized that in spite of all the money, there hadn't been that many exciting, interesting times. She would be twenty-two this month, even though everyone still treated her as if she were a spoiled child. Well, maybe she was, but who had spoiled her? She closed her eyes, running back through the years. Guilt. That was what she remembered most; the guilt she felt because Anne, her beautiful, titled mother had died giving birth to her. Didn't Daddy always remind her of that when Cherish didn't do as he wanted? So with Daddy, she was a dutiful daughter, doing exactly as she was told. With everyone else, however, it was a different story. Of course because of who Daddy was, the others overlooked her headstrong willfulness.

No, there had been one happy memory. She took a deep breath of the scent of burning wood and remembered another crackling fire, another chilly night. New Year's Eve, 1880; the first time she had ever met her future husband—and his older brother; the only other man who had ever kissed her. Even Pierce didn't know about that. It was so special, she had never shared her secret with anyone. Too bad it hadn't been special to him, too. She had hoped . . . well, what did it matter now?

* * *

Cherish was only fifteen years old, but Daddy was allowing her to hostess this big party at their ornate Sacramento mansion. The place had mostly been shuttered and gloomy all these years, but now she suspected Daddy was showing her off to all the California gentry so that when she finally made her society debut, she'd have many suitors.

That night, the house gleamed, looking like a Victorian palace with all its turrets, gingerbread, and stained-glass windows. Daddy boasted he'd built an even finer castle than his older brother had inherited back in England. Daddy, as the younger brother, got nothing and had married a poor but titled beauty. They had come to America. He lost the beauty giving birth to their only child that first year. Amos Blassingame threw himself into business, slowly amassing a fortune in railroads while Cherish was spoiled by governesses and servants, all eager to curry favor with her father.

Such a party! Cherish wore a demure but expensive daffodil yellow dress that went well with her pale hair. Now she stood next to the plump and pompous Englishman greeting his guests. With the New Year's Day custom of young gentlemen calling on eligible ladies rapidly falling into disuse, this was a polite and discreet way to survey future matrimonial prospects.

Tonight the elegant carriages of some of the most important and richest people arrived for the social event of the season. The house rang with laughter and music, dozens of servants hurried about with trays of drinks and long banquet tables groaned under silver platters of food. Even her dour governess, Miss Grimley, seemed almost cordial as she sent maids scurrying for more champagne. A full orchestra played in the big ballroom and carriage after carriage brought new crowds of party-goers sweeping through the ornate front doors, each lady dressed more beautifully than the last. The mayor and even the governor had made an appearance.

Now their starchy butler, Smathers, announced the arrival of the Randolphs of Arizona and their two sons. Daddy took her elbow and hurried to meet them. He shook hands with the man. "By, Jove, Quint, I'm so glad you could make it! And Dallas, haven't seen you in years." He kissed the lady's hand. Cherish smiled and curtsied. The dark older beauty was tall for a woman, with a few gray hairs in her black hair. She might have been near forty but was aging gracefully. She wore a simple but elegant emerald velvet dress. The man was handsome, with gray streaks in his light hair. He might be around fifty, not much older than her own father.

Daddy said, "May I present my daughter, Cherish? Mister and Mrs. Randolph."

Cherish curtsied again. "So delighted to meet you."

"Lord, such a beautiful daughter!" Randolph drawled, "and these are our two sons, Nevada and Pierce."

"How do you do?" Cherish curtsied ever so slightly, looking the two tall young men over discreetly as they bowed to her and shook hands with Daddy. The one called Pierce was evidently the younger. He looked more like the father with his lighter hair and hazel eyes. The older one, Nevada, seemed to have the dark good looks of his mother. The younger son was dressed formally, but the father and Nevada wore well-cut, Spanish-style short jackets and expensive boots.

Dallas Randolph smiled, looked around. "Such a lovely home." She had a husky, charming Texas drawl.

Daddy stroked his mustache. "Thank you, I built it as a gift for my wife, but unfortunately . . . ah well. Monroe and Charlotte aren't up to coming?"

Mr. Randolph ran his hand through his graying hair. "My sister is a bit under the weather tonight, so they send their regrets."

Cherish knew the elderly Monroe and Charlotte Davenport through Daddy's business associates. They had hinted they had two eligible nephews to introduce to her. She sneaked glances at the two young men as the parents chatted. From the ballroom drifted the strains of a waltz.

The younger son bowed elegantly. "Miss Cherish, I'd be honored."

She took his arm, a bit unsure of herself. "Of course, if you'd really like to."

"By Jove, of course he'd like to," Daddy said.

"Indeed," Pierce said.

The older, dark one appealed to her more, but he was regarding her as if she were a small child and he looked a bit bored by the party.

She let Pierce lead her out onto the crowded ballroom floor. People around her were giving her indulgent smiles. She felt like a little girl who was being humored by grown-ups.

Pierce Randolph danced quite well and he treated her as gallantly as if she were a grown lady, not like a pampered child. "I'm so pleased to get away from the ranch," he said, "and more delighted to be in the company of the California capital's most beautiful woman."

Cherish felt a pleasant flush stain her cheeks. He was flattering her, but she was enjoying it. "Really, Mister Randolph, you're the only man who thinks so."

He whirled her around the floor. "Not a bit of it," he said smoothly, "everyone is talking about you. That's a stunning dress."

"Thank you." She could only smile up at him like a silly schoolgirl, dazzled by his sophistication and good looks, although he couldn't be more than three or four years her senior. "Do you get to Sacramento often?"

He frowned. "Most of the time, I'm stuck at our ranch, the Wolf's Den, but now I see I should come and visit my Aunt Charlotte and her friends more often."

He was actually flirting with her. She felt quite desirable and grown-up as they swept around the ballroom. Thank goodness Daddy had sent her to dancing school. "Wolf's Den seems a strange name for a ranch."

" 'Randolph' is an old and honored name," he explained. "It means 'protected and advised by wolves.' "

The Randolphs must have respectable nobility in their background. Daddy would like that. "I heard your Aunt Charlotte say the ranch covers half of Arizona Territory."

He made a wry face. "My Aunt Charlotte exaggerates a bit. It's mostly a wild and desolate place of endless hills, cattle, and wild mustangs."

"You don't like it?" Cherish asked. "I always thought I would love living on a ranch."

"I wouldn't tell just anyone this," he admitted conspiratorially, "but I loathe the place. I have bigger ambitions than riding the range looking for stray colts."

She glanced over and saw his older brother leaning rather nonchalantly against a door, watching the dancers. Somehow, he looked wild and a bit dangerous. She noted many women's heads turning toward him. "Your brother looks as if he'd be right at home on a ranch."

"Oh, he is." Pierce looked at his brother, who smiled and nodded as they danced past. "I don't think he feels at home without spurs and a gun strapped on his hip."

"He usually wears a pistol? How exciting!" She glanced again toward his brother.

"The future, Miss Cherish, is in law and the legislature. Someday, my parents will be too old to deal with that big spread. Then if I have my way, maybe we'll sell the ranch, invest in railroad, mining, and bank stock."

She studied Nevada Randolph out of the corner of her eye. There was something sensual, almost primitive about him; so different from the suave Pierce. "What does your big brother think? He doesn't look as if he'd be the kind to sit behind a desk."

Pierce's smile turned into a frown. "His views carry more weight with my parents than mine, I'm afraid."

Cherish caught the slightest hint of jealousy in his tone. "I'm sure your parents are very proud of both their sons."

"But he's their favorite. Someday, however, I'll show them. I'm ambitious, Miss Blassingame. I was named for a United States senator, and I'm hoping he'd help me if I ever decide to go into politics."

"You're named for Pierce Hamilton?" She was impressed with the grand old man from Kentucky whom she had met in Washington.

"Senator Hamilton is an old friend of my father's. I plan to go visit him while I'm back at Harvard this spring."

She didn't mention that Daddy didn't like Senator Hamilton. He never voted as Daddy wanted him to and when Daddy sent him a large campaign donation, the elderly gentleman had returned it.

"I'm a great admirer of your father's," Pierce said. "I hear that he, too, was a second son who outdid his brother. I can't imagine him willing to stay out on a ranch and raise horses as my father and my big brother are content to do."

She tried not to turn her head to look at the dark, older son. "Everyone should follow his own heart. If ranching doesn't interest you, I'm sure Daddy

41

would introduce you to all the important men in California business."

He smiled and kissed her hand. "Miss Blassingame, you are too kind."

It was a wonderful evening for a fifteen-year-old girl. Of course, as hostess, she had to dance with all the young men and smile at all the doddering old ladies who told Daddy what a "sweet child" she was and the mirror image of her beautiful mother.

Pierce was now dancing with his mother and Mr. Randolph was at the punch bowl talking business with Cherish's father and old bewhiskered Hiram Pettigrew. When Quint Randolph talked, he gestured and she saw the magnificent crested ring he wore gleam in the light. She stifled a yawn and looked around, wondering what had happened to the dark, dangerous-looking son who had not given her the time of day. No sign of him. Now where had he gotten off to? He couldn't have left, his parents were still here. Cherish was a bit miffed that he hadn't asked her to dance. In fact, he had seemed almost bored with the lavish social affair.

Almost defiantly, Cherish sneaked a glass of champagne off a servant's tray. Then she sneaked another, even though Miss Grimley saw her and glared. Daddy would not approve and no doubt Miss Grimley would tell on her later. The champagne made her feel a bit giddy and light-headed.

Out of sheer curiosity, she drifted through the drawing room, then the music room. Madge Pettigrew, Hiram's new red-haired young wife, seemed to be moving from room to room, too.

In each room Cherish entered, people looked up and gushed about what a wonderful party it was. She nodded politely, lifting her full yellow skirts as she moved on to the next room. Curiously, she trailed along behind Madge as the beauty in the blue dress went down the hall. Who was she looking for?

The billiard room? Now why would Madge be headed toward that masculine retreat with its exotic wild animal heads and leather furniture? Cherish tiptoed after her, peeked around the door. Nevada Randolph stood before the big stone fireplace and appeared startled as the pretty redhead rushed up to him.

"Darling, I've been looking all over for you. It's been so long since you've been in town, and I thought we might—"

"Madge, you married last month, remember?"

Cherish put her hand over her mouth to stifle her gasp as Mrs. Pettigrew slipped her arms around the man's neck. "Now, Nevada, darling, there's no reason we couldn't meet sometime. Why, old Hiram has whiskers like a Billy goat. I married him only for his money, and he's too elderly to give me what I really need—"

"You should have thought of that, Madge. I don't mess with married women." His voice sounded as cold as his expression. He attempted to unlock the girl's arms from around his neck. She resisted and rubbed her body up and down his lean frame.

"You aren't afraid of old Hiram," Madge said. "Why, everyone knows you're the fastest gun in three states."

43

He tried to pull away from her. "I don't aim to kill your husband, if that's what you're hoping. It might bring me very bad luck."

"Oh, you're so superstitious! Here, I'll give you some luck!" Then she kissed him in a way that made Cherish gasp at her daring. "Please, Nevada," Madge implored, "we were good together. When I remember the way you used to . . ." At this point the girl whispered in his ear, giggled, and rubbed herself up against him again before kissing him with abandon.

For a moment, he seemed to lose control and his arms pulled her hard against him. Then he took a deep, shuddering breath, reached up and unclasped the girl's arms from his neck. "No, Madge." He stepped away from her. "I do have a few principles."

"Well, I don't, not where you're concerned." She sounded huffy now, perhaps a bit angry. "There's someone else, isn't there? Some bitch who does a better job of clawing your back?"

"No, there isn't. Look, it's over now that you're married. I won't shame my father and the Randolph name; it means too much to me."

"You gallant Southerners and your stupid ethics!" Madge swore and whirled around, swept out of the room, right past Cherish who was hiding behind the door. Cherish peeked around the door, wondering about the dark, worldly man standing before the fireplace. She watched him wander over to a table, pick up the stereoscope and stare at the photo in it with a bored expression. Behind her, the faint strains of music drifted from the ballroom, accompanied

by laughter and light chatter. Her favorite song: . . .
beautiful dreamer, wake unto me, starlight and dew-
drops are waiting for thee. . . .

She really should get back to her guests, Cherish
thought, still dizzy from the champagne. No wonder
Nevada had ignored her, with sophisticated, beautiful women draping themselves all over him. She
shouldn't spy on him, she should go in like a good
hostess and inquire if he were having a good time,
get him to return to the ballroom. Perhaps then he'd
ask her to dance. She wanted to see what it felt like
to be in his arms, if it affected her the way it had
just affected Madge. He had his back to her as he
put the stereoscope down. Cherish stubbed her toe
as she stepped around the door, and immediately he
whirled, grabbing for a pistol that wasn't there.

"Excuse me, Mister Randolph, I didn't mean to
startle you." She was confused and embarrassed.

"Oh, Miss Blassingame." And then more guarded.
"How long have you been hiding behind that
door?"

"I—I was not hiding." She felt her face turn crimson, knowing he was wondering if she had wit-
nessed the passionate scene with the tempestuous
redhead. "I—I was passing by, and caught my toe
on the carpet, that's all." She came into the room,
feeling very young and awkward.

A moment of silence.

"I'm not fond of crowds," he said a bit lamely.
"I had just slipped away to enjoy a cigar."

He didn't look like the type who smoked cigars,
but she didn't say so. Instead, she picked up the

stereoscope off the table, held it before her own eyes, grasping for conversation in the silence. "Ah, are you familiar with John Fouch, the photographer who took this?"

He shook his head, appeared bored with her, and then looked toward the door as if wondering whether he could soon make a polite exit. "To be honest, Miss Blassingame, that scene of horse bones and desolate prairie isn't too interesting."

"Oh, but it's the first photo taken of the Custer massacre site."

"Is that a fact?" Now she had his attention. Of course everyone was interested in what had happened at the Little Big Horn four years ago when General Custer and his command were annihilated. He came over, took the stereoscope from her hand, viewed it again. "I think maybe I had friends and relatives on both sides of that battle."

"Really?" She was intrigued, looking up at him. He was so near, she seemed to feel the heat from his body. The champagne made her feel carefree and almost reckless.

He actually smiled at her. "Yes, really! My mother is half-Spanish, half-Cheyenne, you know."

"And your father's accent sounds Southern. From which parent do you get such an unusual name?"

"Actually, I'm Quinton Randolph the sixth. My middle name is Nevada. I think that's where my folks met. And yes, the Randolphs are old Kentucky gentry. Didn't you notice the family crest on Dad's ring?"

* * *

Ring. Oh, my God. Cherish's eyes blinked open and she struggled to a sitting position, the dream faded. Where was she? By a fire on a blanket in an Indian lodge. She searched her memory. Now she knew where she had seen that gold ring her savage captor wore. A wolf's head crest. That warrior had murdered Mr. Randolph to get it!

Three

Old Ben sighed as he sat down by the camp fire next to the painted brave. "I swear, boy, this time you've really gone and done it!"

"Don't start on me, Ben."

"Don't you use that tone to me," he snapped. "I ain't forgot I put your first didie on your small butt!" He searched through his pockets absently.

The younger man tossed him a sack of tobacco. "You trying to make me feel guilty or obligated?"

"Neither, I reckon," he drawled as he began to roll a cigarette, "just reminding you I knew you before you could walk. Your papa—"

"He's not my father," the younger man snapped and his expression turned stony as he stared into the fire.

Ben looked at him, sighed. "He is as far as he's concerned; as far as everyone else is concerned. If me and him hadn't been there that cold January night you were born with no doctor available—"

"He felt guilty, that's all."

Ben reached out, took a fiery branch from the

camp fire, lit his cigarette, tasted the tobacco as it burned. *Guilt.* It was an emotion he knew well. He'd never told this young whippersnapper about his own younger brother, Danny, who took a bullet meant for him at Gettysburg. Danny was just about this hombre's age when he died; twenty-six. Maybe that was why Ben now rode with this hell-bent boy; someone had to look after him. He hadn't looked out for Danny.

An owl hooted from a scrubby pine tree and the younger man crossed himself automatically. Ben half smiled to himself. The kid's beautiful mother was Catholic and there were habits he'd never lose, no matter how hard he tried to distance himself from his raising. "So now that you've carried her off, what are you going to do with her?"

The scarlet war paint shone in the firelight as he turned his head toward the lodge. "I haven't decided yet."

"It wasn't enough that we rob the old man's trains, you had to steal what he values most."

The other nodded. "Maybe that's why I took her."

Ben studied him. "You shame your family name."

"I have no family name."

How sharper than a serpent's tooth is an ungrateful child. Ben stared into the fire. If it weren't for the friendship he bore the boy's father, he would have ridden away long ago. Ben was no outlaw. "You should have left her on that train; she'll bring you bad luck and you're superstitious—"

"Don't you think I haven't thought of that?" His voice was sharp. "When I saw that private car, I thought I had old Blassingame at my mercy. I never expected to find her aboard and wearing a wedding dress."

"So you thought you could stop the wedding by kidnapping her?"

"I don't know what the hell I thought! Maybe I just figured the old rascal would pay a fortune to get her back."

"You didn't take her for money," Ben chided gently.

"Are you calling me a liar?" The dark eyes blazed. "Men have died for less than that!"

"So kill me," Ben drawled calmly. "Do you fear the truth so much?"

The warrior took a deep breath. "Truth is what set me on this path back in the spring of Eighty-one."

Ben started to speak, changed his mind. *Truth. Honor. Guilt.* He knew things the boy did not know, but Ben was sworn to silence. He was a Kentuckian and his oath was his honor.

In the silence, the fire crackled and somewhere in the distance, a horse whinnied.

The warrior stared into the fire. "You know who she's marrying?"

Ben did know, but he said nothing, merely grunted. He had managed to contact the parents so they wouldn't worry; but it had been several years ago, when the gang was still in New Mexico.

"She's marrying Pierce. Can you believe that? Pierce!"

"It's the lady's choice to make." Ben shrugged.

The other looked at him, smiled without mirth. "Not now it isn't. I've got her."

"Or she's got you," Ben said pointedly. "You can't hold her captive forever."

"Sure I can. No one can find this valley who hasn't been here before."

Lord, he was hardheaded. "So will holding her against her will solve your problem?"

"It'll deprive Pierce Randolph of the pleasure of sleeping with her."

Ben winced at the fury in his voice. The two young men were as different as night and day. "You hate him so much, then?"

"You know I do—and why." Behind the war paint, his handsome face was a sullen mask.

"When he first learned to walk, he followed you everywhere," Ben reminded him. "You saved his life when he fell in the horse tank."

The other cursed under his breath. "If I could have looked into the future, seen what he would do, I would have let him drown."

Even Ben was shocked at the cold fury of his words. "The Good Book says, 'vengeance is mine, says the Lord.' "

"It also says, 'if thy hand offend thee, cut it off.' "

"You're taking us all down the road to Perdition." Ben rubbed his lined face with a weary gesture.

"No one else has to go with me," he said. "Pierce meant to hurt me when he told me the truth—"

"So you take revenge against her, too?" Ben nodded toward the lodge.

"Especially against her. I still keep the letter she wrote me."

Ben had not read it, but he knew about that dog-eared scrap of paper. He must reread it now and then to keep his fury high. "Give it up, boy. It ain't too late. Blindfold her, take her to the nearest settlement and leave her, then she won't be able to lead a posse back."

He laughed, but there was no humor in his voice. "So she can go back and marry him? No! I'll have my revenge!"

"You will if it kills us all," Ben agreed. "Send her back, boy; close the door on what's past. We could cross the border, take it easy in the sun."

Ben had known his reasoning was in vain. The other shook his head slowly. "I want vengeance and the virginity of Pierce Randolph's bride. The only thing that would please me more would be killing him."

"You say that," Ben argued, "but raisin' runs deep; deeper than bloodlines. The man who raised you left a deeper mark than you know—"

"You don't know me very well."

"Don't I now?" Ben spit into the fire, "Boy, I helped deliver you. He's left his mark you can't erase, and he's a gallant gentleman if there ever was one."

"Gallant?" the other snorted. "He killed my father to steal his woman!"

Ben almost told then what he knew. Truth. Honor. Guilt. He had sworn an oath. "I think that even you don't know how much he's put his stamp on your soul; maybe you never will. As for Pierce, should you ever have the chance to kill him, your own heart won't let you."

"With my luck, I'll probably never get the chance to find out."

Ben took out his harmonica, rapped it against his hand. He was not yet sixty, but somehow tonight, he felt very old and very tired. He was almost glad now that his dear, dead Martha had never given him children. His friend's had brought him nothing but heartache. There was no reasoning with the young. "It's been a long day," Ben muttered. "I'm tired. Do what you will."

He got up, weary and bones aching. Wistfully, he thought of his comfortable bunk back at the ranch. He hadn't slept in it since that spring that . . . well, maybe he never would again. He felt obligated to ride with this hell-bent hombre, even if the boy took them all to hell, which was likely. Was it guilt or was it devotion? He was tired of thinking about it. He stretched and limped off to his blankets, playing a slightly off-key version of "My Old Kentucky Home."

Tequila watched from the shadows as the old man left the glow of the camp fire. His stiffness was no more than could be expected from one with gray in his hair. Her gaze returned to the man staring into the fire. *Si*, he was a big, handsome stallion all right.

The Mexican girl thought about the captive he had brought into the hideout tonight and gritted her teeth with jealousy. Here she had been waiting for a chance to leave Jack and become Nevada's woman, and he had brought in some delicate, yellow-haired lady. Still, he had not yet gone to her blankets; maybe Tequila herself still had a chance with the leader.

She adjusted her peasant blouse still lower so that it showed plenty of her ample bosom, shook back her long black hair. With her gold jewelry, she knew she was pretty enough to take any man's eye, *si*, even this gunfighter who still wore his masquerade of a savage. It was late and the camp was quiet. Her own man, Jack, was asleep after using her body for his pleasure. She curled her lip in disgust. Jack was a sweaty pig and he knew nothing of pleasuring a woman, only himself.

Tequila looked around. No one was about to spy and report on her. The old white man and the strange one they called "Mex" were asleep, as were the savages. Jack lay snoring in their lodge. His brother, Charlie, was on guard duty out near the horse herd, he wouldn't see her. She sauntered over to the fire, swinging her hips as she walked. "Hello, *hombre*. You can't sleep, no?"

He frowned. He didn't approve of her, she thought, but that didn't matter. She could change his mind if she ever got him between her thighs.

"No, I can't sleep," he agreed. "Where's Jack?"

His hint was all too pointed. Tequila ignored it, sat down on the ground next to him. "Asleep, snoring like a sweaty pig."

"That's where you should be."

54

"Hah! He wears himself out on me in two minutes, dumps his seed and rolls over. That's not what a woman wants." She put her hand on his bare thigh. She saw his prominent manhood grow hard under the loincloth. So he had not yet exhausted his lust on the pretty captive.

He took her hand, threw it off him in disgust. "If you want a man tonight, go wake Jack up."

"What for?" she sneered, scorn in her voice. "So he can rut on me again and then go back to snoring?"

Nevada shrugged. "If he doesn't suit you, you should move on."

She leaned toward him so that he could see her big breasts in the low-cut neck of her blouse. "I tell you something, gunfighter, when Jack Whitley took me from that cantina last fall, I only come because I think that sooner or later, I belong to you."

"You thought wrong."

She looked up at him under her eyelashes, ran her tongue over her wet lower lip and smiled in a teasing way. "Maybe not, *hombre*. I could please you like no woman ever has. I do things white girls never know."

"I reckon that's why Jack keeps you, then, when he should kick your cheating butt out of here."

"You don't approve of me, no?"

"I don't approve of you, *si*." He nodded his head ever so slightly and returned to staring into the fire.

"I could pleasure you, too. Jack need never know." She twisted her fingers in the heavy gold necklace she wore.

"You don't understand, do you? Jack cares about you and he's jealous as hell. You come to me with the scent of him still smeared on your thighs? *Puta,* I don't do that to a friend."

Whore. She'd been called worse. Tequila laughed, not taking offense. She'd been born to pleasure men. In the poor Mexican village that she came from, there was no other way for an ignorant but pretty girl to prosper. Only one of those hundreds of men had she ever felt guilty about; Antonio Gonzales, that very innocent and idealistic young priest she had seduced.

Tequila looked toward his lodge. "What about the elegant lady?"

"What about her?" he snapped. "I took her to hold for ransom."

"That wouldn't keep you from using her for your pleasure before you return her; she'd be too ashamed to tell."

His expression told her that thought had been on his mind, but he only stared into the fire.

The gold of her bracelet jingled as she reached out, brushed her fingertips across his nipple. "Let me please you," she purred. "I think I could make you forget her."

His nipple went taut and she heard his quick intake of breath. He was a virile man and Tequila sensed he hadn't had a woman in a long time. She knew how to make a man forget duty, honor, everything but the urgency of mounting her warm, ripe body. She leaned forward, slipped the other arm around his neck, kissed him wetly, running her

56

tongue across his lips, probing his mouth. She wanted him, wanted to take his manhood in her lips, drive him to a frenzy. Maybe he would kill Jack for her and she could be his woman.

Instead, he took a deep breath, pulled away from her, stood up. "Stay the hell away from me, Tequila. Jack's a friend of mine."

She looked up at him, enjoying his discomfort and the desire he could not control. His manhood was all too noticeable under the loincloth. He needed a woman. Hadn't she known that from the way he hesitated to push her away when she kissed him, put her tongue in his mouth? He couldn't be that honorable. Sooner or later, he would weaken as men always did, even priests. Besides the fact that this gunfighter looked as virile as a stallion, he was the leader of this bunch and no doubt could buy her trinkets and more gold chains to hang around her neck. If he didn't rape that captive soon, he'd give in to his needs and Tequila would have his hot mouth on her breasts and his hard dagger thrusting into her depths. She could wait. She understood the weaknesses of men.

Cherish watched in horrified fascination from the interior of the lodge. That wanton Mexican girl with all the gold jewelry had done everything but pull the savage down on the blanket by the fire. Cherish saw the ring on his hand gleam as he pulled away from the girl. The girl laughed, stood up, and showed a pair of slim legs as she whirled away from

him. She wasn't wearing any underclothing **and she** evidently wanted the warrior to see that. Cherish studied the ring again. Yes, it was that same ring she had seen on Mr. Randolph's hand that night. How had this savage come by it? The answer was too obvious; he had killed Pierce's father. When? How?

The Mexican girl shook the dust from her full skirt and sauntered away, swinging her hips. The warrior watched her go. She must be his woman; or maybe she was the camp slut who satisfied all the men here. Cherish thought about that. Was that why she was here? Did her kidnapper intend that she service all his warriors? If so, why hadn't she already been put to use by the dozen or so men who had ridden with him?

He was looking her way. Cherish scurried backward, out of his sight. Again she pulled at her bonds with no results. She heard him stand up, saw his shadow fall across the doorway. Quickly, she lay back down on her blanket as if asleep. She glanced at her torn wedding dress. Her breasts were bare, but she was helpless to remedy that with her hands tied. Maybe he would glance in the door to make sure she was there, then go away. Cherish closed her eyes and lay very still, barely breathing.

He stooped and entered the lodge. The girl lay on her blanket by the small fire. He dropped to one knee, stared down at her. He had never seen such a beautiful pair of breasts. They were not huge like Tequila's but they were plenty big enough to fill a man's two hands. The nipples looked like pink rosebuds. He felt himself go hard just staring at them as he imagined lying on her soft body, putting his mouth on those breasts. Certainly no man had ever touched them, or even seen them. Cherish Blassingame was a lady; she would save herself for her marriage bed.

He thought of Pierce and smiled. It would be a worthy revenge to deflower Pierce's bride. He had dreamed of nothing else but possessing this girl from the first moment he had seen her. Well, she was his captive now and at his mercy. There was no reason he couldn't finish ripping that fine white satin from her nubile body, fall on her and use her to ease his throbbing lust.

It would be a fitting vengeance to have her lying there with her virgin blood smeared across the remnants of her wedding gown. Instead of a fine down-soft bed with silken sheets, she could give up her innocence on a blanket by a fire. If she protested, or tried to scream, all he had to do was stuff a scrap of her dress in her mouth again. Then mute and bound, he could tangle his fingers in those long, golden locks, force her thighs apart. He wouldn't be gentle, he would thrust deep into her like a steel sword entering the velvet sheath it belonged in.

More than six years he had waited and dreamed of having this woman in his embrace. That was long enough. Didn't she deserve this for the way she had spurned him? He reached out and tangled his fingers in her hair. So soft; so silky. The slight flutter of her eyelashes, the heart beating hard under that pale, blue-veined breast betrayed her. She wasn't really asleep, she was lying there pretending. He trailed his fingers from her hair down the side of her face to her throat. He felt her pulse pounding hard there. Only a few more inches and he could have his fingers on her breast. She must know it, too; she stiffened, but still pretended to sleep.

Her belly was visible in the torn dress. He resisted the urge to bend and kiss her navel, taste her fragile skin. He smiled sardonically at the perfect vengeance; to send her back to her bridegroom and her snobbish father with her belly swollen big with his half-breed bastard; those fine breasts full of milk to feed his child. Amos Blassingame would go purple with rage at his aristocratic lineage mixed with mongrel blood.

The fire crackled and the scent of smoke mingled with the slight, delicate scent of her skin and silken hair. He was throbbing with urgent need as he studied her; she was his to enjoy as warriors had always used captured enemy females. As badly as he needed a woman, it wouldn't take him long to break through her maidenhead and empty his seed within her. As proud as he was, Pierce might not want her then. Perhaps she would not tell him she had been used for a half-breed gunfighter's pleasure. He would want both Pierce and Amos to know. Maybe he would send the bloodied, torn wedding gown as a gift to Pierce with a card that said: "My compliments on your choice of a wife. She serviced me well!"

Her full, soft mouth trembled ever so slightly. He knew how to humble her. Cherish Blassingame was arrogant, spoiled. That note she had sent him long ago was unnecessarily cold and heartless. He pictured her on her knees before him, still a bound captive. He would make her use that mouth in a way she might never dream of. Yes, that would humble her. And when she was broken in spirit, obedient, used to pleasuring him in any way he demanded, then he would return her to civilization and her bridegroom.

Again she trembled all over. The night air was cool. Was she cold lying here almost naked? He could cover her with his own hot, hard body, warm her skin fast enough. God, how he wanted her!

She trembled again. She was chilled and fearful, too. Despite himself, his resolve began to fade. So very small and defenseless. Slowly he pulled a blanket up over her shoulders. She wasn't asleep, he was sure of it. He didn't want to protect her, he wanted to ravish her, and yet . . . a long time ago, he had kissed this girl and his life had been forever changed. No doubt, she wouldn't even remember it; it obviously hadn't meant anything to her. She hadn't even recognized him, while her image was burned forever in his brain.

Music; yes, there had been an orchestra playing faintly in the background: . . . *beautiful dreamer, queen of my song, list while I woo thee with soft melody.* . . .

Despite his youth, he'd made love to many, many women. They sought him out, knowing he was virile, knowing he could please them. This one had been almost a child, fifteen years old and wearing a dress the color of daffodils; the color of her hair. She had stood innocently in front of a big stone fireplace looking up at him, those same soft lips half parted. She'd had some wine and slightly tipsy, she had thrown her arms around his neck. He hadn't meant to kiss her; he was gallant with the innocent and she was a lady. Women like Madge Pettigrew were more his type. He couldn't stop himself now from leaning over and brushing his lips across hers as gently as he had that long ago New Year's Eve. She might have forgotten, but he would never, never forget the magic of that moment.

In her memory, Cherish was drawn back to that long ago New Year's Eve before the fireplace in the billiard room. She, who had never been allowed a taste of liquor, was more than a little drunk from champagne. Otherwise, she would never have had the sheer audacity, yielding to impulse and throwing her arms around the handsome rake's neck. She had felt him start in shock at her daring.

Why had she kissed him; she who was such a prim, respectable lady? Cherish had surprised herself at her unthinkable behavior. Perhaps it was the unaccustomed liquor, or her own loneliness, or even curiosity, having just watched the embrace between Nevada and the uninhibited redhead. If she had given her motive any thought rather than acting on impulse, Cherish would never have done such a daring thing; the idea was too unconventional, too shocking. It was the only wild, impulsive action she had ever taken in her young, sheltered life.

She had kissed him, standing on her tiptoes to

reach his mouth. Even now, she could feel the hard muscles of his broad shoulders and neck as she held him close, breathed in the masculine scent of him. He smelled of shaving soap, tobacco, brandy, and sun.

And the taste of him! His sensual mouth was so unexpectedly soft beneath her own. She had not realized that the taste of his mouth, the warmth of his body against hers all the way from her ankles to her breasts would make her heart pound so madly. His big body trembled as if he were holding his passion in check; not at all like he had reacted to Madge Pettigrew. His arms came up very slowly and slipped around her, holding her gently against his hard length.

As his lips brushed across hers in a velvet caress, she had felt tenderness, not lust, as he held her as if he would shield her from the world's hurts and disappointments. Forever, Cherish would remember that moment that seemed to last an eternity, yet might have been only a heartbeat long while he held her close and kissed her with a gentle promise of love and friendship such as she had never known in her lonely young life.

Even now, she could taste that kiss, recall with dizzy certainty that this was the man she would never, never forget; the one who had given her her very first kiss. Until the last moment of the final day she lived, Cherish would remember the heady feeling that swept over her in the dashing rogue's arms.

Abruptly, her eyes opened wide with surprise, and

she looked up in disbelief and recognition at the painted savage who bent over her. "Quinton Nevada Randolph!"

Four

"Is it you?" Cherish looked up in amazement at the war-painted face. In the firelight, she thought she saw the dark eyes widen in surprise. Then they turned as black and hard as obsidian. Of course she was mistaken. There was no hint of a smile or of recognition in the hostile face, and yet that kiss. . . .

"You are wrong. I answer to no white man's name."

She felt depressed and foolish. No, of course this savage chieftain couldn't be Pierce's rogue brother. She didn't know where Nevada was, Pierce had been quite vague about it; something about a family dispute. Anyway, why would Nevada be riding with renegades and terrorizing his brother's bride? "Then what are you called?"

He sat back on his haunches, regarded her a long moment, shrugged. "If it pleases you to call me Nevada, call me that."

Nevada. She thought of wild, hostile mustang country, snowy mountain ridges. It fit him. She had been mistaken because both men were dark. She wondered who had taught this savage English. "I am called Cherish Blassingame. My father is a very important man. Send him notice that you have me and he will pay ransom to get me back unharmed." She stressed "unharmed" as she struggled to a sitting position. That was a mistake, she realized too late. Her movement caused the blanket to fall away, revealing her breasts in the torn dress.

He pulled a small knife from his waistband. Oh, my God, he was going to kill her. She licked her dry lips. "Please . . . oh, please. . . ."

His mouth smiled but his eyes did not. "You are not so proud now, are you, Cherish Blassingame?"

She didn't answer, wondering at the challenge in his voice.

He moved, quick as a flash. She didn't even have time to shrink away from him before, knife blade flashing in the firelight, both his arms reached around her. His hard chest brushed her bare nipples in the momentary embrace and she gasped at the unexpected sensation. She waited for the pain of being stabbed, then he settled back on his haunches and it took a second or two to register in her brain that he had cut the ribbon that bound her.

Slowly, she brought her arms before her, rubbed her numb wrists. Now what? He stared at her naked breasts again and she caught the edges of the torn bodice, held it across them.

He grunted. "Come morning, Tequila bring you some of her clothes."

"Thank you." She hesitated. "And then you'll send a message to my father?"

66

"Maybe. I'll think on it."

She was used to people hurrying to do her bidding. His casual disregard would have sent her into a fit of pique if she'd gotten this reaction back in civilization. Here, he was in charge and she was at his mercy. Oh, she hoped the posse and the army had been alerted! She saw a vision of this man in chains being dragged along behind the dust of her horse on the return to Sacramento. He would be begging her to intercede for him, and she would yawn at him groveling beneath her stirrup as she said, "Maybe. I'll think on it."

"Tomorrow I tell you my decision, Cherish Blassingame," he said regally as he rose and left the lodge.

Cherish heaved a sigh of relief. She had at least bought herself some time. In a few hours, Daddy and Pierce would be at the station to greet her arriving train; probably the society editor of the local paper, too. She imagined their consternation when they heard the news.

No, of course the train crew would wire on ahead as soon as they could reach a telegraph line. Even now, Daddy might be sending messages to the governor, maybe even President Cleveland. The Randolphs had influence and money, too. This savage brute was going to pay for what he'd done! Cherish lay down by the fire, still rubbing her wrists as she thought about his punishment with relish.

Pulling the blanket over her, she concentrated on his punishment and wondered how she could ever have confused him with Nevada Randolph. She had only met Nevada a few moments on that long ago New Year's Eve, and she wasn't actually sure she'd know him again if she saw him. Still the attraction had crackled between them and somehow she'd been in his arms, reaching up for his kiss. Cherish felt her face burn with embarrassment. She'd never dare tell her fiancé his brother had kissed her first.

Amos Blassingame poured himself another toddy and settled himself in a comfortable leather chair in his bedchamber, laid aside the book he'd been reading. His insomnia seemed worse lately. Financial problems were beginning to loom.

By Jove, if he could get his hands on that bandit who kept plaguing his trains, he'd . . . Amos twisted his hands together, wishing he had that young desperado's throat in his fingers.

Just who was the arrogant young pup and what had Amos Blassingame done to deserve this? At first, he'd thought the outlaw was merely after the gold, but the deliberate gesture of sending mocking compliments, via the conductor, to Amos and his daughter was a swaggering insult. Investors were getting nervous, companies were hesitating to ship with him, having heard that only Trans-Western trains were targeted. If it didn't end soon, Amos might be headed for bankruptcy and all because of some cocky thief who laughed in his face.

Why? Why? What had made him the object of an outlaw's vengeance? Had he once worked for the railroad and been fired? Had his farm been condemned and sold so Trans-Western's tracks could cross it? Rewards had been posted and raised, then raised again.

Amos chewed his mustache in frustration and gulped his drink. Maybe he should consider laying an ambush, putting a posse on a train. You'd think the outlaw would realize the southern route across Arizona and New Mexico was getting too hot for him with everyone wanting to collect the reward, and move on to some place like Montana or Wyoming. Oh, he was a smart one, that young desperado! At least so far, he and his band of cutthroats had only hit the southern trains, so Amos felt sure it was safe for his daughter and her friends to take the northern route for their shopping spree back East. Besides, she had begged, and he couldn't deny his daughter any whim.

The only face that came to him when he thought about it was Pierce's older brother. Of course that was absurd; the family had plenty of wealth of their own, and Quint Randolph had enough power to ruin Amos should he make such a wild and reckless accusation. Besides, he hadn't a shred of proof. Now that he thought about it, it was a ridiculous suspicion, borne of sheer desperation. He didn't expect to ever see that boy again, as Pierce had said that there'd been a family disagreement and they thought Nevada was in South America. He hoped the rascal stayed there.

In the meantime, if companies increasingly refused to use his trains he'd be ruined financially even though he still had plenty of influence at the state capital.

The wind blew outside and the big Victorian mansion creaked and whispered. He almost seemed to hear the rustle of ghostly skirts.

Anne. Amos fingered his mustache and looked at the small painting of his beloved wife on the chairside table. He felt such guilt. She seemed to be looking back at him so accusingly. Yet Anne wouldn't accuse anyone of anything. She had been one of those sweet, delicate wisps who never took control of her own destiny. She lived to please others. Guilt. Hadn't the doctor warned him Anne was too fragile for childbearing, that he must not lose his head and force his animal lusts on her?

But she was so blond and beautiful and he was young. One night, he drank too much brandy and insisted on his husbandly rights. Weakly and in vain, Anne protested, but he would have her! He hadn't married to live like a monk. Besides, what good did it do for a man to build an empire if he had no sons to inherit it?

By Jove, he had felt such guilt when Anne told him she was in a family way. The doctor had looked at him with grim accusation in his eyes. At least with her already expecting a child, Amos could enjoy her body. He didn't mean to do it again, but he could not control his need. The child grew big in her belly and it moved between them when he used Anne.

There was no passion in his gentle wife. She was obedient and docile, letting him vent his lust on her.

She said nothing, yet her silence accused him. Certainly the doctor had exaggerated, Amos assured her. They would find another doctor, one who was not such a nervous old man. Anne and the child would be fine; she'd see. Next year, they'd have another child and then another. There would be a houseful of strong offspring to carry on the Blassingame name.

The house moaned again in the wind and he sipped his toddy and stared morosely at the painting. Anne had died screaming and bloody, leaving him a bit of a baby girl who looked just like his beautiful, delicate wife. Except Cherish had fire and spirit, not like her docile mother. He had always feared someday his daughter would rebel; he sensed it in her. Guilt was the whip he used on his daughter's soul to control her. Whenever he felt that rebellious spirit about to rise to the surface, he reminded her that Anne had sacrificed her life for Cherish. He told her again and again that he was a lonely man who had lost his wife and sacrificed everything to devote his life to his daughter's happiness.

A small clock on the mantel chimed and he drained his glass and reached for his book again, something about India. He wasn't really reading; all he saw in the pages were dark, swarthy men.

That made him think of that Randolph boy; the dark one who had called on him the morning after the big New Year's Eve party Amos had given.

Nevada. Amos curled his lip at the memory. That was a cheeky one, all right. "Wonder whatever happened to the cocky young bugger," he thought aloud, and then felt foolish talking to himself. He stared at the book without seeing it, remembering that New Year's Day.

Amos had gone to his office, knowing no one else would be there. Maybe he could get some work done. He had no interests outside his railroad empire and his daughter. The servants would be bustling about the house, cleaning up after the party with Smathers and Miss Grimley, directing them. Cherish was going to her friend Hetty's house for tea.

Someone knocked at his office door. Blast it all, who even knew he was here? He opened it. It was that dangerous-looking Randolph boy from the party.

"Yes?"

He doffed his Western hat, appeared ill at ease. "Sir, Nevada Randolph. You know, my father and my Aunt Charlotte and her husband are acquaintances of yours."

"Oh, of course, come in." There was nothing else he could do. Perhaps if he appeared grumpy and busy enough, the young man wouldn't stay long. "How are your folks?"

"Fine, sir, packing to go home to Arizona."

Thank God for that. This young rascal would be gone before he could create any problems. He'd seen the way he looked at Cherish. "Yes, nice people; the Randolphs and the Davenports. Come in." He gestured Nevada to a chair. Probably just dropped by to pay his respects. "You'll be going back to Arizona, I take it?"

The young man nodded as he sat down. "Except for Pierce. He'll be staying with Aunt Charlotte till the end of the week when he takes the train to Harvard."

Amos poured himself a toddy. "Drink?"

"Thank you, sir." He took it. "Wonderful party, Mister Blassingame."

He warmed to him a little, but not much. "I daresay it'll make the society news. I figure if one is going to give a party, it should be the very best." He looked at the boy keenly "Your parents asked you to pay their respects?"

"No, sir." He fumbled with his glass, looked a bit uneasy. "They don't even know I'm here. I'm sure you'll be getting a note from Mother with her thanks."

"Hmm." Just what the devil did this young man want then? He looked Nevada Randolph over and tried to decide what it was that made his hackles rise at the sight of him. "You don't go to Harvard like your younger brother?"

He leaned back in his chair with the lazy grace of a cat. "No, sir, my life is the ranch; Pierce's interests are different."

"He does seem quite ambitious." Now, Pierce Randolph he liked. He could identify with that patrician, well-dressed youth. Money and power would be as important to Pierce as it had been to the Blassingame younger son. He frowned, thinking how his

73

own older brother has inherited all the family estates and title.

"Mister Blassingame, I'll get right to why I'm here."

"I wish you would," Amos said a bit more shortly than he intended, "I have a lot of unfinished paperwork on my desk I had hoped to do."

The young man looked him squarely in the eye. Amos knew what it was now that he didn't like; dark skin. He evidently took after the mother with that brown skin and black hair. No, it was more than that. "Sir, I'll be twenty-one in a few days."

A job. Was Nevada Randolph going to hit him up for a job? He breathed a sigh of relief. "Oh, of course, you're looking for a position with Trans-Western—"

"Sir?"

"Young man, exactly why are you here?" Amos felt increasingly annoyed with Nevada Randolph. It was something he couldn't quite put his finger on.

"I didn't call on you to inquire after a position. In a few days, I'll be twenty-one and in increasing control of the Wolf's Den Ranch. I wouldn't dream of living anywhere else. I love Arizona."

"Good for you! I appreciate a man who clings to his roots." Arizona was a long way from here.

"I'm old enough to marry, but I'm willing to wait."

Amos blinked. The boy was talking in circles. He watched the young man squirm under his curious stare. Did the young pup expect Amos to find him a suitable woman who would endure life on that spread of cactus and wild Indians? "I'm afraid I don't follow—"

"What I'm asking, is permission to call on Miss Cherish." His words tumbled out as if rehearsed. No doubt he had never done this before.

Amos took a deep breath, stroked his mustache and glared at him in disbelief. "Call on my daughter?"

"My intentions are strictly honorable," Nevada explained, leaning forward.

"Are you mad? My daughter is barely more than a child! She won't even be sixteen till May."

"I said I was willing to wait for her, sir. Whenever you think she's old enough—"

"Does Cherish or your family know of this idea of yours?"

"No sir. I thought I would approach you first for your permission. My dad is a Southern gentleman. He would think that the proper and honorable thing to do."

"Hmm, yes, of course." He must handle this carefully. Of course Cherish wouldn't be interested in this dark, wild cowboy—would she? He took a second look at Nevada Randolph and knew exactly what it was that Amos didn't like about him; his proud, bold spirit. This one would be his own man; no one would control or dictate to him. Amos thought of Cherish's own stubbornness, her rebellious spirit. Oh, he could just imagine the sparks flying between them. This wild, virile-looking young stallion wanted to carry his daughter off to

Arizona where his passion could swell her belly with his swarthy offspring.

"Cherish is my only child," he said softly, staring at Nevada Randolph, "and much too young to be courted."

"I said I was willing to wait—forever if need be."

Such passion in his dark, handsome face. "Actually, I had been thinking of sending my daughter away to school." Far away, he thought, where this one could never get close to her. What was the name of that prim boarding school someone had told him about? Oh, yes, Miss Priddy's Academy in Boston. He wondered if he could still enroll her for the spring semester?

"Mister Blassingame, I said I was willing to wait; I'd be patient while she finished her schooling, grew up."

Perhaps he could make this young buck feel guilty. "She's all I have, you know, her name is how I feel about her."

"I feel the same. I promise I would take care of her, sir. I think she'd like our ranch."

"Arizona?" The thought appalled him. "That wild, dangerous place full of savages?"

"There's trouble with the Apaches now and then, that's true, but the Randolphs have always lived at peace with the Indians. They respect Dad and we have no trouble with them; don't expect to."

"But it's so far away," Amos protested. "Since my wife died giving her birth, I have lived for my daughter. Oh, someday, I expect her to marry, of course, but I just always assumed she and her husband would move into my home and we'd be one big happy family."

The young man looked back at him, disapproval in his dark eyes. "Excuse me for saying so, Mister Blassingame, but you can't relive your life vicariously through your daughter. Perhaps you need to find interests of your own."

Amos felt his face redden with rage. He must control his temper. This arrogant, young whelp had just the kind of swaggering manliness that might attract Cherish. She might look like Anne, but she had her father's passion and willfulness. "Thank you for pointing out my failings, Mister Randolph," he said in as cold a tone as he possessed. "No, you may not call on my daughter; not now, not ever."

"Sir, I apologize for letting my temper get the best of me. I meant no disrespect."

"This meeting is at an end." Amos stood up, walked over and opened the door. "I trust you will not want me to report to your father your impudence and insulting demeanor."

The young man was still defiant, but passionately angry himself, as he stood there, a muscle jerking in his jaw. He twisted the brim of his Western hat in his hands. "My father is a Kentucky gentleman of the old school. I would appreciate your not telling him I was here."

Power. This boy cared deeply what his father thought. That gave Amos power. "Then don't call on my daughter. I think we understand each other perfectly. Good day to you."

Nevada Randolph paused outside the door as if

he would argue the point, but Amos shut the door in his face. He went back and sat down at his desk, drummed his fingers. What to do? That young pup was as arrogant and hardheaded as he had been himself at that age. If it weren't for that dark skin—no, of course he didn't want someone with his own temperament for Cherish's husband. Amos would choose a pliant, agreeable sort with money from a good family who would be happy to live in Sacramento in the big house Amos had built as a monument to his wealth; someone Amos could control.

Pierce Randolph. The patrician young face came to his mind. The younger brother. Yes, in a few years, he might consider Pierce. That boy probably wasn't more than eighteen or nineteen himself and had years ahead of him at Harvard. Harvard was in Boston where Miss Priddy's school was located. That would give Pierce ample time to call on Cherish. Of course there were lots of other possible suitors, but Pierce Randolph fit the bill.

Amos leaned back in his chair and folded his hands over his ample belly. Strange the older boy was so dark and the younger one so fair. Everyone said one favored the mother, the other the father. "Hmm," he mused aloud. Was there anything in their family background he could use if he needed to create trouble for the Randolphs? Amos doubted it; he'd never heard a breath of scandal about them; prominent, powerful, and rich as he was himself.

He was worrying unnecessarily, he knew that. Probably he had made his feelings to young Nevada so perfectly clear that the boy would change his affections to some other girl. Still, there was a bit of steel to his jaw, his disposition. Perhaps he had better have that Pinkerton Detective Agency discreetly investigate the family. Knowledge was power and with that oldest son, he was afraid he hadn't seen the last of him yet.

A shutter banged in the darkness and Amos jumped, stared at his book again. By Jove, his worries that long ago day had been for naught. All these years later and Cherish was engaged to Pierce Randolph. He glanced at the small bedroom clock and yawned. In a couple of hours, her train would be arriving. He had better go ahead and shave, get ready. Pierce was living over at the hotel, but of course he'd be moving in after the wedding. The couple would have separate bedrooms. He'd already made it clear to young Pierce that he was not to expect much of a delicately bred lady like his daughter in bed; just now and then, so there'd be grandsons to inherit the Blassingame empire.

He stood up and stretched, went to the window. A horse galloped up his drive and stopped, the rider dismounting in a rush. "What the devil?"

He heard the messenger ringing the bell, ringing and ringing. The sound of old Smathers walking to the door. Then feet hurrying up the stairs. "Mister Blassingame? Sir, are you up? Something terrible has happened!"

* * *

Pierce Randolph rolled over in bed and reached for Madge. "We've still got time. My fiancée's train isn't due in till dawn."

She laughed and her red hair fell down over them both as she mounted him. "Does her daddy allow you to have other women?"

"Matter of fact, I almost think he'd prefer I take my passion elsewhere." He didn't feel comfortable discussing Cherish with an easy slut like old Hiram's wife. He loved Cherish, but he'd been holding his appetites in check for all these years and of course, a man had needs. . . . "After all, one can't expect a high-born girl to do more than submit to her husband's lust. His daughter is a lady."

"And I'm not."

"We both know what you are, Madge." Pierce closed his eyes and arched his body, enjoying the feel of her hot sheath coming down on him. Old Hiram couldn't live forever and then Madge might use that fortune to help Pierce politically. A man had to think ahead.

Madge leaned down and offered him her breast. He closed his eyes and sucked it, pretending it was Cherish who rutted on him. He'd never dared do anything more than hold her hand in all these years, except when he'd proposed and then he'd kissed her primly, not wanting to frighten her. Wasn't she like all aristocratic ladies?

On their honeymoon to England, the old man was coming along, but that was okay, too. After all, Amos Blassingame was paying for it. Pierce was ambitious, but building a fortune came slowly, especially since relations with his parents were so strained, had been ever since . . . well, someday they'd come around; after all he was Quint Randolph's son and blood was thicker than water.

"Ohh, Pierce, you're pretty good," Madge gasped as she rode him hard and he arched his back, trying to give her a little more rod, "almost as good as—"

"Who?" His eyes blinked open and he stared up at the buxom girl. "Good as who?"

"Nothing, forget I said it."

"Nevada," he guessed. "You used to sleep with him, didn't you?"

She giggled and trailed a finger across his lips. "He was good, all right, but he stopped seeing me when I married Hiram."

"That old man doesn't know the difference." Pierce felt that hot anger rise in him. Would he forever be compared to his brother by everyone, even sluts? Pierce always came out second best, even in bed. He knew he wasn't built as big as his brother, but it angered him for this blowsy slut to mention it.

Madge leaned down and ran her tongue along his ear, causing goose bumps down his back. "That's what I thought, too, but Nevada had a sense of honor about it. What's happened to him? Haven't heard you mention him in years."

He reached up and grabbed Madge's heavy breasts, stroking them, wondering what Cherish's were like. At least as a virgin, she wouldn't have any basis of comparison. "I've told you before, there was a family fuss; he left."

81

"Yeah, but you never told me what it was about."

He ran his thumbs over her nipples, knowing that would distract her. He didn't want to talk about his brother; he wanted to vent his lust on this rich, married slut. Besides, he felt a bit guilty about Nevada. No reason he should, he told himself for the one millionth time, even if Nevada had always looked out for his younger brother. Pierce had been right to tell the secret Amos Blassingame had hired detectives to track down.

"Umm, Pierce, that feels good!" In the moonlight, Madge seemed like a pagan goddess of lust, her head thrown back, her body arched so that her long red hair trailed on his thighs and manhood. The moonlight through the window shone on her creamy white skin. "You gonna keep seeing me after you marry that prissy lady?"

"I—I don't know." Cherish was the chaste, unattainable virgin; a prize to be won. Pierce didn't expect her to feel passion and he'd feel guilty about using her for his lust. A lot of men kept a mistress on the side. Maybe Cherish would expect him to also.

Pierce had loved Cherish from the first night he had seen her at her father's party and he was certain he wanted to marry her when they rode the train together when they both went away to school in Boston. His lust and his love were two separate things. All these years, he had waited to take Cherish's virginity, dreaming of owning the desirable maiden. Some nights he woke up in a sweat and trembling, dreaming he was finally between Cherish's thighs after all this time. In a few more weeks, it would finally happen. Until then, he was only human. . . .

"Give it to me, sweet," Madge purred, "oh, Nevada, I love you. . . ."

Damn her to hell, but he was too aroused to stop now. Pierce arched his back and grasped her breasts. Madge was riding him in earnest, coming down on him hard and sure. No, he couldn't expect his future wife to behave like a hoyden, yielding to passion. He loved Cherish, but maybe a prominent, sophisticated man could be forgiven if he succumbed to lust with a hot, willing slut occasionally, as long as he did it discreetly.

In two minutes, he'd be finished, then he'd send her home and sleep awhile before he got washed up, bought some roses, went with old Blassingame to meet the train.

A sudden pounding on the door.

"What the hell?" Pierce swore.

Madge was already grabbing for a robe, climbing off him just as he was about to climax. Her husband? He gestured her to the dressing room as the pounding on the door increased. He walked across the room naked, his swollen manhood jutting out before him. Oh, God, could it be her husband? Talk about bad timing. Should he protect her? Of course not. He'd tell Hiram she'd seduced him. At least the intruder could have waited just a few more seconds.

Pierce opened the door a crack, peeked around it at a pimply faced messenger boy. "What the hell do you mean disturbing a man's sleep—?"

"A message from Mister Blassingame, sir. Something terrible has happened! Miss Cherish's been kidnapped off the train!"

Five

Cherish got very little sleep before the first gray light of dawn. As she roused, the girl she had seen last night entered, carrying a bundle. "Nevada say I give you some of my old clothes," the girl sneered. "You're about my height, but much smaller in the chest." She took a deep breath, showing off her amply endowed bosom.

Cherish started to snap back that she was also smaller in the waist and hips than the Mexican girl, but decided it was not a ladylike thing to do. "Thank you." She accepted the skirt and low-cut blouse.

"You're not welcome, *gringa*. I am called Tequila."

"Tequila?"

"You know, like the drink; men say I affect them the same."

She didn't know what the girl expected her to say. "I am called Cherish, as in loved, adored, and protected."

"Humph!" Tequila shook her raven hair back and

looked at the torn white dress Cherish wore. "Looks like Nevada gave you all night of 'loved and adored.' He was good, no?"

With a shocked gasp, Cherish realized what the tart hinted at. "That's not what happened."

"No?" The girl touched the heavy gold necklace around her own tawny neck. "I think you do not know much about men, *gringa*. If you did, you, too, could wear fine jewelry they give you."

Curiosity got the better of her. "Is Nevada your man?"

"Maybe *si*, maybe no." Tequila cocked her head at Cherish, played idly with her necklace. "He's *mucho hombre*, hey, *gringa?*"

"I—I wouldn't know about that," Cherish snapped. She remembered seeing this girl touching and kissing him last night. For some reason, it annoyed her. This conversation was going nowhere. "Look, I need to get a message to my father. He's very rich and would pay anyone who brought him word. Do you know Sacramento?"

Tequila laughed. "Sacramento? *Si*, I know that town. You waste your time, *gringa*, I no need your money. Jack give me some of train loot from last night to buy more pretties."

She'd try another approach later. Right now, she was hungry and no posse would arrive to rescue her before breakfast. "Is there food?"

"*Si*. Nevada tell me to give you some. Get dressed and come eat." Tequila turned and sauntered out.

Fiddlesticks. She'd hoped the girl might be bribed to help her. If Tequila weren't sleeping with Nevada, maybe it was only because she hadn't yet had the opportunity. Somehow, she was annoyed all over again. Cherish stripped off the torn, smudged wedding dress. Yesterday it had been worth hundreds of dollars; this morning, it wasn't fit to be used for dust rags. She had a sudden vision of the arrogant outlaw tied with strips of her ruined dress. He was standing on a wooden platform. "Do you have any last words?" the sheriff asked, standing before the throng of silent spectators.

"Yes, I beg Miss Cherish Blassingame's pardon a million times for inconveniencing her and causing her to be married in a tacky mail-order catalog wedding dress. Please, Miss Cherish, I beg you, don't let them hang me."

"I'll think about it," Cherish said with a yawn, and studied her fingernails. "Maybe I'll give you an answer tomorrow; maybe I'll let you stand here till hell freezes over waiting for my decision." The hangman's noose, of course, was made from white satin strips torn from the ruined dress.

At least she'd managed to hang onto her shoes in all this, Cherish thought. Tequila looked like she had big feet.

She went outside in the first cool light of dawn. It was an even smaller camp than she had thought. Not more than a dozen lodges, a stray dog or two, an Indian here or there, and a herd of fine horses grazing in the beautiful valley of scrub pine, silver sagebrush, and bright-flowered cactus. In the coming light, snowy mountains and stark cliffs were silhouetted in the lavender and pink light of the coming dawn. Wisps of gold and rose trailed across the horizon to the east. In spite of everything, Cherish thought dawn in Nevada must be the most beautiful sight she had ever seen. Then it occurred to her that she wasn't terrified anymore. Maybe she was just weary or maybe it was because she realized she was too valuable as a hostage for this renegade band to kill her. Rape might be something else again. She wouldn't think of that at the moment.

She walked over to the camp fire where Tequila handed her a tin cup of coffee. Cherish wrapped her hands around the warmth, inhaled the scent, tasted it. The coffee was strong and sweet. Tequila indicated Cherish should help herself to the warm tortillas and crisp fried meat. For breakfast, Cherish was accustomed to weak tea and toast. This hot, delicious meat was juicy, smearing her mouth so that she licked her lips and then felt embarrassment that she had done anything so unladylike as eat with her fingers. Why, Miss Grimley would be horrified.

She looked up as she finished, saw Tequila watching her, hands on hips. "*Gringa,* is your papa really rich and important?"

"Yes," Cherish said with eagerness, "and he'd be willing to pay anyone who would bring him word."

"This is a secret valley," the other said, "he could not find it even if someone told him where you were."

"But someone could lead him and the soldiers here." Cherish leaned toward her. "The reward would buy a lot of gold chains."

"How do I know he's rich?"

"Ask anyone in Sacramento," Cherish whispered, "ask them about Amos Blassingame and Trans-Western Railroad."

A strange expression crossed the dark girl's sultry face. "He your papa?"

"Yes, have you heard of him?"

"Maybe yes, maybe no." Tequila gave her a mocking smile. "Now I think I see why Nevada rob only those trains."

That didn't make any sense. Didn't outlaws rob indiscriminately? Then abruptly, she remembered the reports from the train crews on the southern lines over the past several years. A handsome, dark outlaw with a swagger to his walk would take Trans-Western gold, then bow in an exaggerated manner and send his regards to the president of the railroad and his daughter. It didn't make any sense to her. Why had the Blassingames been singled out?

Had Nevada once worked for her daddy and been fired? Perhaps it was a business dispute over track right-of-way. A chilling idea crossed her mind. She had thought the mixed-blood savage had kidnapped her at random just because she was so noticeable in that white wedding dress. With the luck of the draw, he might have carried off one of her friends. Had he singled her out? Fiddlesticks, that didn't make any sense. "Tequila, are you saying you won't help me, even for a reward?"

Tequila threw back her head and laughed. "In your world, *gringa,* maybe people bow and scrape to you, clean your house, cook your food, do your bidding because they fear your father. Here"—she gestured to the valley that surrounded them—"Nevada rules. His command is law here and it would be more than my life is worth to cross him."

"That simple savage?"

Tequila raised one eyebrow and smiled. "That simple savage is the best-known gun in three states, spoiled white girl. I think I would not let him hear me call him that if I were you."

Fastest gun in three states. In her mind, she saw red-haired Madge's pretty face. Nevada. Could he possibly be that Quinton Nevada Randolph? It had been so long ago and she had seen him so briefly. It was unbelievable that a member of the wealthy Randolph family could have fallen so low as to become an outlaw. She was determined to find out. "Where is everyone this morning?"

Tequila yawned. "The Indians drift in and out, you never know about them. Jack and Charlie are on guard duty, that one with the strange eyes, Mex, is asleep and so is the old one called Ben."

"Where's Nevada?"

"Up by the creek." She gestured with her head. "You waste your time, *gringa,* to appeal to him. When he decides your fate, he will tell you. Women do not lead him around by the nose like the weak men you are used to."

Ignoring the girl's advice, Cherish left the camp and walked up the creek. Up ahead lay a grove of small willows. She heard the splash of water. No doubt he was watering horses. Was there any way she could steal a horse, escape? It would be worth some thought. Like most well-brought-up young ladies, Cherish couldn't handle a gun, but she could ride. In her wardrobe at the mansion, she had dozens of fine riding outfits, many in the daffodil yellow she favored. Her sidesaddle had been custom made by the best saddle shop on the West Coast.

Cherish tiptoed to the grove of willows, peeked through.

Oh my God! Cherish clapped her hand over her mouth to keep from making a noise. She certainly didn't want him to know she was here. The big man stood naked in the creek, washing the scarlet and yellow paint from his face and body.

She must back away, not look. She would die of embarrassment if anyone knew she had seen him. Yet, she seemed to have grown roots to the spot. She couldn't move away, she couldn't even close her eyes. In fact, she felt her eyes widen as she moved closer for a better look. Cherish had never seen a naked man before and this one was all man. Muscles in his wide shoulders rippled as he scrubbed himself, the dawn light glistening on the droplets running down his brown skin. The gold ring shone when it reflected the light. Yes, that was the Randolph ring, all right. How had he come by it, unless . . . ?

His hips were lean and his legs long. His manhood. No, she must not look at that. She shook her head, willed herself to back away, but instead stared. Now she knew what a stallion looked like. One thing was sure, she'd know he'd been there if he took her. His face was half turned away so that she still could not decide if this Nevada was Quinton

Nevada Randolph. She didn't want to believe that Pierce's brother could do such a thing as kidnap his brother's bride.

Something on the creek bank caught her eye. A pistol in a holster near a pile of clothes. If she could get her hands on that, she could hold him at gunpoint, make him do her bidding. In her mind, she envisioned him riding ahead of her out of the valley, hands in the air. His men would watch and let them go because they feared hitting their leader if they fired. She slipped around, grabbed the pistol out of its holster.

At the sound, he whirled around, cursing. "What the—?"

"Now we see who is the captive." She held the gun with both hands, trying not to look at his virile body as she reached for a towel, tossed it to him. "Get out and get your clothes on."

"Or you'll do what?" His tone was arrogant, annoyed. He tossed the towel to one side, started toward her naked.

"Stop or I'll shoot you!" She waved the gun at him. "You won't make any more women happy if I shoot you right in the—"

"You wouldn't dare." He hesitated, began to walk toward her again.

She tried to concentrate on his face, too aware of his nakedness as he strode toward her. "Stop, I say, or I'll kill you."

He paused right in front of her.

"For heaven's sake, put your pants on," she implored.

"No." He surveyed her calmly.

"All right," she backed up several steps, "you can be my hostage and ride out of here naked for all I care!"

He just glared into her eyes, not smiling as he began walking toward her again.

"Didn't you hear me?" She waved the gun at him again. "Stop and keep your hands in the air or I'll kill you."

"Then you won't have a hostage." He was standing almost close enough to reach out and touch her.

She thought about her ruined wedding dress and got angry all over again. "I might think it was worth it."

"You are too gentle; too much a woman, Cherish," he whispered. "It is not in you to do violence."

"Don't try me!" She gritted her teeth and pointed the gun at him with both hands. "I'm capable of pulling the trigger."

"In the first place, I can tell you've never shot a pistol in your whole life and you've already broken the first rule of a gunfighter."

"Which is?"

"If you're going to kill a man, kill him; don't threaten him with words. And second, never let him get close enough to grab your pistol!" His hand reached out quick as a rattler's strike, jerked the gun from her hands.

She turned to run, but he grabbed her and they struggled on the slippery bank. She lost her footing and they both fell, rolling across the grass.

"You sneaking savage! You beast!" She bit and

scratched and fought him, very aware of his hot wet skin touching hers as they struggled. Her skirt edged up and she felt his manhood against her bare thigh. It seemed to burn like a brand there. He easily ended up on top, pinning her hands above her head on the ground. His wet chest was pressing into her breasts through the thin blouse. They both breathed heavily.

"Let me up!" she shrieked. "Get off me! Oh, I'll have your head on a platter, you—you—" It dawned on her suddenly that she was looking directly into his dark, handsome face with no disguising war paint. There was no mistake. It was Quinton Nevada Randolph. Why? How? She must not let him know she was now certain who he was until she could figure out what to do.

"And third, don't get under him, you never know what he'll do." Before she realized his intent, he bent his head and kissed her.

Once again it was New Year's Eve and she was giddy and slightly drunk as Pierce's big brother took her in his arms and kissed her gently. His lips had caressed hers in a way that sent chills down her back. That night, she had had too much champagne or she would have never been bold enough to offer a womanizing man of the world her innocent lips. All that was missing now was the wine, the song, the scent of a fire in the background.

Was she losing her mind? Her eyes flew open and she struggled. What would Pierce say if he could see her lying under a naked gunfighter while he kissed her and she returned the kiss? "Get off me, you—you bandit! I should have shot you while I had the chance."

He chuckled, stood up, reached for his pants. "You aren't the kind who could kill a man," he said, his face grim, "except maybe under very unusual circumstances."

Was he right? Why had she hesitated? A thousand years of British civilization ran in her veins. Maybe he was right, maybe violence was not in her, but by God, she was sorry she had missed her chance just now!

She watched him dress, tight black pants, black shirt open to the waist, fine, handmade boots on small feet. Last, he strapped the pearl-handled pistol low on his hip.

"We need to talk," she said.

"I'll decide that. In case you've forgotten, you're my prisoner." He began walking back toward the camp.

"Quinton Nevada Randolph, don't turn your back on me!"

He paused, whirled to glare at her. His expression was cold, his dark eyes stony. "I am called Nevada; that's all. I answer to nothing else."

Could she have been mistaken? It had been so long since that New Year's Eve and she hadn't seen him since. They said everyone in this world has a double. Could that be the case? Why would he not now want to claim a proud old family name?

He dismissed her with a shrug, started toward the camp. She almost had to run to keep up with his long legs. "Nevada, have you sent a message about the ransom yet?"

He made a noncommittal grunt and kept walking. How did one deal with a man like this one? She was too furious to be cautious. All her life, men had catered to her every whim and in turn, she had always done exactly what was expected of her. Yet sometimes she felt resentment and rebellion building in her soul so strong, she felt she was smothering.

Defeated, Cherish watched him walk away, his hard hips moving in the tight black pants. He walked with the easy grace of a big cat. For a moment, she remembered the sight of him naked, the water glistening on his nipples, the power of his wide shoulders, the sheen of his unkempt ebony hair. She would not let herself think about his male nakedness. Cherish ran her fingers across her lips absently, lost in the remembrance of that kiss. Had it really been just like the one that New Year's Eve? She was no longer sure of anything except that both those kisses were ever so much more exciting than the prim one Pierce had given her to seal their engagement.

Now what? Perhaps there was nothing to do but scout the valley out herself, look around for any possibilities of escape and wait for Daddy and Pierce to find her. She went back to her lodge, surprised Tequila holding the torn wedding dress up before her. "I—I did not hear you come up."

What was this pathetic tart doing? Cherish's heart softened as she realized Tequila was pretending she was a fine lady about to be married. Well, one thing was certain, Cherish thought as she surveyed all that was left of it, she herself would need a new one and where could she get it just weeks before the wedding? "You like it?"

Tequila looked embarrassed at being caught. "I thought maybe it could be mended."

"If you want it, you can have it."

"How much?" the girl asked shrewdly.

"What?" Cherish had so many wardrobes of clothes she couldn't wear them all. It occurred to her she really should go through her things and give some to charity.

"How much money you want?"

"Nothing. You may have the dress." In fact, Cherish wanted to get it out of her sight. For a moment she thought about it, uncertain as to whether it was because it reminded her of the ordeal of her kidnapping—or the fact that she was going home to marry a man her father had chosen for her. She was shocked at her own rebellious thoughts.

Turning, Cherish left the lodge, walked aimlessly around the camp. She tried to seem as casual as she could so no one would pay her any heed while she assessed the number of guards, where the horses grazed and anything else that might help her escape under cover of darkness.

On a big rock on the other side of the pass, she saw two men with rifles. The pair were hard-edged gun toughs and they looked alike, possibly the brothers Tequila had mentioned. On a rise near the horse herd, she saw Nevada and an Indian who might have been forty or fifty years old. With his lined face and gray-streaked hair, it was difficult to tell, but she remembered him taking Nevada's horse when they rode in last night.

The horse herd. Maybe if she could move closer, she could see just how many there were, how well the herd was guarded. She began to pick wildflowers. That should be an innocent-looking enough an activity for everyone to ignore.

Nevada watched the blonde as he rolled a cigarette. What the devil did she think she was doing? Picking wildflowers. It was something his mother would do. He winced, not wanting to think of her.

Kene grunted. "Pretty, but she bring you much trouble, maybe, as another woman brought your father."

"You knew him?" Nevada lit the cigarette.

"I knew him." His face was grave. "We rode together as young warriors. His sister, *Atsa,* and my woman, *Moponi,* were good friends."

"You never talk about those days." He only knew that *Kene* was a Paiute word for a type of hawk.

The older warrior sighed. "Best forgotten; old times gone forever. No longer do the Paiute and their brothers the Bannock and Shoshoni ride wild and free."

"What started that long ago trouble?"

"White men raped both girls and kill *Atsa.* My *Moponi* disgraced; bear half-breed child, run away. I never know what happen to her."

Rape. Wasn't that just what Nevada was thinking about? He smoked and watched the girl in the meadow pick wildflowers. The breeze blew her clothes against her form so that her breasts and hips were outlined. He had waited a long time and he wanted Cherish any way he could get her.

"Tell me about *Timbi*." He knew so little about him, except that Quint Randolph had been his blood brother. Bitterness came to his heart again that anyone could do what one friend had done to another.

"So little to tell." *Kene* shrugged. "Very brave warrior. He helped lead the uprising against whites who dig in the hills for the yellow and silver metal and send magic messages back and forth with galloping horses."

"The Pony Express," Nevada thought aloud. *Kene* was right, it had been very long ago, maybe 1860 or '61. "I have forgotten what *Timbi* means in Paiute."

"The rock. Good name for him. *Timbi* kill many at the Pyramid Lake battle against the whites."

Nevada watched the girl. Her long hair caught the sun and shone like spun gold, blowing out behind her. Yes, he could understand why two brothers could become bitter enemies, fight to the death over a woman. He could understand it, but he could not forgive it.

Kene sighed. "There were more whites the second time they came to fight. We could not win. We scattered and most returned to starve on the reservations."

"Did you see *Timbi* die?"

The handsome older brave didn't answer for a long moment. "The memories are bad; don't ask."

What else was there to know? Quint Randolph had admitted he was guilty.

His Medicine Hat stallion whinnied and tossed its mane, rearing up on its hind legs, pawing at the sky. A dainty palomino mare in heat nickered to the stud. He nickered deep in his throat, prancing sideways. She flung her cream-colored mane like a flirting woman and danced away. The stallion would have her. This was his herd and she belonged to him. He called out to her again and the mare hesitated, arched her pretty neck, dancing in place.

The great horse nipped her neck, shook his fine head, reared on his hind legs. The dainty mare stood still, knowing what was coming, her small hooves stamping. The stallion nuzzled her neck again and she flung her head as he danced about her. From here, Nevada saw the great iron bar of the stud's maleness, engorged and hard as the pinto moved. He nickered once more and then he reared up on the mare, lunging into her. She stood now and let him cover her, plunging into her as he gave her his seed. It was wild and savage and beautiful. In only moments, it was over. The docile mare was again grazing in the meadow, the stud, dominant and possessive of his herd, moved to a small rise where he could stand protectively.

Sky Climber. There was a Paiute legend of a great pinto stud with the same strange coloring. Many tribes thought the markings magic; the shield of color across its chest and head called Medicine Hat. "Was there ever really such a horse as the Medicine Hat stallion called Sky Climber?"

Kene nodded. "Some say he still runs these hills on moonlit nights."

"That can't be," Nevada argued, "it's been too long ago. Horses don't live forever."

The older brave looked at him a long moment. "I have seen him running along the snowy crests, but even I am not sure what I saw. Maybe he is not a horse, but a spirit vision, running wild and free in the Nevada hills forever."

Nevada shivered and crossed himself. He was too superstitious, or maybe too Indian not to believe in spirit medicine. He had never seen this vision, but once when he was in trouble, he thought he heard the spirit horse thundering through the hills.

"Many of the old stallion's colts roam this land," *Kene* said. "You ride one yourself. Maybe through the bloodlines, the great spirit horse can never really die. Horses and men prove their immortality through their sons."

Nevada looked down at his own strong hands. They were brown like *Timbi*'s, but he wore the Randolph family ring. He should take it off, throw it away, yet despite everything, he could not bring himself to do so. Quint had given it to him to mark his twenty-first birthday.

He watched Cherish pick some wildflowers as pink as her lips, place them in her hair. He imagined holding her close, burying his face in her fragrant locks, tangling his fingers as he pulled her close to kiss her. He had wanted her for his own, but somehow, his younger brother was the one chosen to be her mate.

Kene seemed to follow his gaze. "Sometimes a man is so bewitched by a woman's body, he will have her if it destroys him. In the end, a man's honor counts; remember that."

Was he talking about Nevada or about the terrible thing that had happened in these hills so many years ago? Murder. He did not blame his mother; he blamed Quint Randolph, who had no honor. He wished he had not found out.

Nevada watched Cherish and dreamed of making love to her in the moonlight of the meadow, taking her wild and frenzied among the blossoms as a stallion overtakes and mounts a mare. In his mind they were there together, running through the swaying grass under the stars. She wore wildflowers in her long hair and nothing else. When he caught her and pulled her to him, she would be warm and giving, molding herself against his body like a wild thing. The grass felt soft beneath their bare bodies, her hair a tangle of moonlight. When he buried his face in it, he didn't know if the heady scent was the flowers or the silken locks that cascaded down her shoulders and across her full breasts. She held out her arms to him, all satin bare skin and long slender legs locking around his hard driving hips, pulling him down to her. He would please her, pleasure her so that she would whimper aloud. Or was it the breeze sighing? Her breasts, supple belly, and eager mouth were offered for his pleasure. Finally they would mate there on the grass under the stars in a tender ritual as old as time itself.

He realized abruptly that he was holding his

breath, aching with the want of her. He had waited a long, long time to possess this woman. Honor or no honor, he would have Cherish tonight, no matter what he had to do, and damn the consequences!

Six

Amos Blassingame paced his office, impatient for Pierce Randolph to arrive. The sun was barely up and already Amos had gotten the governor out of bed, called his United States senator raising hell that a taxpayer's daughter was not safe on her own daddy's railroad. What was this bloody country of colonials coming to anyway?

His timid male secretary, what in blazes was his name? stuck his head around the door. "Sir, Mister Randolph is here."

"Well, show him in, you doddering idiot, and get that message through to Wells Fargo and the military. Let me know when the governor calls back!"

"Yes, sir." He retreated. His complexion was almost as colorless and drab gray as his suit.

Young Randolph burst into the room. "May I say, sir, that when I was awakened at the hotel with the dreadful news—"

"Yes, yes." Amos motioned him to a chair with an impatient gesture. He had no time now for expressions of sympathy. His success as a businessman had depended on viewing the problem, deciding what must be done, and forging ahead. Quickly he filled Pierce in on the details as he knew them and what action he had taken so far. By Jove, if the men he'd helped elect didn't do something fast, they'd regret it next election.

Pierce cleared his throat. "Now here's what I think we should—"

"I've taken care of things," Amos snapped. How dare this young chap do any thinking at all unless Amos told him to?

The secretary, Timothy Sparrow, was returning with a tea tray. He set it on the big mahogany desk. "Shall I pour, sir?"

"No, Sparrow, leave us." He dismissed him with a wave. "We're not to be disturbed until we're finished talking." Sparrow fled. Amos paused. His chest was hurting again.

"Is there something wrong, Mister Blassingame?" Pierce leaned forward in his chair. "You look a bit pale and—"

"I'm fine," Amos snapped, "just such a shock, you know. Getting where a decent girl isn't safe anywhere. You colonials. . . ." He poured two cups of strong, brisk tea. "Lemon or cream?"

"Er, however you're having yours, sir." The expression on Pierce's handsome face belayed the fact that he didn't care much for tea at all but was not about to tell his future father-in-law.

Amos poured big dollops of thick cream and three lumps of sugar in each cup, passed one to Pierce. "See if that suits you."

Pierce tasted, not managing very well to control the wry face he made. "Delicious, sir. The British certainly have a way with—"

"Yes, yes." Amos sat down in his chair behind the big mahogany desk and sipped his tea out of the dainty cup. His chest began to hurt again. He supposed he ought to go to the doctor, but that bloody bastard would put him on a strict diet and take all the good things away. "Have you heard any more?"

"No, sir, just the message you sent. The word must not be out to the papers."

"It had better not be! I'm a major stockholder in half the newspapers in California. No well-bred girl likes being mentioned in the papers except on the society page. I've already called that social editor and given him some lame excuse as to why he shouldn't go to the station. I told him there was some kind of problem with the engine; train delayed for a while in the desert."

"You won't be able to keep it quiet forever," Pierce said.

"I know that, but I figure maybe we can get her back before word leaks out she's been carried off by the Indians. Scandal; I don't need it in my family." He looked pointedly at the young man. "You know how far I will go to protect me and mine from such."

"I remember." Pierce nodded and sipped the tea. He didn't look as if the memory was a good one, Amos thought. Perhaps he was feeling guilty for his part in it, but it was water under the bridge. It had gotten rid of Cherish's unwanted suitor, so Amos thought it was well worth it—as long as Mr. and Mrs. Randolph never realized his part in it. He had never again discussed it with Pierce since it happened.

Cherish. His plump hands shook a little as he sipped his tea and saw her face in his mind. "There's not much more I can tell you. I spoke with the train crew. Indians waylaid the northern route train in Nevada last night, robbed it and abducted Cherish."

Pierce's face looked incredulous as he set his cup to one side. "My poor darling! But since when do Indians waylay trains?"

Amos shrugged and sighed. "I've had numerous robberies on the southern route for the past several years; just common outlaws. Arizona and New Mexico are such wild, lawless places, even with gunmen like that Billy the Kid dead now. Still and all, there's not been much trouble on my northern route, so I thought it would be perfectly safe for her and her little friends to take that shopping spree back East. I suppose I should have sent an armed escort with her."

"No, don't feel badly, Mister Blassingame, how were you to know?" Pierce crossed his long legs. He wore a stylish waistcoat and the finest silk cravat, Amos noted. "Anyway, she's used to having her own way; we both certainly cater to her. Cherish was determined to have that particular wedding dress even if it delayed the wedding again."

It was a sore point with both men, Amos thought glumly. This wasn't the first time it had been delayed. By thunder, this time, when they got her back safe and sound, they would get this wedding over with. *If* they got her back. The thought made his chest hurt again.

"I've heard of Indians carrying off white girls before, but what I don't understand is why they only took Cherish and not several?"

"Hmm." Amos fingered his gray mustache. "Maybe somehow they realized she was wealthier than the others. Maybe they might even be thinking of holding her for ransom."

"I didn't think savages were that sophisticated," Pierce mused. "Are there any clues at all?"

Amos shook his head. "Very few. The conductor remembered only that the leader wore a gold ring."

"A ring?" Pierce frowned. "I suppose there's some poor white man lying somewhere with his scalp lifted and his finger cut off. That's not much to go on."

Amos sighed and made a helpless gesture. "Come to think of it, the arrogant bandit who usually plagues my southern line was reported to have worn an unusual gold ring. I hope he was the one that Indian killed; would serve him right. I've set a trap for him several times lately, but he's smart and we didn't get him."

"If he's that smart, maybe he's given up his life of crime. I don't remember your mentioning a bandit." Pierce looked blank.

"I thought I had told you about that upstart. He and his gang rob my trains and then send his compliments to me and my daughter." He felt through

108

his pockets for his cigar case, but Pierce was already offering Amos one of his. "Here, sir, allow me." He lit it, too, then lit one for himself. "Well, if the Indians have killed him, I'd call it good riddance. Very small chance it's the same ring."

Amos nodded. "I'm just hoping. Nothing would make me happier than to hear that that cheeky bloke had been tortured and staked out to die and that's how the warrior came by the ring."

Pierce took a deep puff. "Gold rings are everywhere. It could be—"

"The conductor said this one was unusual." Amos savored the taste of the tobacco. "Said it had some kind of family crest, some animal maybe."

Pierce turned slightly pale, ran his finger around his shirt collar as if it were choking him.

"Man isn't safe anywhere anymore. We need to do something about law and order in this country, I tell you; not civilized like England."

"Yes, sir."

"I remember your father wore an unusual gold ring," Amos mused. "You said it had the family crest."

"It—it's been lost; I've forgotten how, stolen maybe."

Amos shrugged. The loss of a ring was not of much importance at the moment when he might have lost his most precious possession—his daughter. "I remember though that you always hoped to inherit your father's ring; surprised you didn't mention it."

Pierce shrugged and blew smoke. "I forgot about

it; there were some family problems, as you know, and we were all worried about Nevada wanting to go off down to South America to punch cattle."

Nevada. Would that young stallion always be a worry to him? He hoped the oldest Randolph son stayed as far away as possible. Still, something about Pierce's expression betrayed that there was still a soft spot in his heart for his brother. He thought briefly about his own older brother. William was a cold one. Still, there had been a few times when they were growing up that the two brothers really cared about each other. Blood was thicker than water, no matter what anyone said. "Does anyone know about that Pinkerton thing?"

Pierce shook his head. "No one. I probably could have handled it better. I was angry and hurt."

"You did just right, Pierce. As long as your parents never know I was the one who investigated." Amos leaned forward across the big mahogany desk.

"I was careful not to mention you."

"Good. Let's keep it that way. We both got what we wanted."

"Sometimes when I see how strained my parents look, I regret—"

"Guilt is the worst thing ever loaded on a human's shoulders," Amos grunted. "If you hadn't told him, someone else probably would have." In truth, he didn't care what had happened to the oldest son as long as the parents didn't blame Amos and the cheeky bloke stayed away from Cherish. "All that's neither here nor there. If that insolent train robber ended up with a gold ring and the Indian killed him, so much the better. When we track those savages down, if it turns out to be the Randolph ring, you'll get it back."

"Thank you, sir." He smiled warmly. "Now what's the next step?"

"I'm waiting for law enforcement and the governor to get back to me. It takes time to mount a posse this big. It may be tomorrow before—"

"Tomorrow?" Pierce without thinking had interrupted Amos, something he'd never had the nerve to do in all these years. His hazel eyes flashed with outrage. "Why, by tomorrow, that savage could have taken her and—"

"I know." Amos closed his eyes and winced. He didn't even want to think about delicate Cherish lying on her back with her thighs spread as Anne used to do while Amos . . . "The governor says they can't move any faster than that, and since it happened in Nevada, it's out of his jurisdiction." Damned politician! Who was friendly to railroads that Amos could put in the state house next election? Somewhere down the line, it might be his son-in-law.

"Nevada." Pierce stood up and paced a little, smoking his cigar. "A lot of wild terrain and untamed mountains. It'll be like looking for a needle in a haystack."

Amos nodded agreement. "You sound as if you've been there."

"No, but my parents have. I've heard them talk about it. Father raised horses for the Pony Express back in Sixty. I don't know how much they would remember about the terrain."

"Have you wired them what's happened?" He watched him, thinking that the information the Pinkerton agency discovered had fractured the parents' relationship with Pierce. That suited Amos fine, the young man would rely more heavily on his father-in-law when he needed money and advice. He wasn't going to lose a daughter, he was going to gain a son in the big Victorian mansion. One big, happy family.

Pierce paused, shook his head. "No, I suppose I'd better. Our relationship is a bit strained, but I figure they'll get over it. After all, I am their son and they like Cherish. Their attitudes will soften when I make a name for myself and present them with a houseful of grandchildren."

Amos didn't want to think about any man sleeping with his innocent daughter, but he did want strapping grandsons to inherit his empire. Too bad immaculate conception was only for miracles. "I suggest you start outfitting us for the posse," Amos said and took a deep puff on his cigar.

"Sir, are you sure you feel like going? You look a bit pale."

In truth, he didn't feel well. If he got out in the middle of that wilderness and had an attack of some kind, he'd slow the posse down. "As much as I regret it, I may have to put you in charge, Pierce, if I'm not up to going."

"You won't regret it, Mister Blassingame." Pierce ran his hand through his brown hair. "I'm certainly ready to go rescue my bride. I'll need a contact at this end to keep in touch with the governor's office and to relay important messages anyway."

"I'll consider it." Almost as much as losing his daughter, he dreaded ending up as a doddering old invalid. Invalids lost their power and others took over their empires, shuffled them to one side. Amos Blassingame wasn't about to let anyone take charge of his kingdom, not for a long time yet. "Check back with me later in the day."

"Yes, sir, you won't regret your reliance on me, sir."

Amos grunted. An idea was beginning to form in his mind. By Jove, young Pierce could come out of this a hero. With that and his attractive looks, family money and both families' power, Pierce could conceivably run for public office and win. As he matured, there wasn't any reason he couldn't be governor. The thought pleased him and it kept his mind off worrying about Cherish.

"Do let your parents know what has happened," he ordered. "There's nothing like trouble to heal old wounds." He wondered whether the second son stood to inherit some, all or none of his parents' land and fortune. As a second son himself, he had some bitter feelings about his older brother getting everything, from the property to the title. As much as he preferred Pierce, Amos didn't want to waste his precious daughter on a chap who brought little or nothing to the Blassingame empire.

"Is there any chance your brother will show up for the wedding?" He intended to make sure he got

Cherish safely married off before that one turned up back on the scene.

Pierce shook his head, looked almost wistful. "I think not. I don't really even know where he is and I don't mention him to my parents. Once we were close, but . . ." He didn't finish.

"Let's concentrate on getting Cherish back and try not to think of anything else." He threw his cigar in the spittoon. "Just as soon as I hear more, I'll send word. Don't worry, Pierce, my boy, I'm sure she'll be fine. Cherish is more like me than her mother; quite plucky."

A muscle twitched in the younger man's jaw and he, too, tossed his cigar in the spittoon. "I'll be waiting for your note. After I've waited all this time for Cherish, I can't bear the idea that some savage might . . . well, you know."

Amos winced. "Don't even think about it." He escorted Pierce out the door, told his secretary again that he wasn't to be disturbed unless the message was from the governor or the army, and returned to his office.

He felt so helpless and frustrated. Always before, money and power had opened doors, solved his problems. He wasn't at all sure it would help this time, and frankly, when he thought about it, he didn't have much faith in his future son-in-law's abilities. Now that older one had seemed so stubborn and independent, so capable of taking care of Cherish. But of course, that was one of the two reasons Amos had disliked him. He didn't want any man to take his only daughter away from him and especially take her far away to that godforsaken desert called Arizona. Nevada's scandalous heritage was the other reason. What was it Pierce had said about notes?

That took him back six years. Should Amos have done what he did then? Wouldn't any father have done as much to protect his only child? No, he wasn't sorry for his action, he just hoped Cherish never found out. How sharper than a serpent's tooth . . . no, she wouldn't be grateful at all for his interference. By Jove, why was he feeling so guilty? Cherish had been far too young and innocent to make an important choice like this alone.

He walked over to the window, stared out at the street scene, not really seeing the carriages and crowds. On the far horizon, the smoke from a train's engine hung like smudge in the midmorning air. He really should be doing something, but what? For once, he couldn't concentrate on business and he felt helpless to do anything about Cherish's plight now that he had called and put fear into public officials. All he could do was wait while the rescue mission got itself organized. He wasn't sure he was physically up to going, but he wouldn't make that decision until tomorrow. In the outer office, the clatter of the typewriter disturbed his thoughts. Frankly, he liked it better when all correspondence was done with a pen.

Correspondence. Could he never get away from the thought of letters and notes, or was it only his own conscience that made him remember? Amos lit another cigar and stared out the glass at the distant puff of smoke from the train.

Six years ago; the first week of January. Amos might not have made the decision to send Cherish so far away to school, but she had mentioned that oldest son of the Randolphs several times.

"Now, Cherish, dear," he had said again as they stood in the station while conductors and porters hurried about. "I know what's best for you, and believe me, someday you'll thank me for this."

"Fiddlesticks! I'll be sixteen in May, and I have no interest in going to Boston; it's too far away." She looked beautiful in a yellow velvet traveling suit, and a big hat with a garland of silk flowers on the brim. So fresh and springlike in such contrast to the smelly, grim station, Amos thought, she even smelled like a flower garden.

"Tut! Tut! I know it's far, my dear, and your daddy will be lonely without you, just as I miss your dear mother."

Cherish bit her lip, seemed to be struggling with a reply. "Aren't there some perfectly good schools in California?"

"Ah, but the best schools are those like Miss Priddy's in Boston." He patted her arm. "Think of it as an adventure. And of course you won't have to travel alone, young Pierce Randolph is on his way back to Harvard and has arranged to take the same train so you'll have a protector. Did you read the nice notes he and his mother sent thanking you for the lovely party?"

Cherish nodded. "Very nice. I don't suppose there was a note from any other gentleman?"

"Well, of course Hiram Pettigrew and his wife sent a note, and—"

"I thought there might have been a note from . . . never mind." She didn't look at him as she fiddled with a button on her waist.

"From who?" he asked innocently.

"I said never mind." She appeared a bit annoyed and upset as she looked up and down the platform.

"I'm sure any young gentleman who was impressed and interested in our family at all would have been polite enough to send flowers or at least a note. Young Pierce sent an expensive bouquet."

"Yes, I know. Remember Miss Grimley has hay fever and was sneezing over them, but she pronounced them lovely. Are you letting that old sourpuss go?"

"Now, Cherish, Miss Grimley has served us long and well. I can't find it in my heart to terminate her; she's such a loyal employee. Perhaps she can take over as head housekeeper, she'll like that."

"I always thought what she really had in mind was being Mrs. Amos Blassingame."

He was astounded and his face must have shown his surprise. It would never occur to him to marry below his social position. Democracy was fine for the working classes, but the Blassingames were distantly related to British royalty. Now it dawned on him why that gaunt spinster had been so very loyal.

"I'm sorry, Daddy, that wasn't kind of me." Cherish hung her head. "Perhaps you are right about my going off to school."

"Aren't I usually right, my dear?"

"It's just that now and then, I'd like to make some decisions on my own without feeling guilty about it."

"Guilty? Now why should you feel guilty, Cherish, dear? You know I've devoted my life to you. Nothing matters to me as much as your happiness."

Cherish took a deep breath, started to say something, looked away. "Here comes Pierce."

"Fine young man," Amos said, beaming, "real future, good family, not a bad choice a few years from now."

Cherish made a noncommittal answer as she dug in her reticule. "Daddy, I didn't have a stamp, would you mail this for me please?" She slipped the letter to him hurriedly as if she did not want Pierce to see it.

"Of course, my dear, I'll take care of it the moment I leave here." He turned to face Pierce. "Well, good to see you again!"

The men shook hands. Pierce touched the brim of his hat with a smile. "Good morning, Miss Blassingame, you look like a breath of spring in that dress; it's just the color of your hair."

Cherish blushed prettily. "Thank you, Pierce, you're so polite."

The train whistle blew and Amos said, "Well, by Jove, it's ready to leave." He shook hands with

Pierce again, wished him luck with his studies and kissed his daughter's cheek.

"All aboard!" the conductor yelled. "All aboard!"

"Goodbye and good luck to you both." He tried to keep his voice light, but now that it was actually time for her departure, he was not at all sure he really wanted her to go off to school and leave him in that big house all alone. On the other hand, if she stayed, that arrogant Quinton Nevada Randolph would attempt to call on her again.

The two boarded. Cherish went immediately to a window. She waved to Amos, appearing both excited and uneasy about going so far away.

Amos pasted a smile on his face and waved back as the train tooted again, began to pull out of the station.

Cherish's lips moved, formed the words, *don't forget to mail my letter.*

Amos nodded, waved reassuringly.

The train pulled away, black gritty smoke billowing back along the wooden platform on that January morning. Around him, people bustled and pushed, but Amos had eyes only for the train growing smaller as it picked up speed. He had work piled up on his desk at the office, but he stood there, forlorn and alone until the train was lost from sight. It's for her own good, he thought stubbornly and turned away. He paused by a trash bin and pulled her letter from his pocket. It was addressed in her sprawling, small script to Nevada Randolph. Amos hesitated only a moment before he opened and read it.

Dear Mister Randolph:

Just wanted your family to know how much I enjoyed meeting you and our conversation in the billiard room New Year's Eve. Perhaps sometime when you are going to be in Sacramento, we might discuss the John Fouch Western photos again. Tell your parents hello for me. . . .

Why, it was almost forward and completely out of character for Cherish. Obviously that brass young pup brought out a rebellious streak in her that if allowed to flourish might even turn his genteel daughter into one of those Suffragettes marching in the streets for Women's Rights, God forbid!

He contemplated her letter for a moment. Cherish trusted him to mail it and of course he would tell her he had. When she got no answer, she would be disillusioned with that older son and the younger one would look so much better to her. Very slowly, Amos tore the letter into small bits and tossed it in the trash. Nevada Randolph would get a letter, all right. Surely after reading it, the young buck would never come near Cherish again, he'd be too humiliated.

Reaching into his pocket, he pulled out the other note, the one Cherish never knew had arrived at the house. Miss Grimley was loyal all right; to the man who paid her salary. Amos frowned as he reread it. Obviously the young upstart was pressing his case. Well, he intended to nip that in the bud!

Dear Miss Blassingame:

I didn't really want to attend your New Year's Eve party, but I'm so glad I accompanied my parents to Sacramento.

I've asked your father's permission to begin calling on you when you're old enough, but he seemed unenthused. I am willing to wait forever if need be if you can offer me any hope at all that there's the slightest chance that you might feel the same. If while you are away at school, you should be kind enough to drop me a note offering encouragement, I will make a trip to Sacramento and see your father again.

Most respectfully,
Quinton Nevada Randolph

That arrogant pup! Try to go behind her father's back, would he? No, Nevada Randolph was not going to get a note of encouragement, but he would get a note that would take care of the problem.

When Cherish didn't hear from him, she'd think he wasn't interested and forget him. In the meantime, young Pierce would be on the scene in Boston and might call on her often at Miss Priddy's. Amos was willing to let nature take its course. Four or five years from now, Pierce might sway her affections. Amos tore Nevada's letter into tiny pieces and threw them in the trash bin. Should he feel guilty? he asked himself as he strode toward his carriage. Of course not, he was merely looking out for his beloved daughter's interests. That young cowboy could find another girl to take far away.

The smoke from the train drifted on the horizon. Amos started, realized he was still standing before the window, looking out at the passing scene. No, he wasn't sorry for what he'd done. Maybe if Cherish ever found out about it, enough time would have passed that she'd understand.

In the meantime, he was losing his mind with worry about her whereabouts. He heard the office door behind him open. "Sir, the governor has sent a messenger."

"Finally!" Amos roused himself from his memory and walked away from the window. "Maybe we can have troops and a posse searching that state by tomorrow. I'm going to make that savage who abducted my daughter wish he'd never been born!"

Dusk spread a lavender haze across the valley. Nevada had waited all day for this. Through these long years he had dreamed of making love to Cherish and since he had kidnapped her from that train last night, he had thought of little else.

His pulse raced as he walked toward his lodge; tonight I'm finally going to make her mine. He frowned. No, she would never be his, but he intended to possess her at least one night. The dangers he faced every day made him a hard-edged realist. Sooner or later, he would have to give her up so she could return to his brother's bed. Nevada smiled but there was no humor in his heart. Pierce might end up with Cherish, but Nevada intended to have her first. He smiled and his pulse pounded with anticipation. Yes, tonight, princess, you're mine!

Seven

Cherish looked up as he entered the lodge. She took a deep breath, seemed to gather her courage. "I've been wondering where you were. We need to discuss my ransom."

He only grunted, watching her pale yellow hair catch the last rays of daylight. Once again he felt the need to hold her, protect her, adore her. He thrust those emotions aside. All he really wanted, he told himself, was to possess her ripe body. "While we discuss this, there's no need for us to make each other miserable. We could go up on a hillside, cook some beef. I have a couple of bottles of good wine I've saved for just such an occasion."

"Where'd you steal the cow?" she sniffed.

He grinned. "Let's just say it followed me home."

"You kidnap girls often?"

"Only when I have good reason." She no longer seemed as afraid of him and he was almost amused at her sudden show of spirit. He had always wondered if there was any real fire behind that perfect-lady exterior. "Come, let's not argue, not when it's going to be such a perfect night."

"I'm not sure I can eat stolen beef."

"Well, you've got a choice, princess, you can starve. We're a little low on supplies."

"I've never had dinner with a bandit."

"Sure you have, I'll bet your daddy brings those corporate types home for dinner all the time."

Her face flushed. "Don't be rude."

"You call me a bandit and then complain I'm rude?" Cherish had more spunk than he had given her credit for. He searched out the bottles of wine, one of whiskey, grabbed a blanket. "I've already got the camp fire going and the steaks cooking." He offered her his arm.

She hesitated, then took it. "All right. Since I must eat anyway. I need the strength to survive until I'm rescued. It will be my deepest pleasure to have another drink at your hanging."

"You do have a sharp tongue, don't you? Very well, I'll drink to that myself; don't ever let it be said I wasn't a good sport." He was more than a little conscious of her small hand on his arm as they left the lodge. "With your tongue like a razor, I may have to pay your dear daddy to take you back."

"It was awful of you to masquerade like a war-painted red devil, ready to take my scalp."

He chuckled. "You should have seen your face; priceless!"

"You think it's funny to scare me half to death?"

He looked over at her and he didn't smile. "Maybe I feel you deserve it."

"Fiddlesticks! I'm not even sure what you're talking about."

Now she was a liar, too. All right, he could play that game. "The law seemed to be everywhere, so we didn't figure anyone would notice a ragged band of scruffy braves. Things were getting too hot along the southern route and the northern run looked like easy pickings. Some of my men are real Indians; Paiutes, mostly. The train through their lands has destroyed scrub pine and prickly pear. They live off piñon nuts and small game that's been scared away by Trans-Western's trains."

She whirled, confronted him. "Are you blaming me for that?"

"No, Miss Blassingame, I blame your father."

"No one can stop progress." Her eyes blazed, her cheeks flushed with anger.

"No, but some thought could be given to the poor devils progress is rolling across."

She tossed her head. "Better be careful, someone might accuse you of being a maudlin, sentimental fool."

He started to say something, decided it wasn't worth the effort to remind her that the last time he had been sentimental, he had made a fool of himself over a fifteen-year-old girl who then laughed and spurned him. A lady's man; a man of the world, done in by a spoiled, spirited girl who was only toying with him.

Everything was quiet as they strolled across the camp, the day lengthening into evening.

"Such a beautiful sunset!" she exclaimed.

"Yes, isn't it?" He looked toward the lavender-and scarlet-streaked sky on the purple rim of the western hills. "The only thing more breathtaking than a Nevada night is a Nevada dawn."

They strolled across the clearing while she studied the sky. "I always dreamed of living in the West."

"You can't get much farther west than California."

"I meant land with no crowded streets to block my view; a place of freedom, no corsets, no governess watching my every move and reporting to Daddy."

Nevada watched her out of the corner of his eye, resisting an almost overpowering urge to sweep her into his arms, kiss her until they were both breathless. *I offered you the West and my heart, princess,* he thought, *and you spurned me with cutting sarcasm.*

Then Amos Blassingame took his revenge. How he must have laughed over the mischief he caused, the terrible conflict he created between me and my brother. He thought of Cain and Abel. Instinctively, he crossed himself, then realized what he had done, glanced quickly to see if she had noticed. She had.

The very last ray of light glimmered on the gold of her hair. Cherish had never looked lovelier than she did at this moment in her simple, low-cut blouse and skirt; no, not even the night of the New Year's Eve party. They passed Charlie eating tortillas and drinking coffee before a small fire. Nevada didn't like the way his eyes brightened as the rangy outlaw's gaze swept over Cherish. He hoped Charlie remembered he, along with his brother, was beholden to Nevada for saving them from a lynch mob. Cherish belonged to him; at least for this one precious night. "Charlie, don't forget it's your turn to stand guard duty later."

"Sure, Nevada." His stare raked across her ripe body. The lean outlaw touched the brim of his Western hat. "Evening, ma'am." He smiled, showing one gold tooth.

Cherish nodded and gave the other man just the hint of a smile. Perhaps here was someone who might be charmed into helping her escape. Nevada escorted her to a rise where a merry camp fire burned. She noticed tin plates and cups. Two big steaks sizzled on the fire, sending up tantalizing scents as their juices dripped into the flames. She took a deep breath and smelled fresh-baked bread.

Almost in answer to her curious expression, Nevada said, "Bread can be baked in an adobe oven. Indians and Mexicans have been doing it for centuries." He spread the blanket on the ground by the fire. "Sit down, Miss Blassingame, and I'll play servant. That should make you feel right at home."

"Oh, but of course! Nothing would please me more than to have you as a servant. Maybe it's too bad slavery no longer exists so I could put you in chains, whip you, and sell you to some horrible plantation."

"Your kindness overwhelms me, princess." His voice sounded cold as he opened the wine, poured it into a tin cup, poured himself some whiskey.

She must have looked aghast because he raised one eyebrow at her. "The good crystal," he said with a touch of sarcasm, "is off being polished by the maid."

Why did he hate her so? She was baffled by his attitude. Even though she'd met him only a few minutes that long ago night, she was certain he had changed dramatically. Quinton Nevada Randolph might be a lady's man and fast with a gun, but he had no need to turn into a bandit.

"Drink up," he said and gestured.

Why not? She gulped the wine, annoyed with him for kidnapping her and upsetting her wedding plans. She imagined Daddy and Pierce's faces this morning when they arrived at the train station to meet her; but of course they had surely received word before dawn. She looked up, spotted her first star of the night as the warmth of the wine spread through her. "Star light, star bright . . ." Cherish paused.

"What did you wish?"

"What did *you* wish?" she challenged.

"Don't be silly, gunfighters don't wish on stars; that's for moonstruck young girls who believe in fairly tales and 'happily ever after.' "

She settled herself on the blanket, sipped her wine, watched him turn the steaks. Maybe she was silly and moonstruck. Somehow, she had expected she'd feel differently, more passionate toward her intended. So far, what seemed the high point of the wedding plans were the dresses and parties and gifts.

Nevada sneaked a glance at her as she sipped her wine. The way she was sitting, he could see the swell of her firm young breasts in the neck of the low-cut blouse. No woman had ever looked so desirable to him and there was none he'd ever wanted so much. He wanted more than that. He had wished on the star, too, he was too superstitious not to, but he would have felt embarrassed to admit it. He had wished that she was his, truly his, and that she would want to stay with him without being held against her will. He had loved Cherish Blassingame from the very first moment her fresh, innocent face looked up at his with those trusting big eyes.

She had been a bit tipsy that night, too, when she followed him to the billiard room. He had a sense of honor about innocent women, and plying them with liquor. She had been the one to raise her face expectantly to his while the orchestra played "Beautiful Dreamer."

He no longer had those scruples, not after the way the Blassingames had treated him; after what Pierce had done. Yet there was one thing he could not bring himself to do; he had to face the fact that he could never force himself on any woman, no matter how badly he lusted for her. No matter how badly he wanted revenge.

Nevada smiled ever so slightly, remembering. Cherish couldn't handle liquor, not even a little. A bit more and she might lose that frosty exterior. He wanted her, but he wouldn't take her by force. He intended to get her drunk and seduce her instead. "Here, princess, have some more wine."

"I thought I'd wait until the steaks were ready." Her face appeared to be slightly flushed.

"It'll be a while yet." He refilled her cup. "How do you like yours?"

"Medium well." She sipped her wine and savored the full-bodied fruity taste. It was a fine wine. No doubt he had stolen it from the private rack on her father's train.

"Then it will be a while," he said and picked up his own drink. "I like mine so rare, a steer hurt worse than that could recover."

Cherish wrinkled her nose; a bit giddy. "Why am I not surprised that an uncivilized bandit eats his meat almost raw?"

"I thought we agreed to a truce over dinner?"

"Did we?" She was beginning to feel a bit reckless as the wine spread through her system. "Why aren't you drinking wine?"

"I prefer whiskey; wine is the sort of sissy thing Pierce drinks."

"He doesn't eat his meat raw, either."

"See? I rest my case." He seemed to be fighting a smile as he sipped his whiskey.

She must remember not to drink too much, Cherish reminded herself. On the other hand, if she could get him drunk, maybe that Charlie who had seemed so friendly might help her escape—for a price.

Just what was Nevada up to? If he was just waiting for the ransom, he didn't have to wine and dine her. The paradox baffled her. And why did he need money so badly if the Randolphs were well off? She couldn't think of any other reason to kidnap her. If he just wanted a woman, several of her friends were prettier than she was, Cherish thought, and while none would admit it under torture, she wouldn't be surprised if several of them wouldn't have jumped at the chance to be carried off by a handsome warrior or bandit. Somehow, she no longer feared for her honor. The Randolphs had Southern heritage; she didn't think Nevada would force himself on her. She looked at him turning the steaks, lithe muscles rippling under his black shirt. At least, she didn't think he'd do anything to soil a lady's honor.

Cherish Blassingame, she scolded herself, if he had any honor, he wouldn't have kidnapped you. You can't trust a man like that . . . could she?

It was comfortable sitting on this blanket by the warm fire in the cool night. A slow and languorous warmth seemed to be spreading through her body. In the moonlight, the camp appeared to be closing down for the night. She wondered which man Tequila slept with and what was happening in that lodge tonight? Images came to her mind of two people locked in a hot embrace and she blinked, glanced toward Nevada. A lady shouldn't think of things like that; it wasn't proper. Here and there a camp fire still burned and one dog barked at the moon. She searched the darkness for the horse herd, spotted Nevada's big stallion grazing quietly among his mares. When she looked toward the pass, Charlie was already up there, sitting guard with his rifle and a cigarette. She began to plan her escape. Of course she would have to wait for Nevada to go to sleep or get drunk and pass out.

She forced herself to smile at him. "I'll have another drink. You having one, too?"

"Sure." He poured them each one before he turned back to take the steaks from the fire. Quickly, Cherish poured hers out in the grass. She was already a little dizzy without drinking any more. Maybe she was more than a little dizzy.

A slow warmth spread through her, down her thighs. She was abruptly aware of her nipples brushing against the thin blouse. Every nerve in her body seemed to be coming intensely alive as her mind grew more foggy. "Here, eat up." He handed her a tin plate of sizzling steak and fried potatoes, passed her the crusty bread, still warm from its place near the fire.

Cherish took a deep breath. She had never smelled anything so good. She cut into it, took a bite. The succulent juices seemed to drip on her tongue. She chewed slowly, enjoying it as she had never enjoyed a meal with Daddy and Miss Grimley. Smathers, the butler, was always hovering in the background.

Nevada smiled and cut into his own steak. "It's the mesquite wood we cook with, gives it that extra flavor."

She had to be careful not to wolf the food down. It had been a long time since she'd been this hungry. Usually she toyed with her food.

He seemed to enjoy watching her eat. "Can you cook?"

She shook her head. "We have a houseful of servants, you know."

"Just what do you do, Miss Blassingame?"

"If it's any of your business, which it isn't, I do the things all my friends do."

"Which is?" He put another bite in his mouth.

"Volunteer work, and of course, society teas. I play croquet and I'm learning to ride a bicycle; it's going to be the new craze."

"Sounds as if Daddy is pretty strict."

Was he making fun of her? "My fiancée thinks it important a lady behave like a lady."

Sweet, I'd like to see you behave like a woman, he thought, but he only grunted and returned to his food. After a long moment, he said, "You ride, don't you?"

On this, she felt competent. She looked him in the eye. "As well as you do, I'll bet!"

He smiled at her cocky challenge. "Good! We'll go riding tomorrow. There's a nice trail through the valley near the lake behind us."

She didn't intend to be here tomorrow if she could escape tonight, but of course she didn't say that. "I might as well. Being held for ransom is really quite dull."

"I'm sorry I bore you."

She almost felt apologetic. When she realized that, she felt annoyed with herself. Why should she feel guilty that she might have hurt her kidnapper's feelings? "You don't seem to understand; I'm on my way home for the biggest wedding California society ever saw."

"I understand. You might be a bit late getting

134

there; I hope the invitations haven't been delivered." She couldn't tell if he were angry or just sarcastic.

There was no point in delving any further into this and angering him. What kind of ransom he was asking for, she couldn't guess, but she didn't think Daddy would have any trouble raising the money. Then he'd have President Cleveland or, at the very least, the governor and the troops hunting this desperado down like a dog. She might as well enjoy the rest of the evening, be civil to him, put him off his guard. She wondered how much whiskey he'd have to drink to pass out. He looked as if he could handle his liquor as well as his women. It might take hours, and she didn't seem to have that much time or that much whiskey. Unbidden, the memory of that Madge Pettigrew kissing him hungrily, rubbing against him, came to her mind. Was he really that good with women? What a shocking thought for her to have! She must have had more wine than she realized.

"Finished?" He broke into her thoughts and she could only be glad he couldn't read her mind. She nodded and he took the plates, set them aside, refilled both cups. "It's turned a little cool."

She felt mellow and relaxed, staring into the fire. "I can smell the scent of wildflowers on the breeze."

"I watched you pick them today," he said, "and imagined making love to you in the middle of the meadow."

She didn't know what to say. Certainly it was not the sort of thing Pierce had ever said to her in all these years he'd been courting her. Pierce had been

135

so chivalrous. Or was it that she didn't appeal to him as a woman the way she did to Nevada? She shivered a little at the thought of making love in the meadow among crushed wildflowers.

"Are you cold?"

"No, I—I don't think so."

However, he had already moved so that he was sitting behind her. He reached out and very gently slipped his arm around her waist, pulled her back up against his warmth.

Cherish started to protest, but the warmth of his muscular body seemed to draw her closer to him. Without meaning to, she leaned against him and he kissed the top of her head. Such a tender gesture from such a brute of a man. She felt his warmth and closed her eyes, still a bit dizzy with the wine. Sacramento and Pierce seemed very far away. This man had kidnapped her, but she felt protected and safe in his embrace. Was she losing her mind? Her brain told her she should move away from him, thank him for the dinner . . . but if she did that, how was she going to get him drunk so she could escape?

He had one big hand in her hair, gently combing it with his fingers. It sent goose bumps up and down her back. "Are you cold, baby?" His breath was whiskey-warm on her neck.

Baby. He was not more than five or six years older than she, but he had so much more experience in living. She started to say no, she wasn't cold, it was something else. She could not bring herself to say anything, afraid he would stop brushing his lips along her neck. Cherish closed her eyes, wondering how many women he had held. Her blouse had fallen down one shoulder and now he kissed there. "I—I don't think—"

"Don't think, Cherish. Just close your eyes and enjoy."

She was enjoying it; that's what made her feel so guilty. "Just because I'm your prisoner, you think you can do anything you want with me."

"I could, but I won't." His lips were brushing across her shoulder again. "Nothing is going to happen, princess, except what you allow."

"You promise? I'll bet you've got your fingers crossed."

He laughed. "Would you take the word of a low-down bandit? Very well, I promise."

This was really quite innocent, she thought with a sigh of relief. Of course she wasn't going to allow anything to happen. She just had to keep him occupied and interested while she got him drunk. "Wouldn't you like another drink?"

"Wouldn't you?"

There was nothing she could do but accept. He didn't let go of her as he reached to refill their cups. "Drink up," he said.

She only sipped hers, but he gulped his down, then very gradually so that she didn't realize it, he was turning her until he kissed her and she tasted the warm liquor on his lips. He was barely brushing his lips across hers. "I—I don't think—" and when she said that, he put the tip of his tongue in her mouth.

Cherish gasped at the sensation. It felt like an electrical bolt of lightning running through her. Gradually, she let him push against her lips until she opened them and his tongue caressed deep into her mouth. She reached up and slipped her arms around his neck, not wanting him to stop, it felt so good. One of his hands tugged gently at her blouse so that it slid down her shoulder.

She gasped aloud as he coaxed her tongue into his mouth and arched her back so her nipples brushed his hard chest. His hands tangled in her long hair and tilted her head so that her white throat was offered up to his mouth in a submissive gesture. His mouth felt hot along her neck as he kissed down and down. Oh, surely he wouldn't go much farther. He had said he would stop when she asked him to, didn't he? She couldn't remember, but she couldn't bring herself to say the word that would tell her if he lied.

Her heart seemed to be pounding so hard, she was certain he could feel it against him as he kissed the hollow of her throat. Oh, surely his mouth wouldn't go to her collarbone, but it did. Only vaguely did she feel his big hand cover her breast. She must stop him, but of course she couldn't say the word "no" because his mouth was on hers again. She hadn't known a kiss could be like this. Yes, she did. Once again she was fifteen years old with a Stephen Foster tune playing softly in the background. His hand caught hers, brought it down to cover his manhood, held it there. He felt as hard as iron and pulsating. Abruptly, she felt dewy wet between her thighs.

His hand returned to stroking her breast. She knew she ought to say the word and maybe she would in another moment, but it felt so good with his fingers kneading her breast through her blouse.

She must be a bit drunk, she decided, but she wasn't thinking clearly enough to be sure.

"Here, baby," he whispered in her ear and the warmth of his breath sent chills up and down her back, "let's just lie down a moment by the fire; you seem cold."

"I—I am," she lied. How could she tell him she was reacting to his animal magnetism? She couldn't seem to stop herself from curling up against him as he lay her down on the blanket. She snuggled against him and his arms went around her most protectively.

He kissed her bare shoulder again. The warmth of the fire against her back was nothing compared to the feel of his long, virile body against her front. Somehow, her skirt had worked up her thighs and he stroked her bare legs. She had the most insatiable yearning to open her thighs. No, of course she must not do that. His fingers now slipped up one thigh and teased under the edge of her lace drawers. She really must tell him to stop doing that, but now he kissed her again while his fingers stroked and stroked under the lace. Surely he wasn't going to touch her there?

But he did. Cherish moaned aloud and pressed herself against his hand.

"Yes, baby," he murmured, "yes, princess. . . ."

She felt silky wet where his fingers touched; silky wet and on fire. Impossible. She couldn't stop herself from pushing against his hand, but she wasn't sure what it was she wanted. He breathed harder and she dug her nails in his shoulders, feeling the rippling muscles there. Whatever was about to happen, she had never felt such an emotion. It was scary. "N-Nevada?"

"Hmm." He was kissing her, pulling at her blouse. Now he had his mouth on her nipple, running his tongue back and forth over it as it swelled with desire. Pierce had never made her react this way, had never tried. Maybe she didn't affect him the way she affected his brother.

Pierce. Was she out of her mind? Her wedding invitations were ready to be sent. The caterer had been selected. How could she be rolling around on a blanket with some dark desperado? Guilt brought her to her senses. She was supposed to be escaping, but he didn't seem on the verge of passing out at all. Abruptly, her head cleared even though he was still kissing her breast with abandon. She reached out, grabbed a rock, took a deep breath. She wasn't sure she could do this. *Cherish, are you insane? He's kidnapped you and you're worried about hurting him?* With that thought, she hit him in the head.

Nevada collapsed beside her. Anxiously, she checked him. No, he wasn't dead, only unconscious. She managed to wiggle away from him, took the pistol from his holster, opened the bottle of whiskey, poured a little on his clothes. Maybe his first thought would be he'd passed out from drinking. She needed all the time she could get.

Cherish stood up, adjusted her clothes, tucked the pistol in her waistband. She was still shaken, knowing she had come awfully close to forgetting how to say the word "no." She hadn't realized it would be so difficult. Well, at least she had a gun, even if she didn't know how to shoot. None of these outlaws knew that, and if she were close enough, maybe it wouldn't matter.

She looked down on the camp. It was late and the camp seemed to be asleep. A few hundred yards away, the horses grazed. Charlie Whitley sat up on a big rock keeping a watch over the pass, his rifle propped beside him. He looked about half asleep. Now what to do? Her nerve almost failed her. If she stepped on a twig or tripped over a pebble as she approached him, Charlie would snap awake. From long habit, he might shoot first and ask questions later. Well, she had to get past him to get out of here and she needed a horse. She paused, looked down at the unconscious gunfighter. She felt guilty in spite of herself. Then she thought about her torn wedding gown and the bridal parties she was missing and got mad all over again. It served him right!

Cherish tiptoed through the shadows. The moon had gone behind a cloud so the darkness hid her like a protective blanket. She had certainly changed in only one night. She hadn't known she could be so bold. Before, she would have whimpered helplessly and waited for Daddy or Pierce to solve the problem. Well, neither of them was here and she was obviously more capable than she had thought.

Charlie was rolling a cigarette. She moved up quietly behind him, her heart pounding in her chest so loudly, she was afraid he could hear it. She heard the match strike, smelled the scent of the burning tobacco, heard him sigh. He leaned back against the rock and smoked.

Now what did she do? She couldn't shoot him without rousing the whole camp and then she'd be caught before she could escape. Besides, she was a gentle person, she wasn't sure she could ever kill anyone, not even someone responsible for destroying her fancy wedding gown. She looked back toward Nevada. From here, she could see the small fire and the shadow of the blankets. It looked like people asleep. If Charlie glanced over there, that's what he would think and wouldn't go investigating.

What to do about Charlie? She didn't have anything to tie him up with. There was only one thing to do. Taking a deep breath, she stepped out of the shadows behind him. "All right, get those hands in the air!"

"What the hell—?" He whirled in surprise. His gold front tooth shone in his weathered face.

"You heard me, and be quick about it or I'll blow you apart." She waved the pistol.

"Girlie, be careful where you point that thing, it might go off."

"Wouldn't that be too bad? I'm getting out of here and you're going to help me." She gestured with the pistol again, too drunk and mad and scared to consider how rash her actions were. Neither Daddy nor Pierce would ever believe she was capable of such action. Come to think of it, they didn't seem to think she was capable of much of anything except being decorative and doing as she was told. Cherish walked over, took his rifle.

"Be careful with that thing; I'll do anything you want. How'd you get Nevada's pistol?"

"Never mind." She gestured toward the herd. "Saddle up a couple of horses, and if you raise an alarm, I'll shoot you."

"Yes, ma'am. Two horses?"

"Well, I've either got to kill you or take you with me. Now move!"

Eight

Cherish kept the gun trained on the outlaw while he caught two horses. Could she bluff him? She wasn't sure if she could bring herself to kill a man. Besides, if she did shoot Charlie, it would bring everyone running so she couldn't escape anyhow. Of course maybe he hadn't thought of that.

He bridled two horses, a black and a buckskin, brought them over. "Saddles are back down in the camp."

She looked in that direction, decided there was no way to get them; too risky. "We'll ride bareback."

"Honey, are you loco? Have you ever ridden bareback?"

"Hush up and let's get out of here." Of course she had never ridden bareback, she'd never even ridden astride.

He spat at her feet. "The only canteen we've got is the one I had with me on guard duty and it's not full—"

"So that will have to do." He was attempting to

144

stall her until help came, she realized, but Cherish wasn't that stupid. She kept the pistol trained on him and gestured for him to mount the buckskin. Even from here, she could see the nervous blink of his pale eyes as he mounted.

"Look, honey, one canteen between us out here in this country—"

"We'll manage." She reached up, took the canteen away from him. What about his rifle? It was tempting, but she couldn't handle it and the pistol, too, on the black. The night seemed as dark as the devil's soul. She was still dizzy from the wine. At least she wanted Charlie on the lighter-colored horse so she could see him on this now moonless night.

Keeping her gun on him, she led the black over to a rock, used it to climb up on the horse. Her skirt slipped up her bare thighs as she sat astride. Cherish had never ridden a horse astride before, but she was desperate enough to try anything. The outlaw's gaze went to her thighs with her skirt scooting up, showing an expanse of long, slim leg. There wasn't anything she could do about that now. My, what would the ladies' garden club think if they could see all this? Last night, she had been a swooning, upper-class lady. Now in sheer desperation, she would have to be bold and daring, make some decisions for herself for almost the first time in her life. She waved the weapon. "Okay; you ride ahead of me down the trail and don't make any sudden moves."

"Just be careful with that pistol, honey," he cautioned again.

"If it does go off, remember it's pointed at you."

"I ain't forgot that."

They rode out through the pass. Cherish felt as if her heart was in her mouth. At any moment, she expected to hear a hue and cry behind her as Nevada and the others took up the chase. Would he be angry enough to shoot her? She wouldn't be at all surprised after she'd hit him in the head and left him sprawled unconscious on the blanket. She took a deep breath of the night air. It smelled faintly of mesquite and sagebrush. Somewhere, a cricket chirped. The moon stayed behind the clouds so she had one thing to be thankful for. Even as they rode down through the pass, she expected to feel a bullet tear into her back at any moment.

She wouldn't think about that; she'd think about escaping and returning to her nice, safe home with its dark Victorian furnishings, pompous butler, and dour Miss Grimley. Safe and secure, yes, it was that. So was a prison. The mansion suddenly was a place she didn't really like.

It seemed forever that they traveled through the rocks and down the trail. Now they rode through shadowy brush and sage. She kept the pistol trained on the rangy man on the buckskin horse. Still no outcry behind them. Was it possible she might actually escape? They rode several miles before Cherish allowed herself to speak again. "Just don't get any ideas, Charlie. Stay ahead of me and keep those hands where I can see them."

He glanced back at her and grinned. "Honey, you ain't takin' me in to no sheriff, are you?"

"I'm not your honey or anyone else's," she

snapped. Her head had begun to clear and it horrified her to think how close she had come just minutes ago to giving her precious virginity to that smooth-talking desperado. "Just behave yourself, Charlie, and keep riding."

He cursed under his breath. "You wouldn't shoot a man in the back, would you?"

"Why not? I'll bet you would."

"The boys'll laugh their heads off that I let a prissy little thing like you get the drop on me. What are you plannin' to do with me, honey?"

"Shoot your head off if you don't stop calling me that. Which way's the railroad from here?"

Charlie turned on his horse and grinned at her. He might have been almost handsome if he'd shave and if it weren't for the gold tooth. "Why should I help you?"

"Because if you don't, I might shoot you."

"Then I wouldn't be of any use at all to you, now would I, huh?"

At least he wasn't so stupid he couldn't figure that out. They broke into a canter as Cherish considered his logic. She was an excellent rider, but she'd never ridden bareback or astride before, so she had to keep her mind on her riding. Just what was she going to do with Charlie now that she had him?

What to do? She had no rope to tie him up and she couldn't stand guard on him continually. Sooner or later, he'd grab her gun. However, if she let him go, he'd raise the alarm. Was there any way to bring him around to her side? She remembered the way he had leered at her. A gentleman Charlie wasn't.

Money. If there was anything outlaws had in common, it must be greed or they wouldn't be robbing trains. Charlie might be lured to help her through a large reward.

They rode until the horses were blowing and lathered before they reined in and walked them to cool them out. She looked back over her shoulder. The trail was empty. She strained her ears, listening for sounds of pursuit. Nothing but the snorting of their horses and Charlie grumbling under his breath.

Money. Daddy thought everyone in the world could be bought. "Charlie, you make much riding with Nevada?"

"Not as much as Jack and me want. Nevada keeps giving it to the Injuns to buy blankets and food."

Robin Hood, she thought. Somehow, it made her see him a little differently. "You ridden with him long?"

"You're just full of questions, ain't you?"

"Aren't you even curious as to who I am?"

"Nope. Nevada's woman is all I heard."

"I am not Nevada's woman." She was almost horrified at how close he had come to seducing her. "My father is a very rich man; president and biggest stockholder of Trans-Western Railroad."

Charlie whistled shrill and low. "God damn, Nevada's got high-dollar taste, don't he?"

"I think that low-down thief intended to hold me for ransom, not realizing my daddy and my fiancé would hunt him down like a coyote. No doubt there's already been a big reward posted for my safe return."

148

"And a bounty on us for bein' part of it?" Charlie looked uneasy again, and his eyes blinked.

"Of course! Daddy will be furious that I was stolen off one of his own trains."

Charlie stared at her. "Good God! I wish Jack knew what we had gotten ourselves into."

He was scared. This was the time to suggest her plan. "There might be pardons and rewards for anyone who helps get me returned safe and sound."

"You suggestin' we cross Nevada?"

She shrugged. "I'm suggesting if you don't want to end up at the wrong end of a rope, you'd better help me."

Charlie laughed. "Me and my brother both already come close to bein' at the wrong end of a rope. Nevada was only riding through Utah as a bunch of drunks was about to throw a lynchin' party with me n' Jack as guests of honor."

"Think about it," she said. "Nevada wasn't too worried about putting a price on you and the whole gang's heads by kidnapping me."

"Now that's the God's truth!" Charlie grumbled.

She'd leave that for him to think about and worry over for a while, Cherish thought as she glanced over her shoulder again. It was a long time till dawn, but Nevada might rouse and find her missing anytime. The head start she had depended on how far she could ride before they realized she was gone and no one on guard duty. "The horses are cooled, let's go."

They rode in silence, Cherish straining her ears for sounds of pursuit. Somewhere a wolf howled,

149

lonely for its mate. Wolves mate for life. She remembered the wolf's head on the crested ring. Would Nevada let her escape or would he come after her? Don't be a fool, she told herself, he's only interested in the ransom Daddy will pay. He was merely amusing himself with you tonight. The horse between her bare thighs felt hot and powerful. It was a sensual feeling. No wonder men objected to women riding astride. She had a sudden vision of her legs wrapped around Nevada's body. She could only imagine the heat and the power of him.

After a while, they had to dismount and walk the horses again. Cherish shook the canteen; it wasn't full.

Charlie snorted. "I told you we'd run short on water, honey. You should have listened to me."

She paused, opened it, hesitated. She couldn't bear to drink after the man. She looked at Charlie. He was watching that canteen, but he didn't ask, obviously didn't expect her to share. "Charlie, isn't there a spring anywhere in the area?"

He scratched his head. "I recollect one, but I'm not sure I can find it. This country, if you don't know it well, can be as dry as scattered cow bones."

She had a sudden vision of them laying out among the silver sage and yucca, gasping for water. "Is there a cantina, a town, anything?"

"Now why should I tell you that?"

"Because you're going to get as thirsty as I am." She handed him the canteen and he gulped some water. She watched it drip down the corners of his mouth and grimaced.

He seemed to notice her distaste, sneered, "There's the Spur, it's a cantina, but we don't have any money and—"

"We'll go there," Cherish decided. "Daddy will see about sending them money to cover expenses."

"Just like that, huh?" The outlaw glanced over at her. "Reckon how much reward your old man is offering?"

Was he being tempted? Outlaws didn't seem to have any sense of honor, she thought, where money was involved. "Big money," she emphasized, "more than you could make the rest of your life robbing trains and banks."

"I keep tellin' Jack, sooner or later, if we don't quit, a posse is gonna get us. I ain't felt the same about Nevada since he killed my buddy, Rod, last fall."

She was shocked, even though she knew Nevada was a gunfighter. "He killed one of his own gang?"

The man nodded. "There was a couple passin' through that Nevada decided to help; an Injun scout called Cholla travelin' with a pretty white girl named Sierra. Rod got into a fight with the Injun over her. Nevada killed Rod."

It sounded almost chivalrous to her. Who was she kidding? "He's just a cold-blooded gunfighter; that's all."

"They do say toward the end of the Lincoln county war, Nevada rode with Billy the Kid and that Cheyenne half-breed from the Indian Territory."

A desperado, that was all he was now, she thought sadly, a cold-blooded, ruthless killer. Nevada was changed from that twenty-year-old boy who had kissed her that long ago night, and it was for the worse. She didn't want to think about him anymore. "Charlie, the law will get you and your brother sooner or later. Think about that big reward my daddy's offering."

Charlie grinned at her, the gold tooth flashing in the weathered face. "Honey, I reckon you're right. I'd like a little more out of life than just a few dollars in my pocket and a bottle of bad booze."

Money could buy anything. She'd let Charlie think on it some more. They mounted up and rode on. The next time they stopped to rest the horses, he reached for the canteen again. Now she was beginning to wish she'd overcome her reluctance, and had drunk some of it.

Cherish had never been inconvenienced, thirsty, or scared in her whole life. She hadn't realized what a dull, safe life she had led. More exciting, scary things had happened to her in this short time since she'd been taken off that train than she had experienced in her whole boring existence. It seemed they had been riding for hours through the barren Nevada landscape, but she had lost track of time. She had drunk too much wine; her head was aching. She began to think about that cantina Charlie had mentioned.

"I been thinkin' about what you said," Charlie said. "Where is it you're tryin' to get to?"

"Sacramento."

"Sacramento?" He didn't say anything else, but he frowned, rubbed his lean, unshaven face.

She relaxed her guard a little. Before this was over, Charlie was going to help her. She wished she'd been paying attention to landmarks. With the moon behind a cloud, the night was so black, Cherish wasn't sure she could lead a posse back to the valley anyway. Something scurried through the dry brush as they walked along. Her heart almost stopped. "What—what do you suppose that was?"

Charlie shrugged. "Could be anything, a lizard or maybe a snake."

"A snake?" She stopped dead in her tracks. In her whole life in town, she had never actually seen one. It couldn't be any more dangerous than the snake who'd just tried to get her drunk and seduce her.

"Don't worry, honey. If we see one, I'll kill it." He chuckled. "Honey, after a few hours out in this chokin' dust, you'd be right glad to drink out of old Charlie's canteen."

She'd have to be dying of thirst, Cherish thought, but she didn't reply. "Your brother going to be upset that you've ridden out with me?"

He glanced at her, wiped his mouth on his sleeve, put the lid back on the canteen. "Ridden out with you? Honey, you had me out at gunpoint."

She'd like to be able to see Nevada's face when he finally came to and realized how he'd come by that lump on his head. "Is that what you'll tell them?"

"It's the truth, honey, but Nevada might be mad as a rattler on a hot skillet. How'd you manage to get away from him, anyway?"

153

She pictured him sprawled on the blanket with a knot on his head. "It's a long story. You can tell everyone you meet that Nevada got outfoxed."

He shrugged. "Outfoxing Nevada is hard to do."

"But it can be done." She was pleased with herself. A few years ago, she wouldn't have had the gall to attempt an escape.

"I gotta hand it to you, honey, I thought you was just pretty, but you're a helluva lot smarter than I first thought. Now put that gun away; you make me nervous pointing it at me, I'm skairt it might go off."

"Just remember I've got it," she cautioned him. She didn't want him getting any ideas about double-crossing her.

"Lady, if you think you can get me a big reward, I have half a mind to help you."

"That's smart, Charlie." She kept her pistol ready. They mounted up again.

"Ma' am, we've got a ways to go to find an army post or the telegraph, but I know where there's help. Maybe with a little luck, we can be far away by daylight and I'll be on my way to bein' a rich man."

Cherish paused and looked behind her. "What about your brother?"

"Jack? Oh, I'll get a message to him somehow and we'll meet below the border; we've got friends there."

"You're not afraid of what Nevada will do to you for helping me?"

He laughed and grinned, his eyes blinking. "Honey, money makes me awful brave. We've been runnin' on borrowed time for some months now, and dodgin' posses and Pinkerton men. We've all been talking about headin' below the border to live in Mexico. I'll tell 'em you put a gun to my head and threatened me. If they all get a share of the reward, I reckon they'll be happy. Nevada can buy himself a pretty blond dance hall girl to take below the border."

She watched the outline of a Joshua tree and smelled the scent of sagebrush. Somehow the idea of Nevada heading off to Mexico with some blond tart annoyed her. "That does rankle me some. I'd like to see him in jail. He had a lot of nerve to kidnap me and upset my wedding plans."

He spat and wiped his unshaven face on his sleeve. "Hell, you can quit worrying about him, ma'am. By daylight, I'm afixin' to take you where you can telegraph for help. In a couple of days, Trans-Western can have you back in your own parlor with this only a terrible memory."

Terrible memory. She remembered Nevada's rancor and his bitterness, wishing she knew just what drove him. What difference does it make? She'd only been half joking about wanting to watch him hang. She'd probably send Daddy to the execution instead. When Nevada was walking up those thirteen steps to the gallows, maybe he wouldn't be so cocky and self-assured. Thirteen steps. He probably wouldn't walk up them; he'd think they were unlucky.

She looked over at Charlie again. She didn't trust him, but he was all the hope she had.

Nevada dreamed lightning crashed and thunder rolled inside his brain; that was why his head hurt so much. Moaning aloud, he gradually opened his eyes. Overhead, there was no moon, but stars twinkled like match flames in the clear blackness of the night. Then how could there be thunder?

He grasped his aching head with both hands, knowing now the thunder was the dull pain in his own brain. Good God! What had happened to him? Where was he? When he turned his head too quickly to look around, it hurt even worse. He was outside, that much he realized. He took a deep breath, smelled the scent of burning wood; took a look around, saw a camp fire with two cups and two tin plates, the remnants of steaks, half-empty bottles of wine and whiskey.

Cherish. Fragments of the early part of the evening came back to him. Drinks and dinner with the blond princess and plans to seduce her. In his mind he saw her fragile beauty, remembered the warmth of her, the silken texture of her skin and the scent of her hair. She had been all he had dreamed; warm and willing in his embrace, her lips opening for his thrusting tongue, the taste of her breasts as she pressed them against his mouth. He relived every memorable moment of the seduction except . . . he noticed now he still had his pants on, so he must not have consummated the act. Surely to God it would have been so wonderful, he wouldn't have forgotten it!

Nevada cursed and sat up very slowly. Had he gotten so drunk, he'd passed out? How humiliating. Had Cherish sneered in disgust and walked back down to the camp, left him dead drunk and snoring? He touched his head, winced as he found a swollen, tender spot. He'd been slugged. His hand went to his holster; empty. What the hell? Very slowly, he managed to stand up. His dizzy gaze swept the camp. No guard. Charlie was supposed to be up in the rocks with a rifle. Nevada remembered now how hungrily Charlie had looked the girl over. Charlie Whitley was woman crazy. Could he have hit Nevada over the head, taken Cherish? Was she being ravished even now down in Charlie's lodge? Nevada gritted his teeth and started toward the camp. If the guard had touched Nevada's woman, he'd die for it and it would be a slow, Indian-style death.

A quick check of the camp revealed both of them were missing. He looked down at his empty holster again. Cherish was a gentle lady who couldn't handle a gun and maybe not feisty enough to attempt an escape. Could Charlie have come up behind them there on that blanket, hit Nevada in the head and abducted the girl? The outlaw had been on the prod ever since Nevada had had to kill Rod last autumn; but it didn't seem likely he'd do something like this. They were gone, anyway, and who knew which one had Nevada's pistol? There was always the possibility that Cherish had either bribed Charlie with talk of a big reward, or held him at gunpoint, forcing him to escort her back to civilization.

Kene came out of his lodge, always alert at the slightest sound. "What is it, my friend?"

"The girl and Charlie are both gone."

"You've searched the camp?"

Nevada nodded and frowned. "I was a fool to bring her into this camp. I knew that wanting her would bring me trouble and bad luck, but I was obsessed. I wanted her enough to forget everything else."

"You are much like your father." *Kene* sighed.

"What do you mean by that?"

"Nothing. Forget what I said."

Nevada started to insist that the warrior tell him what he'd been hinting at, but then old Ben came out of his lodge, yawning and scratching.

"Gettin' so's a body can't sleep," he drawled.

"Cherish is gone, so is Charlie," Nevada snapped.

"Oh, Lord, I knew she was gonna mean trouble!" Ben looked up at the moonless sky. "Dark as a Yankee's soul. Can't trail them till dawn."

"That what I think, too," *Kene* said.

"I can't wait till morning!" Nevada protested. He saw the two exchange glances even as Mex, Jack, and some of the Paiutes came out of their lodges, muttering and asking each other about the noise.

"I'll explain later," he shouted, "the girl and Charlie are missing! We're going to mount up and spread out over the whole valley and hills if need be."

"Charlie?" Jack ran his hand through his tousled hair even as Tequila stuck her sleepy head out of the lodge door. "Naw, not my brother. The little wench has him at gunpoint or he wouldn't do it."

Everyone murmured agreement and Mex said, "Nevada, *hombre,* we wait for first light, *comprende?* We no can pick up a trail in the dark."

By morning, anything could have happened to Cherish. "We're riding out now," Nevada insisted, "as soon as we can get mounted. We'll split up and check every trail and hideout within a hundred miles."

As they turned reluctantly to do his bidding, Nevada thought about Cherish. Out of the frying pan and into the fire, you little fool! Charlie had a thing for pretty girls. First chance he got, the scruffy outlaw would rape Cherish! The thought made Nevada hurry to saddle the big Medicine Hat stallion. He only hoped he would find her in time. Without thinking, he crossed himself and said a small prayer. That innocent girl was going to need all the luck she could get tonight!

Charlie turned his head and watched the girl as they rode through the darkness. Boy, she was a looker, all right. No wonder Nevada had kidnapped her. Had he known she was rich when he stole her from the train? He rubbed his hand across his unshaven face again. Had Nevada planned to collect a big ransom and cut his gang out of it? That didn't sound like Nevada, but there was no way to know.

God damn, he'd like to climb that one, make her lock those long legs around him. She sure was pretty, and classy, too. It wasn't hard to believe she was a rich society gal. Big reward. Too bad he didn't dare go into Sacramento to collect it. The law was actively looking for Charlie and Jack in that town. A fat reward wouldn't do him no good if he ended up hanging. No, he couldn't take a chance on taking her to Sacramento.

Charlie grinned. A bird in the hand was worth two in the bush. There was a cantina only a few miles from here where thieves, rustlers, and gunrunners stopped to wet their whistles and do business. In the old days, it was said even Comancheros rendezvoused there. Anything a man might need or want could be bought or traded for at the Spur Cantina—for the right price.

He watched Cherish as they rode. One of them Mexican bordellos might pay big money for a fair-skinned, yellow-haired gal like her. She might even get sold overseas to one of them harems. Pretty women disappeared all the time and were never heard of again.

She seemed to feel his gaze, turned her head and actually smiled at him. "What're you thinking?"

"How tired and hungry I'm gettin'. Ma'am, there's a cantina I know of a few miles from here, we could get something to eat and rest our horses."

"I don't know. . . ." She looked weary and uncertain.

"There may be someone there who'd carry a message for you; you know, to a fort or maybe reach a telegraph so you can let your poppa know you're all right."

Her face brightened. "How far do you think it is?"

She was going for the bait. Already he could see her in chains and standing on the bar while men leered, felt her ankles and bid on her. Before he sold her, however, Charlie intended to have a sample of her for his own self. "I don't know, maybe mid-morning."

She looked pleased and relieved. "Sounds good to me, but remember, I've still got the pistol."

"I ain't forgot, ma'am, nor about all that money your daddy will pay for bringin' you home safe and sound." He tried his best to sound gentle and trust-worthy. First chance he got when she relaxed her guard, he'd take that pistol.

"I'm leaving it up to you then, Charlie, since I don't have any idea where I am. With no moon, it's hard to follow a trail or recognize any landmarks."

Charlie's groin tightened with anticipation. Next time they stopped to rest the horses, he was going to take that Colt away from that little gal somehow. In only a few minutes, Charlie could use her and get rid of this ache in his groin. He reckoned he could convince Nevada the girl had forced Charlie to take her to a railroad so she could go to California. Nevada never needed to know Charlie had sold the blonde into white slavery!

Nine

Nevada had most of his men mounted and riding out into the darkness within minutes, even though in his heart, he knew that picking up a trail would be nearly impossible until first light. If this had been Arizona, where he grew up, he would have known the terrain as a man knows his beloved's body, but he had not been born in this wild country. There was another reason he was called Nevada.

He winced at the painful memory, but he must not think of his past now. "We'll split up," he yelled, "there's a lot of ground to cover. First one to find anything, fire three shots."

They all nodded.

Nevada named a prominent landmark. "We'll meet there first thing in the morning if no one's found anything. If anyone's missing at dawn, we'll know he's on a hot trail or has run into trouble."

"Or dagnab it, is lost in the hills," old Ben grumbled. Even in the darkness, he saw the troubled look on the old man's face, saw that *Kene* was ready to object but held his peace. Mex, as usual, said nothing as he waited and plaited a hangman's noose from a rawhide string.

Jack's face dripped sweat even though the night was cool. "I can't believe Charlie would do this, even though . . ."

"Even though what, Jack?" Nevada looked at him. "You know, when I saved you two from the lynch mob, you told me you'd been wrongly accused of murder and they wouldn't give you a fair trial. Was there more to it than that?"

Jack hesitated. "No."

"Jack," Nevada snapped and his tone carried the pent-up fury he felt. "Spit it out!"

The other looked away. Sweat beaded on his lip. Nevada saw it even in the darkness. The others leaned on their saddle horns and listened. "Jack?"

"I hadn't done nothin,' but they were gonna hang us both. I tried to tell him he shouldn't, but Charlie has an eye for light-haired women."

"Jesus!" Mex whispered and it sounded loud in the silence.

Nevada saw the fear in Jack's eyes and felt a dread down deep in his soul. "Jack, tell me the rest, or I swear, I'll kill you right here!"

"Charlie, he—he saw this woman hangin' clothes on a line at a ranch on the outskirts of town. We was just ridin' through and I said, 'forget her, Charlie, there'll be a whore in the next town,' but this gal was there alone. She had yellow hair and he had to have her."

In the silence, Nevada seemed to feel his head pounding to the rhythm of Jack's breathing. His stallion snorted and Ben's horse stamped its hooves. "Jack, are you telling me he raped a woman?"

"I tried to stop him, but he had to have her. Knowing how you'd feel about that, I was afraid to ever tell you."

Nevada crossed himself. "Holy Mother of God! I should have let them lynch you both."

"It wasn't me, Nevada," Jack gulped, "but he's my little brother, I always took care of him; tried to keep him out of trouble. One brother's got to look out for another!"

In his mind, Nevada saw Pierce trailing after him, remembered trying to keep him out of mischief, trying to teach him how to stay on a pony. *My little brother.* No one can cause you pain like those you love. He felt his eyes mist and he had to clear his throat before he could speak. "I believe you, Jack. I know you didn't have anything to do with this."

Jack took out a bandanna, wiped his face. "Charlie's innocent, too, you'll see. That gal probably held him at gunpoint, made him take her out of the camp."

"I don't think so," Nevada said. Cherish was such a protected, genteel thing. Could she possibly have more spunk than he realized? More importantly, had she been that desperate to escape his ardor?

"Nevada," Jack said, "if Charlie did this, I couldn't blame you for killin' him; I don't cotton to forcin' a woman. You'll see; it ain't Charlie's doin'."

"We'll see," Nevada said. "If he hurts her, he's a dead man."

"Don't blame you," Jack said again, "but he's my brother; I know he wouldn't go this far."

The others sat their horses. Nevada's word was law and they awaited his orders.

"Spread out," Nevada said, "we've got a lot of ground to cover, trying to pick up some sign. If anyone finds anything, let him fire three quick shots."

Mex put away his hangman's noose. *"Amigo,* you want I should ride with you?"

Nevada shook his head. "We can check more territory if we fan out. By morning, we should know something."

Ben pushed his hat back, began feeling through his pockets. "We could get so spread out, we might not be able to hear shots if anyone finds anything."

Nevada handed him his own tobacco pouch. "We'll do the best we can." His head hurt as he took the tobacco back, watched his men ride off in all directions. Now which trail was the best one for him to take? His head still pounded so hard that it almost blurred his vision. He touched the lump gingerly. Damn that Charlie! He'd better have some good answers. Nevada put the spurs to his spirited stallion and began to ride. He didn't even want to think where that pair might be, what might be happening.

The stallion's hooves pounded like drums in his aching head as the minutes turned into hours, with no sign and no shots echoing to say that anyone else had found a clue either. He'd lost all track of time and distance. It must be the middle of the night. Never had a night seemed so very long. He paused now and then to walk the stallion, cool it out, mounted up and rode on. Ben was right; he'd been a fool to try to track them in the dark instead of waiting for dawn. He'd been too worried about Cherish to think straight. Of all the bad luck. He was superstitious. Hadn't he known that women brought bad luck? He reined in, wondering which way to ride next. The night was still deep and dark around him. Little brothers. Cherish was promised to his, and Nevada had wanted revenge—or was it only that he had wanted her?

Vengeance is mine, sayeth the Lord. The old words came back to him. Well, the Lord would have to wait his turn. Charlie better pray that some of the others found him first, because if Nevada ran across him, Charlie would be headed straight to hell!

Cherish was so exhausted by now, she was almost reeling on the horse, but she knew she must keep riding, for behind her in the darkness, Nevada might be on her trail. She could only imagine his anger at her knocking him in the head and fleeing.

Ahead of her, Charlie turned and looked back. "Are you all right, ma'am?"

She nodded. "I wish I knew what time it was. Once the sun comes up, we'll be much easier to track."

"They got a lot of ground to cover attemptin' to find us," Charlie said. "We got a good chance; especially if we can make it to the Spur."

"The what?"

"The Spur Cantina." He dropped back to ride beside her. "We can get some food and water, rest a little."

"How much farther is it?"

"Oh, just a few more miles; maybe a couple of hours."

"Won't the place be closed down by then?"

He shook his head, "Naw, lots of action around the Spur, no matter what time of the night it is because of the gold and silver mines up in the hills. Them miners got money burnin' holes in their pockets."

She kept the pistol on him as they rode along just in case he tried to trick her. He seemed to notice and laughed. "Hey, don't worry, ma'am, the more I think about that big reward, the better it looks to me. I expect Nevada was going to ransom you and keep all the money his own self."

Was that what he had wanted? She felt disappointed. Yes, of course that was it, money and revenge. He had been ready to seduce her, maybe just for the sport of it. She hated him for it and tried to focus on the fine wedding she and Pierce would have as soon as she escaped.

"Ma'am, these horses are tired and so are we. I know where there's a spring a few hundred yards off this trail; we ought to stop and rest a few minutes."

She didn't want to be alone with Charlie any longer than she had to. "Couldn't we just ride to the cantina you were talking about?"

"Horses might not make it, if we don't stop and rest them; I'm plumb tuckered out myself. Don't you worry none; I think we lost Nevada's bunch out there in the cactus and brush, if they're even aware that we're missing yet."

Charlie was right, she knew that. Both horses were lathered and blowing and her mouth tasted so dry from lack of water, it felt like cotton choking her. She licked her lips. "You say there's a spring close by?"

"Yes, ma'am. Now you won't forget about that big reward when old Charlie gets you out of here, will you?"

"Of course not." She had relaxed her guard some, partly because she was weary and partly because she was certain now that the outlaw was greedy enough that money was more important to him than loyalty to the gang.

He rode out through the sagebrush and she followed him. "Just a few more minutes, miss, and you'll have some cold water."

"Aren't you afraid of Nevada? I've heard he's fast with a gun."

"I'm not so bad myself," Charlie bragged. "Been wantin' to put him to the test for months, but my big brother tells me I'm loco."

Brothers. There was a bond between them that was like nothing else, Cherish thought. She'd never had a brother, though she had wanted one. There were times she felt so alone. Maybe she was better off as an only child; Nevada hated his brother so much that he had stolen his bride. Pierce hated Nevada, too, she could sense it in him, although he never talked about him. What had happened between those two to cause all the conflict?

"There it is—hope it hasn't dried up none since the last time I was here." Charlie urged his buckskin on.

Cherish licked her lips, thinking about water. When she got back to civilization, there'd be a big tub and imported soap. There'd also be a corset and yards of full skirts, all the restrictions that went with being a rich society girl in a city. And there'd be Pierce. Cherish sighed. She couldn't disappoint Daddy. All of a sudden, she didn't really want to return to Sacramento and the dull, restricted life she'd always led. But of course she had to. What else would she do and where would she go if she didn't marry Pierce?

"I see the spring up ahead," Charlie called back over his shoulder.

They were in an area of small hills and arroyos. It was still so dark that if Charlie hadn't been riding a light-colored horse, she couldn't have seen him. He dismounted, motioned to her, "Come on, ma'am, there's water in the spring, all right!"

With a sigh of relief, Cherish nudged her black forward. Her adventure was almost over. In a couple of hours, she'd be sitting in that cantina having some hot coffee and warm food while someone went to telegraph Daddy to send a special train.

Nevada. She hoped she hadn't hurt him, but then, he deserved to be whacked on the head. He had kissed her and . . . no, she must not think of that.

He didn't care about her, she was only the dessert after dinner. He had been amusing himself with her. Why had she let him kiss her, bring her to the brink of passion? It was the wine, she thought, she must be careful not to drink wine anymore. The last time she had had too much, she had ended up letting him kiss her at a party. Fiddlesticks. She'd drunk wine in the past few years and it hadn't affected her like that. She'd never had the urge to throw herself at her fiancé with passionate abandon.

Charlie ran back. "There's water in the spring."

With a sigh of relief, she slipped from her horse, let Charlie lead it to the pool. Maybe he was as eager to help her as he appeared to be because of that fat reward. She still had the pistol in her hand when she walked to the little spring where the horses were drinking. Oh, that water looked good. Charlie was already wiping his mouth on his sleeve. "Here, miss, drink right out the spring above where the horses are gettin' theirs and I'll fill the canteen, too."

She knelt and put one hand in the water. Cold. With a sigh, she lay the pistol up on the rocks, leaned over to splash her perspiring face and drink her fill. "Thanks for finding this, Charlie, I guess I was wrong about you and—"

She raised her head and realized she was looking into the barrel of the pistol. Charlie grinned and the gold tooth gleamed as he cocked the gun. "Now, you uppity little bitch, we're gonna do things my way."

"But—but the reward—"

"I'm wanted in Sacramento for murder, so you can see how I can't go waltzin' in there to accept no reward."

Her heart began to pound in fear from the expression on his face. "Maybe you wouldn't have to go to Sacramento. Daddy would be willing to send the money. Maybe you could just wait here for him—"

"And be a sittin' duck for that posse that's lookin' for you? He'd send the law, not the money. My momma didn't raise no fools."

"Are you taking me back to the hideout then?"

"Hell, no! You think I'm loco?" He held the gun on her while he pushed his hat back. "When Nevada finds you're gone, there's gonna be hell to pay! Nobody takes nothin' that belongs to him without regrettin' it."

"I don't belong to him! You men act like I'm some toy. Come to your senses, Charlie, there's still time for you to get that reward."

"I'm gonna get some money, all right, honey, but I want a little sweet stuff to go with it."

Cherish's blood seemed to freeze in her veins. She took a step backward. "What?"

He leered at her. "Ah, now, honey, don't play dumb, you know what I mean, I can tell by the look on your pretty face!"

Oh, Lord, out of the frying pan. . . . She had escaped being seduced by Nevada and now she was going to be raped by a filthy, ignorant outlaw. The horses. If she could mount up, spook the other horse, she might escape and leave him afoot out here.

He must have read her thoughts. Even as Cherish turned and grabbed for the reins, almost managed to mount, Charlie reached up, grabbing at her. For a long, horrifying moment, she was in his arms with him fighting to mold her against his body, his hands pulling at her clothes, pawing her breasts. She kicked out, knocked him down. He fell into the brush with a crash, swearing. "God damn you, bitch, I'll make you pay for that!"

She attempted to gallop away, but the horses spooked, half reared. Charlie was on his feet, grabbing for her. His hot, sweaty hands were all over her body; she felt them through the thin cotton blouse and skirt. She screamed as he dragged her kicking and fighting off the horse.

"Shut up, slut! If there's any Injuns out there, you'll have them down on us!"

Cherish screamed again, kicking and biting as he dragged her off the horse. Even marauding Indians sounded better than being raped by Charlie. She fought him as he tried to drag her to him with one hand. His clothes felt wet against her skin and he reeked of stale sweat. Cherish brought her knee up, caught him between the thighs. He bent over, swearing mightily, let go of her as he clutched himself.

She turned and ran blindly through the mesquite. She had no idea where she was going and it didn't matter. There were miles of this desolate brush, yucca, mesquite, and cactus. If she did manage to lose herself in it, she'd probably die out here before anyone found her. At the moment, it didn't matter. She'd rather die that way than be raped by Charlie. Behind her, she heard him swearing and threatening what terrible things he'd do to her when he caught her. She ran on, crashing into brush, catching her hair on branches.

Behind her, she heard Charlie coming. "Stop wastin' my time, you uppity bitch! I'm gonna have you, you hear, honey? The madder you make me, the more it's gonna hurt when I get you! You'll die of thirst out there in the prickly pear and you might even like what I'm gonna do!" He proceeded to describe the act in obscene detail as he followed her.

She was out of breath, her sides hurting as she ran, and he could surely hear her loud gasps, but she didn't stop running. Her clothes were torn and her face scratched. Behind her, she heard him coming. She tripped over a rock, fell, knocked the breath out of herself, stumbled to her feet and ran on. She was trying so hard, yet he seemed to be gaining on her. Because of the dense brush, she wasn't making much progress. Behind her, the rapist sounded closer. Every woman's nightmare, she thought, being chased as in her dreams by a man who would do her great harm. And in those dreams, one runs and runs and runs but doesn't seem to get anywhere, while the menace grows closer.

This is about the place in a dream where a woman always wakes up breathless and shaking, she thought. Oh, please, God, let me wake up, let me wake up safe in my own bed, far from here, let me wake up in Nevada's powerful arms. No, no, she didn't mean that, she didn't know what she meant. She ran in terror. The only reason she didn't scream and cry was that Charlie would hear her.

"Where are you, honey? Now, just stand still and maybe I won't hurt you too much when I get you!"

She didn't stop running, but she felt so very weary, she staggered, went to one knee, stumbled to her feet and ran on. She couldn't go much farther, she was too tired. An outcrop of rocks loomed in front of her. Maybe she could hide behind it, maybe she could use one as a weapon, maybe she—Cherish rounded the boulder and collided with a man. Oh, God, he'd come around the other way! She opened her mouth to scream and he clapped his hand over it, twisted her around so that her back was against him and his face close to her ear. "Hush, Cherish!"

Nevada? She realized it really was Nevada holding her against him with one strong arm, his other hand over her mouth. She heard Charlie crashing through the brush toward them. *Nevada.* She almost collapsed with relief, then realized she wasn't any better off, she was still a captive. Why had she felt for a split second that she had reached safety and protection?

Behind them, she heard Nevada's stallion whinny. Immediately, Charlie stopped running. She heard his labored breathing only a few yards away. Nevada muttered a curse against her hair. His horse had spoiled the ambush, Cherish thought.

Charlie yelled out, "Who's there?"

Nevada hung onto her and didn't answer him. "Are you all right?" he whispered against her ear.

She managed to nod.

"Who's out there, damn it?" Charlie called again, but this time, he sounded scared.

Against her ear, Nevada's breath was warm. "All right, princess," he whispered, "I'm going to turn you loose and you keep quiet and move away."

She nodded to show she understood.

He kissed her ear. "If he gets me, you take my horse and ride like hell, okay?"

She nodded again. Very slowly, Nevada took his hand away from her mouth. She was loathe to leave the safety of his big arms, but she stepped into the brush and watched. The moon came out then, big and golden. Nevada wasn't having any luck tonight, she thought. From where she stood in the shadows of a Joshua tree, she figured she was hidden, but now the two men could see each other. Only then did she realize Nevada had a knife. Charlie yelled, "Nevada, is that you?"

"It's me, Charlie."

"Well, glad you got here," Charlie blustered. "She made me bring her; took me out at gunpoint."

"Charlie, why don't I believe you?"

She watched Charlie moving closer. "You got it wrong, Nevada, I had just took the pistol away from her, was getting ready to bring her back to you."

"You had your hands on my woman, Charlie; you're gonna die for that."

"Oh, now, you wouldn't shoot me, would you? Why I'm unarmed; I dropped the Colt back there in the brush when I was chasing her."

He was close now and getting closer. She glanced

at Nevada. He had only a knife. She saw the reflection of light off the metal of Charlie's gun barrel. "Look out, Nevada, he's got a gun!"

It happened in a heart beat. Charlie brought the pistol up to fire even as Nevada threw the knife. Charlie never got a shot off. He dropped the gun, staggered backward, the big blade in his throat. He tried to cry out but he only gurgled in his own blood. Cherish watched, horrified, as he clawed at the dagger in his neck, scarlet blood pouring down his denim shirt. She smelled the warm scent of the blood, started to scream, but clapped her own hands over her mouth as Charlie crashed down.

Nevada ran to her. "Are you all right?"

She couldn't even speak, all she could do was stare up at this big man who spoke so gently to her seconds after he'd killed a man.

"I'd left my rifle on my saddle," Nevada said. He half caught her as she fell. "Oh, Cherish, if he's hurt you . . ."

She couldn't stop herself from weeping now in terror and relief. Nevada swung her up in his arms. "It's all right, princess, you're all right now, he's dead."

She put her face against his brawny chest, let him hold her against him as she wept and he carried her over to the spring.

"Cherish, it's all right! I've got you; you're all right now!" He was kissing her face even as he sat her on a rock, hugged her to him. He went to his horse, got a poncho, came back, slipped it over her head to cover her half-naked body. "He won't hurt you; nobody will ever hurt you as long as I'm here!"

She sobbed uncontrollably as he dipped his handkerchief in the cool water and wiped her face. "I knew he wanted you, but I didn't think he'd do something like hit me on the head and steal you right out of my arms!" He turned away to dip his bandanna in the spring again.

She wasn't a bit better off as his prisoner, she thought. Sooner or later, he intended to enjoy her body, too. She realized suddenly that he had his back to her, that she could yet escape. Even as he leaned over to wring out his bandanna, she hesitated, picked up a rock and hit him on the back of the head. Nevada crashed down like a giant tree. So trusting, she thought regretfully. Then she remembered that she wouldn't be in this horrible predicament if it weren't for him. He wasn't dead, only unconscious.

Now she could escape. Could she ride his horse? Probably too spirited for her. Sure enough, when she tried to approach, it backed away, snorting.

Nevada lay out cold by the spring. When he came to, he was going to have a splitting headache, she thought, and this time he'd know for certain who hit him. She couldn't bear to even look at Charlie lying on his back with the knife in his throat, his eyes staring up at the sky, gold tooth gleaming in his open mouth. She needed a weapon, but she shuddered at the idea of touching that bloody knife. The pistol. It must be under him. Even if she could move his weight, she wasn't sure she could bring herself to touch him.

Cherish led the black over to a rock, managed to mount up. She looked at the rifle hanging on Sky Climber's saddle, but she couldn't get close enough to the spirited stallion to get the gun. Now the other two horses seemed to smell the blood, neighed, reared and galloped away. Cherish hesitated. She was leaving him without a horse, unconscious and stranded in this desolate country. Fiddlesticks. She was in this horrible situation because of him; this was all his fault, it was all he deserved. No doubt Nevada knew this country well or his gang would find him later, but she needed enough time to escape them all. Cherish forced herself not to look back as she took off at a gallop, hoping to find the cantina where she'd be safe until the law could help her.

Ten

Cherish rode blindly through the night. She had no idea where she was or where she was going, but surely sooner or later, she would find a settlement or an isolated ranch where people would help her.

Nevada crossed her mind. She pictured him lying by the spring, hurt and alone. Was she out of her mind for worrying about him? She was nearly raped. It would serve him right if his horse never came back and he ended up having to walk miles for help. She hoped his boots put blisters on his feet.

How long was it until dawn? There was no way to know and she was beginning to lose track of days. By now Daddy and Pierce should have the law and the army scouring the whole state looking for her. Maybe with any luck, she'd run across one of those posses. Maybe someday she would be able to laugh about her exciting adventure, being carried off by an outlaw. Certainly it would be more interesting conversation in her social circle than playing croquet and whether bustles would go completely out of style. But of course she wouldn't be able to gossip about this because it might ruin Pierce's career if anyone knew his brother was an outlaw. No wonder he was telling everyone his older brother was in South America. She was slightly hurt that Pierce had not trusted her enough to tell her the truth.

The breeze blowing against her face felt cool and she was glad she had Nevada's poncho. Cherish topped a rise and almost cried out in sheer relief. Below her was a settlement; what appeared to be a small saloon, maybe a store and a few outbuildings. She was saved! Cherish went down the hill at a gallop. Judging from the buckboards and wagons, the horses tied out front, this rough and isolated place might be one of those that catered to cowboys and men from the mines who were working twenty-four hours a day taking treasure from the surrounding mountains.

She reined in before the saloon, hesitated. It looked like a tough place. Even at this odd hour, she heard laughter and music from inside. A couple of dangerous-looking men stared at her curiously as they pushed through the swinging doors and went in. She must look a sight with her hair in a tangle and wearing a man's poncho. Miss Grimley would not even let Cherish go out without gloves and a parasol. She would probably faint if she could see Cherish out in public looking like this.

Cherish dismounted, tied her horse to the hitching rail. With any luck, she would be on her way home by morning. It couldn't be that far to a Trans-Western rail line, although she hadn't the least idea where she was or how many miles from where she'd been abducted. Holding her head high, she pushed through the doors. The light was dim and the place smelled of stale beer and cigars. Men's heads began to turn toward her and gradually the conversation died. The only women were a couple of slatterns serving tables. Everyone stared at her in a way that made her want to turn and run out.

A short man with a stubble of beard came around from behind the bar, wiping his hands on his apron. Something about the way he stared at her made her skin crawl.

"I—I am Miss Cherish Blassingame," she announced, "and I have been kidnapped. Can someone please direct me to a telegraph office?"

The men stared at her, then began to laugh. A ripple of laughter floated across the saloon. The short man was more than a little drunk. "We don't give a damn who you are, slut, and we got no telegraph. You lookin' for a job?"

"I beg your pardon—?"

A man in back yelled, "Hey, baby, I got something you can do for me! The whores here are pretty ugly and old!"

"You don't understand," Cherish said, feeling her face flush, "my daddy owns the railroad and—"

"And I'm Mrs. Astor's pet horse," the short man snorted. "Where'd you come from? Pretty gals like you don't usually show up at the Spur, but you're welcome to stay." He caught her arm while the others cheered him on.

"How dare you!" She slapped him hard.

He grabbed her, twisted her arms behind her back. "No whore slaps me around. Some man needs to teach you better manners, gal!"

The customers laughed raucously, each making ribald comments about what they'd like to teach her. She tried to explain, but everyone was laughing and shouting, no one was listening to her at all.

"Gal, what're you doin' out here? You get dumped off a stagecoach?"

Cherish struggled to break away from his grasp. Even from here, she could smell him as he held onto her arms. "You pig! I demand you call a sheriff—"

"A sheriff? In the Spur Cantina? Hear that, boys? Our uppity whore wants a sheriff!"

The men roared with laughter again. The drunken bartender pawed at her. "Let's see what's under that poncho, slut." His breath smelled of garlic and cheap whiskey. She winced as he pulled the poncho off. "Well, lookee here what we got!"

She fought to break away from him as she stood there in her torn sheer blouse and skirt. "Let me go! I'll have your job for this!" No one was listening to her, the men were hooting and laughing, making remarks about her revealing clothes.

"Hey, Joe, I'll give you a week's wages for a few minutes of her time!"

Another yelled, "Put the uppity whore where we can get a look at her; stand her up on the bar!"

In vain, Cherish protested, tried to make them understand who she was and that she needed help, that there would be a reward. Either they weren't listening or they didn't believe her.

"Shut up, you loco little slut." Joe ripped away part of her skirt, gagged her with it even as he tied her hands, lifted her to stand on the bar where all could see her. "Now fellas, here she is. Since she's in my place, I reckon I got as much right as anyone to put this whore's time up for bids. Who wants her first and what'll you pay?"

The men cheered. "Hey, Joe, let's see more of what we're getting!"

"Sure, wouldn't expect you to buy sight unseen!"

Before she realized what he was about to do, the drunken bartender reached up, ripped the front of her blouse, leaving her breasts naked and exposed. Even as she struggled to get away, he jerked at what was left of her skirt. It tore with a loud rip, leaving her standing on the bar in her lace drawers.

A sudden hush fell across the room. "Take a good look, boys, you ever see anything so purty?"

Cherish stared out at the crowd. She wanted to scream in protest, but the gag muted her. The men in the shadowy saloon looked at her like a pack of hungry coyotes, their eyes almost seemed to touch her bare, naked breasts.

A man in back yelled, "I'll give a twenty-dollar gold piece to have her first!"

All around her was sudden noise and confusion as men began shouting how much they'd give for a few minutes of her time. How dare they? Daddy would have the whole bunch hanged. But Daddy wasn't here.

Joe held up his hand for silence. "Only fair way to do it is to auction her off."

"Now, Joe, since when is she yours to auction?" A tough-looking *hombre* up front protested. "I figure she drifted in outa the night, she belongs to us all equal, share and share alike!"

Oh, Lord, they were all going to rape her. Cherish had a sudden vision of the dozens of men gathering around her on some cheap cot in the back room, taking turns humping between her thighs, all of them wanting to put their wet mouths, their dirty hands on her breasts. She tried to jump off the bar, but Joe held onto one of her trim ankles.

"See, boys?" Joe guffawed. "She's so eager for you, she can hardly wait to get off this bar and get to it!"

Everyone laughed.

"Now," Joe said, glaring at the motley crowd, "it's my bar and she come in here of her own free will, didn't she?"

There was a murmur of agreement. Cherish tried to get the gag out of her mouth, but no one was paying attention to her. Joe's dirty hand felt hot on her bare ankle. "What am I bid?"

If only Nevada were here, he'd kill this man for touching her. In her mind, she saw his dark face, felt the safety of his powerful arms as he had held her against his chest. Letting him have her body suddenly seemed so much more appealing than being used by these filthy brutes. But Nevada couldn't help her; he was lying miles from here by the spring. Oh, God, what was going to happen to her?

The men were bidding, shouting for more whiskey. Somewhere in back, a man yelled, "I'll give a thousand dollars and a round of drinks for the house if you'll sell her to me!"

A murmur ran through the crowd and all heads turned. The man stood up, pushed through the crowded tables. He was dressed like a rich Mexican *vaquero* and wearing a *sombrero,* but he had red hair and freckles on his swarthy skin above a ragged beard.

Joe's attitude turned respectful. "Senor Juan Kelley, the girl appeals to you?"

He nodded, strode to the bar. "I need a pretty whore for my place in Mexico City. Sell her to me."

"I meant for one night, senor; then I was going to set her free or offer her a full-time job here."

The red-haired Mexican shrugged. "Who's to know if I take her across the border? I'll give ten thousand American dollars and drinks for the house!"

They were actually discussing selling her! Cherish thought in disbelief. She'd heard wild stories about girls being carried off by white slavers for the use of rich men and whorehouses, but she'd never believed them.

"Done!" Joe said. "Unless someone has objections or more money than Senor Kelley."

Cherish tried to object, tried to tear free from Joe's hand, but he was already reaching to lift her down. "Belly up to the bar, boys! Here, senor, take your purchase!"

There was a roar from the crowd as they pushed

forward, eager for the free drinks. Joe pushed her, helpless and bound, off the edge of the bar, the big red-haired man caught her, held her close against him. Cherish struggled, tried to break away, but he held her tightly against him as he counted out the gold. "Give me her poncho," he said, "I wouldn't want her to get cold."

He swung her up in his arms and carried her out into the night. He paused, grinned at her, inspecting her half-naked body for a long moment before he wrapped her poncho around her. "I've made a good purchase; what luck! You, *puta,* are on your way to a new life in Mexico City."

Cherish's heart hammered with fear. Her owner threw her up on a big bay horse, mounted behind her. Now he ran his hands up under the poncho, grunted with satisfaction. "Yes, you're worth it. My cantina's customers are the richest of the ranchers, officials, and army officers. With you servicing fifty of them a day, you will soon earn back what I have paid for you, *puta!"*

With his hand still on her waist, he turned his horse and cantered away from the Spur.

Cherish struggled, tried to break away from his hot, groping hand but she was powerless. Now he had his hand on her bare thigh where the lace of her underclothes ended.

He chuckled. "You can stop resisting, sweet slut! It's all an act, no? *Si,* it makes me want you more."

If she could just get this gag out of her mouth, she would tell him that her daddy and her fiancé would pay fifty times what Kelley had just paid for her. He couldn't get away with this—could he? It dawned on her that the Southwestern desert was an isolated place. It was a long way to Mexico, but there was no reason at all he couldn't take her across the border where she could disappear forever.

He put his bearded face close to her ear as they galloped away into the night. "My brother will be so happy to see what I have brought back to help our business. We are going to put callouses on your back, my sweet, and if you make our customers very happy, we will give you all the whiskey you want!"

In vain, she struggled, trying to break free, but he held onto her tightly and she could not speak. Cherish lost track of time. Alternately, her new owner cantered and walked his big bay horse to cool it out. As the hours passed and the sun rose, he seemed to breathe easier. "It is going to be a hot day," he said. "I think perhaps I will rest and eat through the rest of the day, maybe ride on at dusk."

He was afraid of being seen, Cherish thought. A man riding with a bound and gagged girl across his saddle would get curious looks and questions should he cross the path of a cowboy or a border patrol.

It must have been almost high noon when Juan Kelley dismounted in a shady, rocky area where a small pool of water beckoned. He wiped the sweat from his face and grinned up at Cherish. *"Si,* tonight when darkness falls, we'll ride on. It is much easier to travel in the night where no one will see you, my pet. Not too many days and you'll be across the border."

He led his horse over, knelt and drank from the

pool, let his horse drink. He looked up at her. "Are you thirsty, *puta?*"

Her mouth tasted so dry, all she could think of was water, but she would not give him the satisfaction of an answer. She tried not to look at the pool. He chuckled as he tied his horse in the shade of a mesquite bush by the pool. "After a few more hours, slut, when your tongue is so swollen, you can't swallow, you will be on your knees begging for a sip and willing to do anything to get some water. Maybe after you reach that stage, you will do things to pleasure me without a fight and then, maybe, I will give you a drink."

He reached up, lifted her down, looked into her face as he unwrapped the poncho. He grunted with satisfaction at the sight of her naked breasts. "You are *mucho* pretty, little yellow-haired slut. You will earn money for me and my brother." He spread her poncho under a mesquite bush, lifted her and lay her there. He lay down next to her, put his hand on her bare waist. "When you are thirsty enough to beg for water, you won't look at me like you were looking at a snake. You will get on your knees and beg as my father begged before his *Americano* countrymen hanged him."

Oh, God, was he crazy or only sadistic? Did it matter? Now he pulled the gag from her mouth, leaned on one elbow looking down into her face. "You wonder about me, no? You wonder why a Mexican has a name like Kelley?"

She managed to lick her lips and swallow.

"Frankly, I'd rather not think about scum like you at all."

"Ah, still defiant!" He threw back his head and laughed. "You'll get over it. Until then, I amuse myself with you. My papa was an Irishman from the *San Patricio* Battalion, who deserted to the Mexicans during the War of Forty-eight. The Yankees recaptured most of the Irish deserters and executed them. I was a baby, my brother still in Mama's belly when she stood and watched them hang her man."

She turned her face away, not even wanting to look at his leering face anymore.

"Look at me, *puta,* when I talk to you!" He reached out, caught her face, jerked it around to stare down into her eyes. "Now what will you do for a drink of water?"

She would not even think about water, although the sun was beating down on them and it was a long time until dark. Her arms tied behind her had lost all feeling. Juan Kelley tangled his fingers in her hair until she cried out as he pulled her to him and kissed her. She would not open her lips. He jerked harder on her hair and she cried out against his lips. Then his tongue forced itself between her lips and his red beard scratched her face. Even as she struggled to break free, he rubbed his body up against hers and she felt the hard maleness of him throbbing through their clothes.

Cherish did the only thing she could do. She bit his lips and he swore and slapped her. Her ears rang as she fell back against the ground.

"You *puta* bitch!" He swore in Spanish and wiped

the blood from his mouth. "I'll teach you how to bite! I'll have you begging me not to sink my teeth in your pretty body!"

"Oh, please," Cherish gasped, "I—I'm not what you think. I was kidnapped off a train. My daddy will pay much money to get me back—"

"A likely story!" He sneered as he glared down at her. "What would you be doing at a rough place like the Spur? Besides, even if what you say is true, why should I return you and risk tangling with the law?"

She struggled to break free. "My daddy will pay you well," she said again. "I was kidnapped off a train by a robber called Nevada."

"Nevada?" Kelley put his hand on his pistol holster. "I know that *hombre* well. I always swore I'd kill him if I ever got the chance. Why did he steal you, *puta?*"

Maybe she had his attention and he would listen and believe her. "My daddy owns the railroad. Nevada was holding me for ransom. I was on my way home to be married."

He grinned. "Tell me more, *senorita,* you amuse me, but I don't believe you."

"I—I'm on my way back to Sacramento to be married. My father would pay you—"

"So I have in my power a woman Nevada wants?" He grinned. "That makes you ever so much more inviting, little slut."

If she could ever get her hands free, she would stand a better chance of outsmarting him and escaping. "You win," she whispered. "I want water and food. Untie me and I'll do anything you want."

"Anything?"

"Anything!"

He laughed, took off his sombrero, tossed it to one side. "I knew you were just a clever whore. You'll like Mexico City; I might even let you keep some of the money you earn for me."

She forced herself to smile at him invitingly as he hesitated, then reached to cut her free.

Her arms were aching from being tied. "Can I have water now?"

He shook his head and laughed and a dirty red lock of hair fell down over his eyes. "No, no, little *puta*. First let me see how willing you are to please me; then maybe if I like what you do, I let you have a little sip of water."

Without water, she would die and this desperado seemed crazy or cruel enough to let her. "I—I'm chaste," she said. "I'm not a whore!"

"So you play that game with me again?" He leaned on one elbow and frowned. "What is your name, girl?"

"Blassingame; Cherish Blassingame. My daddy—"

"Ah, Trans-Western Railroad. Suppose I don't believe you?"

"Contact him," she begged, "he and my fiancé are even now gathering troops and a posse to rescue me from this outlaw who stole me from the train."

He glowered at her and his dark eyes turned cold above his freckled, swarthy cheeks. "Once he bested me in a business deal. I have no love for Amos

Blassingame and his railroad. Even if you are his daughter, which I doubt, I no help you."

"Have mercy! At least contact him, ask him if he—"

"Mercy? Amos Blassingame does not deserve mercy, nor does his daughter. I tire of this game, slut. I intend to have my fill of you, now. Maybe after we are safely in Mexico City, I will send Blassingame a note, asking if his daughter is missing, describing you, and telling him how much my customers are enjoying his beautiful child!"

He dragged her to him and the pistol he wore pressed cruelly into her flesh. "All right little *puta,* amuse me for a couple of hours, and if you do well, I will feed you and give you water. Otherwise, you can go without till your tongue swells your throat shut!" He grabbed her, forced her lips apart, ran his tongue deep into her mouth even as his hand went under her back, pulling her to him.

She dare not even bite him, Cherish thought, knowing he might beat her for her defiance. What was she going to do? How she wished she had stayed with Nevada; at least Nevada was gallant enough that he would not rape her. This pig was going to ravish her right here on the ground. His hot hands seemed to be all over her, his bristly whiskers scratching her face.

His hand stroked her bare thigh as he looked appreciatively at her body, visible in her torn clothes. "Slut, you are going to service me a dozen times today before I take you across the border. My brother will want you, too. He likes fair-skinned women!"

She would not be raped. She hadn't escaped from Nevada's capture to lose her virginity to some Mexican-Irish outlaw. She struggled even as he tangled his hand in her hair, and threw his leg across her bare thighs so she couldn't move while he pawed her half-naked body.

Cherish felt, rather than saw the shadow that suddenly loomed across them, blocking out the sun.

Kelley glanced back over his shoulder, equally startled. "What the hell—?"

She looked. A big dark man stood in the rocks behind them, his shadow looming across them. "Nevada!" She felt almost relieved.

In the split second that followed, Kelley grabbed her up, stood with her half-naked body shielding his.

"Well, Kelley, it's been a while."

Kelley swore. "Not long enough! As I remember, you rode on the other side of the Lincoln County War. I should have killed you then."

"I never gave you the chance, but you'll get that chance now, Kelley." His face was grim and he kept his hands out to his sides as if wary and ready to draw. "What you've got there belongs to me and I want her back."

Kelley kept her close against his body. "So come and get her. After I kill you, I'm gonna rape hell out of her and then put her under fifty *hombres* a night!"

A muscle twitched in Nevada's jaw and he shook

his head very slowly. "I'm gonna kill you for just touching her."

Kelley's grip around her tightened. "Lay your gun down, *hombre,* otherwise—"

"Otherwise what?" Nevada's face was set, angry.

"You can't get me without risking her," Kelley reminded him. "You're gonna throw your gun down and let me ride outa here. In a couple of days, your little *senorita* is gonna be workin' a whorehouse below the border."

She was too terrified to say a word. When she struggled, Kelley jerked her hard against his body.

Nevada shook his head ever so slightly. "Set her to one side, Kelley. You always wondered if I was faster with a Colt than you were; we're about to find out."

"I ain't gonna draw against you, Nevada, not when I've got her between us. I can tell by your face you won't take a chance on her gettin' hurt. Throw your gun down."

Nevada hesitated.

"No!" Cherish screamed. "He'll kill you and rape me anyway."

Nevada paused. "No more talk, Kelley." Nevada had his hand out from his holster. "You always said you were faster than I was. Let her go. If you beat me, your reputation is made!"

However, Kelley clutched her even closer against him. "I know how fast you are. You throw down your gun, Nevada, and let me ride out of here, or the girl gets hurt."

He had his hand up under her breast as he

dragged her toward the horses. She was so terrified, she couldn't think straight. When Kelley got her up on a horse, he would blast away at Nevada, and suddenly she knew Nevada wouldn't return the fire for fear of hitting her.

Kelley backed toward his horse, dragging her along. She looked at Nevada with mute appeal. He was going to let Kelley ride out with her. Abruptly, she felt Kelley's hand reach, and in that split second, she realized he was going for his gun.

"Nevada, look out!" she shrieked even as she dropped to the ground.

The guns went off almost simultaneously, the acrid smell of gunpowder stinging her nostrils even as the roar rang in her ears. For a heartbeat she lay there frozen. Cherish screamed as she saw Nevada take a step toward her, totter; scarlet blood smearing his shirt. He'd killed Nevada. She screamed again as Kelley fell across her, his warm blood soaking her clothes.

She crawled out from under him. Kelley's eyes were open and his mouth, too, as if to exclaim in disbelief that the top part of his head was gone. Nevada had gone down on one knee and now the pistol tumbled from his hand. "Cherish—" he managed to gasp. "Cherish, are you all right?" And then he fell forward on his face.

She scrambled to her feet, smeared with Kelley's blood. Oh, God, they had shot each other. She was safe; safe!

No, Nevada was still alive. She ran over, kicked the pistol away from him, picked it up, pointed it down at him. He lay looking up at her, blood slowly spreading across his shirt.

"I should finish the job!" She cocked the gun.

Nevada lay looking up at her, reaching his hand toward her. "Cherish, help me. . . ."

She couldn't shoot him with him reaching out to her that way. Well, it looked like he was wounded badly enough that he'd bleed to death as soon as he lost consciousness. She backed away, avoiding his eyes. She didn't need to kill him. Half naked and smeared with Kelley's blood, she ran to the horses, swung up on Kelley's big bay.

"Cherish. . . ." Nevada lay on the ground still reaching toward her, his face turning pale as his blood ran into the dry sand.

"You rotten thief!" she shouted at him. "You dare to kidnap me and then you expect me to help? To hell with you!" If he bled to death out here, he deserved it. She reined the bay around and nudged it into a gallop. Cherish had escaped at last!

Eleven

Cherish galloped a few hundred yards before she realized that in her haste to escape, she had not taken a canteen, nor had she had a drink of water since last night. She hesitated, reined in. Without some water, food, and at least the poncho to cover her half-naked body, she would not make it through the day, and who knew how long or how far it was until she found help?

Fiddlesticks. She would have to return. Reluctantly, she turned the bay and went back. No doubt Nevada was dead or at least unconscious by now. She didn't want to even think about him, the way he had reached out to her, the way he had risked his life to save her from Kelley. Then she reminded herself that she wouldn't be in this mess if it weren't for him. She fueled her anger with that. Yes, he deserved to die out here. She rode toward the clearing. A shadow fell across her and she looked up. Already vultures circled slowly overhead. Cherish shuddered at the thought of them tearing a human body to pieces. Funny how they spotted the dead and helpless so fast.

Helpless. She thought of Nevada lying there, not yet dead, but too weak to do anything when the vultures landed on him, begin to tear him apart while he still lived. Well, maybe he was already dead. After all, she hadn't killed him, so there was no reason for her to feel guilty. Yet she felt guilty in spite of herself and it made her angry all over again.

She rode in, dismounted. Kelley lay dead with his open eyes staring into hell. Nevada lay still and looked dead from this distance, too. She avoided looking at his body as she grabbed up Kelley's canteen, knelt to fill it as she put her face in the water, and drank and drank. She had never tasted anything so sweet and good. Now she put the cork in the canteen, looked up at the vultures, hesitated. Oh, God, she just couldn't let them eat Nevada. She had to at least bury him; it was the decent thing to do.

She walked over, stood looking down at him, fighting the tears that came to her eyes. Once she would have married this man if he had shown any interest, answered the note a timid fifteen-year-old girl had written. That kiss that had meant everything to her had meant nothing to him. No doubt he had laughed at her when she turned and ran from the billiard room.

As her shadow fell across his body, his eyes flickered open. Oh my God, he wasn't quite dead. He reached up a hand to her and struggled to speak. "W-water . . . please, princess. . . ."

She ought to mount up, ride away and leave him

to die after all the terror and trouble he'd caused her. Who would blame her?

She hesitated, looking up at the vultures flying in ever lower circles. "I wouldn't let a mongrel dog die of thirst!" she scolded him as she knelt and gathered his head into her arms. His pale face was warm against her naked breasts as she held him, put the canteen to his lips. He drank greedily, then looked up as the shadow of the vultures fell across them, tried to cross himself. "For God's sake, finish the job," he gasped, "don't leave me to them!"

She winced. Cherish couldn't kill a man. She got up, started to walk away. He'd be dead soon and he'd never feel the sharp beaks. She had a gun but she couldn't pull the trigger.

He looked at her. "Then leave me a gun with one bullet," he gasped. "I can get the job done. . . ."

What to do? Why was this her problem? She looked from the man at her feet to the vultures overhead. Cherish cocked the gun. He crossed himself and closed his eyes.

What a dilemma. She couldn't ride away and leave him to the vultures nor could she put a bullet through his head. Cherish began to swear. "I'll see what I can do to help; maybe your gang will find you later." She fired three shots at the vultures and they flew away with frightened squawks.

Nevada ran his tongue across his cracked lips. "They'll be back the minute you leave." For the first time, he looked scared. It frightened her to see this big man helpless and afraid.

"Can you sit a horse?"

He managed to smile. "Too weak. If I could, do you think I would have let you ride away?"

"Damn you! We wouldn't be in this fix if it weren't for you!" She turned and walked back toward her horse.

"Cherish . . . don't leave me."

She hesitated, angry with herself for her weakness. "I'll stay a little while." She tore most of her petticoat up for bandages. "It's still bleeding."

"It—it needs cauterizing," he whispered.

She shrank back in horror. "You mean, put a hot iron to it? Oh, my God, you can't expect—"

"Think about your fine wedding dress I destroyed," he muttered. "Think about me kidnapping you."

"On second thought, maybe I can do it after all."

His face looked pale, set. "Just don't enjoy it too much."

She built a small fire, found a knife. While she waited for the knife to heat, she wrapped her poncho around Nevada, who seemed to be drifting in and out of consciousness. It was a shoulder wound, maybe not as bad as she'd first thought from the blood all over his shirt. She found some food in Kelley's saddlebags, and a small pan. Maybe she could boil some beef jerky and get the broth into him. Finally the knife glowed red-hot. "I—I'm not sure I can do this."

His eyes flickered open. "Princess, for once in your life, do something besides be helpless and pretty."

She gritted her teeth at the insult. If it hadn't been

for Nevada, she'd be home eating strawberries and cream, choosing her silver pattern. Helpless and pretty indeed! "Maybe I can manage after all." She took a deep breath. "This is going to hurt."

"I've been hurt worse. Do it." He turned his face away.

She had to admire his bravery, even while smarting from his "helpless and pretty" remark. Cherish took a deep breath and swallowed hard, then she put the glowing blade on the wound.

He cried out and bit down on his lip so hard, it bled. She gagged on the scent of burning flesh, but she didn't give in to the feeling until she was sure she had it cauterized. Nevada was unconscious when she stumbled into the brush and vomited.

She splashed water on her face at the pool to keep from fainting, and wet a scrap of her slip. When she returned, big beads of sweat stood out on his face as she wiped the sweat away. Very gently, she bandaged his wound, tucked the poncho around him and saw to her broth-making.

It was late in the afternoon before he stirred, groaning. He glanced up at the sky as though looking for the vultures. "It's all right," she hastened to assure him, "I'm still here."

"Cherish?"

"Don't try to talk. Here, I've made you some broth."

She cradled him in her arms and spooned it between his lips.

"I—I thought you'd leave."

"Don't tempt me," she frowned. "All I have to

do is think about that dress, and I get mad all over again. Here, eat this broth. When I think you'll be okay, I'm riding out and you're on your own."

"Fair enough. Thanks. I—I never meant to hurt you."

"Shut up and eat your broth." Of course he didn't mean any of it. He was flattering her because he was injured and helpless; knew the vultures would get him if she left. Once it got dark and the birds went to roost, she'd ride out and he'd be on his own.

Night came and he was still drifting in and out of consciousness and shivering. "Cold," he whispered, "so cold. . . ."

She built up the fire and covered him with Kelley's blanket, too. She'd tied a horse to Kelley, dragged his body off into a gully and thrown brush over it. Then Cherish watered both horses and hobbled them so they could graze. What was she going to do? Nevada wasn't in good enough shape for her to ride away and leave.

"Cold," he muttered in his sleep, "so cold. . . ."

She was cold herself. The Nevada night had turned chill when the sun went down and her torn clothes were thin. She wasn't sure she could make it through the night unless she took her poncho or the blanket, but the wounded man needed them both. She drank some of the broth herself, huddled closer to the fire. Never in her whole privileged life had she ever been cold, hungry, or miserable. Pretty and useless. That described her life, all right. Most of the women she knew were just like her. Of course that was just the kind of wife Pierce wanted.

Evidently Nevada expected more from a woman. Damn him anyhow. This desperado had caused all this trouble for her. Of course, he could have let Kelley carry her off and not taken that bullet. Then she reminded herself Nevada hadn't done it for her, he'd done it out of the vengeance he bore her father and his brother. He didn't intend to give his hostage up to another man; that was all.

She was so cold, she was shaking. He was trembling, also. What to do? Cherish was afraid to build the fire any bigger, afraid renegades or Indians might see it and they were helpless here. She huddled closer to the fire, listened to Nevada moan, and prayed for daylight. Maybe the soldiers and the posse who must surely be combing this wild country would find them tomorrow. Then she would be on her way to Sacramento to be married and her captor would be on his way to prison.

Her captor was her captive now. She had the gun and he was at her mercy. She studied his dark, handsome face. Nevada; wild as a mustang in this untamed beautiful country. Yes, the name suited him better than Quinton. He was trembling again and she was so cold, her teeth chattered. She should take the blanket and to hell with him. He'd gotten himself into this spot. She reached for it, then shook her head. Spoiled as she was, she couldn't take a blanket away from a wounded man; not when he'd taken that bullet to save her from that ruthless Kelley.

A thought occurred to her. Oh, God, a lady couldn't do that. No, she'd sit here by the fire and make it somehow. He trembled again. She might make it, but he was going to die if he didn't stay warm. Well, he was unconscious; who would know the difference? Gingerly, Cherish crept under the covers. She was almost naked and she hesitated to move closer. In spite of his shivering, his skin felt hot and feverish. The warmth of his big, brawny body drew her to cuddle up against him. She hardly dare breathe, afraid he would open his eyes and realize she had her naked body up against him. He didn't stir but gradually, he stopped trembling and sighed. Her reputation was safe, she thought with relief, no one need ever know she'd ended up in his embrace. He'd never know himself.

In the meantime, the heat of him felt good to her chilled skin. Though she tried not to think about it, she was acutely aware of his hard, brawny body. What would it be like for him to make love to her? She had a sudden vision of herself locked in his embrace, his dark, muscular body contrasting starkly with her creamy, delicate skin as her pale hair fell down over them both. No doubt he would be a virile and passionate lover. She had not even let herself think about what her wedding night with Pierce was going to be like; very prim and civilized, no doubt. Pierce probably slept in a monogrammed nightshirt.

She bet this primitive male next to her slept naked. When Pierce took her virginity, no doubt he'd be very civilized about it; asking her permission after he'd turned off all the lights. He'd push her nightgown up just past her hips and mount her in a hesitant manner while he kissed her. It would be over in less than five minutes.

What would it be like to be made love to by Nevada? Probably it would be as wild and passionate as the man himself. He would take her on the fur rug before the big, roaring fire, tangling his hands in her hair, putting his tongue deep in her mouth, then kissing her breasts until she writhed under him and clawed his back. She saw herself with her fingers in his black, unruly hair, holding him against her nipple while he sucked it into a sensitive point that made her moan and beg for more. She imagined his face kissing her pale belly, kissing her thighs, kissing. . . . Oh, was she out of her mind? Of course a man never kissed a woman there! Her face burned with shame that she had even thought such a thing.

A lady didn't feel passion; she submitted to her husband because it was her wifely duty. Never in all these years had Pierce let himself give way to passion. He'd only kissed her that once. Certainly he would never kiss her in the way she was fantasizing about. In fact, the thought would probably shock him. Why, what she was thinking was probably not even the way harlots reacted to a man. Yet just lying here next to Nevada, feeling his warm body against hers, made her acutely aware that this was a man. No, more than a man; a mustang stallion of a male.

Fiddlesticks. There was no need to feel ashamed, no one would ever know what she was thinking, certainly not this savage or anyone else. In the meantime, she was only using him for body heat.

Still, it did feel comforting to be curled up in his arms. She snuggled even closer and drifted off to sleep in spite of herself.

She awakened once in the middle of the night. Somehow he had shifted position so that his face was against her bare breasts. Cherish started to pull away from him, paused. Once she had dreamed of holding him close like this and he hadn't cared enough. Yet Cherish found herself embracing him tightly instead of drawing away. She put her arms around him, pulled him closer. While she drifted off to sleep with his face against her breasts, she wondered what it was that had caused the terrible falling out between Pierce and his older brother and why Nevada hated Daddy so much.

Tomorrow morning, she thought; tomorrow morning, I'll ride out and he can look after himself. If I leave him a canteen and some food, in a day or so, he'll be in good enough shape to ride back to his valley.

Damn. The valley. In the darkness, she hadn't seen enough to be able to lead a posse back there. Oh, well, as long as she got away, she wouldn't worry too much about tracking him down and putting him and his whole gang behind bars, even if that would be important to Pierce and Daddy.

When she awakened with a start, it was still dark, but she was staring up into old Ben's pistol barrel. "Okay, ma'am, what's happened here?"

She started to sit up, realized she was half naked.

Nevada still lay asleep beside her. The whole bunch was here; Ben, Mex, Jack, and that Indian with the gray streaks in his hair. She had missed her chance to escape. Cherish sighed. "It's a long story."

Ben and the others surrounded them. "We got time. Suppose you tell me as we rig a travois."

She had stayed to help him and gotten recaptured. She didn't know whether to cry or laugh at the irony of it all. "I suppose we're headed back to your hide-out?"

Ben pushed his battered hat back with the barrel of his pistol. "You got it, Miss Cherish. Sorry, but I don't know what else to do until I get orders from Nevada."

Jack scowled. "What I want to know is: What happened to my brother? We found his body."

Cherish pulled the blanket around her naked shoulders. "I promised him a big reward if he'd help me; he tried to rape me instead."

"Well," Jack said grudgingly and wiped his sweating face, "I suppose Nevada had a right to kill him then. Women always was Charlie's downfall; I warned him a hundred times."

"I don't want to look after him." She looked down at Nevada. "Let Tequila do it."

"Uh-uh, not my woman," Jack grumbled. "I don't want her washing him, handling him; she's got enough ideas already. Gal, he's in this fix because of you; you can look after him on the way back to the valley."

If she had just ridden out and left him to the vultures, she might be safe in Sacramento by now. As it was, she was right back where she started. Cherish sighed in anger and defeat as old Ben tossed her a shirt.

"I should have left him to die," she grumbled as she buttoned the shirt.

Ben said, "I'm wonderin' why you didn't?"

"There were vultures and I wouldn't leave a dying dog to them."

"The boy's tougher than a cheap steak," the old man said, "he'll make it. Men, get some poles and let's rig a travois."

At the sound of the familiar voice, Nevada's eyes flickered open and he looked around. "Ben?"

"I'm here, boy."

"The girl? Did she—?"

"Girl still here," the Indian with the gray-streaked hair grunted.

"She stayed to help you, boy," Ben said, "otherwise, you wouldn't have made it. Should we set her free?"

She watched Nevada's face go cold, hard. "Hell, no, someone's got to look after me while I mend. I like the idea of my brother's pampered bride waitin' on me hand and foot."

Cherish seethed. A slave. he intended to humiliate her, make her beg for her freedom—or barter for it somehow. "You scoundrel! I should have let you die!"

He smiled ever so slightly. "Why didn't you?"

She didn't know herself, but now she wished she had. Why did he hate her so much? What was it he wanted from her?

Within an hour, the men had rigged a travois, buried Kelley, and were on their way back to the valley. The Indian seemed quiet and thoughtful as usual. Mex kept his own council, although she wondered what went on behind his strange eyes. Jack was morose, having just lost his brother; sweat dripping down his face to which he paid no heed. Cherish rode at the back with old Ben, who played off-key tunes on his harmonica as they rode along.

Maybe she could work on the old man; he seemed deep down as if he might be a decent sort. "Ben, you don't seem like an outlaw."

The old man shook his head, slapped the harmonica against his hand. "Wasn't, but someone has to look out for him." He nodded toward the travois.

"What's Nevada to you?"

"Oh, maybe the son I never had; the little brother I might have saved. . . ."

She waited, but he seemed lost in his own thoughts. "Ben, won't you help me?"

He winced and didn't look at her. "Don't ask me to go against him, miss, I can't do that."

"You know who I am, who my father is?"

He nodded. "The blame-fool kid is takin' us all to hell in a hand basket, but most of them was goin' anyway."

She looked toward the men who rode in this gang; hardcases, outlaws, Indian warriors with no future except a grim reservation. The West was taming down and there was no room for most of these. Nevada and Ben didn't seem to belong here at all; neither did Mex, the boy with the strange, haunting eyes who was braiding a little hangman's noose with his reins as they rode. "My daddy won't rest until he tracks me down, you know that, don't you?"

"I know it, miss."

"Then you could turn me loose," she pressed her case, "and there wouldn't be any posse or soldiers combing these hills—"

"Can't do it, ma'am." He was more than polite, he was gallant. "I'm bound to follow Nevada's orders."

She looked at the unconscious man on the travois. "He doesn't need money; I know who he is. Why does he rob the Trans-Western trains? Why did he kidnap me?"

The old man shook his head. "I reckon I don't know if it's revenge or . . ."

"Or what?"

He looked at her with his pale blue eyes. "If you don't know, ma'am, I sure ain't gonna tell you." He touched the brim of his Western hat with two fingers and nudged his horse up to the front of the line so he rode next to Nevada.

Revenge? Greed? Hatred? Lust? She was mystified by the conversation. If he would only name a ransom figure, Daddy and Pierce would pay any amount for her safe return.

Ben could almost feel the girl's stare on his back as he rode alongside Nevada's litter, looked down at the unconscious young man. "Well, Quint," he whispered, "you told me to look out for him, and

I reckon I did a bad job of it." Guilt. The heaviest load a man can carry.

It had been a cold, crisp spring night six years ago when he had walked into the rancher's den. Quint sat slumped on a sofa before the fire, head in hands. Things were overturned, glass smashed.

"Good God," Ben had breathed aloud without thinking.

Quint raised his head very slowly. His eyes were red. "Did old Juanita tell you?"

Ben nodded, started to reach out to the other man, hesitated, stopped. It was an awkward feeling. He wanted to do something to help his old friend's pain, but he didn't know what to do or say. "Quint, I'm sure sorry. Where's Dallas?"

Quint Randolph ran his hand through his hair distractedly. "In the chapel. At least she has her religion to comfort her." He reached for his pipe, his hands trembling as he filled it. "I hope you aren't going to say 'I told you so.' "

Ben shook his head. "You know me better than that." He looked around the smashed-up room. "What happened here?"

Quint lit his pipe. "Somehow, Pierce found out, and he told Nevada. I wish to God I knew who told Pierce, I think I'd kill him myself."

Ben felt through his pockets and Quint handed him his pouch of tobacco. He rolled a cigarette. How many times had he warned Quint he should tell the boys himself before someone else did?

"Lord, I know we shouldn't have tried to keep

211

the secret," Quint said, running his hand over his face, "but how do you tell something like that?"

He didn't have an answer and he knew that sometimes people just need to talk. The older boy was the one he worried about. "So where's Nevada?"

Quint shook his head. "I wish to God I knew! There was a terrible confrontation. I didn't realize Pierce hated his brother enough to hurt him that way."

"And Cain slew his brother Abel," Ben said softly.

Quint puffed his pipe and his hazel eyes filled with tears. "Where did we go wrong, Ben? We tried to do our best for both our sons and somehow, it wasn't enough."

"I reckon millions of parents have said the same thing." Ben was almost glad now that he and Martha hadn't had any children. "Nevada's tough and self-reliant, Quint; he'll make out."

Quint got up and paced the floor. "That's what worries me, Ben. He's good with a gun; too damned good. His Uncle Trace said he was the best he'd ever seen and you know no one handles a pistol like Dallas's brother. I'm afraid Nevada'll join up with outlaws, hire his gun out."

"You want I should see about him?" Ben stood up slowly, looked at Quint's hand. Was it only a couple of months ago Nevada had turned twenty-one and Quint had handed him his own crested family ring that signified the passing of the torch? Pierce hadn't liked that.

"We go back a long ways, Ben, but I can't ask you to do that."

"Somebody needs to. In the meantime, try to understand Pierce's point of view; he's always felt passed over."

"We tried to be fair to both sons, but maybe we felt so guilty about *Timbi.*"

"How sharper than a serpent's tooth. . . ."

Quint's eyes filled with tears again. "Oh, Ben, we tried; we really tried to do the best we could."

"I'll follow Nevada." He stared at the glowing tip of his cigarette. "There's a range war winding down in New Mexico; he might try to link up with that Bill Bonney."

"The one they call 'Billy the Kid?' "

Ben nodded, walked toward the door. "I'll check in now and then." He paused, looked back. "You might tell your missus to say a few prayers for all of us; I think we're gonna need them."

Prayers. Ben looked down at the unconscious man in the litter, back at the girl. Six long years. He was too old for this, but he couldn't abandon the boy. Billy the Kid was dead, the Lincoln County War was over, but still the boy hadn't gone home. He'd been badly hurt and he couldn't find it in his heart to forgive anyone. And now kidnapping his brother's bride might be the final chapter of this bitter tragedy. Why had the girl stayed with him instead of taking the chance to escape? Amos Blassingame's greatest treasure. Was it revenge or lust that had caused Nevada to steal her off that train? Trouble was, before this drama played out, it might destroy them all!

Cherish watched the old man, wondering what he was thinking as he rode next to Nevada's travois, looking down at the unconscious outlaw.

By the time the sun came up over the far hills all purple and pink, *Kene* had blindfolded her. Cherish had hoped they would forget. If she ever got away from this place, she wanted to be able to recognize enough landmarks to lead the troops right to this insufferable outlaw. The only reason she had saved his life, she told herself, was so she could enjoy the pleasure of watching him hang.

Ben still hadn't satisfied his troubled mind when they rode back into the valley.

Tequila came out to meet them, swinging her hips. "What happen? Who shoot this *hombre?*"

Ben shrugged as he took Cherish's blindfold off. "Jack will tell you, I reckon. Charlie's dead."

"It was his own damned fault," Jack said. "I'd do the same if anyone messed with my woman."

Ben heaved a sigh of relief. At least Jack wasn't going to hold it against Nevada; Ben had been afraid he might. He noticed the way Mex was staring at Tequila as he tucked away another little hangman's noose. Strange young fellow; never knew what he was thinking. Ben turned to Cherish. "I reckon it's up to you to look after Nevada."

She bristled, no doubt regretting she had saved the outlaw's life. "He's not my responsibility."

Tequila smiled. "I take care of him."

Jack frowned and wiped the sweat that ran down his face and neck despite the cool morning. "I think you won't. You're my woman; let his own look after him."

"Then he can die," Cherish snapped.

Kene glared at her. "Nevada my friend. He die, girl in big trouble."

Cherish turned in mute appeal to Ben but his grizzled old face was stony cold. "The Indian's probably right, miss. I got no other way to make sure he gets good care and the boy's important to me. I hope you're a good nurse."

Kene nodded. "Take good care. Nevada die; you die!"

Twelve

Cherish watched as they carried Nevada into the lodge. His men glared at her with hostility. If he didn't survive, old Ben might not be able to keep them from killing her. Then it was up to her to see that he lived. "Get me some water, whatever medicine you might have, and tear up some clean cloth for bandages," she ordered.

Tequila sneered. "Since when are you in charge?"

Ben snapped, "I'm puttin' her in charge. Do what she tells you, gal."

Cherish looked at her wedding dress still thrown on the floor of the lodge. "Here, this might do for something, but clean cotton would be better."

The Mexican girl gathered up the torn dress in her arms. "I take; see what I can do. Maybe I got old petticoat I can tear up."

The Indian grunted. "Know little about herbs and poultices from desert plants; I get."

Within minutes, Cherish had Nevada spread out on his blankets in the lodge. "Someone give me a knife."

The old man hesitated, then handed her his. "I reckon if you were gonna hurt him, Miss Cherish, you had plenty of chance when he got shot."

She only nodded as she took the knife and began to cut Nevada's bloody shirt away. "Do you know if he ever got a ransom demand off to my daddy?"

"No, ma'am, I don't. That don't mean he didn't send one of the warriors," he hastened to say when her dismay must have been mirrored on her face.

"Get me some water, Ben, and tell Mex to bring a little more firewood." Ben left to do her bidding. Pretty and useless, wasn't that what Nevada had called her? Maybe he was right. Always before, she would have waited for someone else to do something while she wrung her hands and whimpered. Now if she didn't take charge, Nevada might not make it.

Her life might depend on his, she reminded herself as she pulled his boots off; otherwise, she wouldn't care if he died. Sweat had broken out over his big body and he moved restlessly. He muttered some endearment in his sleep and Cherish frowned. Which one of his saloon wenches was he dreaming of?

They began to bring things; firewood, water, salves. Tequila, with gold chains jangling, brought in a clean white petticoat torn into strips.

"I stay and help," Tequila said.

Cherish gave her an icy look. "I can manage."

"But—"

"I can manage."

Ben chuckled. "Tequila, you heard her. Let's clear

217

out and get some grub. I'll bring you some, ma'am." He gave Cherish an admiring look. "Maybe there's more to you than I thought there was, Miss Cherish."

They all left and Cherish set to work. After only a moment's hesitation, she cut him out of his bloody, dirty clothes. Nevada was dark, big, and brawny. Did Pierce look like this naked? Cherish blushed that she had dared think about such a thing. No, Pierce was lighter skinned and civilized. She tried not to look at Nevada's manhood as she washed him, put a cool wet cloth on his forehead. Now she covered him with a blanket and set about changing his bandage. He moaned aloud. "Princess. . . ."

"I'm here, Nevada." She put her cool hand on his sweating forehead.

"Don't leave . . . don't leave me. . . ."

How could she when she was a prisoner? At least if a posse found them, Nevada would get better medical care. "I'm not going anywhere."

She patted the back of his hand and before she was aware of it, his hand clutched hers. Cherish stared down at the big gold ring he wore. What had happened to set him on the outlaw trail? If things had been different, she might be married to him now instead of planning her wedding to his brother. She tried to pull away from his grasp but he held onto her hand as if he were drowning and her hand was a life preserver. She put her other hand on his forehead and brushed his black hair out of his eyes. He was as tough as old boot leather, still he looked like a small, sick boy right now. She reminded herself that he was her kidnapper and that she hated him, but it was hard to do when he hung onto her hand the way he did.

When he seemed to relax and sink into a deep slumber, Cherish unclenched his hand from hers, built up the fire, and made some broth. Gradually as the afternoon passed, his temperature seemed to drop. When he roused a little, she spooned some broth into his mouth. "Why—why are you doing this?" he muttered.

"Because if you die, I'm afraid of what your men might do to me," she snapped.

He gave her a look of cold contempt. "That's what I thought."

He drifted off to sleep again. Ben stuck his head in the lodge. "You okay, miss?"

"Oh, Ben, what's going to happen?"

He shook his head. "I wish I knew, miss; I just wish I knew," he said with such an air of utter resignation.

"You know Daddy will have the troops and a big posse out?"

Ben rubbed his grizzled chin and nodded. "I know. This is a secret valley; unless someone leads them here, they won't find it."

"You mean, I could be a prisoner here forever?"

"I—I don't know what Nevada's plans are for you, ma'am, I'm not sure he knows himself."

She looked down at the sleeping outlaw. "Can I trust him to do what he says?"

Ben paused. "If you mean, is his word good. He's

been raised by a Kentucky gentleman; you can bank on Nevada's word."

She brushed her hair back with a weary gesture. "I keep waiting for him to tell me what ransom he'll demand. I'm sure Daddy will pay anything."

"Yes, ma'am." He felt through his pockets, and without thinking, Cherish handed him Nevada's tobacco. He rolled a cigarette. "We're running low on supplies, ma'am, and I'm getting ready to send someone out. Is there anything you need for him?" He gestured toward Nevada.

She shook her head. "As you said, he's tough. A little rest and some food will put him back on his feet in no time."

"All right, Miss Cherish, I'll check back with you later." Ben stood up, went outside the lodge, lit the smoke, and thought about her. What in hell was Nevada going to demand by way of ransom, or was he going to keep her? Ben saw nothing but trouble down the road, but then everyone in this camp expected that theirs was a hopeless cause. Who should he send out for supplies? Jack had volunteered, but he wasn't sure whether he could trust him after Charlie's death. The Indians would arouse suspicion if they rode in to buy supplies. Tequila wanted to go, and frankly, Ben would be pleased to get rid of her awhile. He had a feeling that she and Cherish Blassingame would clash soon if something didn't happen.

Mex. The young Mexican with the strange eyes who had joined up with them last autumn. Yes, he would send him along with those two because he'd trust that boy with his life. He went to find him.

"Mex, will you go with them?"

"Si, of course." He set aside the noose he was plaiting. "You and Nevada have been good to me; because of you two, I send *mucho* money to my village."

Ben took out his harmonica. "Always to the village. You payin' for candles; got some priest praying for your sins?"

The boy studied him with his strange, haunting eyes. "I pray for someone else, help build a school in village of Guadeloupe."

Ben scratched his head. "I don't know why you feel it's your duty to build a school."

"A debt of honor," the boy said with a vague wave of his hand. "If something should happen to me, would you make sure that my share goes there?"

Old Ben patted his shoulder. "Nothing's gonna happen to you."

Mex looked at him. "None of us have long to live; but we have chosen this path, each for a different reason. I have almost paid for the school now. This is important to me."

"You know, I don't even know your real name." Ben rubbed his grizzled chin.

Mex shrugged. "Gonzales. That is all you need to know. It is for the honor of the Gonzales family. I'll get ready now."

Ben stood looking after him and brought his harmonica to his lips. Mex was a strange one, all right. He must remember to tell Nevada about the promise. Whatever happened to the Mexican outlaw, the little children in the poor village of Guadeloupe would get their school. He could only wonder about the honor of the Gonzales family.

It had taken longer to organize this expedition than Pierce had expected, but now he was aboard the train with horses and men. Pierce had taken almost a perverse pleasure in wiring his parents about what their favored eldest son had done. Maybe they would finally overlook the family blowup Pierce had caused. Amos Blassingame had been persuaded to stay in Sacramento because he seemed to be in such poor health, and at least he could relay messages and orders if needed.

Talk about a wild-goose chase! For all he knew, his brother had headed off to Arizona or New Mexico with Cherish when he'd taken her off that train. All they could do was search hundreds of miles of desolate country for her. When he found her, he would be such a hero, even in Cherish's eyes. Pierce had sensed she was hesitant about marrying him.

At least Mr. Blassingame respected his true worth. As Pierce stared out the window at the passing landscape, he remembered that the blowup had actually been caused by Amos, but of course Pierce had never told his parents about the Englishman showing up at Harvard that long ago spring of '81. Pierce was still upset over his older brother being given the family ring for his twenty-first birthday.

"Why, Mister Blassingame! What a pleasant surprise! Do come in." He had ushered him into his room. "I just saw your daughter over at Miss Priddy's a few days ago and she didn't say anything about your coming—"

"Cherish doesn't know I'm in town." Amos pulled at his mustache and cleared his throat. "Actually, I didn't come to see her and I'd just as soon she didn't know I've been in town."

"Sir?" Pierce was baffled.

"I came to see you, young man." Amos settled himself into a chair. "I don't want you to feel offended, but since I thought you might become engaged to my daughter, I hired Pinkerton's to investigate your family."

Pierce bristled. "I'll have you know, sir, the Randolphs and the Durangos are cultured, wealthy people."

"So I found out," Amos said, drumming his fingers on the arm of the chair, "except for one small scandal."

Pierce stared at him. "There's no scandal in our family."

"A drunken old Indian woman the detective found says different. Do you know anything about the Paiute Indians around Pyramid Lake?"

Pierce shook his head. Either Amos Blassingame was losing his sanity or perhaps he had been drinking. "You mean in Nevada? I think I've heard my father mention it when he said something about the Pony Express. Father supplied horses for that."

"Hmm. That would have been about Eighteen sixty or sixty-one?"

"Yes. I don't have any idea what you're driving at—"

"Have you never noticed how dark your brother is?"

Pierce shrugged. "He resembles Mother while I take after Father; everyone knows that—"

"Sit down, Pierce, I want to tell you what my detectives have discovered."

Even now, six years later, Pierce winced when he recalled what Amos Blassingame had told him. He had jumped up from his chair. "Sir, you smear my mother's name with your lies. My father is a Kentucky gentleman, he's liable to call you out on the dueling grounds and—"

"Why don't you find out if I lie?" Amos looked at him coolly, drummed his fingers on the chair.

Pierce stared back at the Englishman. If what Amos Blassingame hinted at was true. . . . He wondered if his big brother knew any of this. "I'll go immediately."

Pierce had mixed feelings about the confrontation that followed his trip home. He stared out the train window now and remembered. It had destroyed his relationship with his brother and his relationship with his parents was still strained. However, they would eventually come around. In the story of the prodigal son, the dutiful son had been overlooked, too. It wasn't fair that his parents had always favored Nevada; not fair at all. Sooner or later, they would realize Pierce's true worth. He would make them

224

proud of him when he married into the Blassingame fortune and went into politics. And after all, when Pierce gained control and sold that ranch out from under them, he'd get them a nice little house in Sacramento. Father was getting too old to be riding and roping. Besides, Pierce had some ideas on investing the money the sale of the Wolf's Den would bring.

Dallas laid aside her book and looked out the window at the late afternoon sun. *Ben Hur.* It was a good book, but reading it, she had thought about the territorial governor who wrote it, Lew Wallace, which made her think about the Lincoln County War, Billy the Kid, and her own son. Where was he today and what was he doing? They hadn't heard from old Ben in a long time. He and Nevada might even be dead.

Balderdash. The boy was tough, he'd be all right. The fact that her brother Trace had taught her son to handle a gun was a mixed blessing.

She smiled and leaned back in her chair, thinking of Trace and the Triple D ranch in the Texas hill country between San Antonio and Austin. When her father, old Don Diego de Durango, had sent Dallas off to school before the Civil War began, she hadn't wanted to go. Fact is, she'd been as difficult about it as a steer in a loading chute headed for the stockyards. Miss Priddy's Female Academy in Boston. It probably hadn't changed much in the more than twenty-five years. Had she ever told Cherish Blassingame that she herself had been a student there before she kicked over the traces and ran away?

Afraid to go home and face her father's wrath, Dallas had to find a job. She was tall for a woman, slim hipped and small breasted; a Texas tomboy who could handle a gun and ride like the wind. In desperation, she had cut her hair, masqueraded as a boy, and ridden for the Pony Express. Quint Randolph had supplied horses for the Pony Express. And then the Paiute Indian War had begun.

Dallas frowned, not wanting to remember that part of her life. *Timbi.*

No, she would think of how happy she had been with Quint once they had left the Paiute country. Within months, the Civil War had begun and she couldn't get back to Texas to see her family. Her husband's namesake had been more than four years old and they had had another son by the time the war ended and the family could return to Texas to visit the giant Triple D ranch.

Trace. She saw her brother's dark, handsome face before her now, and her beloved father, that dignified old gentleman with a white mustache. Dallas sighed. So many things had changed when she got back to the ranch, yet so many things were the same. She remembered alighting from the carriage with her small child in tow and Quint carrying the baby, Pierce. Even the *ranchero*'s feisty little Chihuahua pranced around her feet, yipping.

Papa hurried to meet her, along with old Sanchez, the ranch foreman; her brother Trace hugged her, shook Quint's hand. Papa had tears in his eyes. "So

226

much has happened," he said. "I must tell you about your mother and Uncle Luis, Rosa, and little Turquoise."

Trace frowned. "Papa, let's get to that later; first, I want to introduce my sister to my new wife and to our adopted brother."

Cimarron. The name meant "Wild One" in Spanish. The way the girl looked at Trace as she came forward told Dallas everything she needed to know about this couple. Cimarron hesitated, then hugged Dallas. "Everyone has been so worried and the whole ranch took on a fiesta spirit when we got your letter."

Trace pumped Quint's hand. "We're so glad Dallas found someone who loves her." He turned and gestured toward the half-grown boy. The boy looked like he might have been in his early teens. He was a half-breed Comanche with a knife scar on his cheek and eyes as gray as a gun barrel. "This is our adopted brother, Dallas, we call him Maverick."

Maverick hesitated, but Dallas would have none of that. She put her arms around him and hugged him, too, then she hugged her father all over again. "I've dreamed of coming home," she said with tears streaming down her face. "Oh, I've dreamed of coming home, Papa."

The old man's eyes were not dry, either. "But now we expect you to come home often and see us; you and your wonderful husband."

Trace had rumpled Nevada's hair. "And Uncle Trace will see if he can teach your sons to handle a gun."

He had, too. The oldest boy had taken to Trace and had a natural talent for horses and pistols. Between Quint and Trace, Nevada could outdo either of them. As time passed and they went home to visit the Durangos, Nevada looked forward to it. It was the younger son, Pierce, who did not really fit in.

A noise brought her out of her thoughts. Was that old Juanita in the kitchen? No, it was Quint coming in. He looked abruptly old and preoccupied as if something were bothering him. In the past six years, Dallas had watched her beloved husband age before her eyes. Their sons had both brought them some grief. "Hello, darling. Are you ready for supper?"

"Hello, my angel." He came into the den, took the book from her hands, sat down beside her.

"There's something bothering you."

He hesitated. "Now how do you know that?"

She leaned to kiss him. "Quint Randolph, we have been married twenty-seven years, I know what you're thinking before you do."

He laughed but there was no humor in his hazel eyes. "Has it been that long? Seems just yesterday I was falling in love with a boy who rode for the Pony Express; that really worried me."

She looked at the gray streaks in his light hair, the lines around his eyes. "What's wrong, Quint?"

"It can wait until after supper, angel."

She took both his hands in hers. They had weathered so much together, both tragedy and triumph.

She looked around the room. Six years ago in this very room, their whole lives had been torn apart. "Hold me a minute, Quint."

He sighed and took her in his arms, held her very close. "Oh, Dallas, will it never end?"

She tensed. "You've heard something from Ben?"

He shook his head. "No, Pierce. I—I got a wire from him, but I've put off telling you about it."

Pierce. She had mixed feelings about her younger son. He thought they discriminated against him in favor of his older brother. Did they? They had never meant to. Maybe it was guilt on their part that made them treat Nevada differently. "We tried so hard, Dallas."

She felt the tears pool in her dark eyes. She didn't want to ask, but she couldn't let her beloved carry this alone. "What's happened?"

"The Blassingame girl."

Had Cherish changed her mind about marrying Pierce? Dallas supposed Pierce loved the girl, but her older son had loved her, too, and Cherish was part of the tension that had put the two brothers at each other's throats. "The wedding is off?"

"Dallas, she—she's been kidnapped."

Dallas sat up straight and stared into his hazel eyes, wondering if this were a joke. If so, it wasn't a very good one. "Balderdash! She and that silly bunch of society bridesmaids are back East buying a trousseau and—"

"The train was waylaid and held up a couple of days ago. They took Cherish, too."

She looked into his eyes. "Poor Pierce! We must go to him and—"

"Dallas, he—I mean, well, he says the train crew says the Indian who took her wore an unusual ring."

Dallas closed her eyes. She did not want to hear this. It couldn't be . . . he wouldn't. . . . "It was Nevada?"

Quint lit his pipe with a shaking hand. "Who else could it be?"

"But why—?"

"Ransom, maybe."

"Or revenge, or love?" In her mind, Dallas saw another man's face, a handsome Paiute chief who had loved Dallas so much that he threw aside everything to possess her. Yes, Nevada was capable of such passion and anger. She didn't even want to think about that time more than a quarter of a century ago.

"He's capable of it, isn't he? Abducting his brother's bride? It's in the blood." Quint had read her thoughts. They had always been so very close.

Dallas went into his arms, lay her face against his chest as he smoked his pipe. "Oh, Quint, what are we going to do?"

She felt him sigh as he patted her absently. "I don't know what to do except wait for this thing to unfold. Nevada has been ranging all over the West; there's no telling where he's taken her."

Dallas wept for themselves and for their two sons. Somehow they needed to help, but she didn't know what to do. Dallas crossed herself and reached for her beads. What they all needed now was a miracle.

Thirteen

Cherish knew Nevada was greatly improved when a day and a night passed and his eyes flickered open, looked at her. "Where—where the hell are we?"

"Back in the valley. Ben and your gang found us."

He struggled to sit up, but she reached out to restrain him. "You're not well enough to do anything but lie there."

He looked down at her hand on his arm, then up into her eyes. She was abruptly aware of the heat and power of his body, and pulled her hand away.

He smiled ever so slowly, but his dark eyes did not smile. "Well, princess, so we're back where we started."

"Fiddlesticks! Not quite," she said. "I've saved your life, I figure you owe me."

"Owe you? Pretty spunky talk for a captive. As I recall, I wouldn't be in this fix if you hadn't run away."

"Or if you hadn't stolen me off a train," she said. "*Touché*. But on the other hand, if I hadn't taken

231

that bullet to save you, you could be well on your way to a Mexican whorehouse by now."

Even the word made her blush. "You're avoiding the real issue. Have you sent Daddy a ransom note?"

"Now you know I haven't." He reached out, tangled one finger in a lock of her long hair.

She pulled away. "I'm way behind with my wedding plans already. I'm sure Daddy will send the money if you'll just get on with it."

He grinned, although a bit weakly. "Princess, we just relieved your daddy's train of a bunch of money, it isn't as if we're in immediate need of cash."

She swallowed hard to hold back her rebuttal. It wasn't enough that he had robbed Trans-Western trains and thumbed his nose at the Blassingames by kidnapping her, he had to rub it in. "You're going to be tracked down like a dog and killed if you don't free me soon."

"You mean they'll try."

She exhaled in a breath of exasperation. "What is it with you? And why only my daddy's trains?"

"You know the answer to that, princess; you and my little brother."

She didn't know, but she had a feeling that if she denied it, he wouldn't believe her.

"Help me to sit up."

She started to argue with him, decided she didn't care if he pulled the wound open and bled to death. She slipped her arm under him while he put his arm around her shoulders, and helped him into a sitting position. She saw him wince, grit his teeth. His eyes closed momentarily, then he took a deep, shuddering breath. He didn't let go of her, but she pulled away, too acutely aware that he was naked, although a blanket covered his lower half.

He glanced down. "Who took my clothes off?"

Now she really did feel her face turn crimson.

"I hope it wasn't Tequila, because Jack—"

"Tequila, Jack, and Mex have gone for supplies."

"You did it?"

Cherish avoided his penetrating look. "Someone had to."

"I reckon I owe you an apology, princess." His voice was almost gentle. "I really didn't think you were up to doing something like looking after a wounded man."

"It wasn't from the kindness of my heart," she snapped. "Your men said they would kill me if anything happened to you."

He frowned. "I reckon I should have known better than think you might care . . . never mind. How about some coffee?"

"Broth would be better." Her tone brooked no argument as she got him a steaming bowl.

"I'm not sure I can feed myself."

She fed him. Somehow it became a very personal thing; the way he looked at her as she held the spoon to his lips. He had a sensual mouth, she thought, and the memory crossed her mind of him kissing her.

"Why are you blushing?"

"I'm not blushing, I'm just hot near this fire,"

she said. He had the most muscular chest. She imagined herself in his embrace, her naked breasts against his hard flesh. The heat of him against her bare nipples. She must not think of that. It was getting dark outside. How many more days before the cavalry arrived to rescue her?

He finished the last of the broth. "What's the chances of getting a steak?"

"You must be improving," she said. "I should have known you were too tough to die."

"Your kindness overwhelms me, princess." Before she could move away, he reached out and caught her hand.

His big hand covered her small one and she was too aware of the heat of his fingers. "Now about the ransom," she said.

"Hmm."

"There's so much left to be done on wedding arrangements and such." His fingers stroked the back of her hand in a way that unnerved her.

"Are you that anxious to sleep with my brother?"

"What an impertinent thing to say!" She jerked her hand free.

He smiled. "I'm not a polished gentleman like Pierce."

"To put it mildly," she sniffed.

"About the ransom; what would you be willing to pay?"

She looked at him, baffled. "I have no money with me; Daddy will have to send it."

He shook his head. "What I have in mind, only

you can give." His hand reached out again, caught a curl between two fingers.

"I don't know what you're talking about."

"Sure you do. I could take it anyway." His fingers were on her throat, stroking there.

She tried to pull out of his reach, but the wall of the lodge was behind her. "Then why haven't you?"

"Because, princess, I want you to give; I don't want to have to take." Her pulse seemed to pound against his fingers as they moved lower on her throat.

"How dare you even suggest—!" She clenched her teeth and willed herself not to slap his hand away.

"You asked what the ransom was; I'm telling you." His fingers stroked her throat until she could hardly think of anything else but his touch.

"Are you saying that to let me go, I'm going to have to . . . ?" She couldn't bring herself to say it. Cherish looked pointedly at his injured shoulder. "You're hardly up to—"

"Let me be the judge of that." His fingers were stroking along the open throat of the shirt she wore. It sent chills down her back.

"You could have—could have had your way with me from the first moment you got me here."

"Maybe you're hard of hearing," he said. "I said I want you to give; I don't want to take."

"I—I don't know what you're talking about." Was it getting hotter in here? She couldn't bring herself to pull away as his fingers stroked below her collarbone.

"Sure you do, I can tell by that horrified ladylike expression on that pretty face," he whispered. "And if you don't I'll spell it out for you. I want you to take your clothes off, get in my blankets, and share a night both of us can remember."

"I believe it's called a nightmare."

"No, princess, it's called passion."

"You aren't serious?" She pulled back as far as she could from him, but the lodge wall was in her way. His fingers still stroked along her skin.

"Oh, but I am."

"Are you saying that if I—I sleep with you, you'll let me go?"

"Sleep isn't what I had in mind." He caught her chin with his fingers, turned her face so that she had to look at him although she didn't want to. "One night. One night, Cherish, is all I ask, and then with the coming dawn, I'll blindfold you, take you out of this valley and turn you loose."

"Of all the—!" She brought her hand back to slap his insolent face, but he caught her wrist.

"You asked. I sense passion behind that delicate, beautiful face, but I don't think my brother will ever bring it out."

"And you will?" Her tone was scathing.

He smiled ever so slowly. "I'll certainly enjoy trying."

"Why are you doing this?" she cried. "There's women aplenty who'd be thrilled to end up in your bed. I saw how that Mexican slut acted—"

"I want you, Cherish Blassingame; I've wanted

236

you since that first time I kissed you at the New Year's Eve party."

She saw it all clearly now. "It's revenge you're after. You're out to get even with your own brother."

"Maybe, but that's not your business."

"You must hate Pierce very much."

"I have my reasons; your father, too." His fingers dug into her small wrist and his eyes were cold and hard as obsidian.

She tried to pull her wrist free, but he was strong. "How can you ask that? Pierce would know. On our wedding night, he'd know that you had been first—"

"Pierce? I doubt it, but that's a gamble you'll have to take. He'd probably never know the difference."

"And what if he does?"

Nevada smiled. "Then I'll have had my revenge on everyone concerned."

She managed to pull away, sobbing and angry. "What have we done that you hate us so? How can you ask this of me?"

"Because I want you, princess," he whispered. "I've always wanted you. I want to kiss you like you've never been kissed, leave you breathless, bring you to passion—"

"Even Pierce has never dared speak so boldly!"

"I'm sure little brother is the perfect gentleman and you're looking forward to your wedding night."

She only stared at him in disbelief, astounded that he could be so cold, so cruel.

"Not looking forward to it? I thought so."

She hated his glib expression. "It's not like that

at all! I love Pierce. We expect to have a very solid marriage."

"Sounds like a stock merger."

"Well, Daddy says—"

"Don't you ever think about what it would be like to marry a man who would stand up to Daddy? Who could make you feel like a woman, or are you really only a china doll after all?" Before she realized his intent, he reached up, caught the back of her neck, pulled her down to him, kissed her. His mouth tasted hot as a branding iron across her lips, his tongue pushing insistently against them, then slipping inside. Her breasts pressed against his hard, naked chest.

She attempted to pull away, panicked that he was building a fire in her that she hadn't expected, that seemed as if it could rage out of control. She was engaged to Pierce Randolph and she must take him the gift of her virginity. How dare this brazen outlaw expect her to play the whore for his lustful pleasure! She brought back her fist, hit his wounded shoulder.

"God damn you—!" He fainted dead away.

Good enough for him, she thought with grim satisfaction, then noted his pale color and immediately became concerned. If he died, his gang would seek terrible retribution. Cherish lay him down, checked his bandage to make sure he hadn't started bleeding, covered him up.

What on earth was she going to do? Did Nevada lust for her that much? If she could believe that he at least cared for her. . . . She shook her head. No, it was just that he hated his brother. What a terrible revenge; to demand a bride's virginity. If he sent her back to her bridegroom with his child in her belly, would Pierce know the difference, or would he think it was his own and assume its dark good looks came from its grandmother, Dallas?

Cherish paused to look at the setting sun with all its pink and purple. How many more days would she be a prisoner here? She had no doubt that in this secret place, she might never escape unless Nevada let her go. One night in his arms and he would free her at dawn. Well, fiddlesticks and damn it, it was out of the question! Of course she wouldn't even consider it. Maybe he had been joking. She remembered his expression. No, he hadn't appeared at all amused. She stood there in the lavender and gray haze of dusk and looked toward the west, wondering when help would arrive or even if Pierce were leading the posse anywhere near this hidden valley. Nevada was right; she could be trapped here as his prisoner forever unless . . . no, she would never, never pay his price!

Pierce hunkered down before the little camp fire, looked toward the setting sun and cursed. Damn, nothing had gone right. A section of track was out, so the posse's train had been delayed and now he realized the troop of cavalry the army had sent was led by an incredibly stupid young captain. No one in the bunch, including himself, actually knew this area. They could spend weeks wandering around in this godforsaken land without finding anything at all.

What was he going to do with Nevada when he caught him? Pierce smiled at the thought of his parents finally seeing his brother as he really was; a discredited outlaw. What about the newspapers? Would the scandal hurt his political and social ambitions? Amos Blassingame was a powerful ally; maybe he could keep the papers from ever pointing out that the two were brothers. Besides, maybe Nevada would get killed in the capture and Pierce wouldn't have to worry about him at all anymore.

He hadn't always hated him. Pierce remembered almost fondly that Nevada and old Ben had put him on his first pony. The hate came gradually as Pierce realized that he was never going to be able to compete with Nevada for his parents' affections, never going to top his older brother at anything. He poked up the camp fire, remembering that New Year's Eve party where he'd first met Cherish Blassingame. What a prize she was for an ambitious young man.

Pierce cared about Cherish; he really did. It was the fear of competing with his older brother for her affections, as well as his jealousy, that made Pierce take the information Amos had given him in Boston, go back to the ranch and confront Nevada with the startling discovery.

Nevada had been sitting in the den, looking over ranch ledgers when Pierce walked in. "Little brother?" Nevada half rose from his chair. "I'm certainly surprised to see you home. Sorry no one was at the station to meet you, but we weren't expecting—"

"Where are Mother and Dad?" Pierce asked. Now he was having second thoughts about what he had come to do because of the way Nevada was pumping his hand, genuinely happy to see him. He had an abrupt memory of being pulled from that horse tank; yet gratitude finally becomes a very heavy burden.

"There's a festival going on at the village." Nevada smiled and Pierce noticed the crested family ring on his finger. Father would be turning over control of the ranch to Nevada. Why did he always get the nod of approval while the real Randolph was passed over? Nevada said, "I thought it was a quiet time to catch up on the paperwork."

Pierce went over to the sideboard, poured himself a whiskey. "Competent Nevada giving his whole life to this sorry spread of cactus and yucca. Haven't you ever thought about selling the ranch, brother?"

"Sell the ranch?" He looked surprised, then laughed. "Not much of a joke, little brother." He came over, clapped Pierce on the back.

"I'm not joking," Pierce snapped and gulped his whiskey. "The folks are not young anymore and they won't always be able to keep the Wolf's Den running well."

Nevada looked at him strangely. "But they've got us."

"Us? You mean *you*."

"You're talking loco, Pierce. Half of everything will be yours someday, you know that."

Pierce sipped his whiskey and looked at him a long moment, trying to decide if he should hold his silence, burn the damning proof Amos Blassingame had given him. He shook his head, wanting it all; all the proceeds from the ranch, his parents' approval, the hand of Cherish Blassingame. "It all should be mine."

Nevada laughed good-naturedly and sat down on the corner of the desk. "Now, baby brother, I always shared my toys with you, even when you wanted them all; maybe even helped spoil you, but—"

"Stop laughing at me," Pierce snapped. "All they ever saw was you; you were always their favorite. Even the hired help liked you best."

Nevada raised his eyebrows at him. "Pierce, is there something wrong at school; maybe bad grades? You come home from Boston unexpectedly, walk in here as angry as a bee-stung bronco and start laying into me."

Did he have the nerve to say it? There was still time to mutter an apology, keep the secret. Nevada reached in his pocket for tobacco and the last rays of the sun gleamed on the big gold ring. The Randolph family ring.

Pierce took a deep breath. "Amos Blassingame came to see me a few days ago."

"He was up in Boston, I presume, to see his spoiled daughter?" Good, Nevada wasn't interested in her then. Pierce had had a glum feeling that if

Nevada wanted her, with his way with women, Pierce wouldn't stand a chance.

"Cherish Blassingame is a beauty and a good match for an ambitious young man," Pierce said and drained his glass to bolster his courage. "In a few years, if she'll have me, I might marry her."

Nevada merely grunted and finished rolling a cigarette. "I had no idea you were interested in her, little brother."

"Please stop calling me that!" Pierce almost screamed it at him. "Everyone thinks of me as your little brother. I'm tired of always being in your shadow."

His brother paused with a match ready to light his smoke; shook it out. He reached his hand to Pierce, paused, dropped it to his thigh. "I—I'm sorry, Pierce, I had no idea you felt that way. I'm sure none of us ever meant to—"

"Nobody around here ever has any idea about how I feel about anything!" he confronted Nevada. "Did you ever think to ask?"

Nevada tossed the unlit cigarette into the fireplace, put his hand on Pierce's shoulder. "I don't know what's got your back up, Pierce, but I care about you; I've always cared about you, that's why I've always done the best I could to look out for you—"

"I am sick and tired of being reminded how much I owe you; even my life!" Pierce jerked out of his grasp. "Besides always living in your shadow and knowing the folks think more of you than they do of me, I have to feel eternally obligated."

"Damn it, settle down." Nevada sounded as if he were finally becoming nettled. "Anything I ever did for you, I did because you're my brother, Pierce, not to make you feel obligated, not so I could feel superior or please the folks."

Nevada might kill him for what he was going to say, but it was going to be worth it after all these years. "Amos Blassingame hired the Pinkerton detectives to look into our family background."

Nevada frowned. "What on earth for? The snooty old son of a bitch has a helluva lot of nerve. The Randolphs and the Durangos are above scandal and—"

"Not quite." He leaned with both hands on the desk and smiled at Nevada, savoring the pain he was going to cause him.

"What's that supposed to mean? Pierce, have you gone loco?"

"Have you ever wondered why you're so dark while I have Father's light hair and hazel eyes?"

Nevada shrugged. "I take after Mother, everyone knows that."

"You've heard the story of how our parents met?"

The other sighed and rubbed his forehead as if he were running out of patience. "Yes, she cut her hair and rode for the Pony Express and Dad was providing the horses. So what?"

"During a big Indian war in Nevada," Pierce said.

"I think I've heard them mention it." He laughed. "Next thing, Pierce, you'll be telling me I'm a foundling someone left in a mailbag. Is there a joke in here somewhere and I've missed it?"

"Father had a blood brother, a Paiute warrior named *Timbi*."

Nevada cocked his head, nodded. "We've all heard that. *Timbi* was killed in that Indian war. Dad thought a lot of him. Surely you didn't come all the way home from Harvard to talk about Dad's old friends and Western history?"

"History is important when it has a bearing on the future." Pierce licked his dry lips, nodded toward a leather case. "The Pinkerton man tracked down an old drunken Indian who was there; who told him what really happened. It's all in that case I brought with me."

For the first time, Nevada frowned. "I don't know where this conversation is going, but I'm beginning to think I don't like your inference—"

"Damn it, I'm trying to tell you something!"

The silence was ominous. Nevada crossed himself automatically and Pierce couldn't resist a sneer. "You're as superstitious and backward as any greaser on the place, as any old Injun—"

"By God, Pierce"—Nevada grabbed him by the front of his shirt, half lifted him from the floor—"whatever this is about, you'd better tell me and tell me quick!"

He realized suddenly that the man who held him was bigger, plus strong from years of ranch work while he'd been reading books and writing poems at college. "The Paiute chief had a woman. His friend wanted her."

The look on Nevada's dark face was terrifying to

see. He shook Pierce like a rag doll. "Tell me, by God, tell me this rotten rumor—"

"Listen to me, Nevada," he gasped, "at least listen to me! Quint Randolph killed *Timbi* so he could take his woman; she was expecting that Indian's child—"

"You lie!"

Pierce saw the blow coming, but he wasn't fast enough to avoid it. Nevada's big fist, driven with all the power and anger of denial, caught him on the chin, knocked him across the desk. He felt the pain as he fell across the bookends and papers went flying, a lamp crashed to the floor.

"By God, I'll kill you for smearing Dad—!"

"He's not your dad! Don't you understand?" Pierce was in a fury himself, tasting the coppery warm blood from his cut lip that now made a crooked scarlet trail across his white shirt, onto the carpet. "You're *Timbi*'s son; you've got no right to the ring, the ranch, even the name!"

Nevada swore as he grabbed him. "I'll kill you for your rotten lies!" He hit him again.

Pierce tried to defend himself, but he was no good with his fists. He felt his body cringe in protest as Nevada slammed him backward. A small table overturned, then a chair. He clenched with Nevada, hung on for dear life as they struggled, fell across a small chair that shattered beneath their weight. Nevada was going to kill him, he knew that, but somehow, the anguish in the dark face, the revenge, made it all worth while.

Pierce wiped the blood from his mouth. "You can

kill me," he gasped as he staggered to his feet, fell against a table as more glass and knickknacks clattered to the floor, "but you can't change the truth. Quint Randolph wanted Dallas and he killed *Timbi* to take her. He's raised you because of his guilty conscience. You're not a Randolph, you're an Injun! You hear? A gut-eating, bloody Paiute!"

With a scream of hatred and anguish, Nevada charged him again. It was worth it, Pierce thought, as they meshed and battled about the den, overturning furniture, breaking glass, knocking paintings from the walls, it was worth it to finally be able to tell Nevada that the man he worshipped was not his father at all.

Nevada swore and knocked Pierce across the room. "It isn't true! I'll ask them; you'll see; it isn't true!"

Pierce retreated, his whole body a mass of pain, his fine waistcoat torn and bloody. "Ask them, then, see if they deny it!" He turned and stalked from the house, feeling both guilty and triumphant.

And now the final chapter was about to unfold. Pierce huddled closer to the camp fire. This posse would rescue Cherish, Nevada would go to jail where he belonged. Maybe even his parents would see that Pierce was really the child who should get the whole inheritance. Cherish would look on Pierce as a hero; so would her father and the newspapers. Amos surely had the power to keep the outlaw's relationship to Pierce out of the papers. Nevada would be just some renegade outlaw Injun.

Pierce looked around the camp and smiled. So what if it did take a couple of weeks to track his brother down, rescue the girl? The publicity was going to make him a legislator, and maybe some day, with Amos's help, governor of California. He'd have the Randolph inheritance, the Blassingame fortune, and Cherish in his bed besides. Yes, he was glad he had done it. There was no looking back now!

Fourteen

Nevada moved restlessly in his sleep, as his throbbing shoulder brought him awake. He opened his eyes, looked around at the interior of his lodge and the small flickering fire. What had happened? He closed his eyes, feeling pain. What had he been dreaming? Oh, yes, about that terrible night that Pierce had come home from Harvard. He and his brother had had such a terrible fight, almost destroying the den. Pierce had left, bloody and angry.

Pierce must have hurt him in that fistfight more than he thought; his shoulder was throbbing with each beat of his heart. What was the fight about? Pierce had accused their parents of awful things. Once again he drifted back into the memory of that horrible afternoon.

After Pierce had stormed out, Nevada had collapsed on the sofa, picked up the leather case. *Where had Pierce gotten this stuff?* He thumbed through it with trembling hands while looking around the wrecked den. Mother was going to be furious over the damage, and Dad, too, although

Quint hardly ever got mad. As he thumbed through the papers, his eye caught the ring he wore. Of course he was a Randolph; if he weren't, Quint wouldn't have given him the family ring. He had to be Quint's son; he worshipped the man. Quint wouldn't lie to him, neither would Dallas. He began to read the papers in the case.

It was dark and he was still sitting there staring into space when he heard his parents' buggy arriving out front. He couldn't bring himself to move.

He heard Dad open the front door. "Well, angel, it was a nice festival, but I'm glad to be home. Funny, no lights lit."

He heard them stumbling around in the front hall, heard Quint fumbling with an oil lamp. Still he couldn't move.

"Nevada?" His mother's voice. "Nevada, are you home, dear?"

They came into the room, Dad carrying the lamp. Quint paused in the doorway, held it high. "Oh, Lord!"

"What is it, dear?" Dallas peered around him. She was tall for a woman and still pretty, even though she had a gray hair or two, Nevada thought dully. Yes, he could imagine that many years ago, a man would kill another to possess her.

He heard his mother's gasp of dismay as Quint held the lamp high, seemed to see him slumped on the sofa for the first time. "Good Lord, Nevada, what happened here? Are you all right, son?"

"I—" He tried to speak and couldn't. His soul was in too much pain. He watched the man set the lamp on the desk, stumble through the wreckage to light the big oil lamp that hung from the ceiling. "Pierce was home," he said.

His mother cried out again as the light brightened and she saw the whole room. "My God, what's happened here? Son, are you all right?" She ran to his side, sat next to him, peered into his face. "You're hurt! Oh, Quint, he's hurt!"

Quint threaded his way through the overturned furniture, looked around, concern in his hazel eyes. "What happened? Looks like a war exploded in the den."

Nevada tried to pull away from his mother. "I'm all right; there was a fight."

Quint ran his hand through his hair. "I'd say that's the understatement of the year, son, are you all right?"

"Don't call me that! Don't you ever call me that again!" He wanted to lash out at them both for their lies; for hurting him.

Quint's eyebrows went up in amazement. "I beg your pardon?"

Nevada stood up, grabbed the case, tossed it into his mother's lap. "Pierce told me the truth; he told me about *Timbi*."

He saw the couple exchange glances.

Quint said, "I don't know what you're talking about, son."

"I said don't call me that; not ever again! You lied to me; you both lied to me!"

Dallas said, "Son, don't use that tone of voice to your father."

"And you," he sneered, turning on her, "you're no better than he is, sleeping with him after what he did."

"Boy," Quint said, his tone measured, controlled fury, "you won't speak to your mother that way, no matter what this is about. I'm not too old to thrash—"

"Are you going to kill me?" he shouted at him as he confronted him. "Will you kill me as you did *Timbi?*"

Even in the lamplight, he saw Quint's face go pale. "Who—who told you that?"

"It's true, isn't it? I can see it in your eyes. You wanted his woman and you took her; it's all right there in those papers—"

"Nevada," Dallas blurted, "Quint didn't—"

"Hush up, angel," Quint said. "I'll handle this."

"It is true!" Somehow he hoped they would deny it, but there was no denying the horror in both their faces. "I'm not your son; all these years you've lied to me! I'm *Timbi's* son, aren't I?"

Dallas buried her face in her hands. "Oh, I knew we should have told you, it was just such a terrible—"

"You are my son," Quint said with anguish in his eyes, "I breathed life into you myself one terrible January night when Dallas went into labor and there was no one there but me and old Ben."

"I'm not your son—"

"You are my son; you bear my name," Quint was

weeping now as only a strong man can weep. "You were sired by my blood brother, but you are mine, I have imprinted everything I ever knew on you; I breathed life into you and held your tiny body against me to warm you when you came into this world all blue and lifeless. I willed you to live!"

Dallas went to his side, put her arms around him. She was weeping, too. "Oh, Quint!"

"I've been living a lie," Nevada whispered. "I'm not a Randolph. Pierce jeered when he told me; I'm a bastard, a Paiute bastard."

Quint came to him, put his hand on the boy's shoulder, but Nevada pushed it away. "You are not a bastard; you bear my name. As far as I'm concerned, you're as much a Randolph as Pierce; maybe more so."

Nevada shook his head. "No, you never cared about me, neither of you. It's guilt, that's what it is—guilt because you killed him!"

Quint made a futile gesture. "Please try to understand. How could I tell you about *Timbi,* we were in a life-and-death fight out there at Pyramid Lake. He wouldn't let me walk away."

"Because you were trying to take his woman, that's it, isn't it?"

Dallas wept. "No, Nevada, that's not how it was! Quint didn't—"

"Hush, Dallas. He's upset; he'll get over it." Quint looked from one to the other. "Look, son, I know finding this out has been a big shock and I can't imagine why Pierce would—"

"He wanted me to know. He resents me, I suppose he's always resented me and you two felt guilty about me. I hate you for that; for lying to me."

Quint reached out to him. "I'm sorry, Nevada, maybe we didn't handle it right, we didn't know how to tell you. Maybe we made a mistake, hoping we could keep the secret, but—"

"I know now why Cain killed Abel," Nevada said and gritted his teeth. He had never felt such bitter fury. He started for the door.

Quint blocked his path. "Son, don't go. You can't leave like this, we've got to talk—"

"Get out of my way or so help me God, I'll kill you!"

"Nevada, please—"

He hit him then, slammed his fist into the older man's face as Dallas screamed. Once he had idolized this man and now. . . . Blindly, he ran through the house and out into the darkness. Somewhere, a coyote howled. He had never felt so bereft, so alone. Torn from a secure environment, abruptly he had no identity at all. If he was not Quint Randolph's son, who was he? What would he do? Where would he go? He ran to the barn, saddled his big Medicine Hat stallion, rode out at a gallop. He could handle a pistol with the best of them and the Lincoln County War was just winding down. Killing for hire was a suitable calling for a Paiute bastard. No wonder Cherish Blassingame had scorned him. Her father was the one who had dredged all this up, and his dear little brother, Pierce, had relished telling it.

He rode blindly toward New Mexico. It was hours later that he realized he still wore the Randolph ring.

He started to take it off, throw it away, but could not bring himself to do so. No, he told himself as he struck out across Arizona, he would wear it to remind him of what had happened and from this day forward, he would not use the name Randolph; it was not his to use. *Nevada*. That wild terrain was the stronghold of the Paiutes, land of his dead warrior father. Nevada; a good name for a gunfighter. That one name was all he needed; he had carried it for six years now.

His eyes flickered open as Cherish Blassingame came into the shadowy lodge. He had forgotten how beautiful she was with the firelight shining on her yellow hair. Quinton Nevada Randolph might have hoped to marry her, but a gunfighter named Nevada could only possess her momentarily. It would have to be enough. She could buy her freedom at the cost of her innocence. He didn't intend that she should leave this camp until he mounted her, took that virginity that Pierce had waited all these years to possess. It was Nevada's terrible revenge against them all.

He watched her lie down on a blanket near him, close her eyes. She looked tired, fearful. Everything in him made him want to reach out to her, hold her close, tell her she was safe, that everything would be all right. If he did that, would she snuggle against him, soft and warm as a yellow kitten and say, I didn't mean what I said in my letter. You are the one I want; the one I've always wanted.

Who was he kidding? His mouth twisted into a sardonic grin of pain. Cherish didn't want love and devotion, she wanted aristocratic bloodlines and social position. If Nevada turned her loose, she would flee back to his brother and her daddy's mansion without a backward glance or even a sigh for what might have been.

Nevada reached out and stroked a lock of her hair. It felt like silk. He had never wanted to possess a woman as much as he wanted this one. She was lying so that he could see the swell of her breasts and he felt himself go hard, thinking of how she would feel against him and how those breasts would taste. He imagined tangling his fingers in her hair, forcing that hot little mouth to caress his manhood. He would dominate her, force her to do things to him that she would never dream of doing to a man. No, he didn't want her that way, he wanted her to want him; to love him with all her heart and soul and come into his arms with a willing passion.

He couldn't have that and he knew it. At best, he could only demand she pleasure him for a night in exchange for setting her free. Pierce Randolph's society bride would be the gunfighter Nevada's whore for a night. Revenge, yes, it would be so sweet. Cherish would finally pay the ransom rather than be his prisoner forever. Nevada hadn't had a woman in a long time and his desire made his pulse pound. If he couldn't put any weight on that shoulder, he would have her ride him so that he could watch her face, reach out to stroke her full breasts. Her hair like yellow silk would fall down like a haze around them both. He wanted to wipe her virgin blood from his body with that torn, fine wedding dress, send it back to Pierce with a note telling him this was repayment for the revenge he owed him.

Something alerted him. Nevada looked around. Cherish still slept. Maybe he had imagined it or dreamed it. He struggled to his feet, stumbled outside. It must be very late. The camp was silent and asleep, the sky like a basket of broken bits of crystal against a dark sky. He looked toward the hazy hills, barely outlined against the moon. What was that? A wisp of fog, perhaps. Without thinking, he crossed himself as the image grew clearer. A Medicine Hat stallion running along the faraway ridge, yet its hooves seemed to make no sound. It paused on a ridge, flinging its head and its mane seemed like a tangle of stardust.

A spirit horse. That was all it could be; one of the medicine visions that warriors prayed for. It turned and looked at him before it reared up on its hind legs, pawing the sky. For a long moment, there was nothing but the dreamlike paint horse pawing at the air while meteors and falling stars seemed to flow from its activity. A great peace descended over Nevada. The spirit horse seemed to be one with the universe and now he was, too, as if the image was bringing him a message from his father's people. The great stallion rose up on its hind legs again, pawed the air. Then it took off running, almost flowing along the ridges, highlighted by the moon, until finally it faded and disappeared into the mist hanging over the hills.

Nevada stared at the empty ridge long after the apparition had disappeared. Now he was not even sure what he had seen. There were legends in the mountains about a great chief whose soul had taken the form of a mustang stallion so he could run wild and free forever. Could it be—? No, he had imagined it. The ridge appeared starkly empty in the moonlight. Still the peace fulfilled him and he knew he had had a medicine vision such as warriors used to pray for. What did it mean?

Abruptly he felt weak and a little dizzy; realized he stood alone staring into the blackness of the night at something he was no longer sure he had seen. He returned to his lodge.

Cherish sat up abruptly. "Are you all right?"

"Do you care?"

"Only as long as my life depends on your health."

"That's what I thought." He sat down next to her, breathing heavily. "I reckon I'm weaker than I thought." He collapsed with his head in her lap.

She started as if to pull away, then put her fingers on his forehead. "At least you're not feverish."

Nevada closed his eyes, enjoying the touch of her fingers stroking his face, the warmth of her body under his head.

An old poem his mother used to recite came back to him abruptly, about a man and a woman whose paths crossed only momentarily long before: . . . *God pity them both and pity us all who vainly the days of youth recall, for of all the words of tongue or pen, the saddest are these, it might have been* . . .

"Oh, Cherish, I wish. . . ."

"You wish what?"

"Nothing. I'm feeling a lot better."

"Is that supposed to be good news?"

"You've got an acid tongue, princess. Pierce Randolph deserves to have to live with you."

"Then you're setting me free?" Her fingers paused on his forehead.

"When you pay the ransom," he reminded her. "You decide when that will be."

"I hope you've got plenty of patience," she said. "I imagine the cavalry will find us before that happens."

He smiled up at her in the darkness. "I wouldn't count on it. There's only one way you'll leave this valley, Cherish; with my seed running down your thighs."

"You're crude!" she snapped and dumped his head from her lap, turned her back and lay down.

Somehow, he wasn't worried. Time was on his side while he waited for his shoulder to heal. Cherish Blassingame was his captive forever, because her would-be rescuers did not know the secret trail into this valley.

Mex watched Tequila's back as she poked up the fire and poured herself a cup of coffee. He didn't trust either the slut or her lover, Jack. By noon tomorrow, they should be buying supplies and returning to the valley.

The two were laughing about the posse that might

259

be vainly combing the hills, making jokes about being hanged. Mex rolled himself a cigarette. "Either of you ever actually see a man that's been hanged?"

"Me and my brother was almost lynched once." Jack sipped his coffee. "That's as close as I want to get."

Tequila looked at Mex with interest. "Have you?"

He nodded and the old memory returned. *"Si.* His face was all discolored, his tongue swelled, eyes and mouth hanging open as if he tried to scream and the rope cut the cry off."

Tequila shuddered and the heavy gold chains on her throat and arms jangled. "You never mentioned that before. Hey, *hombre,* let's talk about something else."

Mex smiled. "Now it doesn't seem so funny, no?"

"Let's stop talkin' about hangin'," Jack grumbled. "I think maybe I'm gettin' as superstitious as Nevada. Mex, it's your turn to stand guard."

He nodded, always obedient; never quarrelsome. He knew the *gringo* thought of him as a greaser kid, but it didn't matter. Mex had no argument with Jack; it was Tequila he had planned all these months for.

Mex took his rifle, climbed up on a high ledge where he could see anyone who rode near the campsite. In the shadows on a blanket near the fire, he could see Jack and Tequila making love. He watched as detached as he might watch a bitch in heat being mounted by a male dog she had attracted. She was clawing Jack's sweaty back and the *gringo* had his mouth on her big breasts. The firelight reflected off her jewelry as she and the outlaw meshed and bucked and writhed.

Gold. The slut would do anything to get it, with no conscience as to where it came from. Mex sighed and rolled himself a cigarette, wondering if he would get his chance on this trip. He had followed her for several years now, waiting his chance. The gold Tequila wore belonged rightly to the peasants of the village of Guadeloupe.

It was a poor village, all right; so very poor and hopeless. However, there had been a new and very young priest who had been born in this village and now returned with such vision, such hope. His innocence inspired them to believe that here was a man who was actually of God, that he was blessed. In turn, they began to believe in themselves; to hope. *Antonio Gonzales.*

The young priest brought honor to his family and his village, who were the poorest of the poor. If Antonio could get educated, become a priest, they could do great things, too. Miracles still happened after all. What they needed, the young priest said, was a school. He was so inspired, so blessed, that gradually he convinced them that they could change their fate; that each of them could make something of himself, too. They must begin with a school.

Ah, it was hard. The village had so little money. The priest's little brother was so very proud of him and full of hope for himself. He might become a teacher or a doctor. Who knew what heights an educated man might rise to?

Mex smoked his cigarette and stared into the

darkness, his hands reaching for a bit of rawhide to braid into a noose. It had taken several years for the poor villagers to accumulate the gold. All had sacrificed much, worked extra hard, done without, sold precious possessions. Finally the money was gathered and given into the priest's keeping. On the morrow, Father Gonzales would journey to Mexico City to buy books for the school they would begin in the old church.

There was only one person in Guadeloupe who was not interested in the school, a hip-swinging young slut who earned her money on her back. She had often glanced toward the young priest with lustful interest; his little brother had seen her. He did not worry; his brother was pure and noble.

No man is above being tempted by a Jezebel. Mex sighed and crushed out his cigarette, toyed with the little noose.

It had been dawn in the village when the little brother awakened to the strange sound of the church bell. It was almost as if someone pulled the rope sporadically. Today was the day Antonio was going for the books and he had told his little brother he could accompany him. Perhaps Antonio was ringing the bell to call everyone to an early mass for blessings before he left. Such a strange sound the bell made. When the villagers went out into the square, they could see something hanging in the bell tower at the end of the rope. When the wind blew, the limp black thing jerked the rope and clanked the bell. Even now, sometimes when the wind blew, Mex could hear that bell, see that face.

Mex watched the two by the camp fire. Jack and Tequila had finished their rutting and slept now. In a few hours, it would be dawn and the trio would be on their way. Mex hadn't quite decided how he would deal with this, but he had waited a long, long time for vengeance.

Tequila yawned and sat up, looked around at the ashes of the camp fire, at the *gringo* pig asleep next to her in the gray light just before dawn. She was tired of Jack Whitley, but she wasn't sure how she would ever get rid of him. She had had her eye on Nevada for a long time, but he had no interest in her. She would pay him back for that; she had a plan. All she needed now was someone who would help her get rid of Jack.

Jack awakened, scratching himself. "Fix us some breakfast, Tequila. Then I want to check the terrain out ahead before we move on. Traveling in daylight is risky. There's probably troops and lawmen combing the whole state looking for that girl the boss kidnapped."

She obeyed, filling the coffeepot, slicing bacon. "You mad at Nevada over your brother?"

Jack frowned. "Yeah, although I know Charlie had it coming. I'd feel the same way, baby, over a man tryin' to get between your legs." He reached out and grabbed her breast, but she pulled away from him.

"Don't, Jack. There's no time for that now." He was such a sweaty pig and she'd gotten most all the loot he'd hoarded over the last few months. Time to find a new man who had gold to spend.

"You're right, baby. Once we get the supplies and get back to the valley, I'm gonna put callouses on your back and a baby in your belly. It's about time you gave me a son."

Tequila shuddered at the thought of herself big with this pig's child. What Jack didn't know was that she had aborted herself twice of his bastards. There was always an old woman around some of these cantinas who knew what to do. "Call Mex in and I'll feed him, too."

"He's a strange one, ain't he?" Jack stood up, signaled the boy up in the rocks. "He's about the only man I ever seen who didn't look at you like he'd like to throw you down on your back."

Tequila poured coffee, turned the sizzling bacon over. "He's got strange eyes; I think he probably sleeps with men."

Jack laughed. "You're probably right, baby, because if you don't interest him, no woman could. I'll bet you could tempt a priest."

She didn't laugh. "I did once."

The three of them ate and Jack got ready to ride out. Mex was probably the only male Jack wasn't jealous of. It was probably true that the boy with the haunting eyes liked men better than girls. Tequila smiled to herself. That was almost a challenge.

When Jack rode out, Mex took care of the horses while Tequila packed up the camp. She had an idea to make a lot of money. That *gringo* girl's torn wedding dress was carefully folded in Tequila's saddlebag. She got it out now, spread it and looked at it. Yes, it was enough to convince the girl's father, all right, especially since it was torn. "Hey, Mex, you realize we never have got to know each other very well?"

He hesitated, looked surprised at her flirting tone. "You had plenty of men around you. I didn't think you knew I was alive."

So perhaps he might be interested in girls after all. She gave him her most engaging smile, let her blouse slip down off one shoulder, revealing a lot of breast. "Jack will be gone maybe an hour."

"So?"

"We could get to know each other very well in less time than that."

"Why the sudden interest?" He walked over, stared down at her as she packed the tin dishes.

Tequila played with the heavy gold chain around her neck, leaned forward a little more so that he could see her nipples. She wore nothing underneath. "I'm tired of Jack. I'd like to be someone else's woman now."

"Jack would kill you if he heard that; you know how jealous he is."

"Not if someone killed him first. He wouldn't expect you to be a danger." She smiled up at him, thinking that she knew he saved his money from the raids so he should have plenty to give her. She often wondered what he did with it.

Mex knelt beside her. "If Satan ever takes female form, I'll bet it's you, Tequila."

"I'm flattered." She smiled, reached out, put her hand on his arm. "You ever think what it would be like with me?"

Those strange eyes seemed to bore into her. "*Si,* I've thought more about it than you know."

She took his hand in hers, put it on her breast. "What would you give to find out?" she purred.

His fingers moved to play with the heavy gold chain around her neck. "You have a hunger for gold." It was a statement, not a question.

"I won't be young forever," Tequila shrugged, "and if men are willing to give it, I take it."

He tangled his fingers in the chain, pulled her up to his lips. "You would tempt a saint," he whispered, "and cause a man to forget his honor."

She laughed softly as she kissed him, running her hands up and down his arms. "Let me show you."

She pulled him down atop her on the spread-out wedding dress, his fingers still tangled in the gold chain. "Is this how you got this," he asked, "for tempting a man past endurance?"

"Of course!" She hiked up her skirt and pulled down her blouse so that the hand tangled in the chain now lay on her naked breast. She would pleasure this strange boy and take his money, then go on to Sacramento with the dress after he killed Jack for her. She pulled him down to kiss him.

"This gold around your neck belongs to the village of Guadeloupe," he whispered.

"What?" Her eyes blinked wide.

"You seduced an innocent priest," Mex whispered.

She was alarmed. He was more strange than she had thought. "How do you know that?"

"Did you lure him into giving you the school money as you are luring me now?"

"There must be a mistake." She looked up at him, trying to figure out how to deal with this. This *hombre* was more than strange, he was loco. "Look, Mex, I make love to you for nothing; you just enjoy me."

"I intend to." He grimaced as he played with the chain on her slender neck. "There is also a debt of honor to be paid."

"Let the priest pay; he gave me the money."

Mex shook his head. "He's already paid too much. He could not be buried in holy ground and his family's disgraced. The town lost more than its gold; it lost its hope."

She felt a sudden rush of terror as she looked into his haunting eyes. Tequila began to fight to get out from under him as he twisted the chain. "Please, *hombre,* I swear—"

"You will soon know, *puta* bitch, how it feels to be hanged." He twisted the chain and she felt it cut into her neck. "I wonder if your eyes will bulge out and your tongue turn black?"

Tequila struggled for air, clawing and fighting him, grabbing at the gold chain cutting into the flesh of her neck. Was he playing games and trying to scare her? "W-Why?"

"You wouldn't remember me as Sancho Gonzales, would you?" He smiled and twisted the chain. "I'm Father Antonio's little brother!"

She tried to beg, to scream out, but the heavy chain cut into her flesh, choking off any cry. Air; she had to have air! Everything seemed to be dimming, going dark, while she fought to break his grip. However, it was a fine, heavy chain that the village's money had bought and it would not break. She tried to protest, to pray, but he was cutting off her words as he choked her very slowly and deliberately. Tequila was losing consciousness and she needed a miracle. This loco *hombre* intended to kill her!

Fifteen

Jack watched from the trees as Mex tightened the chain. The slut! Offering herself to another man the minute Jack turned his back. Even this strange young *hombre* was not immune to her lure. He couldn't shoot Mex from here without risking hitting Tequila. Jack saw the butcher knife gleaming by the bacon. He ran across the camp, picked up the knife, stepped up behind Mex. With one quick move, he slashed the boy's throat.

Warm blood gushed out on Jack's hands, cascaded onto Tequila's naked breasts, that white fabric she lay on. Mex half turned to look up at Jack, trying to say something, reaching to him. He could only gasp for air like a throat-cut lamb.

Jack sneered. "You stupid greaser! You're just like every other man when it comes to Tequila!" He brought his foot up, planted it against the boy's chest, kicked him off the girl. Mex lay on the ground gasping his life away as his blood pumped out into the sand with each heartbeat.

Tequila struggled to sit up. "Jack! Oh, Jack! Thank

the saints you came!" Her neck looked red and bruised where the heavy gold chain had cut into it. "The *hombre* was raping me! I tried to cry out for help!"

He didn't believe her, he had been watching too long from the bushes. "Well, baby, I'm glad I got here in time." He forced himself to smile. "I expect you to be very grateful."

A look of distaste crossed her face. *"Si,* of course, Jack." She rubbed her throat, looked toward the dead body. "I don't know what made him try to rape me."

"As I always said, baby, you'd tempt a saint."

Tequila shuddered. "It was his brother Mex was talking about last night. He seems to think I knew him; that it's my fault he hanged himself."

She could do that to a man; drive him to desperation. Jack was not going to be able to hold her, he knew that. He'd seen the way she looked at every man, especially Nevada. Jack loved her, but he could not deal with her cheating anymore, the way other men always wanted her. "What're you doing with that girl's wedding dress?"

She looked down at it. The expensive white satin had a scarlet smear of blood on the skirt now. "You do believe me about Mex, don't you?"

"Sure, baby."

"I'll prove it's you I really care about, Jack. Did I ever tell you I know that girl's papa?"

"No. I reckon now you'll tell me you used to sleep with him, too?" He had already decided what he was going to do. If he couldn't keep her, he didn't want her sleeping in any other man's arms.

She laughed. "Just once. I was a maid cleaning his offices for a while. He's just a lonely, fat old man. I seduced him on the sofa in his office."

"And he gave you money?" Jack reached out and caught the gold chain between his fingers, wondering how much she would have gotten for selling him out to Mex.

Tequila nodded. *"Si*. His name is Amos Blassingame and his Trans-Western Railroad has its office in Sacramento."

"So?"

"Don't you see?" Her eyes widened with greed. "No one can find that valley without someone to lead them in. The old man will be offering a big reward."

He tangled his fingers in the chain so casually, she didn't even seem to notice. "Are you saying we double-cross Nevada?"

She shrugged and he saw the jealous glint in her eyes. Tequila would drop him for Nevada if she could and he knew it. "Why not?" she said. "After all, Nevada killed your brother."

Somehow he couldn't fault Nevada for that. Nevada had killed Charlie for the love of a woman. Jack loved Tequila like that.

She smiled. "We take this dress to the old man as proof we know where she is. When he sees that blood, he'll go crazy, thinking Nevada has raped or wounded her. He'll pay anything to get us to lead him to that valley."

"Very clever," Jack said. "We get away with the money and the troops ride in with blazing guns and wipe the whole gang out. Very neat and tidy."

"Isn't it, though?"

"And how long after that before you lure some man with your body into killing me?" He played with her gold chain.

Her face paled. "You got it wrong, Jack, I love you." She reached up to kiss him and he let her, savoring her mouth and the memory of all the times he had held her in his arms. But she didn't love him; she never had.

"You'll tempt no one else, baby," he whispered. "Why couldn't you be content with me?" And then he tightened the chain.

For a long moment, she stared up at him in surprise as if she didn't quite understand the words he had just said. "Jack, I swear—"

"Goodbye, baby," he whispered. He closed his eyes as he twisted the chain in his big hands so he wouldn't have to see her face as it discolored, as her eyes bulged and her mouth came open like a doomed fish thrown up on a riverbank, gasping for air. Tears ran down his sweating, weathered face as he slowly choked her. She whimpered and clawed at him, but she was small and no match for his strength.

Jack didn't look at her after she quit struggling. He put his head in his hands and shook, sorry now, yet past feeling almost anything except relief that he would never again have to worry about her betraying him. He took her necklace to remember her by, put it in his shirt pocket. Somehow, it was comforting to have it. Tequila had put some bad scratches on his face that stung now as sweat ran down it.

Should he bury them? Jack paused, shook his head. He didn't have a shovel. Besides, if anyone found the bodies, they would think the two had killed each other.

He was still numb and without emotion as he took the torn wedding dress, stuffed it into his saddlebag and rode out. What to do? He couldn't go back to Nevada after killing Mex. His mind went to Amos Blassingame. Jack wouldn't have to sell his friends out, he would only pretend he was going to lead the posse to the valley, take the reward and run. Maybe somewhere far from here, he could begin a new life.

When he walked into Blassingame's office the next afternoon, Jack carried the saddlebag. "We need to talk."

The old Englishman set down his teacup, his nose wrinkling in distaste. "By Jove, how'd you get in here, anyway? I'll have my secretary call the guards to—"

"I've got something you'll want to see," Jack said as he threw the saddlebag on the desk, began to pull out the torn white satin. "I know who's got your daughter and an idea on how to get her back."

"See here, young man, everyone's trying to take advantage of me with cock-and-bull stories about seeing my daughter. . . ." His voice trailed off and he gasped. "That's the dress Cherish showed me in the designer's sketch."

Jack nodded, spread it out. The scarlet stain had turned almost black, but there was no mistaking what it was.

Amos gaped at the dress, back up at the scruffy desperado. The dress had been an original, there couldn't be another like it, and that stain. . . . For a long moment, his chest hurt, and his head swam. He thought he might faint. "Where—where did you get that?"

"I reckon now you'll believe I know where she is." The outlaw flopped down in a leather chair, reached to help himself to an expensive cigar from the humidor on Amos's fine wood desk.

Blood. There was blood on that torn, dirty dress. Almost petrified at the realization, Amos noticed for the first time that the outlaw had several bad scratches on his face. Amos had a sudden vision of his delicate daughter fighting for her life as this scum murdered her. No, he was saying she was alive. Then at the very least, she'd been . . . "Are—are you saying you can lead us to her?"

"For a price."

"You'd barter a girl's life for money?" His chest began to hurt again.

"Don't act like no saint with me, old man." He lit his cigar, leaned back in his chair with a comfortable sigh.

What would it take to buy this thug? He could only stare back at the other man and wait. "I—I don't even know your name."

"Jack Whitley; not that it matters."

He studied the man, wondering how he had found Amos. Had Cherish sent him? "Is my daughter all right?"

"Depends on what you mean by 'all right,' " The outlaw smiled and fingered the scratches on his unshaven face. "An Injun's got her and the way he was lookin' at her—"

"Don't tell me the details; I can't bear it." Amos drummed his fingers on the desk, staring at the ragged fabric. "I see no reason to pay a rotten thief like you; the army and the posses will—"

"Never find her." The other grinned, flipped ashes on the expensive Persian carpet. "Only people who have been in that valley can find it again. You don't even know which state to look in."

It was true. The last wire Pierce had sent him suggested the posse was hopelessly lost and arguing among themselves. "I see. How much do you want?"

"Ten thousand dollars."

"Ten thousand—?"

"Ain't she worth it?" The outlaw smoked and waited.

"Yes; yes, of course." He vowed at that moment that he would place double that amount on this outlaw's head, and on the kidnapper's head, when Cherish was safe. "All right. I'll make arrangements.

You'll have to go meet her fiancé and the posse, lead them to her."

"When do I get the money?" He took a deep puff on the cigar.

"Half now," Amos said, "half when I get her back safely; just in case you were thinking of taking the money and double-crossing me."

The surprised expression on the other's sweaty face told him that was exactly what the outlaw had been planning to do. "You're pretty smart, old man."

"I bloody well didn't build this empire on soft stupidity," Amos snapped. "I'll have to wire her fiancé and make some arrangements both to get the money and for you to take the train and meet him. Right now, he's wandering around out there lost."

"I told ya." The outlaw grinned, tipped his hat back. "I'll keep in touch." He stood up.

Amos nodded, watched him saunter from the office. He had never felt such frustration and anger as he did now, staring at the outlaw's arrogant back as he left the office, then at the torn and bloody dress. Cherish might already be dead and this cold-blooded thief only using the dress to milk money from her grieving father. No, Amos wouldn't even consider that possibility. That only left one other way that skirt could have been bloodied. Pierce might not want to marry her now if she'd been used for an outlaw's pleasure.

He should summon the sheriff to stop this man and—no, he wouldn't learn Cherish's whereabouts that way. Amos gritted his teeth in sheer rage. He

276

would have his revenge if anything had happened to his innocent daughter. He drummed his fingers on his desk, thinking. Yes, he would arrange for the money all right, but he didn't intend that this outlaw should ever enjoy spending one dime of it. He reached for a pencil, scribbled a note telling Pierce that Jack Whitley was coming. In it, he added a carefully worded message to let Pierce know that he didn't expect Whitley to come out of this alive.

With all that confusion, once Cherish was safe, it might just happen that someone in the posse accidentally shot the informer in the back. Who would question it? Amos stood up, deciding to take it to the telegraph office himself. Right now, it was important to get Whitley on a train. Before this was over, Amos intended every one of that gang should feel his vengeance. As for the kidnapper, Amos intended to see him hang!

In the lodge, Cherish watched Nevada's face as she changed the bandage. "It's healing amazingly well; you must be as tough as a mustang."

"I'm Indian, remember? Not some prissy dude like you're used to. I can't stand any more of this sitting around. Let's go riding."

"With that shoulder?"

He shrugged. "It's almost well. Besides, Ben or *Kene* will saddle us a pair of horses."

"Oh? Do you want my company or are you just afraid I might escape if you leave me alone too long?"

"Maybe both, and I can't risk you escaping again; I've got only one shoulder left and it's my gun hand."

"Such charming flattery sweeps me off my feet," she said acidly. "However, I'm bored, so I'll go tag along for want of something better to do."

He frowned. "Thanks a lot!"

They went out to the horse herd where *Kene* saddled Sky Climber and a dainty Medicine Hat filly. Nevada even attempted to help her mount, but he was awkward with his injured shoulder.

He was a strange man, she thought as she watched him swing up on his big stallion with the easy grace of a man born to the saddle. She wouldn't want to admit it, but she found him intriguing, too. That made her feel guilty. Daddy would say she was an ungrateful, unappreciative child if he knew how often she had thought of Nevada even though Daddy had handpicked Pierce for her husband.

They rode out into the valley at a walk, paused to look over the view of wildflowers, silver sage, and cactus. They were far beyond the camp and might as well have been the only two people in the world this sunny afternoon.

Nevada sighed. "Reminds me a little of the Wolf's Den ranch. Pierce and I used to ride together as boys. . . ." A frown crossed his handsome face.

She couldn't contain her curiosity. "You were friends that night you came to our home in Sacramento and enemies by spring. Once you must have cared very much about each other."

278

He leaned on his saddle horn. "Once maybe we did, or at least I thought . . ." He spoke softly as if speaking to himself. "No one would have ever believed we would have such a terrible disagreement." He seemed to be lost in memory and his face saddened.

"What happened?"

Immediately, his eyes turned hard, expressionless. "That hardly concerns you. Besides, don't be so innocent; you know what happened."

She started to protest that she had no idea what he was talking about, but he had already started out again at a lope. She, too, took off across the valley, enjoying the ride immensely and she almost forgot she was a captive. Her hair came loose from its pins and her skirt hiked up because she rode astride. Loping along beside him seemed like the most natural thing in the world to do. She savored the freedom of enjoying the ride, not having to act like the perfect lady. Certainly there were years of that ahead of her after she married Pierce. She felt Nevada watching her and glanced over. He acted almost awkward at being caught staring. "What is it?"

"Nothing." He shook his head. "I had almost forgotten what it was that intrigued me about a spoiled little princess from Sacramento."

"And did you remember?" she joked lightly, but his face was thoughtful.

"Yes, I remember; I remember too well."

Something about the way he looked at her made her feel self-conscious. The look was almost tender. "Race you to the creek up there!" She pointed toward the distant water and before he could react, she nudged her mare with her heels and took off at a gallop.

"No fair, you didn't give any warning!" he yelled behind her, but she only laughed and kept riding. She heard him urging his great stallion on and the thunder of hooves behind her.

She knew a lady wasn't supposed to enjoy competing with a man, but she had never enjoyed anything so much. Cherish was determined to beat him, make him eat her dust. "Come on, Ink Spots, keep going!"

But about that time, her mare shied at a snake and Cherish found herself flying over the mare's dainty head, landing on the ground. Even though there was a carpet of lush grass and crushed flowers to cushion her, she was momentarily stunned. Behind her, she heard Nevada's voice as he thundered up, swung down. "My God, Cherish, are you hurt?"

She didn't feel like opening her eyes. She lay there with the wind momentarily knocked out of her.

"Cherish, princess, answer me!" He was cursing as he knelt by her side, gathered her into his arms as best he could. "If you're hurt, I'll never forgive myself."

The concerned tone touched her and she slowly opened her eyes. "I—I think I zigged when I should have zagged."

He crossed himself, looked relieved. "This may be your lucky day. Are you all right?"

Out of pure contrariness, she decided to prolong

his anxiety. "I—I'm not sure." Somehow, his arms felt warm and comforting around her. "I'd feel better back home."

He raised one eyebrow at her. "You must not feel too bad if you're trying to strike deals with me. You scared me to death."

"I should be so lucky!" She was annoyed with him for seeing through her ruse, and maybe with herself for wanting to lie there in his embrace rather than hop right up and insist she wasn't hurt.

He caught her hand and she decided not to pull away. Maybe she could soften him up by appealing to whatever honor he once had had and he'd change his mind and free her. He brought her fingers to his lips and kissed them gently.

"You surprise me," she whispered.

"Why? Because you don't think a savage could be capable of tenderness? Have you forgotten that New Year's Eve?" She felt the blood rush to her face and he eyed her curiously. "You haven't forgotten."

"Of course I have!" she blustered. "It was a silly, schoolgirl thing."

"Maybe to you."

Of course he was lying, attempting to soften his image as a robber and kidnapper. Not that it mattered; it was all water under the bridge. He still had hold of her hand and she was looking up into his eyes. She must be nice to him and maybe he would relent and turn her loose. Cherish wasn't quite sure whether he was drawing her to him or whether she did it without thinking, but abruptly she was in his embrace among the soft grass and wildflowers and he was kissing her.

She felt giddy with the sensation of his lips brushing across hers. It wasn't the passionate kisses he had given her when they were both half drunk by the camp fire the night she had escaped, it was a tender kiss of a man who really might love a woman. His tongue caressed her lips until she opened them. She hadn't meant to do that, but now his tongue touched the insides of her mouth and his hand was cupping her breast. She found herself pressing against that hand, her heart beating faster. His fingers slipped inside her shirt, catching her nipple between his fingers, making it swell with desire. She had a sudden image of his dark face against her white breast. Without meaning to, she reached up and unbuttoned several buttons and with a sigh, he put his mouth there.

She cradled him in her arms like a baby, offering him her breast, urging him to nurse it. She felt hot all over as he sucked hard, his arm going around her to pull her against his mouth that was hot and wet and wanting. She did not think; she only felt, wishing she had milk to nourish him as she bent her head, kissed his ear, ran her tongue into it.

"Oh, Cherish . . . princess . . . my princess . . ." His hand slipped down to push up her skirt. She knew she should make him stop, but she was his captive and if he desired her, he could do anything he wished. She kept telling herself that so she wouldn't feel guilty about wanting his hand to stroke her thigh, wanting him to touch her in even a more intimate place. Her body seemed on fire as his hand caressed her thigh and moved higher.

Oh, surely he wasn't going to touch her there. Then his mouth sucked her breast again and she didn't care what he did with his hand as long as her body stopped this aching. With a shuddering whimper, she let her knees fall open and his thumb touched the bud of her femininity. Pierce had never dared touch her this way, she would never have dreamed of letting him do the things Nevada was doing with his hand, or his mouth. She couldn't stop herself from making little noises in her throat as his fingers touched her and his demanding mouth sucked each breast into two blazing points of desire.

She felt him fumbling with the buttons of her shirt and then slowly, his lips kissed down her bared belly. She closed her eyes and felt the tip of his tongue in her navel, teasing and caressing there. Cherish was past shame, past anything but wanting him to do whatever it took to stop her from trembling the way her body was at this moment.

Oh, God, what was he doing with his mouth now? She felt him kissing her thighs and she couldn't stop herself from letting them fall open, tangling her fingers in his dark hair, urging his mouth to move even higher.

His breath was hot as his lips teased up her thigh. She could feel her pulse pounding as she arched her back and offered him the most tender part of her flower. When he kissed her most intimate place, she was so shocked, she gasped, but she didn't stop him. What surprised her most of all was that she wanted him to touch her with his mouth again, and she pulled him closer. He caressed her with his tongue and then the hard blade of it slipped inside and teased her body with its wet, velvet touch in the most intimate of kisses.

Dimly, she reminded herself that she must stop him. No, she couldn't stop him; she was his prisoner and he was bigger than she was. He could use her for his pleasure and she need not feel guilty. Pierce would never know. Somehow, she would fool her bridegroom on their wedding night. Cherish was feeling urges she had never felt before, didn't even know her body was capable of. She wanted this man to lie on her, take her in his embrace, make her submit to his superior strength and size. She wanted him to put his child in her body, protect and adore her. She could sleep safe and secure in his arms because she was his mate. He would keep her near him always, kill any man who looked at her with desire, and most of all he would make love to her continually, love her as she had never been loved, teach her passion so that she wanted him to . . . wanted him to what? She pulled away from him, breathing hard.

He laughed softly, but he was gasping for breath, too. "You've got some feeling for me, princess, I can see it in your eyes. You're shocked yourself, aren't you?"

"I—I'm only being nice to you so you'll let me go. I—I can't help it if you force yourself on me!"

"If you think I'm going to forget myself and rape you, my elegant miss, that's not going to happen.

You're not going to be able to tell the world and your conscience I took you by force."

She pulled down her skirt with an angry gesture. "You—you were making me submit to you."

"Is that what that was just now?" He leaned back against a log and rolled a cigarette, but she noted his hand shook. "Forcing you to submit? Are you lying to me or yourself?"

"You're playing with me and I don't like it!"

He paused and frowned. "You did the same to me once, and laughed because I thought it might be more than that."

What on earth was he talking about? She hadn't laughed at him that New Year's Eve, but it didn't matter now. She was going to wed this outlaw's brother and lead a nice, ordinary upper-class life. She absolutely refused to give her virginity to this vengeful desperado as ransom. "You misread what just happened here. I thought if I was nice to you, you might let me go."

He put the cigarette in his mouth and lit it with an awkward hand, checked the match to make sure it was out before he tossed it away. "Is it so distasteful to you then to endure my embrace?" Was he angry or hurt? She couldn't be sure. "In case you've forgotten, Cherish, I've set the ransom price. You can either pay it willingly or you can stay here forever!"

Sixteen

Pierce glanced up at the sun, over to the cavalry officer as the troop paused to rest their horses. He read the wire the handsome young captain had just handed him. "A guide?"

He read it again. Amos was sending one of Nevada's own men out on a train to show the troops where to go to trap the outlaw. The sun beat down on them, making sweat run down his back. Pierce hated dirt, manual work, sweat and horses.

"Looks like we'll have to wait for this guy to show up then," the captain said, took off his hat, brushed his light-colored hair out of his pale blue eyes with a weary hand. He turned and gave orders to the sergeant. All down the line, the order went out to dismount.

Pierce scowled as he reread the paper. It was about time he got a break in this kidnapping. The posse and the troops had been wandering around for days, quarreling among themselves about who was in charge and probably resenting that they were out on this wild-goose chase looking for this spoiled heiress. No one seemed to know which direction to take or even which state or territory the outlaws might have holed up in.

He tried to read between the lines, wondering what it was his future father-in-law was trying to tell him about the guide. He had a distinct feeling when he finished reading that Amos wouldn't mind at all if the informer caught a bullet and didn't come back alive to collect the promised reward. That didn't bother Pierce's conscience one bit. Only old-fashioned people like his parents had a black and white morality. If Pierce was going to be a success in politics, he'd remember that there were lots of areas of moral gray, especially where money was concerned.

Pierce took off his expensive hat, wiped his brow with a fine linen handkerchief and dismounted. Somehow, he had a distinct feeling that there was something that Amos hadn't told Pierce. Had Cherish been hurt? Surely if that were the case, old Blassingame would have told him. "I suppose we might as well pitch camp then," Pierce grumbled, "and wait for this Whitley fellow."

The captain nodded. "Yes, sir, Mister Randolph."

Pierce didn't like him and sensed the feeling was mutual, although the officer was being scrupulously polite; almost too polite.

The captain said, "We'll camp. Maybe by tomorrow or the next day, the guide will get here and lead us to this hideout."

Pierce smiled and nodded, but there was no humor in his heart. All he could think of was how he planned his revenge. He intended to be rid of his black sheep brother forever!

Quint Randolph looked at the message in his hand again as he stood by the hitching rail of the ranch veranda. So far, he hadn't told Dallas about this new wire from their younger son, yet he knew he must. They had been married more than a quarter of a century and he loved her more than he had loved her the day they wed. He didn't want to share this information that would hurt her, and yet she needed to know.

The Arizona sun felt warm on his back. *Timbi.* None of this might ever have happened if he hadn't saved *Timbi's* life all those long years ago. If he could have looked into the future and seen the grief the Paiute chief would bring, would Quint have saved the Indian's life that hot day or would he have ridden away and left him pinned under that dead horse to die slowly of thirst?

Quint had been out in Nevada with Dallas to see how his horses were doing as mounts for the Pony Express that warm spring day in 1860. He had left her at one of the stations while he rode out to search for a legendary wild mustang stallion known as Sky Climber. If everything said about the Medicine Hat's speed was true, he wanted that stallion in his breeding program. He rode toward the hostile arroyos and cliffs, hope beating high in his heart.

He rode for a couple of hours, spotting only a rattlesnake and the biggest scorpion he'd ever seen scurrying into the rocks. The sun beat down hotly and he reined in, sipped the tepid gyp water from his canteen, made a face. A man had to be plenty thirsty to drink gyp water with its strong mineral taste.

The holster hung heavy on his waist. He unbuckled it, hung it on his saddle horn, pulled his hat down over his eyes and rode on. Maybe the stallion didn't exist. Suppose he spent all this time and didn't even see it?

Then he spotted the tracks of unshod ponies and horse droppings. An experienced tracker could tell how far ahead of him a herd was by the freshness of the droppings. Hope rose again as he realized a herd—or was it only an Indian war party—had passed this way less than an hour ago? Quint urged his mount on.

In a moment, he heard a scream of defiance, of challenge, and jerked up. He blinked, almost not believing what he saw. Watching him from atop a cliff was the biggest, most magnificent black and white pinto stud he had ever seen.

The pinto reared on powerful hind legs and whinnied again as if questioning Quint's right to invade its domain. He stared at the big horse, more than sixteen hands high and finely built, its long mane and tail blowing in the late afternoon wind as it reared and pawed the air in that peculiar climbing motion.

"Sky Climber," he whispered, and then realized

he had been holding his breath as he stared at the great horse. A broken rawhide lariat dangled from the stallion's neck and the light gleamed on the unusual shield markings on its chest.

The wind came up again, bringing a coolness to Quint's perspiring brow and blowing the horse's mane and tail straight out like proud banners.

And Quint knew that, except for Dallas, he had never wanted anything as much as he wanted this horse. No wonder men had risked death and had spent fruitless months on vain attempts to capture the stud. He vowed right then that he would catch and break the horse, take it back to add its great bloodlines to those of his own fine horses.

He stared transfixed as the magnificent horse reared up and challenged him again, trying to climb the sky, and then wheeled and took off at a gallop.

That broke the spell. Quint spurred his own horse forward, knowing that unless he had incredible luck, he could never get close enough to lasso the stud. There was probably no horse that could outrun the big devil. His only chance might be to corner the stallion in a canyon, and the pinto knew the hills better than Quint did.

The herd. The Medicine Hat would have a little herd of mares nearby, colts and fillies grazing peacefully. That was why the big horse stood guard on the rise, to protect his harem. Quint reached for his lariat. The herd might slow the big stud down enough to get a rope on him.

The stallion stretched out in a lope. Quint spurred his horse even faster, galloping after him up the ridge. When he hit the flat plain, he saw the big horse running without effort ahead of him, nipping and urging on his mares, hanging back to stay between Quint and the little foals that ran on unsteady legs.

Quint almost cried out in exaltation. Because of that herd, he might manage to get close enough to get a loop over the stallion's head. Otherwise, he wouldn't have a snowflake's chance in hell of catching it.

The horses galloped across the small plain in a cloud of alkali dust, their hooves beating like war drums against the ground. The dust blew back, clinging to Quint's sweating face and lips, but all he could think of was getting a rope on that horse. The Medicine Hat galloped so effortlessly that Quint began to appreciate why it was a legend in Nevada.

Closer. Even closer. He urged his weary gelding along, smelling the sweat of its lathered body, the dust that blew back at him from black, bay and pinto mares. The little colts and fillies were tiring fast; the stallion seemed almost desperate now to keep itself between them and Quint. Several colts bore the medicine shield coloring of their sire.

Quint felt both excitement and shame that he might be taking the sire from the herd, leaving mares and colts unprotected. He told himself that sooner or later another stud would add the mares and babies to its own harem.

Closing ground fast on the great horse, Quint felt a deep admiration as he reached for his loop. Sky

Climber could avoid capture easily by galloping away and abandoning his family, but the big stud refused to do that.

The wind changed suddenly and whatever scent it brought to Quint's gelding caused it to start and lose stride, neigh and prick its ears in the direction from which the wind blew.

"Damn it!" Quint cursed and reined in, knowing the chase was over for the afternoon. His horse was too winded to take after the herd again now that Quint had lost that split-second chance to get a loop over the stud's head. His shoulders slumped in defeat as he watched the little herd disappear down a ravine.

Quint took a deep breath, gasped at the sweet, decaying scent the hot wind carried. Something lay dead upwind, and the smell had startled his mount. Buzzards rose up and circled lazily, throwing black shadows across him as he squinted skyward.

What was it the filthy devils had been feeding on, or were about to feed on, when the galloping horses had startled them away? Whatever it was might not even be quite dead, they might be tearing at living flesh. Suppose it was a man?

Quint shuddered at the thought, urging his horse to lope over the ridge to investigate.

Lord, what was that? He didn't really need to ask. Even from here, he recognized the still form of a roan horse, a rider. They were both obviously dead and the buzzards had been feeding off the carcasses.

The thought made Quint a little sick. He'd at least bury the man. It wasn't decent to leave him for the buzzards.

He urged his gelding down the ridge, although the horse shied from the reek of the rotting horse.

An Indian. Quint stared down at the half-naked, magnificent brown body. What had the warrior been doing out here alone and what had happened to him?

Then he noticed the broken rope tangled around the bodies, remembered the loop around Sky Climber's neck. The dead roan's head lay at an odd angle on the steep rise. Quint pictured the scene; the brave chasing the wild stallion, the roan tripping as the stallion broke the line, the fall.

The warrior's fingers moved ever so slightly. Good Lord, he was alive! Quint dismounted, ran over, felt for a pulse. When he touched the brave, dark eyes slowly opened, looked up at him for a moment as if not quite sure who Quint was or what had happened.

Then the Indian glared hatefully and managed to say in English, "I kill you, *tavibo,* if you don't kill me. . . ."

Quint knelt, frowned at him. "You've got more guts than sense." He studied the situation, realized the brave's leg was trapped under the dead horse. "For your sass, I ought to ride out and leave you lay."

The handsome face contorted in pain and fury. "I expect no better from a white."

"Then I'm going to disappoint you, Chief," Quint said. "I wouldn't leave a rattlesnake trapped for the buzzards to eat alive!" He went to his horse, got a canteen, and came back to kneel by the brave.

The Indian was all but dead. A less magnificent specimen would already have died under the hot sun. Quint gathered the big body into his arms, held the canteen to the Indian's lips.

The brave started to grab it, then turned his stoic face away. "You poison me."

Lord, why do I bother? Quint shook his head. "Look, I drink from it myself, see?" He took a sip, then held it to the brave's lips.

The warrior grabbed it from his hands, gulped the tepid liquid down.

"Easy, not too much at first." Quint pulled the canteen away, wet his bandanna, wiped dust from the brooding brave's face. Then he gave him another drink. "How long you been here?"

The brave blinked, found the strength to raise up on one elbow. "Yesterday I chase the great Medicine Hat stallion. My horse slipped."

"Is your leg broken?"

The Indian considered, shook his head. "A big rock, the same one that ripped my canteen, is holding up most of its weight. Why do you stop to help me?"

Quint tipped his hat back. "Damned if I know! I'm beginning to think I must be loco."

He stood up, surveyed the situation a moment, then strode over, took his loop, put it around the dead horse, and swung back up on his mount. "When I've dragged it far enough, you move quick." Quint backed his horse and dragged the roan just a few inches, but it was enough. The Indian managed to crawl free.

Quint swung down from the stirrup. Now what was he going to do? Two men, one horse. He couldn't leave the brave, but he'd have to abandon his horse hunt if they rode double out of here. When he turned around, he saw that the Indian had crawled over and picked up the knife and lance that had lain only a few feet away. He could throw either before Quint could move.

"And now, white dog, I take the horse and your scalp!"

Quint cursed himself for his carelessness. His guns were on his saddle. "I saved your life and you do this? Where is your honor?"

The brave hesitated. "You are right. I owe you my life."

Quint breathed a sigh of relief as the man slowly lowered the lance.

"You are very different from the whites I have known, except for the Mormons a long time ago," the warrior said in halting English as if he had not used the language in a very long time. "Who are you?"

"Quint Randolph."

The brave considered, then he seemed to notice the gold ring for the first time. "It is a sign." He gestured with the knife. "What does your name mean?"

Quint shrugged, still wary. The brave still might change his mind and attack him with the long lance.

"Quint? It's a very old Latin name meaning 'five,' you know, the number. 'Randolph' is Anglo-Saxon and it means—"

"Five? That is the magic number of my people, the *numa* that you whites call Paiute. The medicine vision is fulfilled!"

He staggered to his feet, and would have fallen but Quint caught him, lowered him to one knee. Very slowly, the Indian held out his hand. "Quint Randolph, I am *Timbi,* a chieftain of the Paiute."

There was still conflict on his face as if it cost him a great deal to make this gesture of friendship to a white man. Quint wondered suddenly what had happened to create such hatred in him.

Quint took his hand. *"Timbi?"*

"It means the 'rock.' "

So this was the Paiute troublemaker who might create problems for the Pony Express and the whites pouring into the area. What he should have done was put a bullet in the Indian's brain while he had him down and helpless. But even as he thought that, Quint knew he could never have done it. Like *Timbi,* he was a man of honor. "Well, *Timbi,* what am I supposed to do with you now?"

The Indian tried to scramble to his feet, but he was too weak. "If you think to capture me, take me to the whites so they can lock me in a filthy cage—"

"If I had meant you harm, I would have let the buzzards finish you. It looked like they were about to eat you alive." Undecided, Quint glanced up at the sun. "I think you need food and rest. We could ride double back to the station—"

"No!" The dark face went grim and *Timbi* pointed in the other direction. "Go Paiute camp."

Some other white man would probably ride out and leave the hostile chieftain. After all, Quint had gotten him out from under the dead horse; was it his responsibility to carry him back to the Indian camp? Suppose the Paiutes decided to take him prisoner or kill him?

Timbi seemed to sense his hesitation. "I owe you my life, so I am indebted to you more deeply than the brother I never had. You have my vow you will not be harmed in our camp. My honor demands I repay you or give you back the life you saved."

Quint grinned wryly, ran his hand through his hair. "I don't know how the hell you'd do that. But okay, I'll take you back to your camp. Maybe while I'm there, I can convince your people to let the Pony riders alone."

He put his shoulder under the Paiute's arm, helped *Timbi* up on the gelding. "As tired as my mount is, I reckon I'll have to walk."

Quint dug in his saddlebags, got out some beef jerky, handed a strip to Timbi, took one himself. It tasted salty, smoky, and delicious as he chewed on it and turned the horse in the direction the Indian had pointed. "Strange how I ended up finding you; it was almost as if the pinto led me to you." He started trudging along, leading the horse.

"I had a medicine vision," *Timbi* said behind him, biting off pieces of the jerky. "It was almost as if I were the horse. We blended and became one, an eternal spirit of the desert running along the cliffs forever."

Quint shrugged as he walked. "Not a bad way to spend eternity."

"You were chasing the stallion? So was I. That is my broken loop on his neck."

Quint trudged on. It was late afternoon but still hot. "I hear the Indians regard that horse as big medicine."

"Yes, maybe no one is meant to capture the Spirit of the Sierra Nevada."

Quint looked back over his shoulder at the man in the saddle. "I hate to disappoint you, friend, since you think your soul is someday going to merge with his, but I have plans for that big stud. He would make a wonderful herd sire; bring new blood to my stock."

"You would lock him in a pen far from his mountains?" *Timbi*'s face, when Quint looked back, was dark with disapproval.

"He'd have a good pasture, the best of food. He'd never have to look after himself anymore."

"And all he would have to give up is his freedom. That's what the white man has offered the Indian. Tell me, Quint Randolph, if you were *Timbi,* would you lead your people up to Pyramid Lake to join old *Poito,* the one the whites call *Winnemucca,* to live with his band like stupid sheep on a reservation?"

Quint didn't like the logic of the comparison. "The government is only thinking of the welfare of your people and of the safety of the Pony riders."

Timbi made a derisive sound. "When anyone offers to feed me, clothe me, look after me, I have to

298

ask, what is it he wants? If my people, if any people accept, they should not be surprised to find out what they have traded away is their freedom, their right to come and go as they please."

"The whites mean you no harm, *Timbi*. There's room for all in this giant land."

"The desert may look big, but it is as fragile as a butterfly's wings and can support only a few people. The poison from the mines has already polluted a stream, killed my whole family, save for one sister. For this I have sworn to kill white men, to fight them with my last breath!"

Quint felt troubled. Had he made a mistake in saving the handsome, moody chieftain? "I thought we were friends?"

Timbi looked back at him, stormy conflict in his dark eyes. "You and I are friends, Quint of the magic number who was sent to save my life by the horse spirit. But other white men and Timbi are not friends, can never be friends."

If Quint had known then. . . . He glanced up at the sun, realized he had been standing in the ranch yard, remembering his Paiute friend who had ultimately made Quint a blood brother. It had all ended so tragically. Even *Timbi*'s little sister, *Asta,* was dead. Who knew what had happened to *Asta*'s friend, *Moponi,* and her young husband, *Kene,* the Sparrow Hawk?

In the end Quint had captured the great stallion and then given him his freedom, although he did capture several Sky Climber colts and brought them back to Arizona. Maybe the great spirit horse still ran the snowy peaks at night in the wild state they'd used as a second name for Dallas's first-born child.

Nevada. Timbi's spirit might still be there in the mountains he loved, running wild and free forever. Besides the colts, Quint had one thing to remember his blood brother by; his son.

Yes, he and Dallas had Nevada, and though the boy had brought them grief, he had also brought them a very special love. Quint had bonded with the boy as he had never really bonded with the younger son of his own blood. He must remember that, it would help get him and his beloved wife through the next few days.

He must tell Dallas about the wire from Pierce. Quint put the message in his pocket, went into the den. She looked up from the book she was reading. "Hello, dear. It's unusual for you to be home in the middle of the afternoon with as much work as there is going on right now."

He shrugged and sat down next to her on the sofa. "The hands can handle most of it. I'm getting to be an old man, angel."

"Balderdash. You're twice the man that most of our young cowboys are." She put down her book, held out her hands to him.

"Spoken like a loyal wife." He took her hands, glanced toward her book. "What are you reading?"

"Still reading *Ben Hur;* it's quite good. So unusual for a territorial governor to pen a best-selling novel."

300

He picked it up, pretended to look at it. "Maybe Lew Wallace was just trying to get his mind off the Lincoln County War and outlaws."

"It helps some," she admitted with a weak smile. "Oh, Quint, I'm so worried."

He took her in his arms and kissed her forehead. Had that gray always been in her black hair? Somehow to him, she was still the tall Texas tomboy who had cut her hair, dressed like a boy, and rode for the Pony Express. He loved her now as he had when she was only eighteen, more than a quarter of a century ago. "Everything will be all right."

She lay her face against his chest. "I wish I could believe that. Where did we go wrong, Quint? We tried so hard with our children, yet they've brought us nothing but grief. I feel both guilty and cheated."

"There's hundreds, if not thousands, of parents just like us, if that's any comfort, wondering what they could or should have done differently." He held her close and thought of the old verse: *How sharper than a serpent's tooth. . . .*

"Quint, don't you think it's time you told me whatever it is you've been hiding the last several days?"

He started to deny it, then took her dear face between his two hands and looked down into her eyes. "Angel, you know me too well."

She looked for a moment as if she had hoped he would deny that he was hiding anything. Fine lines around her expressive dark eyes deepened. "What is it?"

"I've gotten a wire from Pierce. He's out with

301

the posse traversing over three states trying to track down Cherish and Nevada."

Dallas shook her head. "After six years on the run, Nevada knows every hidden valley, cave, and pond like the back of his hand. I doubt anyone will ever find him if he doesn't want to be found."

"Good Lord, I wish that were true, but there seems to be an informant who's going to lead them to him."

Her lip trembled. "Someone will get hurt. I'm really worried about Cherish Blassingame. How could anyone have done that to his brother?"

"Someone who didn't know the details might have asked the same question of me that time. I think like Cain and Abel, Nevada and Pierce are determined to finish this thing once and for all. I'm afraid that one might kill the other over Cherish."

She blinked and tears gathered in her eyes. "Quint, dearest, I—I can't bear to lose either of my boys, yet I know Nevada would rather die fighting than end up in prison."

He leaned back on the sofa cushions and took out his pipe. "If I could reason with them, maybe this could end without someone getting killed, but we don't have any idea where Nevada and his gang are holed up. We haven't heard from Ben since they were in New Mexico."

She lay her face against his arm, enjoyed the scent of his tobacco as he filled his pipe, lit it. She loved this man as she had never loved another, more than she loved her sons. "I wish neither of them had ever met Cherish Blassingame, then maybe we could have kept both of them content on the ranch; there never would have been all this conflict between them."

He shrugged, smoked his pipe and hugged her to him. "Maybe it was our fault, angel, for not telling them about Nevada's past, about what really happened at Pyramid Lake that day."

"You shouldn't have let him think you killed *Timbi*," she said.

"Better he think that than be devastated by the whole truth; I'm not sure he could deal with that. Besides, he and Pierce were always as different as night and day. Sooner or later they would have come into conflict just as *Timbi* and I did."

"And for the same reason," she said, "over a woman you both loved. I've always felt guilty about that."

"Nonsense." He took the pipe from his mouth, rumpled her hair. "You couldn't help it that my blood brother wanted my wife bad enough to steal her and was willing to kill me to keep her."

She tried to hold the tears back, but she thought now of that long ago day and the emotions returned. "Oh, Quint, hold me. Hold me and tell me that you love me; that our love will stand up against anything, even our family falling apart, our sons ready to kill each other."

He set his pipe in the ashtray on the sofa table, gathered her into his arms. "Oh, angel, please don't cry! It hurts me to see you cry."

"If only all that hadn't happened, maybe our sons would both be yours and—"

"He *is* my son, Dallas, as far as you and I are concerned. *Timbi* gave me back the life he owed me, you know that. I raised Nevada as my own, gave him my name, breathed life into him when there was no one else to save a sickly newborn. Now I'm not sure that if I could have looked into the future and seen what kind of grief he would bring his mother, that I wouldn't have let him die."

"Don't say that! You love him as much as I do, maybe more."

He nodded. "Pierce is jealous of him and maybe with good reason. I tried, God knows I tried to treat both boys fairly. But when I'd look at Nevada, I'd see my blood brother and there was something special there."

"If only I'd never ridden for the Pony Express, none of this would have ever happened," Dallas mourned. "If only we'd stayed East and—"

"Remember what we discussed that long ago day, angel? When we rode away from the Paiutes at sundown, we vowed that nothing could ever come between us and that we'd close the door on our past."

She remembered. Quint had been haunted by guilt when she'd first met him. He'd felt responsible for the death of his first wife. "We said that 'if only' were the two saddest words in any language because the past is set in stone and can't be changed."

"That's right. It's still true," he whispered. "All we can do is forget what's past, look toward the future and hope for the best."

She wiped her eyes, attempted to give him a brave smile. "That's hard to do when your children are bent on destroying themselves and maybe their parents along with it; it doesn't make you feel much better."

"It's all we've got, Dallas, that and our love." He kissed her very gently and she returned his ardor. Twenty-seven years he had been making love to her and she never tired of it even though they were both getting gray in their hair and lines around their eyes.

"You know, the young think they are the only ones who know about passion," she said. "They think they discovered it."

Quint smiled. "Mature love can be even better," he said, "speaking of which. . . ."

He stood up, swung her up in his arms. "The help is gone for the afternoon and I have an idea for what to do with a couple of lazy hours."

"Oh, Quint, your arthritis will be hurting with your carrying me like some young cowboy."

"Today, I feel like some young cowboy, and you're as pretty as you were when we met."

He carried her down the hall to their room. They made love in a slow, easy rhythm that brought them both to passion; a leisurely sharing, not like two hot, young things in a hurried frenzy that was over too soon. They knew each other's bodies and souls because they were friends as well as lovers.

Dallas kissed the gray on his temples and loved him as she had loved him the very first time so many years ago and smiled to think that grown children would be shocked that parents still felt young inside even if their bodies belied it. After they made love, Quint dropped off to sleep, but Dallas could not nap. She was worried about her sons and what they might do to each other, angry with them for causing Quint grief. He'd been a good father, he didn't deserve this heartache.

She rose and went to the window. The sun was setting in the west, all pink and orange and purple. It was under just such a sundown that the last terrible chapter had been played out with *Timbi* all those many years ago. Now history seemed to be repeating itself; *Timbi*'s son kidnapping a girl whom he wanted and betraying a brother to get her. Was it love or was it vengeance? Yet her own blood ran through this renegade son and Quint had raised him as his own. Surely Quinton Nevada Randolph could not walk away from all that?

Where could he be? If only she and Quint could find him before the posse did, they might yet stop the bloodshed, save his life, and free the girl.

Dallas closed her eyes and leaned against the window, crossed herself, praying for a miracle. Where was Nevada? Three states was too large an area to search and they hadn't heard from old Ben in a long time. In her mind, she saw that final sunset, saw the snowcapped peak where she and Quint had buried his blood brother. Quint said *Timbi* had said he wanted to be that great medicine horse that galloped through the mountains. Did that wild spirit still run the Sierra Nevada at night and did he call out to his own, drawing his blood home like a salmon would migrate to a place it had never been?

And suddenly, the miracle happened and she

knew! She ran to the bed, shook Quint. "Get up, dearest, we've got to go. It just dawned on me where Nevada has taken her. We've got to get there before that posse does!"

Seventeen

Pierce didn't like the look of this outlaw, Jack Whitley, who had just ridden out to meet the posse. He had shifty eyes, sweated like a horse, and had deep scratches on his face. Had Cherish put those scratches there? He didn't even want to think about it. Amos didn't have to hint to kill this son of a bitch the first chance Pierce got, the thought that this low-life thug might have enjoyed the future Mrs. Randolph was reason enough for Pierce to kill him.

"So you're the fellow who knows where the girl might be held." He forced himself to smile and shake hands with Whitley. Pierce would have to be cordial . . . until Whitley no longer served any useful purpose. "Where is this place?"

Whitley shook his head. "You don't think I'm stupid enough to tell you that, do ya? If you knew, you wouldn't need me."

As shrewd and distrustful as Whitley was, his ancestors must have either been outlaws or politicians, Pierce thought. "My, you are distrustful! All right, you lead us, and I'll reward you when I know she's there and safe. How far is it?"

The outlaw rubbed his unshaven face, looked up at the sun. "I reckon maybe we can be there by tomorrow evening."

Pierce nodded. Tomorrow evening, Cherish would be back in his arms and they could continue the wedding plans. Was it really his older brother who had kidnapped her or was some other swarthy outlaw wearing that ring? He wished he knew. One thing was certain, he hoped the kidnapper put up a fight. Pierce planned to kill him.

Nevada looked up at the sun. "What do you reckon has happened to Mex, Jack, and Tequila?"

Kene looked somber, shook his head.

"By cracky, they should have been back last night." Ben paused in playing his harmonica.

The Paiute said, "Maybe they get drunk, end up in white man's jail."

Nevada crossed his fingers, laughed. "That's possible, but somehow, I've got a bad hunch about this."

"Fifth month," *Kene* reminded him, "five lucky for our people."

Ben spat. "But maybe not for us white eyes. You don't suppose they would betray us?"

"Mex? Never!" Nevada said. "He's a strange one, all right, always sending his share of the loot to that little town across the border. Jack, I don't know; he might be upset about his brother, but he'd feel he owed me because I once saved him and his brother from a lynch mob. Tequila would sell out Jesus Christ for some jewelry; Delilah and Jezebel could have taken lessons from her."

Ben looked toward the blond girl frying meat over a camp fire. "Wonder what kind of reward her old man is offering? Wonder—?"

"No." Nevada shook his head. "Neither Tequila nor Jack would know how to reach her father. Maybe like *Kene* says, they're sleeping off a drunk and will ride in tonight or at the very least, tomorrow morning."

Ben began to search through his pockets absently and Nevada automatically reached into his own pocket and handed the old man a pouch of tobacco. Ben said, "I've half a mind to send someone out lookin'."

"Me, I go," *Kene* said. "I take several warriors, see if we find any sign of camp. Maybe stray soldiers or robbers got them."

"Okay, you do that," Nevada said, "maybe we're getting worried for nothing." He turned and looked toward Cherish, watching the way the sun caught her hair. She was the most beautiful thing he had ever seen.

"Boy," Ben drawled as he rolled a cigarette, "ain't you ready to turn her loose yet? We still got time to skedaddle across the border into Mexico. Between her daddy and your brother—"

"I don't have a brother," Nevada snapped.

"Have it your way." The old man sighed as he lit his smoke. "I hope sleepin' with her has been worth

310

what it's goin' to cost. I'll bet every inch of three states is being combed by troops and lawmen with orders to shoot on sight."

Nevada watched the way she moved as she poked up the fire. "I didn't steal her to sleep with her, Ben. I took her for the ransom and revenge."

"Uh-huh. If you say so." The old man sounded dubious.

Kene cleared his throat. "I knew your father, *Timbi*," he said. "A woman was his downfall, too. She meant more to him than anything and it got him killed."

He didn't want to think about his warrior father being murdered by Quint as *Timbi* tried desperately to hang onto Dallas. Maybe he was no better than Quint Randolph had been. "This isn't about lust or love, it's about big ransom and revenge."

Ben sighed. "I feel like I'm on a ride straight to hell and it's movin' too fast to get off."

Nevada whirled on him. "Damn it! You can get off any time, old man, any of you can who don't want to ride with me!"

Instantly, he regretted his sharp tone. "I—I'm sorry. I'm on edge lately." He looked toward the girl again.

"We understand," Ben said, "you've got an itch that needs scratchin' and that itch has long yellow hair. If nothing else, boy, take her a couple of times and then let's leave her at a settlement as we skedaddle to Mexico. She'll keep her mouth shut."

"That's not what I want; I wish it was that simple." He felt annoyed with his two friends and him-

311

self. He didn't know exactly what it was he wanted from her. Yes, he did know. He yearned for her to want him or at least pretend to, if only for one night.

Ben smoked. "You're as hardheaded as a mustang, boy. Whatever you decide, we'll stand by you."

Kene nodded. "Me, I take men, go looking for Mex and Jack."

Nevada grunted, hardly listening as the two turned and left. He was too preoccupied by the girl to worry about the trio being a few hours late. Ben was getting nervous as a whore in church on Sunday. In the past, he would have been concerned himself, but he didn't want to even think that things might have gone wrong. All that obsessed him was possessing Cherish Blassingame for a night. Once he had lain between her thighs, he'd worry about the future. He ought to just rape her and be done with it.

He shook his head. Maybe the gallant Southern upbringing of Quint Randolph had rubbed off on him after all. Rape wasn't an act he could even fathom. He wanted Cherish to make passionate love to him and he didn't want to argue about whether it was lust or revenge that drove him.

Cherish saw Nevada in conversation with the Indian and the old man, wondered what they were discussing. Maybe they were talking about terms of the ransom or when they were going to set her free. Nevada surely couldn't be serious about his demand; not when he realized Daddy and Pierce would be willing to pay a fortune to get her back unharmed.

The other two walked away and Nevada came toward her. He moved with an easy gait, the pearl-handled Colt tied low on his hip, the gold ring gleaming on his hand. She reached for a tin plate. "You want some food?"

"Si." He poured himself a cup of coffee. "I have to hand it to you, princess, you aren't nearly as spoiled and useless as I first thought."

"Is that supposed to be a compliment?" She dished up fried beef, some bread she had cooked by burying it in the coals.

"Take it like you want to." He took the plate, began to eat. "This reminds me of meals at the ranch sometimes when my folks . . ."

His voice trailed off and she almost felt sorry for her kidnapper. "Nevada," she whispered, "why don't you go back to the Wolf's Den where you belong?"

"I don't belong there; I belong here with my people." He gestured toward the hills.

"Nevada, you're kidding yourself. You remind me so much of Quint Randolph—"

"Stop it, Cherish. I'm nothing like him; couldn't be."

"No, I guess you're not. He's a Southern gentleman, gallant and polite." She sipped her coffee. "You won't be satisfied until you or Pierce is killed over me."

His laugh was harsh, without mirth. "Don't flatter yourself, princess. There's more behind this trouble between Pierce and me than possession of a woman."

"You're breaking your parents' hearts."

"They've washed their hands of me and me of them." He sounded more sad than bitter.

"I doubt that," Cherish said as she ate. "No parent ever really gives up on a child, Nevada, they keep trying, hoping things will work out—"

"Will you stop?" He glared at her. "You may be operating under a load of guilt, but not me, lady."

Guilt. Of course that was how Daddy had controlled her all these years. It wasn't really her fault that her mother had died. "Nevada, it isn't too late," she said, "if you'll turn me loose, I'll swear you didn't kidnap me, that I went with you willingly."

He paused, looked at her over his coffee cup. "That would cause a scandal in the papers, now wouldn't it? Pierce would be fit to be tied; might even break the engagement."

"But you'd be off the hook," she insisted. "You could surrender, make amends for whatever you've done, straighten your life out."

"Oh, sure. If they didn't hang me for my outlaw past, they'd at least send me to jail."

She leaned forward eagerly. "But your folks and my daddy are rich and powerful and then there's Senator Hamilton who might write a letter in your behalf. The money could be paid back and maybe you wouldn't have to go to prison for long—"

"I got news for you, princess." He set his plate to one side. "One day behind stone walls would be too long for a wild mustang like me. I don't ever intend to be taken alive. If I reach that point where I'm about to be captured, I intend to use my last bullet on myself."

314

"Oh, Nevada, think how your folks would grieve. Any coward can kill himself. It takes guts to face up to what you've done and take your medicine."

"Spoken like a protected society girl who has no idea what a hellhole a prison can be." He finished his coffee. "You're not worried about my fate, princess, you're just trying to escape and figure out a way to get back to Pierce. I have no doubt you and your daddy would be the ones out at the state capital making sure I got hanged."

There was no reasoning with him, Cherish thought. Whatever he had once felt for her was gone now in his bitterness and hatred. He didn't want her body because he loved her, it was revenge against Pierce. "You haven't changed your mind about the—the ransom?"

"Did you think I had?" He looked into her eyes.

"I merely hoped you'd be reasonable and realize how much Daddy would be willing to pay—"

"I don't want Amos Blassingame's money," he snapped. "I want his daughter's innocence. Nothing else is acceptable."

She closed her eyes against the hardness of his handsome, dark face. If she could only believe that he might care something for her rather than wanting to deflower her strictly for revenge. "And if I say, 'no,' I could be your prisoner forever?"

"Remember, forever is a long time to be held prisoner." He smiled. "We've discussed this before."

She knew that, it was only that she kept thinking he'd reconsider this merciless idea, but there was no softness in this renegade. She took a deep breath.

"So you're saying that if I come into your blankets tonight, let you—let you take me once, you'll free me tomorrow?"

He shook his head. "I didn't say once, Cherish, I said 'all night long' and I'll let you go at dawn."

All night long. He looked virile enough to take her a dozen times in those long hours between sunset and daybreak. "You're despicable. You want me to give myself to you like some harem slave girl entertaining a sultan?"

"Only if you want to go free."

"That's a pretty damned high price to pay."

"Is it?" He looked at her a long moment. "Your daddy and Pierce would probably give me a hundred thousand dollars to turn you loose with your virtue intact. I could buy the services of a dozen of the best whores in San Francisco or New York with that kind of money."

"Then for God's sake, why don't you?" She was angry with his cold stubbornness.

"Because, Cherish," he said very slowly, "I'd rather have your body under me for one night. Now that should flatter you. Pierce surely doesn't put that high a price on your charms."

"Am I supposed to be flattered?"

"Suit yourself, I reckon. Just remember, you're going to be my prisoner for many years."

Changing Nevada's mind was as impossible as moving a mountain, she thought with dismay. She was going to have to give him what he wanted, or she was going to be held prisoner for an indeterminate amount of time. As long as Pierce never found

out, there would be no repercussions. "All right"—
she threw up her hands in defeat—"but I hope you
know I'll hate you for this."

He smiled slowly. "I thought you'd finally see it
my way."

"Don't you feel even the slightest shame at ma-
neuvering me into this position?"

"I'm not as gallant as my brother," Nevada said
and rolled a cigarette. "I don't have any qualms
about it at all. In fact, I haven't had a woman for a
very long time, princess. I expect you can look forward to at least a dozen times tonight."

She felt her face flush. "I'm not looking forward
to it at all. There's a difference between bowing to
defeat and looking forward to being used as a plaything."

"I'm not forcing you; it's your choice."

"I won't even dignify that with an answer." She
wanted to attack his glib, self-satisfied face with
her fists and nails. Instead, she gritted her teeth.
"All right, it's agreed, then. I'll get myself all bathed
and perfumed, present myself in your lodge at sundown like a harem slave presenting herself to her
master. Then at dawn, you'll provide me with a
horse and an escort out of here?"

"Done. You have my word on it." He smiled easily.

"Your word," she sniffed. "I suppose I have to
hope you'll keep it, although a man who'd demand
a chaste girl play the whore for his entertainment
doesn't have enough scruples to keep his word."

His face looked as hard as stone. "Don't talk to
me of 'scruples,' princess. I used to believe in them

and then I found out how far people like your father and Pierce were willing to go, what they would do to anyone who got in their way. I'm merely playing the game by their rules now."

"I'll be in your lodge tonight at sundown then." She turned and flounced away.

Nevada watched her walk, the easy grace of her hips, her trim legs under the skirt. For just a moment, he felt shame that the girl was finally accepting his conditions for her release. Once he had loved this girl and would have done anything for her, but she had scorned him. You owe me this night for your cold scorn, princess, he thought. Yet even thinking of her naked in his arms didn't bring him as much pleasure as expected.

Yet he wanted her, whether for lust or revenge, he wasn't sure himself anymore. It didn't matter as long as she ended this ache in his groin. Like a seldom-used stud horse, he was virile and ready to commit the ultimate revenge on Pierce Randolph as his own father had done Quint. If he were lucky, Nevada hoped to be able to put his child in her belly tonight. Without thinking, he reached out and knocked on the wooden lodge pole. Pierce would unsuspectingly raise that son as his own; but Cherish would know as Dallas must have known. Every day, Cherish would look at his son and remember that night in Nevada's arms. And if Pierce finally did realize, he would be in the same trap Quint Randolph had been in, thinking about his brother lying between his woman's thighs; dreading every day that this would be the day that his son discovered the truth as Nevada had discovered it from a taunting younger child.

A younger child. Of course when she went back to marry Pierce, he would sleep with her; it would be his right as her husband. Nevada didn't like to think of Pierce or any other man making love to the blond princess. There was nothing to do the rest of this long, hot afternoon. Nevada thought about it. If he was going to make love all night, he needed to be fresh and rested. He went into his lodge and lay down, took a long, refreshing nap.

The day seemed to drag for Cherish. She felt as if she were going to be executed at sundown. Once she would have dreamed of going into this man's arms, surrendering herself to him . . . that was a long time ago when she had thought he might love her, too. It was one thing to surrender herself to a man who loved her enough to risk his life to steal her off a train. It was quite another if the man was only doing it for revenge. She still wondered what had happened that had created this hatred between brothers.

In the late afternoon, she found a secluded place on the creek, bathed herself with soap and perfume that Nevada had borrowed from Tequila's lodge. She also took a sheer, daffodil nightdress with a wrap to go over it. She spent the last hour before sundown in Tequila's lodge, brushing her hair until it shone, using the perfume she found there. She had always worn her hair up and now she put it in a French twist, put on the nightdress and the wrap.

Cherish waited until after dusk before she took a deep breath and walked the few hundred yards to Nevada's lodge. There was little activity in the camp besides the usual guards posted in the rocks and a few men around camp fires. No one paid her any heed. Perhaps none of them really saw her in the growing darkness. She entered Nevada's lodge, heart beating hard. "I—I'm here."

She realized then that the lodge was empty. Fiddlesticks. She hardly dared to hope. Had he had a change of heart, was he suddenly ashamed of himself for his unchivalrous bargain and had reneged? She looked about. Maybe she'd find a note that said: "You're free to go. I've decided it was too much to ask of a lady."

But even as she inspected it, she realized the lodge had been spruced up as if for a tryst with a merry fire, a platter of food, a bottle of wine. Her gaze went to the shadows. A bed had been prepared with clean blankets. Her heart sank. He did not mean to let her out of this bargain after all.

"So you did come." She whirled at the sound of his voice and he entered the lodge, bare-chested above his pants, black hair damp. "I thought you might back out."

"I don't suppose you've changed your mind about this?"

"Not hardly." He came in, sat down by the fire. "I was down at the creek cleaning up." She watched

320

him open the wine, pour two glasses. He gestured her to a spot next to him.

She hesitated, sat down, took the wine.

Nevada frowned. "I like your hair down." Before she could move, he reached out, took the clasp from her hair, smiled in evident approval as the long yellow locks cascaded down her shoulders. "That's more like it. Here." He filled a plate, held it out to her. "If you're going to amuse the sultan, you might as well eat the delicacies, too."

"Hummingbird's tongue and honey cakes?" she asked sarcastically.

He chuckled. "How about roast smoked stolen beef and prickly pear preserves instead?"

"I like it when you laugh," she blurted, "you ought to do it more often."

A look of great sadness crossed his dark face. "Princess, I haven't had anything to laugh about in a long time. Now eat your food."

She ate to fortify herself for what she knew would be coming later on. The food was good; much heartier than the delicate city fare she was used to. "This is an excellent wine."

"It should be," he said, grinning, "the boys took it out of your daddy's private stock on the train."

The nerve of this thief! She drained her glass and the wine made her bolder. "What I've never understood is why you hate my daddy and Pierce so."

He ate in silence and she was not sure he would answer. Finally he said, "Didn't my brother tell you?" He finished his food, set his plate aside.

Cherish shook her head, sipped her wine. "Just

said there was some kind of family fuss and that you had gone off to South America to work on a ranch."

Nevada leaned against a backrest, and drank his wine. "Pierce will make a great politician. He's willing to do anything to get what he wants and he lies like a rug."

"You're a fine one to talk!" If the wine hadn't been getting to her, she wouldn't have had the nerve to dispute him. "I would say that sleeping with your brother's bride is about as lowdown as a man can get!"

"Once a long time ago, I thought you might someday be my bride, princess, but then, I underestimated what your daddy and my dear brother were willing to do to keep that from happening."

She was baffled. "I have no idea what you're talking about."

He studied her. "You know, I could almost believe you. Of course you know that Amos went to a lot of trouble to find out my background and that Pierce could hardly wait to tell me?"

"Tell you what?" She was fascinated by this mystery.

He took a deep, shuddering breath and looked away. "That Quint Randolph is not my real father."

"Of course he is," Cherish said. "Pierce looks like him and you look like your mother—"

"And my real father. No wonder Pierce didn't tell anyone else, he didn't want the scandal to be whispered about, afraid it might cost him votes someday."

"I don't know what Daddy's got to do with—"

"He's the one who tracked the information down and gave it to Pierce. My dear brother could hardly wait to tell me."

"Tell you what?"

"That Quint had stolen Dallas from a Paiute chief named *Timbi*."

"Then Quint isn't—? But he raised you."

"Guilt, that's all. They kept the truth secret, but Pierce enjoyed telling me; I could see it in his eyes."

"So now you intend to repay his treachery by sleeping with his bride?"

He nodded. "He deserves it."

"But I'm innocent in this."

"Are you?"

She didn't know what to say. With the wine, her mind wasn't working very well, and she couldn't imagine why Daddy had cared enough or hated this man enough to investigate, to tell Pierce the scandal. She hadn't realized Pierce was capable of being so cold-blooded except that she knew he felt his parents favored the older boy and that he was jealous of Nevada. "So I'm to be your revenge?"

"That was the bargain; one night."

She noticed her hand was trembling and she set her wine glass down. "You have no shame to demand this. Very well, if I must fulfill this cold-blooded deal—"

"You won't get off by shaming me, princess; I've waited too long for this." He leaned back. "Stand up, take off that wrap thing. I want to see what I'm getting."

She hated him for acting as if he were buying a very high-priced whore for the evening. It had grown dark outside and the lodge was lit by the flickering flames of the fire. She stood up and very slowly took off the wrap, stood there in the sheer yellow nightdress.

"Turn around." He gestured.

He could see right through the lace nightdress, she realized that, but there was nothing to do but turn slowly around, let him inspect her. She felt like a slave on the auction block. All she could be grateful for was that her long hair hung down over her shoulders and partially hid her body.

He surveyed her with evident approval. "I didn't think I would ever say this, but you're prettier now than you were that night when I kissed you before the fireplace."

"I'm surprised you remember that New Year's Eve; I didn't think it meant anything."

"Maybe. You were almost a child, wearing a daffodil dress, much this same color. You were spying on me, so big-eyed and innocent. The orchestra was playing 'Beautiful Dreamer'."

She blinked, more than a little shocked that he remembered such small details. "As I recall," she said acidly, "you were in the midst of a passionate embrace with Madge Pettigrew and I interrupted you."

"She was kissing me, not the other way around," he pointed out. "When you kissed me, I felt like a cradle robber."

"I—I had had too much wine. You must have known I had never kissed a man before."

He stood up slowly. "Then maybe it's only fitting that the man who got your first kiss be the one who takes your virginity." He took her small face between his two big hands and kissed her very gently, brushing his lips across hers.

Without meaning to, she leaned into him, giddy with the sensation, the touch of his hot mouth on hers. His tongue brushed along her lips and without even thinking about it, she opened them.

With a groan, he pulled her against him while his tongue went deep into her mouth and she slipped her arms around his neck. Only as he molded himself against her, was she abruptly aware that he was naked from the waist up and that his manhood was swollen big and pressed against her body through the sheer nightdress. She felt the ribbons of it begin to slide down her shoulders as he lifted her with his great strength so that her breasts were almost to his mouth.

"Wrap your legs around me," he ordered.

She did and his big hands cupped her small bottom as the nightdress slid up her thighs. The top of the bodice slipped down, so that her breasts were offered up to his eager mouth as a feast. He was sucking them now, hard, and without meaning to, she clasped his head against her breast, willing him to continue the sensation he was building in her.

But instead, he released her, let her slide slowly down his body until she was on her knees before him like a virgin priestess before a pagan fertility god.

She clasped him about the hips, looking up at him from her position on her knees. His maleness was big, hard, and erect. She was Woman, worshipping that rod which gave life.

"Cherish," he whispered, "you know what I want, don't you?" He tangled his fingers in her long blond hair.

She knew even if he hadn't been pressing her face to his groin. She molded her half-naked body against his bare legs and kissed his throbbing scepter. With a groan, he tangled his hands in her hair, pressing himself against her lips, wanting her to give him the Ultimate Kiss.

She realized then that she loved this man, had loved him since she was fifteen and had been lying to herself about Pierce Randolph. Yet Nevada didn't love her, he was using her in cold, calculating revenge. Even knowing that, she wanted him.

She kissed it, ran her tongue around its long, throbbing length while he gasped and shuddered. Somehow it thrilled her to know that even as she gave him this gesture of complete surrender, she was the one in control; he wanted her past all reason.

He reached down, lifted her, swung her up in his arms. They were both covered with a fine sheen of perspiration and he was gasping for breath no less than she was.

"You little minx," he whispered. "As innocent as

you are, you know how to make me want you more than I ever wanted some high-skilled whore."

"Isn't that what I'm doing tonight; playing the harlot for a set price?"

"That's how you see it, isn't it? The aristocratic white girl submitting to the Injun savage so he'll let her go?"

She wanted to tell him that she loved him, that she had really always loved him, but he cut off her words with his mouth. He kissed her, almost brutal with his need. Against his great strength, she was powerless, and she knew it.

He carried her over to the blankets, laid her down. "Princess, you are going to take me a dozen different ways tonight," he whispered. "My brother may get you the rest of your life, but you'll remember that, for a few hours, you were possessed by a real man!" His lips went to her breasts and belly.

Any time now he would deflower her, she thought with mounting excitement. Somehow she knew she wouldn't be able to stop this inner ache until he put that hard dagger of flesh deep inside her, poured a torrent of hot seed deep into her womb, kissed and sucked her breasts until they were raw.

"You were going to make love to me to save my injured shoulder," he said. "That was the deal."

Before she could answer, he rolled over on his back, lay there naked looking up at her. His maleness seemed big as a sword. "Make love to me, princess. Let me know that having you in my arms for one night is a better bargain than all that money your daddy would pay me."

He was determined to make her feel like a whore. Despite what she felt for him, he thought of her as a vessel for his seed, a pretty toy to be used for his vengeance. There seemed to be nothing she could do but obey. She knelt next to him and kissed his nipples. With a groan, he caught her, held her face against his dark chest. She nipped him there, felt him writhe with pleasure from her sharp teeth. Somehow it pleased her that she could drive him so wild with desire.

"Now straddle me," he ordered. "I've waited a long time to bury myself in you. Impale yourself on me."

Cherish hesitated. A woman can give her virginity only one time. By all rights, it should be given to her husband. That was part of her value; the pleasure and vanity of a man knowing he had been the first. It would all be over in a moment. All she had to do was straddle his lean, dark body, impale herself on him and ride him while he caught her breasts in his two big hands, massaged and squeezed them. Once she had given him the ultimate gift of her virginity, he would let her go free in the morning.

Just as she was about to straddle him, she heard noise and confusion outside in the dark camp, a galloping horse, a man shouting.

Startled, she looked at Nevada but he was already sitting up, cursing as he grabbed for his clothes.

She listened to the shouts outside, but understood little. Nevada was jerking on his pants, his hard maleness jutting out before him with his need still unfulfilled.

"What's happened?" she asked. "What is it?"

"Sounds like *Kene*." He reached for his boots. "Sounds like he's found our missing people and the news isn't good!"

Eighteen

Cherish grabbed her robe, wrapped it around her. "What do you think—?"

"It's *Kene*. Something about finding bodies. Stay here," he ordered. "I'd just as soon my men didn't see you like that; you're desirable enough already." He leaned over, kissed her forehead, and strode out into the night.

She reached up and touched where he had kissed, moved by his gentleness. How could he be so savage and vindictive one moment, so protective and tender the next?

Cherish peeked through the entry at the crowd of men gathering around the big camp fire. Was the valley about to be invaded by the posse in time to save her paying the ransom? She remembered the past few minutes and the pulse-pounding excitement. Caught up in the touch of him, the taste of his lips, she had been as eager as he was. Or maybe it was only the effects of the wine? At the very last possible moment, the rider had come galloping into camp with news. Her virtue was saved . . . at least temporarily. Cherish felt amazed that she wasn't quite certain whether to be relieved . . . or disappointed.

Nevada strode out into the cool night, still barechested though he had stopped to pull on his boots. His men gathered around *Kene,* who had just slid from his galloping horse in the camp circle. Some seemed to notice Cherish peeking around the entry of his lodge, smiled and nudged each other.

Somehow it annoyed him that they might think she was some cheap whore amusing him. He hadn't realized she still meant something to him other than vengeance, until he saw the men nudging each other and scowled blackly at them.

He pushed through the crowd where Ben and the Paiute stood in excited conversation. "Okay, *Kene,* what is it?"

"I find Mex and the girl," he said, gesturing, "both dead. Buzzards been at them, so not sure what killed them."

Mex. Such a strange boy, but they had shared food and danger many times. He felt a sad emptiness. Too many men died in this outlaw life; he was weary of it. "Any sign of Jack?"

Kene shook his head. "He may be there dead somewhere and I overlook him to get back and tell you."

Ben rummaged through his pockets and Nevada sighed and handed him his tobacco pouch.

"Ben, what do you think?"

"I think we need to get the hell down to Mexico like I told you in the first place."

Nevada looked around at his men. "He may be right, boys. Any of you wants to pull out, go ahead, I won't hold it against you."

There was a buzz of Indian and Spanish as some of them conversed, argued.

Ben rolled a smoke. "There's probably troops or a posse to our south; searching for us now if Jack has sold us out; make it hard to get through them to the border and it's a long way."

"Not if we break up and go one or two at a time, or we could head north. *Kene,* your men could escape into the Black Rock Desert; army not likely to follow them there."

Kene shook his head. "Like walking across hell," he said. "We stay here. One place as good to die as another, and we will die rather than go back to reservation."

Ben blew smoke. "We may be gettin' excited for nothin', boy," he drawled. "Always a possibility that bandits got 'em or that Jack caught Tequila offerin' herself to Mex, killed them both in a jealous rage, lit out."

Nevada didn't say anything. Those were two possibilities. The third was that Jack had been captured by any posse that might be combing the area to the south. Maybe Jack was loyal enough that he wouldn't give them any information. Of course posses had been known to do whatever it took to get information out of a suspect. "What do you think,

Ben? I wouldn't blame you for pulling your picket pin, heading for Mexico."

"I let one young pup get hisself killed because I didn't look out for him, I ain't gonna feel guilty for doin' that again. Besides," his pale eyes twinkled, "I've half a mind to stay just so I can say 'I told you so.' "

Nevada slapped him on the shoulder warmly. "You old codger. I don't know what I'd do without you. Remember, if anything happens to me, we promised Mex we'd get his share of the loot to that little town for its school." A thought occurred to him. *"Kene,* was Tequila still wearing that gold necklace?"

The Indian shook his head. "It gone; I could tell that."

Ben breathed a sigh of relief. "See? We're gettin' excited for nothin'. What we have here is just some common bandits."

Nevada looked around at his men. "You know this country as well as I do. If you clear out right now, you've got a chance; if you wait a few hours, you might be trapped in this canyon and have to fight your way out."

Kene shrugged. "Paiutes stay. Other choices no better and besides, old man may be right; maybe only bandits."

"Okay, we're agreed then," Nevada said. "We'll know by late tomorrow if it was bandits or the army because by then the whole countryside may be crawling with lawmen."

Ben said, "We'll double the guard and see what

333

we can do about fortifications. Most of those troops will be Yankees and I didn't get to kill enough of them in the war anyways."

Nevada swallowed the lump in his throat. "Old man, I never said it before, but I appreciate your staying by me all these years; I know you didn't have to."

"Aw, go along with you." Ben cleared his throat and blinked rapidly. "Who else would I bum tobacco off of?"

Nevada turned to his men. "We may be getting excited for nothing. *Kene,* send out some scouts, and Ben, you see to the fortifications and guards. If there's no soldiers or a big posse, we may want to lay low for a few weeks until things settle down again."

The men nodded and scattered except for Ben. He looked toward Nevada's lodge. "So what do you intend to do about her?"

Nevada cursed under his breath. He had come so close to taking her. If *Kene* had come only a few minutes later, he could have had the pleasures of her body at least once. Now . . . "I don't know, Ben, this isn't my lucky day, is it?"

"When you do stupid things, don't blame it on bad luck. You'll have to get her out of here before there's shooting."

"You're acting like a hysterical old maid," Nevada scolded. "There may not be a posse within a hundred miles of this valley."

"But if there is, and he's a mind to, Jack knows the way in," Ben reminded him.

"That's right." Nevada looked reluctantly toward his lodge.

Ben smoked and his gaze followed Nevada's. "Still not ready to give her up, are you?"

He realized abruptly that he never wanted to give her up. He was fooling himself that it was because of revenge. Maybe he had been fooling himself from the very start. "She hasn't fulfilled her end of the bargain yet," he mumbled, thinking how much he'd like to go back to her arms. If there was no posse coming, he could make love to her all night long tomorrow night . . . and have to return her to Pierce the next day.

"What you thinkin' about, boy?"

"When a man gives his word, is it binding?"

"You know it is. Quint taught you that."

Nevada might not be sired by Quint Randolph, but Quint had raised him and left more of his stamp on him than the warrior father Nevada had never known. "Suppose he changes his mind?"

Ben looked toward the lodge. "If you're thinkin' what I think you're thinkin', forget it, boy. You can't take a girl, especially *that* girl, on the outlaw trail with you."

"It was just a thought."

"Well, don't think it. Her papa and your brother would tear up the whole Southwest lookin' for you like they're doin' right now. I never should have let you take her off that train."

Was he ever going to spend a night in her arms? Tonight was lost, but maybe tomorrow night. . . .

He couldn't think any more about that now. Nevada sighed and turned his back on the lodge. "We've got some planning to do. Let's get with it."

Dallas looked at her reflection in the train window as it pulled away from the station and headed west into the night. With any luck, by tomorrow night, they hoped to be in the Nevada town nearest the lake where maybe they could rent a buggy and head up to the hidden valley. They might have to drive most of the night, but maybe they'd be there by dawn day after tomorrow. She could be wrong; maybe that wasn't where the climax of this drama would be played out. More than a quarter of a century ago, there had been another life-and-death fight at that place between two brothers, one of them white, the other Indian.

So very long ago. That drama had begun late in the afternoon before sundown. She had been in that valley with *Timbi,* living as his woman because he had wanted her enough to hold her captive. . . .

It had been late afternoon and the slate-colored sky had finally started to clear, although the ground was still wet and slick from cold rain.

A brave shouted from the rocks. "A white man rides toward us!"

She felt *Timbi* stiffen. "A white? Is he a scout?"

"He does not try to hide. He rides boldly as if he wants us to see him. Shall I shoot him?" The man raised his rifle.

Dallas knew *Timbi* was about to assent from the look on his stern face. "Oh, *Timbi,* don't murder him! Perhaps he wants to parley."

He smiled. "I will humor you, my spirited one." Then he turned and yelled up at the man in the rocks. "Let him ride in. We will see what it is this bold one wants."

They waited, watching the man up in the rocks, little *Wovoka's* father, squinting to perceive the rider they could not yet see.

"Timbi," the man yelled, "there is something more. The white man rides the medicine horse!"

Amid a flurry of excited talk, more men climbed up into the rocks to stare at the man moving closer.

Timbi frowned. "The Medicine Hat stallion? But of course that's impossible. You are wrong!"

But the man turned and yelled again, *"Timbi,* it is our *nermerberah*—your blood brother!"

Even as Dallas stared curiously, *Timbi* seemed to falter. "N-no, that can't be so! He must only resemble him!"

"I thought you didn't have a brother. A white man?"

Timbi shook his head, not looking at her, staring into space. "I owe him my life, so it's taboo to kill him."

Dallas stared at *Timbi,* horrified. "Kill him? Why would you want to kill him?"

"Because I'm sure he comes to kill me!"

"Timbi," shouted a warrior, "what shall we do? He will be in the camp in a few heartbeats."

"Does he come alone?"

"He comes alone."

"Then let him come," *Timbi* said with grim finality. "It is time we ended this so I won't have to spend the rest of my life listening for every footstep, awaiting that time when we will fight to the death."

She ran over, grabbed his arm. *"Timbi,* what is all this about? Surely this can be settled without bloodshed—"

"No, it cannot." As he looked at her, deep sorrow etched lines in his face. "He comes for you, Dallas, and because of you, one of us will kill the other."

"Me?" She touched her chest in surprise. "But I've never even met your blood brother!"

He came over and put both his hands on her small shoulders. "Listen to me, Spirited One, and know this; what I have done, I did for love of you, and I would do it again, no matter how dishonorable it may seem."

She looked up into his dark, tragic face. "You're talking in riddles. I don't understand—"

"Dallas, listen." He took her small face between his two big hands. "I tell you, he comes for you. But when he finds out you carry my child, he won't want you. No white man wants a woman who has been a brave's squaw."

She looked past his shoulder, saw the barest outline of a big man on a pinto stallion just at the edge of the camp. Then she looked up at *Timbi,* not understanding. "Why would he want to take me? I don't know him."

His face seemed grim as death. "Hear me! I did

338

it for love of you, and would do it all over again. I hope you will understand and not hate me."

"Hate you, *Timbi?* I don't hate you!"

"But you will soon. When you see him, you must tell him to turn around and ride out, that you carry my child and that you love me and want to stay with me."

What on earth was he talking about? It didn't make any sense to Dallas. "Why must I tell him this?"

"Pony Girl, I lied when I let you think I might let you leave." His expression was tragic. "If he tries to take you out of here, my men up in the rocks will shoot him down. He will never leave this camp alive!"

Dallas pulled away from him, turning to look in puzzlement at the big man riding into the camp. "But no white man knows I'm here, and—"

"Somehow he found out. Remember, if you value his life, you must pretend you care nothing for him so he will ride away without you."

She was utterly bewildered as she turned and stared at the big man riding closer. She felt *Timbi's* hand tighten on her arm.

"Remember," he whispered.

She stared at the profile of the big man on the giant stallion, blinked, stared again.

It couldn't be. . . .

The man dismounted at a distance, tied up the strangely marked horse.

No, it was a mistake, something she had prayed for so hard, she now imagined it. He was tall and broad shouldered; that was why he reminded her so much of. . . . But Quint was dead. Her hand went to the ring she wore on a thong.

Then he strode toward them in that easy, long-legged gait that was so familiar to her. It couldn't be! Tears blinded her so that she could see nothing but his vague outline.

She felt *Timbi*'s hand tighten on her arm, saw the warriors up in the rocks ready their weapons.

"Remember," *Timbi* whispered, "convince him to leave this camp if you value his life!"

Quint! Quint! It was a good thing *Timbi* had hold of her because her first impulse was to race toward the big man, screaming his name.

She whirled on *Timbi*. "What is this about? You told me he was dead! You told me—"

"Silence!" he commanded, and they both turned to face the white man as he strode up.

Dallas's heart was in such turmoil, she was not sure she could stop herself from racing into Quint's arms. She looked at the Paiute's grim face. She had never hated a man as much as she did at that moment, knowing she was going to have to deny her real love to save his life.

Then Quint stopped, stared at her, his mouth opening in surprise. "Dallas?" For a split second she thought he would run to her. "Angel, I thought you were dead, and—"

"No, I just ran away," she answered coldly, folding her arms across her chest to keep from throwing herself into his arms. "I—I decided our marriage was a mistake."

340

Mistake? Never! she thought. Till death do us part. But I will make this sacrifice, dear one, to save your life.

He stared at her, wide-eyed, and the hand that he ran through his hair trembled. "Good Lord! Dallas, you can't mean that!" He turned and smiled at the warrior. "Brother, I can't thank you enough for finding her. Here I thought you'd been involved in her death! Why if I hadn't found out in time—"

"Save your thanks," *Timbi* said coolly. "She has something else to tell you."

Quint looked from one to the other. "What is all this?"

Dallas didn't look him in the face. She knew if she did, he'd know she lied. "Actually, Quint . . . well, I can't think of an easy way to tell you."

"Tell me what?" His voice had a decided edge to it as he looked down at her. He began to curse. "I ride in here, find my woman alive, and my blood brother hasn't bothered to send me word—"

"Tell him, Pony Girl," *Timbi* said.

The lie. She was going to have to lie to him to save his life. He would ride out of here hating her forever, cursing her each time he thought of her. But nothing was more important than saving Quint's life. Dallas took a deep breath, forced herself to stare into Quint's eyes. "Quint, I . . . I'm *Timbi*'s woman now."

He reacted as if she'd hit him hard across the face with a gun butt, staggered backward two steps. "What the hell—? What did you say?"

Timbi nudged her. "Tell him again, Dallas."

341

"God damn it, I heard her! I just don't believe what I hear!"

For a split second, she thought he would throw himself at *Timbi*. She glanced up at the warriors in the rocks with their rifles, stepped between the two men, wanting to throw herself into Quint's arms, to kiss away the anguish in his eyes. "It . . . it just happened, Quint. *Timbi* saved me from the Pit River tribe after they captured me."

Timbi reached out, put an arm around her shoulders. "You heard her, Quint. She's my woman now, and has stayed of her own free will when she could have come back to you if she'd wanted to. Isn't that right, Dallas?"

My love's life might depend on what I say, whether I manage to convince him. She could feel the tension in *Timbi*'s arm. "That's right." She even managed to look Quint in the eye without blinking.

Dearly beloved, we are gathered here today before God and these witnesses. . . .

"Dallas, my God! How could you? You're my wife!"

She knew if she hadn't been standing between the two men, Quint would have already thrown himself at the Paiute. Pain battled fury on his face. "We're married!"

Do you, Dallas Durango, take this man . . . ? Oh, yes! Yes! Yes!

"Not as far as I'm concerned, Quint," she answered coldly and *Timbi* pulled her close against him. She could feel the big knife he wore pressing against her side. She must get Quint out of here

342

before *Timbi* and his men killed him. "Quint, I . . . I think you should know that I'm happy here and I intend to stay."

What God hath joined together, let no man put asunder.

"Besides, I . . . I'm expecting *Timbi*'s child."

The sound he made was halfway between a curse and a sob. His face turned ashen. "My blood brother. My woman. Why, I ought to—!"

"No, Quint!" Again Dallas moved between them. "I . . . I've made my choice. I made a mistake, marrying you! I'm half-Indian myself, you know, and *Timbi* and I have much in common."

We've both betrayed you, she thought in anguish, but I never meant to.

"I loved you, Dallas, more than anything in this world!" He gestured toward *Timbi*. "And I saved his life! If only I'd known then—"

"Remember what we said about never looking behind you," she snapped. "Now why don't you get on your horse and ride out of here?"

He stood staring at her, fists clenched. "I love you, angel, and I'd do anything in the world to make you happy. If you want him, I won't try to force you to leave with me."

His shoulders slumped as he turned back toward the big stallion.

Dallas felt *Timbi*'s arm relax on her shoulders, yet she was so blinded by tears she could barely see Quint's big form as he walked toward his horse. The love of her life was leaving her behind—forever.

343

But she had saved his life and that was all that mattered.

A warrior grabbed the stallion's bridle, and the horse laid back its ears, snapping, hooves flaying. The man stumbled backward, and the rifle he held slammed against the ground and discharged, the shot going wild and echoing through the hills.

Quint grabbed the reins. "Sky Climber lets no one but me get too close to him!"

Then one of the braves on the rocks yelled, "The white army comes at a gallop!"

Timbi let go of Dallas, pushed her away, jerked out his knife. "My white brother whom I trusted!" he snarled. "You said you came in peace, but you actually bring the white army to kill us!"

"Quint, look out!" Dallas screamed.

He turned. *"Timbi,* no. I told them to wait while I parleyed so no one would die!" Quint unbuckled his gun belt, let it drop to the ground. "I disarm myself to prove my good faith! I'll ride out and try to stop them—"

"No, I will not be fooled by your lies!" *Timbi* advanced on him, knife flashing in the light as the late afternoon storm clouds parted and the sun broke through.

Dallas clasped her hands over her mouth to hold back her sobs. *"Timbi,* let him go! I promised I'd stay if you'd let him live! Let's escape before the soldiers come!"

In that split second, Quint seemed to read her face, to understand the sacrifice she'd been willing to make. "Why, you rotten—!"

He charged *Timbi* and they meshed, fought; *Timbi* slashing with his knife.

"Stop it, both of you!" Dallas cried, but all she could do was watch helplessly as they fought a life-and-death battle. The warriors in the rocks were now preoccupied with the white men galloping toward them. The firing between the two groups began, rifles echoing through the hills.

But Dallas cared only about the fight between the two men who loved her. She watched them, torn by her emotions as they struggled, went down, rolled in the dirt as they fought—her husband and the father of her unborn child. And she didn't want either of them to die.

Timbi regained his feet, slashed at Quint, Quint dodged.

"White dog! You'll never take her away from me! I'll kill you first!"

Quint grabbed *Timbi*'s wrist, stopping the sharp blade in midswing, and they seemed poised for a heart-stopping minute as they struggled. Both men were big and powerful. They were evenly matched, and they fought for more than their lives, they fought for possession of the woman they both loved.

She didn't know what to do. There was no way to stop them. All she could do was watch. In the distance now, she saw the cavalry and the volunteers galloping forward, shooting at the braves up in the rocks. The Indians were shooting back. It would be all over before anyone could get here to stop this fight.

And now Quint lunged, throwing *Timbi* off balance, the knife clattering away into the rocks. *Timbi* went down, slamming his head against the ground, temporarily stunned.

She saw the rage on Quint's face as he grabbed up a stone, stood for a long moment over the fallen man. She held her breath as Quint brought the rock back to crush *Timbi's* skull.

"My blood brother," he said softly. Then very slowly, he let his hands drop and tossed the rock to one side. "Even now, I can't kill you!"

With a sigh, he turned away, clutching at his arm. His blood-soaked shirtsleeve was evidence that an old wound had reopened during the fight.

"I won't let you leave here alive!" *Timbi* stumbled to his feet. "Only if you are dead can I make her mine forever!" He grabbed up the knife, charged blindly at Quint's undefended back.

"Look out!" Dallas screamed, and Quint half turned, throwing up his arm to defend himself, but the knife caught him in the shoulder. He was fighting now for his very life.

The noise increased as the army overran the Indians' positions in the rocks, charged forward, the Paiutes scattering. But the white force wouldn't get here in time.

She ran over, picked up Quint's holstered pistol from the ground. She would scare *Timbi,* demand that he drop the knife, let Quint go.

Timbi's face was distorted with insane jealousy and fury. "And now, white dog, I kill you, claim the woman and the stallion!"

She cocked the pistol, aiming it at the two men. *"Timbi,* no!"

He looked at her even as he brought the knife down in a final swing toward Quint's heart. She saw the surprise on his dark features, as if he had not thought of the gun or of Dallas turning on him.

In that split second as the knife flashed down toward Quint, Dallas chose between the two men. . . .

The train whistled long and low, bringing Dallas out of her memory with a start.

"Angel, what's the matter?" Her husband smiled at her.

She looked over at his dear face, saw the gray in his hair and thought of all the years they had been together through happy times and tragedies. "I was just remembering. . . ."

He must have realized what she had been thinking about because he slipped his arm around her shoulders and hugged her close. "I know; I know. I've wished a million times that things had turned out differently. He was the only brother I had. If only—"

She put her finger across his lips, blinked back tears. "Remember we swore that day we would not regret that which we cannot change?"

He nodded. " 'If only'; the two saddest words in any language. People bring themselves a mountain of grief that way, don't they?"

For a moment, she almost hated her two sons for the pain she now saw in her beloved's hazel eyes. They had sacrificed and worried and loved their children, and this was how they were repaid. "Oh, Quint. Suppose we don't get there in time? Suppose—?"

"Good Lord!" He ran his hand through his hair distractedly. "Remember people also bring on a lot of unnecessary pain borrowing trouble by worrying about the worst possibilities before they happen . . . *if* they happen."

She nodded. "Yes, we'll reach the valley, rent a buggy."

Quint smiled, but it looked forced. "We'll get there in time, Dallas, and we'll straighten this whole mess out, rescue Miss Blassingame, somehow get both our sons back."

She laid her face against his coat and the strength of that broad shoulder comforted her as it always did. "It's almost as if we're replaying that same time all those years ago with two brothers ready to kill each other over a girl they both love."

He kissed her forehead. "Let's hope not. Surely we can talk some sense into them both, get this all worked out, if we can get there before the posse and the troops."

She looked up at him, her heart twisting in pain. "Oh, Quint, dearest, suppose we don't?"

Nineteen

It was morning when one of the Paiute scouts rode in. Nevada saw him reporting to *Kene* who hurried over. "Him say many bluecoats and star chests maybe a day's ride. They look for sign and tracks."

Damn the luck. Nevada tipped his hat back. "Was Jack with them?"

"Don't know."

Nevada sighed. His luck was finally going to run out . . . or maybe it was just God finally getting even with him? He crossed himself. "By the time we decide whether Jack's leading them here, it will be too late to escape. If they're just searching without a clue, we can stay until they go away and they'll never find this valley."

The Paiute nodded. "No matter."

"It matters to me," Nevada said. "If the soldiers come here, it will be because I took the girl. We could have lived like bandits and rustlers for years without them bothering to do anything. I'm sorry, *Kene*."

Kene shook his head and Nevada noted the gray streaks in his hair. The Paiute was not a young man anymore. Living the way Nevada was going, he didn't expect to live long enough to have gray hair. Right now, he'd be pleased to look in a Gypsy's tea leaves and see that he was going to make it to twenty-seven.

Kene smiled somberly. "No need be sorry; spring is a good time to die. My friends mostly killed at Pyramid Lake; this as good a place as any to end it."

"We're in a box canyon," Nevada reminded him, "if your braves delay and the soldiers are coming, it will be too late to change their minds at the last."

"I'm tired." The Indian sighed. "All my warriors tired and lost hope long ago. If we be asked to ride the spirit trail tomorrow or next day, we go out with good fight."

Nevada held out his hand. "I'm not sure I ever thanked you, *Kene,* for everything. We all take too much for granted, thinking we'll thank people tomorrow." They shook hands solemnly.

"You are *nermerberah,* Indian's friend, brothers," *Kene* said, "as your father and the brown-haired white man were brothers."

A thought occurred to Nevada. "I know my father, *Timbi,* was a man of honor. Did you see him die?"

The brave hesitated. What was it that he was holding back? "I was there. One was a man of honor; the other threw away his honor because he wanted the woman."

Yes, that was the way Nevada had been told, all right. Maybe Nevada was no better than Quint Randolph after all, stealing his brother's woman.

There was no time to worry about that now. Nevada scuffed the toe of his boot in the dust. "Maybe the soldiers don't look for us. Anyway, if Jack isn't with them, they'd never find this place."

"True; but no matter. Warriors living on borrowed time now. Better short, free life than return to reservation." *Kene* cocked his head. "Most my braves stay. What you do?"

"I—I haven't quite decided. Let's talk to our men; let each make his own choice."

They left the circle. Nevada followed the faint sound of that off-key harmonica to where Ben sat leaning against a tree, playing "My Old Kentucky Home."

Nevada nodded a greeting. "One of *Kene*'s men has spotted a posse and soldiers who may be here by dark if they come this way."

Ben slapped the harmonica against his hand, put it in his vest, began to feel through his pockets. "They may be just out on a picnic, knowing damn Yankee soldiers."

Nevada shook his head. "Not with our luck; they're probably looking for us. Damn it, Ben, don't you ever carry tobacco?" With an annoyed gesture, he handed the old man his own pouch.

Ben laughed. "I never can rightly remember where I left mine." He shook some tobacco out into a paper, handed the pouch back. "Pierce or Jack with them troops?"

"No one knows yet."

"Your own brother won't shoot you, boy. Pierce'll give you a chance to surrender." Ben rolled a cigarette expertly.

"Will he?" Nevada looked Ben in the eye and after a pause, began to roll a cigarette himself.

"He won't forget he owes you; you saved his life once. He's shore 'nuff got that much honor."

"Has he?" Nevada thought of Quint, the *nermerberah*, the blood brother who had killed *Timbi* so he could have Dallas.

Ben nodded and smoked. "When it comes right down to it, I'm not sure if Pierce would kill you, but I know you couldn't kill him."

"Unless I get him in my gun sights," Nevada said dourly as he stuck the smoke between his lips, lit it.

Ben snorted in derision. "Tough talk. He's your baby brother, and I know you better than you know yourself; you couldn't do it to save your own life."

"Cain did."

"You ain't Cain," Ben said, "you're Quinton Nevada Randolph. You couldn't hurt Pierce. To you, he'll always be that little brother you taught to swim in case he fell in any more horse tanks."

Maybe old Ben didn't know the whole scandal. Hell, what difference did it make now? "He better not try me," Nevada snapped, "I've waited six years for the chance."

"If you had been gonna kill Pierce," Ben drawled, "you would have already did it that day at the ranch.

Now him killin' you, that's a plumb different story. You're more like Quint than Pierce is."

He remembered that Quint had killed his blood brother so he could have his woman. "You know, maybe I am like Quint after all."

Ben looked toward the lodge. "What you gonna do about her?"

"We can use her to barter for our escape if they corner us." Nevada blew smoke like an angry dragon. "They won't shoot with us using her for a shield."

"Uh-huh, tough talk again." Ben leaned against the tree and smoked. "You wouldn't put any woman in that kind of danger. Quint Randolph didn't raise you that way and the apple don't fall far from the tree."

"Unless maybe there's a worm in it." He ground the cigarette out.

"What's that supposed to mean?"

"Nothing. Forget it." He, too, looked toward the lodge. "If we try to get away, she'll slow us down. If we stand and fight, she might get hurt." He thought about it. It came to him suddenly that he felt very protective toward the spoiled heiress . . . or was he only remembering a shy young girl who had obeyed an impulse and kissed him that New Year's Eve?

"Turn her loose, boy." Ben smoked and looked at him. "It's about time to pay the piper for the sins we've committed. No use her gettin' hurt, too."

Nevada didn't answer. He pictured Cherish going free, returning to Sacramento to marry his brother.

His groin made him almost painfully aware that he had come within minutes of taking her virginity before *Kene* had ridden up to tell of finding Tequila and Mex's bodies. He looked up at the sun, wishing he knew for certain if the soldiers were coming here. By the time they found out, it would be too late. He still had time he could spend in her arms.

Ben sighed. "We maybe could escape from this trap."

Nevada shook his head. "I've given everyone a chance to clear out; I wish you'd go, Ben. You could always return to the ranch and sign on as foreman again."

"Can't yet. I promised Quint," Ben blurted, "I—"

"What?"

"I reckon now that we're only a few hours from bein' buried on the prairie, I might as well tell you. That day you left the ranch, I promised Quint I'd stay by your side, look out for you till we both go home or die. I figure it ain't much different than putting didies on newborn bottoms or teachin' two little boys to ride a pet pony."

In his mind, he saw his dad. No, Quint Randolph wasn't his dad . . . except in his heart, maybe, he would always be. Nevada blinked rapidly. He must have dust in his eyes or they wouldn't be blurring with tears. "I should have known he'd do that."

"He cares about you, boy. Always did; always will."

"It's guilt, that's all."

"Maybe he should have told you the secret, Nevada, but I reckon he was a'feared you'd hold it

354

against him. We all can look behind us and see the mistakes we've made and wish we could change them."

"That's God's truth." Nevada reached out, knocked on the trunk of a small, twisted tree. If he had his life to live over, would he have let Pierce drown or stolen Cherish?

In his mind, he saw himself and his little brother begging the ranch foreman to put them up on a horse and Ben lifting them both onto an old, gentle mare. He heard his own voice: "Hold on to me, Pierce, I'll look out for you."

My little brother. How had it come to this? Did Pierce regret it as much as he did?

Ben said, "We could still all split up, make it across the border."

"Every man can do what he wants," Nevada said as he made a weary gesture. "Me, I'm tired of running, always looking behind me. I've got some regrets, Ben, but it's too late."

"It ain't never too late, boy."

"Yeah, it is," Nevada said and stared off at the horizon. "Quint wouldn't want me back now and even if he did, as you said, we owe the piper. I'd rather take a bullet than go to prison."

"I don't know if I ever told you this," Ben said, "but you remind me some of my little brother, Danny."

"Ben, I'm much obliged for everything you ever did for me. If you make it through this and I don't, tell Dad . . ."

Dad. He faced the truth then. Quint Randolph had

355

raised him. He'd been more of a father to him than he'd ever had a right to expect.

Ben said, "You were always the most stubborn little cuss, even when you was little. Pierce would always try to finagle and charm his way or talk me out of something, but you was hardheaded and independent. Danny was that way, too; took a bullet meant for me. Talk about regrets. . . ." He took out his red bandanna, blew his nose.

Nevada felt awkward, watching the wiry old coot struggle with his emotions. "Hell, Ben, we're too ornery to kill, and it's bad luck to think about it."

"Sure." He got out his harmonica again. "You gonna tell the lady what's goin' on?"

"I don't know." He turned uncertainly toward the lodge. "Reckon I at least ought to go see about her." He turned and walked away with Ben's off-key playing echoing in his ears: . . . *weep no more, my lady, oh, weep no more today, we will sing one song for my old Kentucky home, for my old Kentucky home far away. . . .*

Nevada went to his lodge. He should free her so she wouldn't be caught in the cross fire once the fight began; turn her loose so she could sleep in Pierce's bed. A man with any sense would use her as a shield to get him out of this fix. Nevada shook his head; Quint had put more of a stamp on him than he realized. Besides, Nevada was tired of running. Sooner or later, there had to be a showdown and it might as well come sooner as later. The sun hung at high noon like a twenty-dollar gold piece in a pale blue sky. By night, the Western horizon would look like a giant paint pot of bright colors spilled across the sky. *Timbi* had died about sunset. Maybe his son was meant to die then, too.

He crossed himself and thought of his mother. He tried not to think of Dallas too often. Somehow, Cherish reminded him of her although Dallas was tall and dark-haired while Cherish was petite and blond. He'd like to see his mother one more time. Funny how precious a man's life seemed to him when he could almost count the grains of sand that were left in the hourglass. He had so many regrets, so many guilts, so many things he'd do differently if he could. Nevada would not live to have gray hair like Quint, or get married and have children. Maybe it was just as well. Children so often turned out to bring heartaches and disappointments, and he wasn't sure they were worth that gamble. He wondered if Quint now felt the same way. But you had to give to get; no love offered, none received.

Like *Kene,* he was weary of running one step ahead of death and disaster. He might as well make a stand and die in this valley. He entered the lodge and she looked up. Nevada always forgot how beautiful she was until he saw her and then that feeling came over him all over again. Lust for her body, he thought, and then his heart told him that now that his hours were probably numbered, he should stop fooling himself. What he felt for Cherish wasn't lust. . . .

"Is something wrong?"

"What makes you ask?"

"Your face; something's happened, hasn't it?"

357

He chuckled in spite of himself. "You remind me of my mother. Dallas always knows what Quint is thinking, I reckon because they've been together so long."

"Or maybe they're just so in tune with each other's souls?" Cherish said.

Nevada shrugged. "One of our scouts has spotted some troops a few miles from here."

"Oh?"

Damn her for looking so hopeful. "Don't know if it's a regular patrol or they're looking for us; lot of them."

She shook her hair back. "Has your famous luck run out?"

"Could be; doesn't matter. No gunfighter or desperado expects to live to be an old man. About last night. . . ."

Her face colored and she looked away. "I—I really tried to keep my part of the bargain."

He felt like a leering rakehell. "It was a devil's bargain, not worthy of being kept. I'm going to turn you over to the posse when they surround this place."

"Hoping I will beg for mercy for you?"

He shook his head. "No need. I don't expect to survive this shootout and I'd rather be killed than go to prison."

Cherish looked up at him. She should hate him, she knew that, but that wasn't the way she felt, and she didn't want him to die. "It shouldn't have come to this," she said. "If only you had expressed some interest in me—I was more attracted to you than to Pierce."

"The way your daddy rebuffed me and almost threw me out of his office when I asked him if I could call on you—"

"You asked to call on me?" She blinked. "He never told me that. I thought I might get a note from you, at least."

His brow furrowed. "Cherish, I wrote you a note."

She shook her head. "Daddy and the servants said no letter came. . . ." A horrible suspicion began to build in her mind.

"I find it hard to believe you never got it," he said, "when you wrote me back with such a mean, cold letter."

"Mean? I thought it was more than encouraging."

"You must be joking!" He looked angry. "I can look at it even now and get angry."

"I—I don't understand."

He reached in his shirt pocket, held up a folded paper. "You call this encouraging?"

"Let me see that."

"Why? You should know what it says—"

She jerked it out of his hand, stared at the familiar, small scrawl. "Miss Grimley." She looked up at Nevada and the dismay began to build. "Surely Daddy wouldn't ask my governess—"

"Are you telling me you didn't write this?" He grabbed her shoulders.

"Nevada, that's Miss Grimley's handwriting, but I can't believe she'd . . ."

"I wonder what Amos promised her?" Nevada began to curse under his breath, took the paper from her, tore it into a million pieces. "Why didn't it occur to me?"

"Fiddlesticks! My daddy wouldn't—"

"Not to keep me out of your life?" He whirled on her. "Think, Cherish! Don't you see what's happened here? It would be funny if it weren't so tragic!" He collapsed on the floor, put his head in his hands.

The realization was numbing; almost as if she'd lost someone she loved very much. In a way, maybe she had. Could her father have betrayed her trust, coldly lying to her, manipulating her and her life as he always had; probably the same way he had done her mother?

She expected no better from Miss Grimley. The pitiful old maid had probably hoped Amos Blassingame would reward her with marriage, so maybe he had betrayed the governess, too.

Her heart ached as she stared now at the man sitting before her with his head in his hands. They'd lost time, precious time to be together; and time is the one thing that can't be bought or sold. "Six long years," she whispered with growing horror, "six years we could have had together that we can never reclaim. More than two thousand miserable days and lonely nights I've cried into my pillow, slept alone and dreamed. . . ." She was weeping now in disbelief. "I can't believe Daddy could have done this."

Nevada's face registered the anger and hurt he

360

felt, too, as he reached out and brushed a tear from her cheek. "The way I feel at this moment, I could kill him! But maybe I can't blame him; you were so young and there were so many men who wanted you."

"Did you—did you want me?" Cherish stared at him, then at the scraps of paper scattered on the floor. From this moment on, Cherish would never feel the same blind, obedient trust in her father. Amos Blassingame wasn't God after all; he was only a plump despot willing to do anything, even break his adoring daughter's heart, to hang onto her.

She looked at Nevada again. "You didn't answer my question."

"All right; I'll admit it. I wanted you from the first moment I saw you when we walked in your front door the night of the party."

"You never even asked me to dance, and there were women hanging on your arm and flirting with you every chance they got," she accused him.

He looked a bit shamefaced. "I don't have the polish Pierce has and I don't dance as well. Besides, you were so very young for a man of my rather dubious reputation, as your father pointed out."

She could only look up at him in unhappy disbelief. Now she realized why Daddy had been so eager for her to go off to Boston, far away from the older son, but close to the younger one's college. Daddy had always made her feel so guilty, so obligated, that she never thought for herself or argued with anyone. She did as she was told, only rebelling occasionally like a spoiled brat.

"Nevada, no one has ever told me why you and Pierce argued, why you left home."

"It doesn't matter now." He shook his head, clenched and unclenched his fingers. "It's too late; too late for anything."

Too late; a posse was coming. That meant she would be freed unless this band of renegades tried to evade them. She looked at Nevada's weary face. "You're not going to flee, you're going to stand and fight, aren't you?"

Nevada shrugged. "I'm tired of being an outlaw, always on the run, expecting to catch a bullet anytime. And most of my men feel the same."

"You'll all be killed."

He ran a hand through his hair. "So what? After what we've put you through, that should delight you."

What kind of fool was she that the safety of this ragged band of Indians and desperados seemed more important than the more obvious fact that she would soon be rescued? "You're going to use me as a hostage; a human shield to escape—?"

"No, princess, I'm going to turn you over to the posse before the shooting starts."

"In hopes the law will go easier on you."

He started to say something, hesitated. "Of course." His voice was cold, businesslike. "A dead hostage isn't any good to anyone; it'd just get me lynched by that mob."

"Why, I'm sure a posse would never—"

"There won't be anyone to stop them," he said matter-of-factly, "and your father and Pierce will probably be relieved that they don't have to deal with a trial."

"Pierce wouldn't stand by and let them—"

"I wish I could believe that. Once Pierce and I were like any two brothers, and then something happened."

"Me?"

"You were only part of it."

She wondered, but he didn't elaborate even though she waited.

She heard commotion outside and Nevada shouted, "What is it?"

The old man stuck his head in the lodge, touched the brim of his weathered hat. "'Scuse me, ma'am." To Nevada, he said, "Well, we can quit worryin,' I reckon, about whether we're going to escape or not; that decision's been made for us."

Nevada looked from one to the other. "How far?"

"Still a few miles maybe but coming on fast."

Nevada's face fell. "Are Pierce and Jack with them?"

The old man nodded. "Appears so."

"My brother still feels some affection for you, Ben, from our childhood." He looked toward the afternoon sun. "After a while, before it gets so dark that the posse can't tell who's coming down the trail, I'm going to send you out with Cherish under a white flag."

Free. She was going to be free. Why didn't her heart race with excitement? Why wasn't she thrilled?

"Boy," the old man drawled, "I know you think I'm too old to be any help—"

"It isn't that," Nevada said, "but Cherish will need someone to escort her."

The old man was fumbling through his pockets again. "Uh-huh. I reckon I know what you're tryin' to do. It's not as if I'm not obliged for tryin' to save my old hide, but I'd just as soon stay here and try to keep the posse from shootin' you in the back."

Nevada handed him a pouch of tobacco. "I'm too old to put a didie on, Ben."

The old man rolled a cigarette. "What I didn't do for Danny, maybe I can do for you."

She looked from one to the other. "Ben, why don't you all surrender? Surely—"

"Beggin' your pardon, ma'am, but I'm not sure we can trust that bunch out there not to put a bullet in our backs; we're worth as much dead as alive."

She put her face in her hands. "Because of me. There's a big reward on you because of me."

Nevada snapped, "Don't flatter yourself! They've been after us for years, ever since we began to rob your father's trains."

And he only robbed Trans-Western trains; again because of her, she thought. "I don't want anyone's blood on my hands. I'm sure when I tell them I wasn't harmed, they won't do anything—"

"Beg your pardon, ma'am," Ben said as he smoked, "but without Quint along, there won't be anyone to keep them from doin' whatever they decide to do. I'm not sure we could even count on the army to protect us."

Nevada shook his head. "After the fight Quint

and I had, he wouldn't lift a finger for me, even if he were here."

The old man frowned and smoked his cigarette. "You know him better than that. As far as he's concerned, you're his son, always will be. Nothin' can change the way he feels about you."

Nevada didn't answer, but she read his emotions in his strained face. No matter how much he denied it, he cared about Quint Randolph. He stared up at the afternoon sun. "The day'll soon be used up. Ben, I want to get her out of here before it gets so dark, they might fire on her by mistake. See if you can find me a sheet or anything that we can use as a flag of truce."

Ben nodded and walked away.

Nevada stared after him. "Ornery old coot," he muttered, "never has any tobacco on him and his damned harmonica drives me loco."

There was so much to say between them, yet so little to say. They stared at each other in awkward silence. She was a society debutante set to marry his brother in the biggest wedding the West Coast had ever seen. He was an outlaw with a price on his head. Like he had said, it was too late; forever too late.

"I—I didn't really fulfill my part of the deal."

"You came awfully close," he murmured and his hand reached out and played with a stray curl. "A devil's bargain to snare an angel. It wasn't as if you didn't try. The timing was bad; rotten luck for me."

She felt her face flame. Torn between relief and

an emotion she couldn't identify, she realized she just might escape this captivity with her virtue intact.

Outside, she heard confusion and shouts as the defenders readied themselves to make a stand in this canyon. Nevada gave her a halfhearted nod. "I've got to go see about arrangements to give our guests a warm welcome."

"You aren't going to kill somebody?" Her horror must have shown on her face because he paused.

"Too sweet and gentle for this rough and tumble life," he said. "I don't know why I ever hoped you might fit in on an Arizona ranch."

She almost told him then that inside, she was no fragile shrinking violet, then realized it didn't matter now.

He left to talk with his men about fortifying the canyon.

Time was ticking away and she was helpless to stop it. With a sigh, she finally went to help old Ben find something to use as a truce flag.

Ben looked as sad as she felt. "There's a lot of soldiers out there waitin' and they've closed the trap. By cracky, miss, I never thought it would come to this."

"Oh, Ben, you realize he doesn't intend to be taken alive."

"He won't listen to me," Ben said. "He might listen to you."

"Me?" She touched her bosom in surprise. "Me? Why would my opinion carry any weight with him?"

Ben looked at her a long moment. "If you don't know, I reckon you don't feel the same or you'd know what I mean."

He didn't elaborate. Not that it mattered. A couple of hours more, maybe, and she'd be free to go on with her life as it had been all these years. Suddenly, that didn't sound too satisfying. Always men had told her what to do, and always she had been the obedient female. Guilt and upbringing had made her that way. She had rebelled in the only way she knew how, by being spoiled and difficult.

Ben went off, saying he had to saddle her a horse. After Ben left, she prayed, but she wasn't certain what she was praying about or for whom? She watched the men hurrying about, dragging wagons and gear to the rocks to use as barricades. Cherish took a deep breath of the sweet desert air. Yes, she could live happily on a ranch, but unfortunately, Pierce wanted to be in a big city where the power and money were. She watched the sun move across the sky, wished she could command it to stand still. Now in the distance, she saw Ben saddling the little Medicine Hat mare, rigging a white sheet on a stick.

Nevada came for her. "I want to get you out before sundown."

"They won't attack in the dark, will they?"

Nevada shook his head. "They'll wait till dawn, I reckon. They may have a little cannon and they'll blast us to pieces when they get it into position. That's not your worry."

Of course it wasn't. He and these others had brought all this on themselves. If they survived capture, they'd be hanged anyway. She looked up at him, not even wanting to think how she felt toward Daddy and Miss Grimley for what they had done. No doubt they would both say it was for her own good.

"Nevada. . . ." Too much time had passed to change anything. She wasn't even sure how she felt about this man. But he had made one sacrifice, he was returning her to her bridegroom with her virtue intact. "I wish . . ." She wasn't even sure what it was she wished.

She glanced around. Everyone's attention was on the men who might be out there beyond the pass. Ben was playing that harmonica again. Nevada was right; he didn't play very well. . . . *beautiful dreamer, awake unto me, starlight and dew drops are waiting for thee. . . .*

Nevada put his hands on her shoulders, thinking she was still the most beautiful woman he had ever seen. "Oh, Cherish. . . ." He paused, not really sure what to say, except that he didn't hate her anymore. Maybe he never had. He'd only been fooling himself. At least he'd done one honorable thing; he hadn't taken her virginity.

In the background, the harmonica played their song. She closed her eyes. He looked down at her, wondering what she was thinking. Had she ever really cared for him at all? Silently, he cursed her father for his harsh determination in keeping the two apart until it was too late, much too late, to recapture all those years that were gone.

"Dad always said 'if only' were the two saddest

words in any language," Nevada whispered, "but years from now when you have children and grandchildren, think kindly of me, because if things had been different . . ."

She looked up at him and swallowed hard. "You didn't steal me for revenge or the ransom, did you?"

He shook his head. "I reckon I didn't even know that myself until this very minute. But a man just can't take something because he wants it. He can call it anything he wants, but it's not honorable. Maybe like Ben said, Quint has marked me with his Southern ways."

"Nevada, under cover of darkness, we could slip out of this valley, go across the border."

A hope flickered in his heart. "Would you do that for me?"

She nodded.

Then reality set in and the hope died as the light was now dying in the Western sky. He shook his head. "It wouldn't work; I'd be a wanted man and I couldn't ask you to live on the run. A man has to pay the piper for what he does, princess, there's no way around it. But this is for old time's sake." He bent his head and kissed her; a final kiss for him to remember in those last minutes before a bullet got him in the morning. He brushed his lips across hers gently, savoring the warmth and the softness and the scent of her. It was as wonderful as he remembered, when he'd been a man of the world and she was a big-eyed innocent in a delicate yellow dress.

She clung to him and he realized she was crying; maybe it was relief that she was finally returning to Pierce or that her virtue had been spared. He reached up and unclasped her hands from around his neck. "Come on, princess, I want to get you out of here before it gets dark."

He let go of her, strode to the rocks and shouted out. "Pierce! Pierce Randolph, are you out there?"

The shout echoed and re-echoed through the rocks and canyons. In the twilight of the vast Nevada wilderness, he saw horses. Here and there was a slight movement in the sagebrush. Yes, there were men hiding out there. Finally the shout came back, "Yes, I'm here! Is Cherish all right?"

"She's all right and I'm sending her out! Pass the word for everyone to hold their fire!"

"Agreed. We'll settle our scores later!"

Later, later, later . . . the echoes rang through the rough, hostile canyons.

His own men were positioned along the rocks of the pass, watching Nevada for any orders. There was no way of telling how many soldiers and lawmen were out there in the sagebrush and they were smart enough to stay out of rifle range until they had time to regroup and bring up a cannon.

Ben led the little mare over and Nevada lifted Cherish to the saddle. "I'm making you a gift of the mare; I know you liked her." He handed her the white rag tied to a stick. "You'll be all right, Cherish."

She hesitated as their hands touched, looked as if she might say something.

"I'm sorry about the fancy wedding dress; I know you can't replace it."

"It—it doesn't matter." She had tears in her eyes. "Nevada . . ."

"Don't say anything," he whispered, "you'll make it harder for me. I'm sorry about everything." He reached out and gave the mare a slap and she took off at a canter down the trail, the white flag blowing out behind and Cherish's yellow hair reflecting the last rays of the sun. Nevada watched a long moment, not sure as he took a deep breath if it was the desert blooms or the scent of her skin he remembered most.

Goodbye, princess, he thought, crossed himself and said a little prayer for her. He wanted her to be happy, wanted it more than he wanted his own happiness. However, he couldn't bear to watch her ride to the end of the trail, see Pierce lift her from the horse and embrace her. He blinked the sudden mist from his eyes as he watched her and then turned and walked away from the rocks. He didn't want to see Pierce take her in his arms and kiss her.

And so it ends, Nevada thought, or at least until dawn when the slaughter starts. Pierce had the woman Nevada loved and all Nevada had was her memory. It would have to be enough.

Twenty

Nevada stopped next to where *Kene* sat in the rocks. "Well, at least I did one thing right; I sent her back to my brother."

Kene nodded. "You have more honor than your father."

"You mean my adopted father," Nevada corrected him as he rolled a cigarette.

The other man shook his head. "*Timbi* did not send the girl he stole back to her man. His blood brother had to fight him for her."

Nevada paused with the cigarette halfway to his lips. "Don't you have that backward?"

Kene's weathered face saddened in the twilight. "*Timbi* was my friend, but I thought you knew he died without honor. He stole the white man's woman and would not let her go."

Without honor. Well, maybe Nevada was more like his real father than he had thought. Ruefully, he lit the cigarette, looked around at the gray and blue shadows of night creeping across the barren landscape. "It doesn't matter now, I reckon. Funny how different things look to a man when he knows he won't see another sunset."

He watched *Kene* twist a little hangman's noose in his strong brown hands. "Where'd you get that?"

The other shrugged. "Mex. Him left these everywhere."

Nevada smoked and contemplated the little noose, put his hand on the other man's shoulder. "I'm sorry, *Kene,* I know he was almost like a son to you."

"No sons; brothers all scattered now, may not be alive. Most our people scattered or dead, as we soon will be."

He didn't really care much anymore. Without Cherish, life didn't seem worth living anyway. "If Jack was guilty, I'm sorry we won't be able to take revenge on him. Did you ever find out why the kid made the nooses?"

Kene nodded. "Know a little. I tell him we try to get his money to town for school."

"Maybe Cherish or someone will do it if we don't make it."

Cherish. She should be in Pierce's arms by now. He was glad he had walked away from the rocks so he wouldn't have to see it happen.

Cherish rode her little mare down the trail through the rocks, holding her white flag high. In the twilight, she could barely see the vague outline of men in the sagebrush and mesquite, the last rays of daylight reflecting off the small cannon. Tomorrow morning, the troops would blast the stronghold into a pile of rubble.

She should be glad of that. It served them right for kidnapping her; and yet . . .

She would not think of any of that now, she would think of how fortunate she was to be free and her virginity intact, her life spared. She felt every man's eyes on her as she walked her mare down the trail. Behind her, the off-key notes of Ben's harmonica drifted out over the valley in the still air . . . *beautiful dreamer, queen of my song, list while I woo thee with soft melody. Sounds of the rude world heard in the day, lulle'd by the moonlight have all passed away.* . . .

She was almost out of range of the rifles in the rocks behind her now and her heart beat hard with excitement and anticipation.

Ahead of her, she heard Pierce's familiar voice yelling, "Watch out now, everyone hold their fire until Miss Blassingame is safe, then we can open up on the stronghold!"

Without thinking, she slowed her mare to a walk and looked toward the day dying all pink and purple on the Western horizon. In another five minutes, dusk would turn to dark and it would be too late to attack the bandits' hideout. The army and the posse would have to wait until dawn. She was buying the renegades another eight or ten hours of life. Cherish wasn't sure why she did it, and she didn't want to think about it or the men in the stronghold.

Yes, up ahead, she could see Pierce, staying back until he was sure she was out of range of the bandits' rifles before rushing out to meet her. Nevada wouldn't have thought of his own safety, she decided, he would have thought of hers. At least she was coming out of this not much worse than she went in; minus one destroyed wedding dress, but there were always dressmakers in Sacramento.

No, nothing had changed. Her virtue was safe and she and Pierce would get married after the posse killed his brother and hanged any survivors. She held onto her white flag, thinking as she rode toward the troops that her life would continue just as it always had, except that Pierce would probably go into politics. She could be quite an asset to him with her money and social contacts. She wondered suddenly if Pierce really loved her or was marrying her for what she could bring to this union. Did it matter? Instead of Cherish Blassingame, she would be Mrs. Pierce Randolph and she would be just what she always had been, a pretty accessory for a man's home.

Pierce was running out ahead of the troops, coming to meet her. "Cherish, thank God, you're all right! They'll pay for this in the morning when we blast them all to hell!"

She looked down at him as he reached for her mare's bridle, and suddenly, she had to know. "Pierce, what was it you and my father told Nevada?"

"I don't know what you're talking about." He grabbed at the dainty mare's bridle.

"I mean the night you two had that big fight."

Her horse danced nervously about, resisting Pierce's attempt to grab it.

"Oh, he told you about that, did he?" Pierce's hazel eyes shone in triumph in the dying light. "All right, now you know that he's sired by an Injun! Amos found out and told me."

His cruelty appalled her. "He didn't know and you told him?"

"Damn it, Cherish, let me help you off that horse. What do you care about that desperado?"

As he reached for her, she asked herself that question: *What do you care about that desperado?*

I love him, she thought with sudden clarity, I love him! And even as Pierce grabbed her mare's bridle, Cherish struck him with the white flag, and let go of it as he stumbled backward, tripping and falling in a tangle of white cloth as she reined her horse around.

"Go, girl!" she shouted and whacked the startled little mare with the reins. The mare responded with all the blood of her swift sire and took off back up the trail at a gallop.

Behind her, she heard Pierce shout, "She's gone loco! Someone stop her! Someone stop that girl!"

No, they weren't going to stop her! Whatever time Nevada had left, she was going to spend it in his arms! In the growing darkness, soldiers and lawmen were racing toward her, trying to head her off, stop her horse. The looks on their faces told her they thought she'd gone temporarily insane from being held captive. A soldier ran right out in front of her horse. The mare reared, but Cherish hung on and

376

slashed the man across the face with her reins. "Let go of me, let go, damn you!"

He fell backward and the mare almost set him aspin brushing past him. All around her were shouts. "Stop that girl! Stop her, she's gone loco!"

Cherish's heart beat hard as she hung on for dear life and urged the mare onward. No, she hadn't lost her mind, she'd suddenly found it, and by God, she was going to follow her heart! She was tired of being decorative, submissive, and obedient. There was only one man in this world who really appreciated her feistiness, and she was going back to him if she got a bullet in the back for doing so!

Cherish galloped up the trail in the almost darkness, barely able to see the outlines of Nevada's men in the rocks. "Hold your fire!" she yelled. "I'm coming in!"

They seemed to realize then what she was doing. A cheer began to grow as she galloped toward them. Cherish's heart cheered with them. Whatever happened tomorrow, she and the man she loved had tonight!

Nevada paused in his conversation with *Kene,* startled. "What the hell is that about?"

The men were cheering up in the rocks. What had happened? What was going on? He turned and ran for the pass, *Kene* behind him. He got there just as Cherish's mare thundered through the pass.

He ran to meet her. "Good God, did the mare run away with you? Are you okay? Why—?"

But Cherish was sliding from the mare into his arms, her heart singing. "I'm back. I've made my choice!"

In the starlight, he looked confused, baffled. "What's going on? If the mare ran away—"

"No, the mare didn't run away, I did!" She threw her arms around his neck.

He looked completely bewildered. "Cherish, this is loco. You mean you deliberately came back? You can't—"

"Fiddlesticks! I'm tired of men always telling me what to do. We're not far from the twentieth century, I intend to start making my own choices!" And she kissed him.

For a split second, he was stiff with surprise in her arms, just as he had been that long-ago night before the fireplace in the billiard room. Then he murmured something, pulled her into his embrace so tightly, she could scarcely breathe as he kissed her, deeply, thoroughly, lovingly.

Around them, Nevada's men cheered.

He held her against him a long moment and she reached up and felt the tear on his cheek in the moonlit darkness. "Princess, you're loco. We're going to die here at dawn, I won't let you stay—"

She gestured toward the starlit night. "If you send me along that trail in the darkness, you run the risk of some trigger-happy *hombre* shooting me by mistake."

"That's so," he admitted. "All right, then, I'll send you out at first light. It won't be hard for you to

378

convince Pierce that you were under stress or that high-spirited filly ran away with you."

She laughed, feeling happier than she had ever felt in her life. "He might be vain enough to believe that, even though I did hit him with the flag!"

"You little devil! Maybe I underestimated you; you're a lot like my mother."

She laid her face against his big chest. "You always saw more to me than just a cute, fluffy thing to decorate a man's parlor."

He looked down at her. "So now what?"

She looked toward the starry Nevada night. "We've got eight or ten hours until daylight, maybe, and six long years to make up for."

He shook his head. "No. If you're feeling guilty, just because I probably won't make it through sunrise, forget it. I brought this on myself."

She reached up and touched his dear face. "Nevada, I know about Pierce finding out your secret, telling you."

He swallowed hard. "The scandal doesn't shock you?"

She shook her head. "I think Quint Randolph is one of the most noble, honorable men I ever met."

In the moonlight, she saw the tears glistening in his dark eyes. "I've been a fool, Cherish, an ungrateful child, and now he'll never know."

She put her finger across his lips. "He'll know; I swear it. We'll tell him together."

He shook his head. "Those hours till dawn are all the time I have left, Cherish. I'm going down in a blaze of gunfire in the morning."

She looked around at the men in the rocks. Like Nevada, they had all made the same decision. She didn't intend to survive without him, but he needn't know that. "Then we have tonight," she whispered, "and I have been waiting for it six long years!"

"Cherish, are you sure?"

"I'm sure. Very, very sure." And she kissed him again.

He hesitated a long moment, then he swung her up into his arms. "Whatever happens tomorrow, we have tonight!"

With his long strides, he carried her to their lodge and lay her down on the blankets. "I've dreamed of this moment all these years," he whispered, "and believe me, it will be the last thing I remember tomorrow as—"

She reached up and put her finger across his lips. "Don't say it," she murmured. "Make love to me tonight as if it was our wedding night, the very first time for the rest of our lives. No regrets, nothing but that we love each other."

"If I could, princess, believe me, I'd marry you."

"And I take you to have and to hold," she whispered, "till death do us part."

In the firelight, she saw his eyes. *Till death do us part.* Tonight was all they were ever going to have.

"Are you sure you don't want to reconsider? Tomorrow, you may regret—"

"Never," she said and she kissed him with the pent-up passion she had been saving all these years and that she was certain Pierce didn't even know she was capable of.

His mouth seemed to burn like a brand into hers as she pushed the tip of her tongue between his lips, thrusting rhythmically deep into his mouth. He gasped at the sensation and pulled her even tighter against him so that his tongue touched hers, sucked hers even deeper while one of his hands covered her breast, the other cupped her small bottom. "I haven't had a woman in a long, long time, Cherish," he said, "and even then, everyone I've ever had these past six years, I pretended was you, because I never in my wildest dreams thought you would be mine."

She began to unbutton his shirt. "We've got so much time to make up for, so many memories to create."

"No, so little time, Cherish." She knew from the look on his face that he expected to die at dawn after he'd sent her back to Pierce, and that he thought his brother would never know she'd spent the night in his arms.

Whatever happened, this was her man. If she couldn't save him by any means, fair or foul, she'd die with him. When she had his shirt unbuttoned, his brawny chest exposed, she put her lips on his nipples while he writhed and gasped at the pleasure she gave him.

"Princess . . . my princess. . . ." He kissed her eyelids, her cheeks. His hot mouth tasted her ears until shivery feelings ran up and down her back.

She began to unbutton her own shirt, wanting his mouth all over her. "Nurse me," she begged him.

"Put your mouth on me and suck them until they hurt!"

His mouth felt very hot and wet on her breast and his hand massaged her other breast like a kitten kneading for milk. Against her belly and thighs, she felt the heat of his big manhood throbbing and hard. "I want you so bad," he gasped, "that I'm afraid I'll hurry through it, take you in a heated rush instead of making it last. . . ."

"We've got all night," she reminded him urgently, desiring him as much as he wanted her. Her pulse seemed to pound like a war drum in her brain. "We'll do it again and again and again."

To make up for all those times in the future that we won't have, she thought, then brushed that fact away. *Tonight.* They had tonight and that was more than some lovers ever had.

He was kissing his way down her belly now that he had thoroughly laved both her breasts with his tongue. Cherish felt warm and wet between her thighs. She unbuttoned his pants and touched his hard maleness. He was so large and she wondered how her small body could ever accommodate him. Even if he tore her open, she would give herself to him.

His fingers went to stroke between her thighs, his thumb teasing the bud of her womanhood until she trembled with need and anticipation. She took his big manhood in her hand. It throbbed and the tip was wet with the seed he had to give. She remembered the stallion topping her mare out on the range.

She would be like that filly, offering her velvet vessel up to this virile male animal.

He rose up on his knees, slowly stripped off his clothes until he was naked in the firelight. She saw a dark, broad-shouldered stallion with his rigid manhood jutting out before him, ready and hot for this mating. "Cherish, are you sure?"

In answer, she stood up, pulled off her own clothes so that she stood naked in the firelight.

With a groan, he pulled her body against his mouth, kissed her from navel to knees, whirled her around and nipped her small hips, while his big hands covered her naked thighs.

"Take me," she commanded, "I've waited long enough." He whirled her around again, kissing her between the thighs as she crumpled in his arms, slid to the blanket.

"Then open for me, princess," he whispered, "if you want me."

Willingly, she let her thighs fall apart and closed her eyes.

"No, look at me," he commanded, "I want to see how you look as I take you."

She was abruptly hesitant, realizing how big he was, how small she was. Still, she reached up, caught his waist with her hands as she looked into his eyes and pulled him slowly down. He hesitated at her opening, his wet, hard maleness against the petals of her femininity.

A woman gives her virginity but once, she thought, and this is the man I choose. With that thought, she wrapped her slim legs around him, arched her body up and slowly pulled him down into her. Oh, he was so big. She felt almost as if she were being impaled by a sword. She felt him touch against the veil of her maidenhead and he hesitated. "Take me!" she begged. "Oh, take me. . . ."

His hands slipped beneath her slim hips, tilting her up for his full penetration. She felt him pause against her virgin silk and then he broke through and went deep into her, filling her, fulfilling her. He lay there a long moment before he began to ride her slowly. "You're so small," he whispered, "so small. . . ."

And he was big, but, ah, it felt so good! She held him against her body with her legs locked around his hard-driving hips, digging her nails into his back while he rubbed his hard chest against her breasts and kissed her mouth, her cheeks, her eyelids. She couldn't get enough of him. "Harder!" she demanded. "Ride me harder!"

"I—I'm afraid I'll hurt you."

"Hurt me; hurt me good and deep!"

What she demanded, he could give her. With long, hard thrusts, he rode her, driving deep into her velvet vessel, his lean, powerful hips slamming into her as she arched under him, her body trying to suck the virile seed right out of his male dagger. In the firelight, they were both covered with a fine sheen of perspiration as they meshed and mated. She could feel him slamming deep inside, up under her navel with his stallion's rod.

"Something's happening to me," she gasped. "I—I don't know what—" She began to feel heated spasms radiating from her lower body, radiating like molten fire through her thighs, belly, and breasts.

"Wait for me, baby," he begged, "wait for me so I can go with you. . . ."

She didn't know what he was talking about except that he was ramming into her harder and harder, but not hard or deep enough yet. She dug her nails into his back, wrapped her legs around his body, bucking under him, urging him in harder and deeper. She felt him begin to convulse inside her and her own body responded by attempting to squeeze his, wanting the seed he had to give.

"Oh, Cherish," he whispered. "Oh, Cherish, princess. . . ." He went rigid, hesitated, gasped, then went rigid again, began to give up his seed.

The heat that was radiating in ever-widening circles from her belly roared into flame. She stopped fighting it, clenched onto his body and was swept away like riding the burning lava from an overflowing volcano. She had never felt anything like this before, it was frightening and it was magnificent. Her body squeezed him even more tightly as she felt his hot seed begin to pulsate into her womb.

They lay there a long time before her eyes blinked open and she realized she lay naked, holding Nevada in a tight embrace in her arms on the blanket by the fire.

"Cherish, baby, are you all right?"

"I love you," she whispered and kissed his face, his mouth. "I love you so much!"

"And I always loved you," he said and began to

kiss her all over again. "Oh, princess, this is going to be a night to remember . . . for both of us!"

A last night, she thought. All these years she had waited and now she finally knew what love was all about. Only one night. Yet maybe she was luckier than most. Many women never knew what love, real love, was all about. This then made it all worth while, and she wouldn't trade one night in Nevada's arms for a lifetime with someone else.

He began to make love to her all over again and she reveled in it, clawed his back in a frenzy of desire and passion. *All night,* she thought, *we've got all night.*

Kene squatted in the rocks and watched for movement out among the troops that trapped them here. He looked around at Ben and the other men scattered along the pass. Ben's off-key music drifted on the still desert air. From here, *Kene* could see the moonlight gleam on the shiny cannon the soldiers had brought. Abruptly the moon went behind clouds. It was dark now; dark enough for what he must do. He stared at the little hangman's noose in his hand; one of Mex's nooses. The shy boy with the strange, haunting eyes was young enough to have been his son, but all *Kene's* blood was scattered or dead.

He studied the little noose again and thought about the school Mex had talked about. In the blackness of the Nevada night, *Kene* was at home as the scorpion and the rattlesnake were at home. He had something he had to do by way of vengeance. Ben would try to stop him, tell him it was too dangerous, but after all, he was going to die tomorrow anyway.

He tucked the little noose in his knife scabbard, told one of his braves where he was going in case he didn't make it back, and crawled across the rocks and down. On the desert landscape below him, the sage gleamed almost silver, the Joshua trees as stark as skeletons. Somewhere, an owl hooted to foretell someone's death. A coyote howled and it echoed and re-echoed across the hostile landscape. The scent of night-blooming cactus blended with the scent of the breeze across the mountains.

Jack always rode a pale buckskin horse. *Kene* searched the sagebrush for the mount, saw it grazing peacefully on the sparse vegetation. His chances of making his way out there to Jack among all the soldiers and lawmen were small, but he had a debt to pay for a boy who couldn't do it himself. *Kene* looked toward Nevada's lodge.

Goodbye, my friend, he said silently, *you might stop me if I told you where I was going.* He hoped Nevada and the girl were finally experiencing that love that he and his little wife, *Moponi,* had had before she'd been raped by the whites so long ago and had run away. She must be dead now.

Kene scurried through the rocks like a desert lizard, taking advantage of every shadow to hide himself. His heart beat hard, not with fear, but with excitement. As a warrior, he had been in battles, been wounded and killed many men, but this would be his last fight and he knew it. Tomorrow, if there

387

was any Paiute left alive at the end of the day, they would be lynched or shipped to a reservation. Better he should die tonight in fulfilling his obligation to Mex, take some of the enemy with him.

Kene moved across the ground as shadowy dark and dangerous as a giant tarantula scurrying across the hostile rocks and sand. Near him, a white man suddenly roused up, but as he grabbed for his gun and opened his mouth to shout a warning, the Indian cut his throat from ear to ear. Hot blood poured on *Kene*'s hands and now the only sound the *hombre* made was a soft gurgle as he died.

Kene wiped his knife on the man's shirt, tucked it back in his belt, looked around. The soldier's horse was tethered nearby, grazing peacefully. It looked up and snorted at the scent of blood. *Kene* paused. The thought occurred to him that he could easily mount that bareback horse in the darkness, pull its picket pin and take off at a gallop. Taking advantage of the surprise, *Kene* could run away and escape the death that awaited his men in the morning; or at least delay it. While the thought tempted him, it wasn't honorable, and he was most of all a man with honor. That was why he must do this thing for Mex; seek revenge on his slayer.

He crawled along the ground, heart still hammering hard. Near him lay an old fat man with a badge and white beard snoring and asleep in his blankets. A deputy. This man he knew. *Kene* would never forget the faces of those who had helped kill the Paiutes at Pyramid Lake so long ago. He cut the man's throat with one slash, leaving scarlet blood staining the white beard. The man's mouth and eyes opened and closed in the darkness like a fish gasping for air, but no air came.

Kene's hands were stained with blood. The coppery, sweet scent came to him when he took a deep breath. Again, the man's horse snorted at the scent. It was a good strong bay gelding that might carry him many miles, but *Kene* thought only of his mission. Any man he killed tonight would be one that would not shoot at Nevada's men in the morning. If he could help them a little, even if it cost his life, it was to be expected from a warrior.

He saw a Medicine Hat gelding grazing, knew that Nevada's brother must be asleep nearby. He was not sure he would know the young man if he saw him except that he might look like *Timbi*'s *nermerberah* from long ago. *Kene* shook his head, decided against taking revenge. Nevada's brother was his own to make peace with or kill.

He saw the buckskin gelding staked out ahead. *Kene* paused, listening to it crop grass, snort, and stamp its feet as it caught the scent of fresh blood on him.

Jack rolled over in his blankets, muttered a curse. "Damn horse, settle down."

It would be so much easier to cut his throat, but it was important that it be done a certain way. Slowly, *Kene* slipped the braided hangman's noose from his belt. Jack turned over again, the sweat on his face gleaming in the dim starlight. Something on Jack's person reflected light. *Kene* stared a long moment before he realized the object hanging from

Jack's vest was Tequila's gold necklace. If he had wondered if Jack were guilty of the two killings, now he knew. He must get that necklace. The gold would help the little school Mex had mentioned. It would be fitting, too. Mex had told *Kene* about Tequila.

He readied Mex's little rawhide noose in his hands and shook Jack awake.

The man blinked sleepily, then his eyes grew wide with fear and disbelief as he looked up and saw the big shadow, the hangman's noose dangling over him. He appeared to try to scream but he only gasped as if in a nightmare.

"From Mex," *Kene* said, and slipped it over the man's head, jerked it tight. Jack clawed and fought him, struggling for air as the rawhide cut into his throat.

He was strong, *Kene* thought, stronger than he had expected. However, Jack was at a disadvantage, trying to fight *Kene* off and get his fingers under the rawhide that was cutting into his neck, breaking his windpipe. "You were way past time to be hung," *Kene* whispered through clenched teeth. He put all his strength into killing the man. Jack's horse snorted and Jack thrashed about. The struggle sounded loud in the desert stillness, but *Kene* couldn't stop until he had finished his mission.

Abruptly, Jack gurgled one more time and died. *Kene* sighed, let go of the cord, realized he was shaking. He took the gold chain from Jack's pocket, looped it around his knife scabbard. No one had sounded an alarm. He was still alive. *Kene* smiled to himself. Maybe it wasn't meant for him to die tonight. He would live to fight beside Nevada tomorrow if he could work his way through the sleeping troops and back up the rocks to the stronghold. Maybe. . . .

A pain more horrible than anything he had ever felt hit him in the back. Agony like coals in his guts. He must not scream, it would alert his enemies. Warriors never cried out, no matter how much they hurt. What had happened? He clawed toward his back, trying vainly to stop the pain that impaled him. The stronghold. If he could get back to the stronghold, he would be safe. His legs didn't seem to work. In spite of his agony, *Kene* began to crawl on his belly, reaching, reaching toward his friends. And then it hurt too much and he was too weak to crawl; all he could do was reach silently toward the rocks where Nevada and his friends waited. He wanted to die with them. He wanted . . .

Pierce swore as he stood with feet wide apart, staring down at the Indian who lay on his belly before him. Pierce shoved hard on the rifle butt, rammed the bayonet even deeper into the man's back. The brave tried to crawl away, but he was impaled against the ground and all he could do was struggle and reach.

Good thing the noise of the thieving bastard killing Jack Whitley had awakened him, Pierce thought with satisfaction. At least he'd saved Pierce the trouble of having to kill the informer so they wouldn't have to pay him the reward. "Thanks, Injun," he muttered and twisted the blade again.

The Indian didn't move this time. Pierce planted one of his fine, handmade boots against the man's ribs, pulled the bayonet out, wiped it against the prone body. "What in hell were you doing out here?" he asked aloud, then felt like a fool for talking to a dead man. He'd been out here killing and stealing gold and a horse so he could escape. Then why was the man headed back up to the canyon when Pierce killed him? That didn't make any sense.

Pierce cursed and looked up toward the stronghold. Where was Cherish and what was happening up there? She must have been temporarily hysterical or a little crazy to turn her horse and return there . . . or maybe he'd misread it. The filly had run away and taken the girl back up there with Cherish trying vainly to stop the horse. Yes, that had to be what had happened, all right.

Pierce looked toward the canyon. It was still a long time until morning when the army could blast that whole bunch to hell. He'd have to make sure they rescued Cherish before the fighting started. He looked toward the canyon. Would Nevada dare—? No, of course not. He didn't even want to consider the thought that crossed his mind. Cherish Blassingame was going to be Pierce Randolph's wife. Like any respectable woman, she'd have the common decency to kill herself if she were despoiled by a savage. Pierce had waited a long time to deflower Cherish, he wouldn't even think about being cheated of that privilege.

The captain called, "What's going on? I heard noise."

Pierce looked at the two dead bodies, wrinkled his nose at the scent of blood. What the hell was going on up there in the stronghold between Cherish and his bastard brother?

"Nothing happening, Captain," he shouted, "just killing vermin, that's all!"

Twenty-one

They made love all night and finally, Cherish drifted off to sleep in Nevada's arms. Nevada didn't sleep. He lay there holding her, watching her lovely face in the flickering light of the lodge fire. All these years he had loved her and now he had finally possessed her for one night. He would die at dawn when the soldiers attacked his stronghold, but at least he would have her memory to hold onto those last few minutes of his life.

Very gently and tenderly, he leaned over and kissed her forehead. *Beautiful dreamer.* She smiled in her sleep and he wanted to hold her close in his embrace, protect her from anything that might hurt her. She would weep for Nevada, but eventually he would only be a faded memory. It was a great temptation to take her with him, sneak past the soldiers and escape to Mexico. However, he couldn't leave his men behind to die and they couldn't all escape under cover of darkness.

He sat up, wondering what time it was. Funny how important minutes seemed to a man who didn't have many left. Nevada rose, put on his gun belt and went outside in to the cool desert night. Ben's music drifted in the night: . . . *weep no more my lady, oh, weep no more today. I will play one song for my old Kentucky home, for my old Kentucky home far away. . . .*

A horseshoe Nevada had nailed to a tree for good luck seemed to mock him as it shone in the starlight. No, he was lucky; very lucky. He had been loved by a princess for a few hours. No prince could ask for more. His men were still at the barricades. He found Ben. "Anything happening?"

The old man shook his head. "Reckon they're waiting for dawn like we are. *Kene* is missing; I think he went out last night to do some scouting or maybe to get Jack for betrayin' us."

"He hasn't come back?"

Ben felt through his pockets and Nevada automatically handed him a pouch of tobacco. "No. Figure one of those *hombres* might have got him, hope he got a few. Maybe one of them was Jack."

Kene. His last link with his father's people. He thought about the things he had learned over the last few hours. *Timbi* hadn't been a man of honor after all. Nevada had tried to send his brother's fiancée back to him and she had returned to Nevada's arms. She was his woman just as he had dreamed all these years. Nevada took the sack of tobacco, stuck it in his pocket. "What time is it?"

"My watch has stopped," Ben said, peering at the eastern horizon, "but I'd say less than an hour till dawn."

"Rustle up some grub for the men then. No man ought to die on an empty stomach." Strange, he thought, we'll all be dead before midmorning, and I'm worried about bacon and biscuits. It was the little things that made life worth living, things like a woman's love.

Ben rolled his cigarette, lit it. "When you sendin' her out?"

He looked at the blackness of the eastern horizon and then toward his lodge. "First light. I'd be afraid to send her out before then, afraid the other side would shoot her, not realizing who she was." He knelt by the camp fire, poured two steaming tin cups of coffee, started back to the lodge. He had only a few more minutes to spend with her and then she would be out of his life forever. Pierce wouldn't let the soldiers fire on the camp until Cherish was safe . . . unless someone out there got jumpy and started shooting. Once that bunch began firing, they'd be hard to shut down and he didn't want the woman he loved caught in the deadly cross fire.

Nevada stooped, went through the door in the lodge, sat down next to Cherish, sipped his coffee. It was strong, hot, and bracing. He watched her dear face, wishing he had the rest of his life to awaken with her by his side instead of this one time. Her eyes flickered open and when she saw him, she smiled.

He smiled back. "Good morning, sleepyhead, want some coffee?"

"I had the most wonderful dream." She sat up, full of bright enthusiasm. "We were on your parents'

396

ranch with our children! We were riding across the land and . . ." The smile faded suddenly as she seemed to remember reality. "Are they still out there?"

He handed her the coffee and tried to make light of it. "You didn't really think they'd go away?"

She took the coffee, sipped it. "What time is it?"

"Not long until dawn."

"It was the most wonderful night I've ever spent," she whispered, "I didn't want it to end." Tears came to her eyes.

Oh, God, if she cried, he might break down, too, and then it would be almost impossible to say good-bye to her, send her to safety. "Here, here, none of that." He caught her small face in his big hand and turned it up to him. "All good things must end, Cherish. All I ever wanted was one long night in your arms and I've had that. I told you then that if you paid the ransom, with the dawn it would be over."

She appeared to be trying to pull herself together. She cleared her throat and pulled away from him. "That's right, you did, didn't you? The trouble is, I didn't know how much I cared about you."

"Keep that memory, princess," he whispered, "keep it locked tight and secret in your heart of hearts. A memory is something that no one can ever take away from you."

"I don't want to go. I want to stay with you."

He shook his head. "You are the very best of me, Cherish, the hopes I had when I was younger, before I went wrong somehow. I want you to live and go on for both of us. At first light, I'm going to send you out. Go to my parents, they'll help you do whatever you want to do with the rest of your life. You can't be forced to marry Pierce."

She set her coffee aside and took his arm. "You're right. I'm going to take charge of my own life; find my own destiny. I don't love Pierce; I won't marry him. I'll go home to my father and tell him so."

"My, you are suddenly getting quite independent!" He was trying to keep things light, but it wasn't working too well.

"Maybe you can make a deal with Pierce that will save your life, let you and your men ride out and escape to Mexico—"

"No, baby,"—he shook his head—"the law wouldn't go for that even if he was agreeable, which he won't be. Pierce and I both have forgotten the things an honorable man taught us. He's my brother and I love him, and maybe he still cares about me, too, but I think he's so jealous, he'll never be satisfied until I'm out of the picture completely."

She wept now. "If you die, I won't want to live!"

He pulled her to him, held her close, kissed her hair as she cried. Oh, God, this was going to be so hard, to send her away, but he must. "You will live, Cherish, and go on. Remember we had one night together and some people never get a night like that, not in their whole long, boring lives." He took the big wolf's head ring off his finger, slipped it on hers. "This is the most valuable thing I own, baby; I didn't realize it until yesterday. A man loved me enough to give me his name and raise me as his own, made me his heir. And I repaid him by breaking his heart."

She looked down at the ring. "There's no changing your mind then?"

He shook his head and pulled her against him more tightly. "Even if my men wanted to surrender, they won't be given the chance, and I'd rather die than go to prison." He reached down and put his hand on the pearl handle of his Colt. "Let's just watch first light break over the hills and pretend we're on the Wolf's Den Ranch watching the sun rise like any old married couple who has fifty years ahead of them to look forward to."

For a moment, he thought she would protest, then she straightened her small shoulders and took a deep, shuddering breath. "All right."

They went outside and turned toward the east. Over the silhouette of the far hills, the first shadowy gray light spread. *Nevada dawn.* In another quarter hour, the sun would peek from behind those hills in a glorious pastel pallet of pinks and blues and lavenders before the bright gold of day broke across the valley.

He stood holding her very close, wanting to imprint the warmth, the softness of her on his body, his memory, for whatever time he had left. Soon he would put her on a horse and send her out of the stronghold, but for these few minutes, she was his and his alone. Nevada pulled her very close and kissed her. "I love you," he murmured. "I loved you from the very first moment I saw you, princess."

"Oh, Nevada . . ." She almost broke down, then

seemed to realize it would waste these last few moments they had together and swallowed hard, clung to him. "I love you, I'll always love only you!"

Pierce stood next to the captain, looking toward the eastern horizon. "It'll be full daylight in a few minutes, and surely to God he'll send her out before the fighting starts."

The young officer looked at him in the grayness of the coming light, curiosity in his pale eyes. "What actually happened last night with her?"

Pierce wasn't quite sure himself. "Her horse ran away with me trying to stop it. That flapping flag spooked it, I suppose. It took her right back up into their stronghold and then I guess she thought it was dangerous to try to ride out again after dark."

"Oh, of course. For a minute, last night, it appeared she was actually wanting to go back—"

"Now, that's a damn fool thought when everyone knows she's been kidnapped and held for ransom," Pierce snapped. Of course her horse had run away with her. The more he thought about it, the more reasonable the explanation seemed. Either that, or her delicate, aristocratic constitution had shattered under all this stress and she didn't know what she was doing. Well, she'd be all right with some rest. They might have to delay the wedding a week or two, but she'd be all right. That trip to England would do her good.

It was almost light. A soldier came riding up at

a gallop, pointed toward the rear. "There's a buggy coming with an older couple in it."

He knew immediately. Mother and Father. He had never felt close enough to Quint to call him "Dad," as Nevada did. It wasn't fair, wasn't fair at all. He wished they hadn't come; they would beg for mercy for their favorite son.

There was some sort of commotion toward the front of the lines and men began to shout.

The captain scratched his head. "What's all that about?"

Pierce couldn't understand a lot of the shouting either, the tired soldiers sounded almost hysterical. "Something about finding men in their blankets with their throats cut!"

"I'll go see." The captain swung up on his bay horse, left at a gallop, but already, Pierce could see the young, inexperienced officer wasn't going to be able to deal with any real trouble. The men were afraid and thought the Indians had gotten out and invaded their lines, were all around them. He hadn't yet told the captain about the informer and the Indian Pierce had killed last night.

Had that Indian killed those men or were there really warriors crawling among the soldiers in the darkness? Once Pierce got Cherish out of that stronghold, he didn't care if the novice, panicky troops blew that place to hell without giving the bandits a chance to surrender. When Quint and Dallas got on the scene, they'd try to stop the slaughter and Pierce didn't want that. He had some misgivings about his brother, but he felt deep in his heart, this thing between them would never end until one of them was dead.

A shot rang out, a soldier firing wildly. "Damn fools!" Pierce cursed. "Not yet! She's not out of there yet!"

Another shot. The soldiers weren't sure who was shooting in the dark gray morn. They thought they were being fired on by the enemy.

"No! No!" Pierce protested, but the captain had his hands full. Around him, panicked men were grabbing for their rifles and the howitzer was being wheeled into place. "Stop!" Pierce shouted. "Not yet, you fools!" But the firing built as the weary, confused troops fired at shadowy sagebrush moving in the breeze. The siege was begun, whether he liked it or not.

Up in the rocks, Nevada heard the first shots in disbelief, whirled. "No, not yet!"

Ben ran to him. "It's started, boy, don't know what happened down there, but the fight's on!"

"I've got to get Cherish out of here!"

Cherish grabbed his arm, shook her head. In her heart, she was glad he couldn't send her away. "I can't leave, it would be death to try to ride out of here now."

She saw the truth of her words reflected in his dark eyes. Behind him, the sun rose and the light across the mountains and valleys reflected the blush of a new day.

He put his arm around her protectively and

crossed himself. "It looks like you got your wish, princess." He led her to a place of safety in the rocks. "Stay here! Either I'll come get you after a while, or . . ." He hesitated, "Well, Pierce will look after you."

"But, I—"

"Cherish, are you my woman?" He looked down at her.

"I am!" she responded with a fiery assertion.

"Then do what I tell you. I can't worry about your being hurt and this fight, too. Now stay down or a stray bullet may get you!" He kissed her, pushed her into the rocks, turned and ran toward the rimrock.

The firing built as the cornered outlaws and Indians returned the volley in the coming dawn. Bullets whined past, ricocheted off rocks. Here and there, she heard a shriek or a moan as men fell wounded or died. She had to help. Cherish crawled out of the protection of the rocks, peeked over the rim. Below her, she saw soldiers and lawmen scattered out in the brush, returning shots. A quick look told her they vastly outnumbered the defenders of the stronghold. The morning light reflected off the brass buttons of the soldiers as they wheeled their cannon into position. It was only a matter of time.

She wasn't afraid as she ran to get canteens, tore up her petticoat for bandages. Once she would have been hysterical at the sound of a pistol shot, but she was Nevada's woman and he needed help. Around her, men were bloody and dying as the bullets flew. The scent of gunfire smote her nostrils and she

403

coughed and ran on, taking a drink of water to this man, stopping the bleeding of another with her tourniquets. She paused next to old Ben.

"Miss, you know how to load guns?"

She shook her head. "Show me! I'll do anything to help!"

He gave her an admiring glance. "I thought he was a fool at first, now I know what he saw in you. Pierce don't deserve a feisty little thing like you!"

She loaded guns, wrapped wounds, held canteens to dying men's lips. Once Nevada looked up and their eyes met. "I thought I told you—?"

"You need help," she said, "and I'm going to help you." She paused, knowing she must look a sight with blood and smoke smearing her face and clothes, but he smiled at her as if she were the most beautiful thing in the world.

"Remember I love you," he shouted. She nodded and ran on. A shell from the howitzer landed nearby, blasting three lodges away and shaking the ground. It got two of the Indians. Cherish ran to them, but they were both dead. Coughing on the dust and smoke, she went to help reload, carry water to wounded men. The cannon roared again and shook the earth when the shell landed. Horses reared and neighed, running about wildly.

It wouldn't be long now, she thought, almost in a daze with all the dust and smoke, screams and blood swirling around her. Nevada's men were outnumbered and outgunned. It would all be over before the sun was an hour old. At least they had last night to remember. He had made love to her a dozen

404

times. That memory would have to last her the rest of her life.

Another shell struck nearby and a man screamed and fell dead. She ran to Ben. "Can I reload?"

He shook his head. "We're almost out of shells, miss, it won't be long now." He looked pale, but calm and resigned.

"Oh, Ben, if you would run up a white flag—"

"No, they intend to wipe us out once and for all." He felt through his pockets, smiled sheepishly. "Never seem to have any tobacco when the boy ain't around." He put his gnarled hand on her arm. "I'll do the best I can for him, Miss Cherish, but you may have to get on your knees and beg Pierce to save his life."

"I'll do it. I have no pride if it'll help him, but I'm not going to marry Pierce, no matter what."

Ben smiled at her. "You don't disappoint me, ma'am, you're worthy of him after all!"

Cherish heard a dying man moaning for water. She found an Indian with his buckskins drenched in blood from shell fragments and held the canteen to his lips. He drank deep, smiled up at her in appreciation and died.

It wasn't fair; wasn't fair at all. Pierce and the army must know how few these men were, how little they had by way of ammunition and weapons. It was sheer vengeance on Pierce's part. She began to hate him as she had never hated anyone. Whatever happened to her, even if she ended up as a cloistered nun, she would not marry the man who was out there with those troops so cold-bloodedly planning this slaughter.

She paused to peer over the rim of rocks. The soldiers, encouraged by the weakening firepower against them, were beginning to move up. The cannon roared again. All around her was smoke and fire and death. The scent of powder and blood stung her nostrils as she breathed. Behind her, men and wounded horses screamed. Nevada, cool and calm, shouted orders over the confusion, but his dark face was blood and smoke-smeared. He looked like a man who expected to die momentarily and only hoped to take as many enemy with him as he could. He had moved to where all his men could see him, balanced on the rocks so that they cheered.

Cherish glanced back toward the soldiers. One had crawled up among the rocks unnoticed. She saw the glint of sunlight reflected on his rifle barrel. Only old Ben was anywhere in the vicinity, she realized abruptly.

"Look out!" she screamed at Nevada, as the soldier aimed.

Only old Ben seemed to hear her. He scrambled to his feet, threw himself in front of Nevada even as the rifle cracked.

Ben stiffened, grabbing for his chest as Nevada caught him. One of the Indians picked off the soldier who tumbled all the way down the rocky wall.

Cherish ran to Nevada, who cradled the old man in his arms. "Oh, Nevada, I saw it, but only old Ben acted."

At the sound of his name, the pale eyes flickered

open and he smiled up at them. "Boy, you—you all right?"

Nevada nodded, looked over at Cherish. She saw the scarlet stain spreading across the old man's shirt. Nevada had to swallow twice before he got the words out. "I—I'm all right, old pard, you took the bullet meant for me."

"Knew there was a reason I had to stick around all these years," Ben muttered and bright blood ran from the corner of his mouth. "I let Danny down, but I didn't let you down, kid."

"No, you never let me down, Ben, I could always count on you."

Cherish was crying now. The tears were dripping on the old man's face. Ben reached a feeble hand toward her. "Count on her, too, boy," he whispered, "she's just like your mama . . . tell Quint I done the best I could . . . think my harmonica is hurt?"

Cherish reached into his pocket, held it up. It had taken the bullet, but it hadn't stopped it.

Nevada said, "Hang on, Ben, we'll get you some help. I'll buy you a new harmonica, and buy you a ton of makin's so you can have all the smokes you want—"

"No fun 'less I can bum them off you. . . ." The old man smiled weakly. "Go home, prodigal son, you got the best dad a man ever had. . . ."

Nevada shook his head. "Too late, Ben; I've disgraced him."

"Never too late," Ben whispered and they had to bend close to hear him above the shouts and firing. "Parents always forgive . . . tell Danny I'm sorry. . . ."

He was lost in a long ago time, she realized. Cherish bent close. "He knows, Ben, can you hear me? Danny knows you did the best you could. Don't feel guilty anymore, it's such a heavy burden. Can you hear me, Ben?"

But Ben smiled and was gone; gone to that faraway place where there is no pain, no guilt, no heavy burdens. And maybe, just maybe, his little brother Danny was waiting to welcome him after all these years.

Nevada was crying now. "Stubborn old coot," he whispered, "never had any tobacco, always bossing me around like I was a kid in diapers."

They held hands across his body and wept together for the man who had sacrificed his life to save Nevada's.

She realized abruptly that they were the only pair left alive. Shells and bullets still whined around them, but there was no return fire. Everyone else in the stronghold was dead.

Nevada staggered to his feet. "It's over, Cherish. I'll signal them to stop firing so you can ride out."

She caught his arm. "What about you?"

"You know the answer to that. I won't be taken alive."

"Oh, Nevada, I'm begging you!" She was on her knees, holding onto him. "I love you and if you won't surrender, I'll die with you!"

"No, you won't. I won't allow it!" He was trying to wrest her arms away. "I'm sending you out."

"I won't go unless you tell me you'll surrender to Pierce. Your dad will see that you get a fair trial, he has money and influence, he'll—"

"I can't expect him to do anything for me."

"But he will," she begged, "you know he will! Give me your gun, I'll ride down there and tell Pierce you'll surrender to him."

"I—I can't."

"Do you love me?" she implored.

"Oh, God, Cherish, you know I do, but you can't ask this of me—"

"I ask—no, I demand!" She stood up and confronted him, eyes blazing. "If you love me, I demand you surrender or by the Lord, I'll kill myself the minute they shoot you down!"

He stood there, wavering. Around them the firing had stopped as the troops seemed to realize there was no one returning fire. "Cherish, I can't let you die. Let me send you out under a flag of truce."

"I don't want you to die, either!" Her eyes blazed. "I'm selfish, I know, but as long as you're alive, even if you're in jail, I have hope that someday we'll be together. Give me that pistol and let me negotiate your surrender, or so help me God, I'll kill myself five minutes after they put a bullet in your brain!"

She meant every word of it and she knew by his face that he believed her. His smudged and bloody face went deathly pale. "Princess, this isn't fair."

"It's important to me that you live; I'd do anything to save your life!"

Behind him, the smoke cleared and the sun rose

all pink and yellow across the Nevada hills, glorious as a new day, an old love.

The invaders' guns were silent, waiting to see what happened next. Cherish had already decided what she was going to do, what sacrifice she would make to save him. "Give it to me." She held out her hand for the pistol.

Nevada hesitated, then very slowly, he pulled it from his holster, handed it over. She took it, tore off a piece of her petticoat to use as a truce flag and swung up on the little mare. "Wait here," she said.

She rode up over the rim, hesitated only a moment silhouetted against the rising sun, the tattered white scrap blowing out beside her like a proud banner. She waited, making sure all below saw her, realized who she was before she cantered down off the rocks toward the soldiers. In the distance, she saw a buggy with two people in it coming hard, but they wouldn't get here in time, she knew. Whoever was in that buggy would arrive too late to stop or change the outcome of this drama.

Pierce sat his own pinto mount, galloped out ahead of the soldiers to meet her. "Cherish, what in God's name—?"

"Pierce, do you still want to marry me?"

"You know I do, but—"

"Nevada is up there. He's the only one left alive and he's unarmed; I have his pistol."

Pierce's eyes widened and he smiled.

"Not so fast," she said, and blocked his gelding's path with her horse. "If you will go up there, accept his surrender, and promise me you won't harm him, I'll still marry you, but I must have your word—"

"What do you mean you'll *still* marry me?"

She dare not tell him everything. Her heart belonged to Nevada forever, but she would keep her promise, give Pierce her body for his pleasure if it would save the life of the man she loved. "Just what I said. You accept his surrender, let him live, and I'll marry you. Things will be as they always were. Otherwise, the wedding's off!"

Pierce stared into her face, a slow, horrible realization setting in. She had slept with his bastard brother! All these years Pierce had honored and respected her, going to whores with his passion rather than despoil her chastity. He had waited patiently to get her in their marriage bed to claim that which was rightfully his, and now Nevada had stolen that treasure from him. Always Pierce came in second to Nevada! His parents loved this bastard more than they loved him. With the crested Randolph ring, Quint had handed over the control of the ranching empire and everything that went with it to the bastard who was not even his own son.

The ring. He noticed it suddenly gleaming on the fourth finger of Cherish's left hand. His agonized gaze went to her face. She didn't have to tell him, he could read it in her eyes. He might get her body, but her heart and her virginity belonged to Nevada. A rage began to build in him, a rage past all reason. He would never really have Cherish or his parents' love because of that damned Injun bastard. "I—I promise," he said, and urging his horse, brushed past hers. He felt her gaze on his back as he held up a hand to stop the others from firing or advancing and then with his hand on his pistol butt, he started up the trail.

He was going to kill Nevada when he got there. The rage in him turned into a cold, all-consuming fire. He was going to gun him down like a dog and no one could see it and no one would know. He would say Nevada had a hidden gun, and even she might believe that. Pierce was going to be a hero and slay the bandit. Maybe even his parents would believe that Nevada had tried to kill him. Would she believe it? She would have no choice but to marry him, her father would pressure her to do so. Yes, he was going to be rid of his brother once and for all and end up with the money, the inheritance, and the girl.

Twenty-two

Cherish watched Pierce ride toward the hilltop with mixed feelings warring within her. If she had told Nevada what she paid for this bargain, doubtless he wouldn't have let her make it. This was her decision to make. If agreeing to marry Pierce would save his brother's life, she would keep her end of the deal, marry him, be a dutiful, obedient wife and hostess, let him rut on her body every night while she thought of Nevada, and even produce children for him. While Pierce's child sucked her breast, she would close her eyes and pretend it was Nevada's.

She and Nevada would keep their word. Would Pierce? Of course he would. Then she thought of the angry light in his hazel eyes, the suppressed fury in the set of his mouth and wondered again.

He was approaching the top of the hill. Around her, the soldiers were picking up their dead and wounded, giving her curious looks. She must look a sight with her ragged petticoat as a truce flag, smeared with blood and smoke, a pearl-handled pistol tucked in her waistband.

Behind her, she heard the squeaky wheels of the buggy coming fast. Cherish turned. From a distance, she recognized the set, drawn faces of Quint and Dallas Randolph. Poor things! By the time they arrived, this whole drama was going to be finished. She half turned her mare to ride out to meet them; then something within her made her uneasy as she looked again toward the hill. What was happening up there? Any moment now, Pierce should be reappearing with his prisoner. The longer she watched, the more uneasy she became. Nudging her horse into a lope, she started up the trail to witness Nevada's surrender for herself.

Nevada had thrown a blanket over old Ben's body. Now sick at heart at the death and destruction surrounding him, he waited for Pierce to arrive and accept his surrender. It had been a long time since he had been without a weapon at his side, but of course, he wasn't going to need it now.

Pierce rode through the pass and toward him. There was a rifle laying next to one of his fallen men not a hundred yards away, and for a moment, he was tempted to race for it. No, he had given Cherish his word. The years ahead of him loomed long and dark behind bars and again, he wished he had fought to the death. But for Cherish's sake, he would surrender. His shoulder ached and he realized for the first time he'd been wounded, lost some blood.

Pierce dismounted; stood there a long moment. "Nevada?"

Nevada held his hands away from his sides. "I'm unarmed, brother, just like she said."

Pierce's hazel eyes glinted with anger and the muscles in his jaw twitched as he drew his pistol, advanced on Nevada.

Nevada shook his head, kept his hands away from his sides. "No need for that, Pierce. I gave her my word."

"Your word! My dear brother." Pierce smiled sarcastically, but there was no mirth in his cold eyes. "You were always so honorable."

Pierce didn't put away the pistol. Something about his expression made Nevada uneasy. "Look, Pierce, I promised—"

"And you wouldn't lie, would you? My, such a Southern gentleman. You were always more like Quint than I was myself."

"I wanted him to be proud of me."

Pierce said, "I'm so damned weary of trying to live up to you, continually being outshined by you."

"We're brothers, Pierce," he said softly. "I always wanted the best for you."

"You were always Father's favorite, he gave you his ring."

His expression made sweat begin to run down Nevada's back. "I never meant it to be that way, Pierce, it was just that I was more like him—"

"More like him? Damn it, you're an Injun bastard! And I always had to feel obligated to you for saving my life, getting me out of scrapes—"

"That wasn't my fault, Pierce." He began to have the eerie feeling that Pierce didn't intend to take him prisoner at all, that something terrible was about to happen. At the very least, he deserved a fighting chance rather than be shot like an injured horse. He had a sudden image of himself lying dead in the dirt with Cherish looking at his body. What lie would Pierce tell her? He didn't want her to think he had given her his word and then broken it.

"It is your fault that you stole my woman," Pierce said, "took her right off the train. Have you had her?"

Nevada hesitated. He couldn't bring trouble and disgrace to the girl he loved. "No."

Pierce laughed. "You're a rotten liar, brother, you haven't had nearly as much practice as I have. She loves you, you know that?"

His arm was bleeding and aching. "No, she doesn't care about me, Pierce—"

"The hell she doesn't! You know the deal I just made her? She's going to marry me to save your life. Think about that brother; your woman lying with her legs spread for me every single night. Every year, she'll produce a son for me, and when I make love to her, I'll make her regret each time that she ever surrendered to you!"

Nevada flinched. He didn't mind dying, he had expected to die today, but he didn't want to be executed in cold blood, and the image of Cherish being brutally raped every night by his brother was more than he could bear.

"Bothers you, does it?" Pierce smiled. "Good!

Now, brother, I'm going to give you a chance. You turn and run and see if I can shoot you in the back before you get to one of those weapons." He was standing very close now and he gestured with the pistol. "I'll tell her you tried to escape and I didn't have any choice but shoot you."

Time. He had to buy some time until he could figure out what to do. "Cherish won't believe you."

"It doesn't matter," Pierce said, "she's a dutiful, guilt-ridden average girl. She'll do exactly as she's told."

Nevada shook his head. "She's changed, Pierce, she's more woman now than you can handle and no one will ever control her again . . . except maybe by love."

"By God, don't you tell me about Cherish Blassingame." Pierce waved the pistol wildly. "I've been engaged to her for years and now you steal her off a train, take her virtue, and throw her back to me with your kisses still on her mouth so she can beg for your life!"

"Pierce, at least give me a chance." Nevada tried to keep his voice calm. "Don't just execute me."

"But you're better with a gun than I am," Pierce said, "you're better at everything than I am, even in bed maybe? Was she good, brother? Did she whimper and claw you when I've never gotten more than one very cold kiss from the virtuous ice queen?"

"I love her, Pierce," Nevada said, "and if I weren't headed for jail, I'd marry her in a minute." He edged a little closer. Could he possibly grab that gun? They were about the same size except Nevada's muscles were hard from years on the range and Pierce had been spending his time in offices and parlors. Yet Nevada's arm was almost useless. He knew he had no chance in a fistfight, still he was going to have to try.

"Run now, big brother, run!" Pierce gestured with the pistol. "Let's see if you can get anywhere near those weapons before I shoot you in the back. They'll probably give me a medal for killing the bad train robber who tried to escape from the brave future governor. Why, I'll bet even Father and Mother will believe me when they arrive."

His brother meant to kill him. Nevada hesitated. He had no chance if he ran, nor any better one if he tried to take Pierce's weapon. At least that way, he would be shot from the front instead of the back. What to do? He remembered an old trick the cagey Pierce used to play on his trusting older brother.

Abruptly he stared past Pierce's shoulder. "What's that? Look!"

Pierce, startled, half turned to see what had taken his brother's attention. At that moment, Nevada took a wild chance and grabbed for the gun.

With his arm injured, he was at a disadvantage. Pierce recovered himself, slammed Nevada backward while he cursed. "So you want it this way, do you? Good!"

Nevada dived in under Pierce's hands, grabbing for the Colt as he caught Pierce's legs and the pair went down. The pistol flew through the air, landed a few feet away. The movement hurt his arm so badly, Nevada could not keep from crying out.

Pierce smiled as he stumbled to his feet. "Hurt, did it? I'll show you what hurt really means!"

He kicked Nevada's injured arm as Nevada rolled away from him. His whole right side felt on fire and for a split second, he thought he would faint from the agony. He willed himself to stay conscious as he staggered to his feet. Now he meshed with Pierce and the two fought, both seeing the pistol lying a few feet away, both trying to reach it. "Pierce," he gasped, "don't do this! We promised Cherish—"

Pierce snarled, "Who keeps their word to a woman? I'll tell her you tried to kill me and I had to shoot you!"

They went down, struggled. Nevada's arm was bleeding again and he was in so much pain, his vision was hazy. The pistol looked a million miles away, reflecting the early morning light. Many years ago he'd been a big brother teaching his little brother to fight so the school bullies wouldn't hurt him, and now it was being used against him.

Pierce struck him in the face, knocking him backward. "I've learned pretty good, huh, big brother? I had a good teacher!"

Nevada was so very weary, and his shirt felt drenched with fresh blood from the wound. His strength was failing him, he could feel it ebbing with his blood. Cherish, he thought, Cherish. She'd think he broke his word to her.

A knife. A big knife lay forgotten and reflecting light in the rocks, much closer than the pistol. Both of them seemed to see it at the same time.

***

Cherish rode back through the pass to the sounds of shouts and cursing. She spurred her horse forward, even as she heard the older Randolphs laboring up the rocks behind her. They weren't going to get here in time. Whatever was done, Cherish was going to have to do. She swung down off the mare, frantic with indecision.

Nevada's pistol; she still had Nevada's pistol. For only a split second, she watched the two brothers fighting to the death. Nevada grabbed a big knife from the ground, staggered to his feet, stood swaying for a long moment. Then he threw it away in disgust. "I can't kill you, Pierce, no matter what you've done. You'll always be my little brother."

Nevada turned and holding his wounded arm, started to walk away.

With a cry of rage, Pierce pounced on the knife. "I'm sick of your honor, of always living in your shadow!"

His arm came up, the sunlight glittering on the blade as Cherish ran up to them, pulled the pistol from her waistband and screamed, "No, Pierce!"

"You haven't got the guts, Cherish." Even as he spoke, his arm came down, the knife flashing toward Nevada who half turned, reaching in a vain attempt to deflect the blade with his injured arm.

Always she would remember that moment with two brothers in a life-and-death fight so close she could almost touch them. All she could see was that knife flashing down at the man she loved. Just before the blade hit home, she made her choice in a heartbeat. Without even realizing she did so, Cherish pulled the trigger.

The shot roared in her ears and the gun recoiled with a brutal jerk. The scent of the powder made her gasp. For a moment, they all stared at each other in horror. Then Pierce grasped his chest where the scarlet spread across his shirt, looked up at her in shocked surprise and slowly crumpled.

Cherish stared at the gun in her hand in stunned silence. She, like Pierce, never would have thought she had the nerve . . . until the life of the man she loved had hung in the balance. With an anguished cry, she threw the gun from her, ran to where Nevada was gathering Pierce against him.

Nevada was crying. "Oh, Pierce, why did it come to this? My brother; my little brother!"

Pierce's eyes flickered open weakly and he looked from one to the other. Cherish began to cry. "I didn't mean to, Pierce! Oh, I didn't mean to hurt you!"

He reached out and touched her face. "You love him, really love him, don't you? I knew you always would, unless I got rid of him forever. . . ."

Cherish heard a sob, looked around. Quint and Dallas Randolph ran toward them. "Oh, Lord," Quint gasped, "what happened? What happened?"

He knelt by Pierce's side as Cherish stood up. "I knew it would come to this," he whispered and she realized how much gray he had in his hair and how very sad he looked. "Oh, I was afraid it would come to this!"

Pierce's eyes blinked open. "You—you loved him better than me; I hated him for it."

Quint swallowed hard, shook his head. "No, parents try to love their children alike, but sometimes we fail." He reached across his dying son and put his hand on his other son's shoulder. "I reckon we were unfair to both of you, trying to keep the secret."

Nevada nodded. "About your killing *Timbi?*"

Dallas was sobbing as she knelt and took her dying son in her arms. "Oh, Nevada, I killed *Timbi!*"

"Angel," Quint protested, "you shouldn't have—"

"I killed him," Dallas wept. "Quint tried to keep my sons from knowing; took the blame himself."

Cherish gasped and Dallas looked up at her, tears running down her face. "Yes, like you, I had a split second to choose, just like you did." She held her dying son close. "Oh, Pierce, perhaps I didn't love you enough . . . maybe we were bad parents . . . maybe . . ."

"Cain and Abel," Pierce whispered. "I knew you loved him more than you loved me. . . ."

"We didn't," Dallas wept. "Oh, we tried to be fair to you both. Pierce, we love you, you hear me? Maybe we showed it more to Nevada because we felt so guilty about his father's death!"

Quint took one of Pierce's hands in his own. "We love you, son, we truly love you. We'll get a doctor; give us another chance to show you."

Pierce's eyes flickered open and he looked up and smiled weakly at both of them. When he spoke, his voice came so faint, everyone had to lean forward

422

to hear him. "Why—why didn't you tell me before?"

"Oh, Lord," Quint was sobbing, "we took it for granted you knew!"

"And now I do . . . Dad. . . ." Pierce sighed and the life went out of him with that last faint breath.

Dallas convulsed with sobs and Quint put his arm around her.

Nevada stood up slowly. "This is my fault, all my fault."

Cherish ran into his arms, hugged him against her. "He was trying to kill you; I never realized how much you meant to me until that moment!"

Quint held Dallas close. His eyes were wet and he looked old. "No, maybe it's my fault. Maybe we should have told Nevada the truth from the beginning, but how do you tell a beloved child that he's not your son by blood and that his mother killed his father to protect me?" He was sobbing now. "I was afraid you'd hate us both."

Guilt. All of them feeling guilty, Cherish thought dully, and who was to blame really? She wasn't sure anymore except that she knew she would never forget that moment as she made her choice and killed a man.

"Son," Quint said and reached out a hand to Nevada.

"Don't call me that." Nevada turned away. "I've brought you heartache and grief; I've gotten Pierce and old Ben killed and humiliated a proud name."

"We love you anyway," Quint said softly.

"Yes," Dallas said, "we love you anyway. Love

isn't something like water from a pump that can be turned off and on at will; we love you, son, we'll always love you; that's what parents are for."

Nevada broke down and cried then; not for himself, but for the dead and the hurt and the misery he'd caused.

The law let him stay long enough to help bury Pierce and old Ben. His brother looked so very young in death. Memories. He washed Pierce's face, brushed his brown hair from his eyes. He could almost hear his toddling steps, his lisping voice; *Let's go ride, Nevada, help me up on pony. . . .*

I'll always be there, little brother, just call my name when you need me.

They wrapped the two in blankets and put Ben's old harmonica in his pocket. Just before they began to fill the grave, Nevada reached in his pocket, took out a full pouch of tobacco, leaned over, tucked it in Ben's vest. "Ornery old coot," he whispered.

The breeze came up as the soldiers filled the grave and it almost seemed to Nevada that he heard a ghostly harmonica playing: . . . *weep no more my lady, oh weep no more today. We will sing one song for my old Kentucky home. . . .*

Nevada took a deep breath and squared his shoulders. "Dad, I'd be much obliged if you'd look after Cherish. I want all of you to forget about me. I've got a debt to pay to society. Those who think they can escape paying the piper are wrong." He turned and held out his wrists to a lawman and the captain who stood respectfully waiting. "I don't know which of you I'm supposed to surrender to, but I'm ready to go."

He could still hear Cherish's and his mother's sobs as they snapped the handcuffs on him and led him away. He didn't look back. There was no point in prolonging this. He wanted to make a clean break.

Cherish was calling his name as he swung up on his horse and with an escort of troops, started away from the valley toward the grim prison he knew awaited him.

Epilogue

Daybreak. Spring 1892.

Nevada grasped the bars of his tiny window. The sun would soon rise over the far hills. Already the sky's gray reflected pale pink and gold. Dawn, his favorite time of the day. How many of them had he seen through prison bars in almost five long years?

Too many. However, this one was special. It was the very last sunrise he would see from a cramped cell. Nevada sighed as he buttoned the cheap suit the warden had sent, picked up the small valise. So few possessions, he thought, and almost five years lost from his life. Nevada turned to the waiting guard. "I'm ready."

The fat man yawned and stepped aside, followed Nevada out of the grim cell and down the dark hall. Footsteps echoed on the stone. No doubt he's seen men come and go, Nevada thought, and most return. Not me, Nevada vowed, I'm going straight and lose myself in some faraway place where no one knows me. Never again will I be caged.

Their boots rang loudly in the silence as they walked past shadowy faces behind iron bars. How many men had Nevada known in this prison; the innocent, and the guilty? Some would never leave here, even in death. Outside these walls lay a small graveyard where some he had known now rested. Others had escaped, been hanged or had years left to serve.

He could not think of them now. Nevada, carrying his small valise, entered the warden's sparse office, waited to be invited to sit down. The man's face was as gray as his hair. In a way, he was a prisoner here himself. He looked up, gestured Nevada to a hard chair. He signed the paper on his desk with a flourish, pushed it toward him. "I know you're eager to be on your way, Randolph."

Nevada nodded, took the paper, stared at it. He folded it, put it in his pocket. Today he felt as old as the warden, although Nevada was only thirty-one. Prison had a way of doing that to a man.

"You've been a model prisoner, Randolph, I hope we won't ever see you again." The warden smiled a rare smile and offered him a cigarette.

"Don't worry, you won't," Nevada promised himself aloud as he took the smoke, leaned forward to accept the light.

The man lit one for himself and leaned back in his chair, blew smoke toward the ceiling. "You're a lucky man."

"Lucky?" He didn't feel lucky. Once he had been superstitious. Behind stone walls, he had kept his religion, gradually let go of the other.

"Lucky," the man said again. "Besides time off for good behavior, don't you realize you'd be serving a lot longer stretch if rich, important people hadn't paid back that money, used their influence—"

"I didn't ask them to," Nevada snapped as he took a deep drag on his cigarette and savored the taste.

"You're a hardcase, Randolph, harder than most."

"It takes a hardcase to survive in here, you know that." He sighed and watched the first pale light wash against the grim wall behind the warden's head.

"You should have at least seen your visitors or read your mail. I hated to send it back unopened." He put his feet up on his scarred desk.

He didn't say he couldn't bear for those he loved to be embarrassed, humiliated by visiting this place. "Better they should forget me; I've shamed them."

"You aren't the first to make a mistake," he shrugged, "and you won't be the last. Your folks came many times, even though you wouldn't see them. That girl, Cherish, came with them and—"

"Don't mention her; her name shouldn't even be spoken in a sewer like this." *Cherish.* He hurt deep inside just thinking about her. They had all finally stopped coming because he wouldn't see them.

"All right. You're a proud, stubborn fool to let her get away."

"That's my business." Almost five years. Five long years. By now, she had surely found a man who deserved her. Nevada didn't want her to wait for a convict out of pity.

428

"I feel sorry for you, son." The warden smoked and watched him.

"Don't." Nevada stared at the glowing tip of his cigarette. "I brought this all on myself; there's no one to blame but me. A man does wrong, he has to be willing to accept the consequences." He had thought he would be eager to leave, but now he lingered over his smoke. What was it like out there? "I broke the law and I've paid the price."

The warden nodded. "You've done that, all right. You'll find it's a different world from the one you left."

That was why he lingered. He had been inside these walls so long, he wasn't sure what he would do, how he would survive on the outside. "Who's president now?"

"Harrison, but it's an election year and Cleveland's running against him. There's been a land run in Indian Territory, and before it's over, it may be a new state called Oklahoma."

"Impossible!" Nevada sat up straight in his chair. "That belongs to the tribes as long as the grass grows and the rivers flow."

"Maybe, but it's happened anyway." The warden leaned back in his chair and the light from the window spread a little more behind him. "There's been a massacre of the Sioux up at Wounded Knee, South Dakota; seems one of our local Paiutes, *Wovoka,* started it with something called a 'Ghost Dance.' "

Nevada shook his head. "I've met *Wovoka,* he's not the type to lead an uprising."

"Not sure exactly how it happened. The old West

as you knew it is almost gone, Randolph. People and barbed wire everywhere. West isn't wild anymore, except for a few scattered outlaws like Butch Cassidy and his gang."

"Never heard of him." Nevada tossed his smoke into the spittoon.

"You may yet," the warden said. "However, civilization is coming to the West slowly but surely." He snubbed out his cigarette with his boot, slid an envelope across the battered desk.

Nevada took it, slipped it in his pocket without opening it, stood up slowly.

"You got any plans?" The warden stood up, too.

"I—I don't know; thought maybe I could get a job punching cattle on a ranch somewhere where nobody knows me."

"There's not much money in that envelope,"—the other man gestured—"maybe enough for a ticket and a few meals. There's a train goes through Reno this morning. There's a ride waiting to take you there."

"Then I'd best be going." He picked up his valise, turned toward the door.

"I'll walk you to the gate. If I was you, I'd think about going home."

Home. He had to blink to keep back the tears of emotion that clouded his eyes at the thought of the Wolf's Den Ranch. About now, his mother would be pouring the steaming coffee and old Juanita would be frying eggs. His dad would be sitting at the head of the table, talking about the day's chores. "I got no home anymore."

"That's not what your folks said."

"I disgraced them by making the front pages, ending up in jail."

"You ought to at least go see them."

He had caused them too much pain; he didn't want to inflict any more. He wouldn't even think about how he'd hurt the girl he loved. "No."

"Stubborn to the end." The warden shrugged and walked with him down the corridor and out into the grim prison yard. In the growing light, Nevada saw the guards in the tower looking down at them, light reflecting off their rifle barrels. The bleak stone walls glowed almost pink with the first rays of dawn as the pair strode to the giant gate.

He was almost scared at the thought of freedom. For five years, he had not had one moment to call his own, and now he would be walking as a free man into a world that had changed. Where would he go? What would he do? He knew what he must not do; he must not go anywhere near Sacramento. If he did, he would be tempted to see her, and Cherish was better off without him. Nevada took a deep breath. Today the air smelled fresh and sweet with the scent of desert wild flowers, chaparral . . . and freedom. Only a few steps and he would put this grim, dingy place behind him.

The warden held out his hand. "Luck to you, son. You've paid for your mistakes, don't repeat them."

They shook hands awkwardly, solemnly.

"I won't be back," Nevada promised. "I'm closing the door on my past."

"Maybe you shouldn't close the door on the

whole past," the other said and signaled the guards to open the gate. "Keep the good memories, let the others go. Forgive yourself, son. Remember the prodigal son went home."

"I've done too much to be forgiven for." Nevada shook his head.

"Even the thief on the cross was forgiven," the other reminded him.

Without thinking, Nevada crossed himself. "Maybe God can forgive the pain I've caused; I don't expect them to." He watched the big gate creaking open.

"Your ride's waiting outside."

"Thanks." Nevada held his valise and watched the gate swing.

"Go out and face the world, son, and may God take a liking to you from now on."

He nodded absently, staring at the gates as they swung. He was free; free. So many, many mistakes; such bitter regrets. How sharper than a serpent's tooth. . . . A man who had not sired him had taken him for his own and Nevada had hurt him; betrayed his love. Never again would he have the privilege of calling Quint Randolph "Dad."

Nevada took a deep breath, straightened his shoulders now as the gates swung wide, walked through them without looking back. The rising sun blinded him a moment with its pink and golden light. *Nevada dawn.* Today he was a free man. If only . . . no, he must not think of her. Surely she had forgotten him by now. He stood there savoring the heady air of freedom, listening to the gates clang shut behind him. Now where was that ride that waited for him?

"Nevada?"

He half turned to face a woman stepping out of the sunrise. The light blinded him and he blinked. Then he realized she had yellow hair and wore a dress the color of daffodils.

Cherish. He fought to control his reaction. He wanted to run to her, sweep her up in his arms, kiss that soft, sweet mouth. He gritted his teeth and swallowed hard. He must not accept her pity. "You didn't need to come; I know it's over. I wasn't planning to bother you."

Tears welled up in her eyes and he wanted to wipe them away, kiss them away. "For me, it will never be over, Nevada; not as long as I live."

Pity. He could accept hatred, but not her pity. "I feel guilty enough, Cherish, without your coming here." He struggled to keep his voice cold. "You're well rid of me. I told you when I was sentenced to begin a new life."

She took a hesitant step forward, clasping and unclasping her small hands. "I came to see you at first; so did your folks."

"Must you remind me?" He grimaced, thinking of his beautiful mother coming to a place like this, knowing he was locked in a cage. He hadn't wanted any of them to see his disgrace. He put down his valise, kicked at the dirt with his worn boot. "You should have taken the hint. I don't love you; I never did. You were part of my revenge, my rotten revenge."

433

"I—I don't believe you." Her small chin came up proudly.

He must make her believe him; it was better that way. "Believe me," he said, "I don't want you, Cherish. You were just a toy, one night's amusement to me."

She took another step forward. "Look me in the face and tell me you don't love me, that you never loved me."

He took a deep, ragged breath. Oh, God, this was so very hard, but he must do it for her own good. Nevada hesitated.

"Fiddlesticks! You can't say it! You know what your trouble is, Quinton Nevada Randolph?"

"I'll bet you're about to tell me, princess," he said. She hadn't changed a bit; still the sweet, bossy little imp he had known so very long ago.

"You're right," she snapped. "Your problem is you can't forgive yourself so you can't believe anyone else could forgive you."

"Are you quite finished?" He managed to keep his voice cold.

Now her spirit faltered. "I—I suppose I am. Your folks are hoping I'll bring you home to the Wolf's Den."

"You know better than that." He picked up the valise again.

"They've aged, Nevada," she said softly, "oh, they've aged so much!"

"Don't you think I know that? It's all my fault."

"Quint's not in good health and they need help

434

running the ranch. I've been some help, but they need you."

"I'm the one who brought them this heartache, remember?" He started walking toward town.

Behind him, she said, "I have a buggy parked around behind those trees; if you won't change your mind, at least let me drive you to the station."

"Fine, I don't want to miss my train." He made a gesture of dismissal. "It's for the best, Cherish, someday you'll realize that. Your father would die at the thought of us together."

"He's changed, too, Nevada; it was that or lose me. You see, I'm not Daddy's little girl anymore; I make my own decisions—"

"Well, I'm making this one for you." He turned toward the trees where she'd said there was a buggy waiting.

"I've been living on the ranch with your folks, waiting for you to get out."

"So now I'm out." Away in the distance, he heard the faint echo of the train whistle. In the stillness of the desert, the sound carried across many miles. "We'd better hurry, the train won't wait."

He walked toward the clump of trees. If he could only maintain this pose until he could get on that train. He loved her enough to make this final sacrifice for her. They had no future together and she would realize that soon. It would hurt too much to lose her a second time.

"Oh, Nevada." She was weeping now, running to keep up with him. "Won't you change your mind? Look!" She held up her hand, and he saw for the first time that she still wore the wolf's head ring. "I thought we'd get married—"

"Married?" he scoffed, "A proud Blassingame to an ex-con?" He looked straight ahead, striding toward the thicket.

"There's a reason," she said, almost running to keep up with his long strides. "I—I brought someone with me."

His parents. Oh, God, she had brought his parents. Nevada hesitated. If Dallas and Quint were sitting in that buggy, he'd lose his resolve to get on that train and he must; he must. "Why the hell did you do that?"

"We'll have this out!" She caught his arm, whirled him around, her eyes blazing. "Tell me that you don't love me, Nevada Randolph!"

"I—I don't love you."

"Damn it, look me in the face and say that! You're a lying, double-dipped yellow dog!"

He didn't know whether to laugh or cry. "You sound just like my mother. Dallas is beginning to rub off on you." He tried to walk past her, but she blocked his path, bristling like a small kitten.

"Look me in the eye and tell me you lied to me that one night we spent together; that you never loved me."

Instead, he marched around her toward the buggy, tears blinding him. He must not weaken and admit that he had never loved another woman as he had loved her, as he loved her now. The words he had said to her that Nevada dawn had come straight from his heart. Somewhere in the distance, the train

436

whistle drifted on the air. If he hurried, he could get to the station before his resolve failed completely.

He stumbled to the buggy, blinded by tears, threw his valise in the back. As he started to swing up on the seat, he blinked in disbelief. A dimpled little girl sat in the buggy wearing a pale yellow dress just the color of daffodils. The tot had dark eyes and long dark curls, otherwise, she was a miniature of Cherish. So she had married after all and had brought her child to show him. That hurt too much.

The child looked up at him with a dimpled smile. "Hello, mister man," she lisped. "We're waiting for my daddy. Do you know my daddy?"

No, it couldn't be. He couldn't even think it. Nevada had to swallow twice to speak. "Who—who are you, little princess?"

"Dawn Anne Randolph," she announced, "and I'm more than four years old." She held up four chubby little fingers.

Very slowly, he turned and looked toward Cherish, a question in his eyes.

Cherish nodded. "That night, yes. I—I tried to tell you, but you wouldn't see me; wouldn't read my letters. You're such a damned pigheaded fool!" She began to cry and she wasn't the only one.

"Why are you crying, Mama? Why is the man crying?"

"Dawn, honey," Cherish said, "meet your daddy."

"Oh, Cherish, I never dreamed! I didn't guess! How can you forgive me?"

"Because I love you," she whispered and held out her arms.

He swept her into his embrace, kissing her as he had dreamed of kissing her all these long, lonely years. Now he embraced them both, alternately kissing and hugging them.

She kissed him again, reveling in the taste, the feel of him. "I never stopped loving you, Nevada Randolph. When you love someone, nothing can change that; no matter what mistakes they make. Your parents feel the same."

He cried then as he had not cried since his brother had died in his arms. "I—I've made so many mistakes," he admitted, "and I didn't want your pity."

In the distance, the train whistled again; a little closer this time. Nevada raised his head and looked in that direction. She had done everything she knew to keep him. If her love and their child couldn't bring him home, there was nothing else to do, but she would love him till the longest day she lived.

He looked toward the wisp of smoke drifting over the far hills from the train. Nevada climbed up on the buggy seat, held out his hand to her. She climbed up on the seat next to him. He slapped the bay horse with the reins and the buggy pulled away, headed up the dusty road away from the prison.

The sun rose over the distant hills. Cherish put her hand on his arm. The wolf's head ring gleamed in the morning light. "Oh, Nevada, dearest, we can close the door on the past if we love each other enough. This can be the beginning; not the end; the beginning!"

Little Dawn Anne looked from one to the other. "So where are we going now?"

Nevada put his arm around Cherish, held her like he would never let her go, leaned over to kiss his child. "Dawn, sweetheart, we're all going home!"

To My Readers

For those who haven't read my earlier books, the one you have just finished is a sequel to my Zebra novel about Dallas and Quint Randolph, the Pony Express and the Paiute Indian War: *Nevada Nights* (ISBN 0-8217-2701-X).

The Trans-Western Railroad is complete fiction. The line that ran through that area was the Central Pacific (now the Southern Pacific), which I mentioned in my story of an escaped Apache scout, where Nevada himself first entered this series, *Apache Caress* (ISBN 0-8217-3560-8).

Trains have played such an important role in Nevada's history that a train adorns its state seal.

The first organized band of train robbers were the Reno brothers and their gang, who robbed a passenger train in Indiana in October 1866.

The very first Western train robbery happened in November 1870, just east of Verdi, Nevada, in the general area where our story takes place. While the robbers were caught and most of the money recovered, one-hundred-fifty of the twenty-dollar gold pieces were never found. Possibly buried near the robbery site, those coins are now worth half a million dollars in today's market. If you're a treasure hunter, good hunting and let me know if you find the money!

In spite of all the movies you may have seen about Indians wrecking and plundering a train, only one time in history did that actually happen. The Cheyenne were the only Indians to do it. Someday maybe I'll tell you that story.

I mentioned an actual obscure Old West photographer, John H. Fouch, in that billiard room scene for a reason. He really did take the first photo of the Custer's Last Stand battle site at the Little Big Horn. Actually he took two photos. I have seen the one because it belongs to a fellow member of the Order of the Indian Wars who collects Fouch photos. Somewhere in an old trunk in an attic or basement, or in a dusty swap shop, other Fouch Western photos are neglected and forgotten. Maybe you or a friend has that rare missing second photo of the Custer battle site? If you have any knowledge of Fouch Western photographs, I'd be delighted to hear from you.

Another time I may tell you more about the Lincoln County War and the territorial governor, Lew Wallace, author of the classic novel, *Ben Hur.* Yes, that's the one made into a movie twice, the second starring Charlton Heston and won eleven Academy Awards.

Billy the Kid was part of that Lincoln County range war before he was killed by lawman Pat Garrett in July 1881. He was not left-handed, no matter what some movies and Western novels claim. In the only known photo of Billy, he holds a rifle in one hand. A sharp-eyed historian recently realized all these years we have been looking at that glass plate photo reversed. He noticed it because he suddenly saw that Billy's shirt buttoned on the wrong side.

By the way, "gunslinger" and "gunfighter" are Hollywood terms. Old-timers called such a man a "gunman," "shootist" or "shooter." Neither did a shootist wear his gun low, or go in for a "fast draw." Fast was not nearly as important as being accurate. Nor in all the history of the West was there ever a single *High Noon*-type gun duel such as you see in the movies where two men faced off in the street to settle who was the "fastest." The famous writer, Jack Schaefer, author of *Shane,* offered a long-standing reward to anyone who could prove such a "fast draw" event ever happened and when he died, the money had never been collected.

The *San Patricio* Battalion of the Mexican War is shrouded in legend. Probably because they felt a kinship with the Mexicans who were also Catholic, these American, but mostly Irish troops, went over to the other side and supported Mexico. When the Mexicans lost, the U.S. army punished many of the deserters with whippings and branding a D across their cheeks. Some thirty of these American soldiers paid the ultimate price and were hanged.

If some of the minor characters named in the story you have just read seem familiar, many such as the Durangos and Randolph family, Pierce Hamilton, the Apache scout, Cholla and his white love, Sierra, were characters in some of my earlier stories. Most of these are still available from Zebra Books in my on-going Panorama of the Old West series. The novel you have just finished reading is #11 in the series. Yes, there will be more based on actual Western and Indian history. Look for a new story about every eight to ten months. Many of my previous titles have been reprinted and may be ordered directly from Zebra for the cover price, plus 50 cents each for postage, or ask your local bookstore for: *Cheyenne Captive, Cheyenne Princess, Comanche Cowboy, Bandit's Embrace, Nevada Nights, Cheyenne Caress, Quicksilver Passion, Apache Caress, Sioux Slave, Half-Breed's Bride,* and Zebra's *1991 Christmas Rendezvous* short-story collection.

If you would like a newsletter and an autographed bookmark, write me in care of Zebra Books, 475 Park Avenue South, New York, New York 10016. Please send a stamped, self-addressed long envelope. Readers in Canada and foreign countries need to accompany theirs with postal vouchers sold at your post office I can exchange for American stamps. U.S. Postal Service does not allow me to use foreign postage. I always answer my mail, so if you don't hear from me within several months, consider the letter lost and write again.

If you are interested in further research on some of the history I covered in this story, I suggest these books: *Sand In a Whirlwind,* the Paiute Indian War of 1860, by Ferol Egan, University of Nevada Press, *Historical Atlas of the Outlaw West,* by Richard Patterson, published by Johnson Publishing Company, and *A Treasury of Railroad Folklore,* edited by B.A. Botkin and Alvin F. Harlow, published by Bonanza Books.

What story will I tell next? Thousands of you loved my first novel, *Cheyenne Captive,* the story of a Cheyenne Dog Soldier, Iron Knife, who kidnapped a Boston socialite, Summer Van Schuyler, off a stagecoach and kept her for his own. *Cheyenne Captive* won both the *Romantic Times* magazine Best Indian Romance By a New Author award and the *Affaire de Coeur* Magazine Gold Certificate award voted by their readers as one of the Ten Best Historical Romances of 1987.

Many of you wrote to ask what happened later to the couple and begged for a sequel, wanting to know about their children and whether Iron Knife would ever meet his sister, Cimarron, the heroine of *Cheyenne Princess*. At long last, by popular demand, here comes that sequel!

The Cheyenne live here in Western Oklahoma and they still gather around the powwow fires at night to tell the old medicine tales. When an old one finishes, he will say, "That is my story. Can anyone tie another to the tail of it?"

Then another story will begin and when he finishes, he will say, "That is my story; can anyone tie another to it?" Sometimes the tales go on all night, but they must stop at dawn because it is taboo to tell the stories in the daylight.

Yes, I can tie the tales together one after another until I have told you many, many romantic legends of the West. My Oklahoma home is built on land where war parties once roamed. Sometimes late at night in my study, I hear the ghostly drums echo. From my window, I seem to see phantom warriors crossing through the blackjack trees, galloping across the prairie and into the misty past. The ghosts of the Old West are waiting for us in late summer or early autumn of 1994 as this saga continues.

Come ride back in time with me. . . .

Georgina Gentry

PASSIONATE NIGHTS FROM

PENELOPE NERI

DESERT CAPTIVE   (2447, $3.95/$4.95)
Kidnapped from her French Foreign Legion escort, indignant Alexandria had every reason to despise her nomad prince captor. But as they traveled to his isolated mountain kingdom, she found her hate melting into desire . . .

FOREVER AND BEYOND   (3115, $4.95/$5.95)
Haunted by dreams of an Indian warrior, Kelly found his touch more than intimate—it was oddly familiar. He seemed to be calling her back to another time, to a place where they would find love again . . .

FOREVER IN HIS ARMS   (3385, $4.95/$5.95)
Whispers of war between the North and South were riding the wind the summer Jenny Delaney fell in love with Tyler Mackenzie. Time was fast running out for secret trysts and lovers' dreams, and she would have to choose between the life she held so dear and the man whose passion made her burn as brightly as the evening star . . .

MIDNIGHT CAPTIVE   (2593, $3.95/$4.95)
After a poor, ragged girlhood with her gypsy kinfolk, Krissoula knew that all she wanted from life was her share of riches. There was only one way for the penniless temptress to earn a cent: fake interest in a man, drug him, and pocket everything he had! Then the seductress met dashing Esteban and unquenchable passion seared her soul . . .

SEA JEWEL   (3013, $4.50/$5.50)
Hot-tempered Alaric had long planned the humiliation of Freya, the daughter of the most hated foe. He'd make the wench from across the ocean his lowly bedchamber slave—but he never suspected she would become the mistress of his heart, his treasured sea jewel . . .

Available wherever paperbacks are sold, or order direct from the Publisher. Send cover price plus 50¢ per copy for mailing and handling to Zebra Books, Dept. 4393, 475 Park Avenue South, New York, N.Y. 10016. Residents of New York and Tennessee must include sales tax. DO NOT SEND CASH. For a free Zebra/ Pinnacle catalog please write to the above address.

Taylor—made Romance From Zebra Books